The Sowers Trilogy

WHERE
FREEDOM
GROWS

BONNIE LEON

B&H

**BROADMAN
& HOLMAN
PUBLISHERS**

Nashville, Tennessee

© 1998
by Bonnie Leon
All rights reserved
Printed in the United States of America

0-8054-1272-7

Published by Broadman & Holman Publishers, Nashville, Tennessee
Acquisitions Editor: Vicki Crumpton
Page Design: Anderson Thomas Design
Page Composition: Leslie Joslin

Dewey Decimal Classification: 813.54
Subject Heading: FICTION
Library of Congress Card Catalog Number: 98-15558

Library of Congress Cataloging-in-Publication Data
Leon, Bonnie.
  Where freedom grows / Bonnie Leon.
      p. cm. — (The sowers trilogy ; vol. 1)
  ISBN 0-8054-1272 (pbk.)
  I. Title. II. Series: Leon, Bonnie. Sowers trilogy ; vol. 1.
  PS3562.E533W47   1998
  813'.54—dc21

                                              98-15558
                                                   CIP

1 2 3 4 5 02 01 00 99 98

WHERE
FREEDOM
GROWS

$\mathcal{A}$CKNOWLEDGMENTS

Thank you, Mary, Diane, Nancy, and Teddy. It was not by chance that you became a part of my life during the writing of this book. With God, nothing is an accident. As you've labored beside me, I've sometimes wondered if you might be angels.

Your sacrificial dedication is rare, and I am truly indebted to each of you. May the Lord bless you.

$\mathcal{P}$REFACE

I N THE DAYS WHEN WAR WAS A
fading memory, and heroes, like Charles Lindberg and Amelia
Earhart, established their names in the history books, and people
trusted their leaders, unexpected storm clouds gathered. Two
powerful countries stood upon a perilous precipice.

Stalin ruled the Soviet Union with a cruel hand, his own
neurosis feeding an insatiable hunger for power and control. In
an insane race to compete with world technology, he
implemented one Five Year Plan after another. Farmers were
ripped from their land and forced to labor on collectives.
Others slaved to build factories, modern railroad lines, and
dams. The appalling cost to the Soviets, their lives.

During his twenty-nine-year rule, more than twenty
million Soviet citizens were slaughtered as he fed his need for
dominance. Even those who were loyal and believed in his

leadership were often deemed enemies and joined the innocent in the grave.

In spite of the oppression, many of the people continued to live, to love, and to honor God, their strength and endurance an inspiration.

Halfway around the world, on Black Tuesday, 1929, the United States was forced to face the financial repercussions of years of gluttonous waste and the naive belief that never-ending prosperity was something to be expected. The seemingly invincible country was driven to its knees. In the decade that followed, drought and hunger cut across the land, randomly taking victims.

Yet, in this time of desperation, hope grew and hard times revealed the nation's valiant heart. Trust in God and in each other blossomed as people endured and upheld one another.

Two continents, two people. One God, one faith.

CHAPTER 1

September 1930
Moscow countryside

Tatyana uncurled her long legs and tensed her muscles. She let her book rest in her lap and studied a thread of sunlight stretching across the tufted rug in front of the wood stove. It reached beyond to the oak floor in the tiny kitchen where the aroma of hot bread filled the cottage.

"Tatyana, I need you to collect the eggs," Galya Letinov said.

When Tatyana didn't reply, Galya stepped into the room, her hands resting on her hips. She smiled at her daughter. "Books, books, books, is that all you intend to do today—read?"

Tatyana studied the tall, slender woman whose bright green eyes so resembled her own. Playfully, she flipped her long blonde hair off her shoulders, stood up, and smiled. "It seems to me, when you were teaching, you didn't believe broadening one's mind was a waste of time." Before her mother could answer, she continued. "They are wonderful, the writings of Anna Akhmatova and Boris Pasternak." She recited the last verse of Pasternak's *The Drowsy Garden*.

> Where the pond lies, an open secret,
> Where apple bloom is surf and sigh,
> And where the garden, a lake dwelling,
> Holds out in front of it the sky.

"It is beautiful, but isn't there something more interesting to read? What of the writings of Patonov and Pilnyak? They are true artists."

"Mamochka, you know I love their works, but . . ." She wrapped her arms about her chest, closed her eyes, and gently rocked back and forth as if listening to a symphony. "Poetry sings." She looked at her mother. "Can't you hear the music in the words?"

"I hear, but I do not have your special ear," Galya said.

Remembering the many hours spent with her father in review of the great writers and their works, and the times she'd listened with her family to the symphonies and ballets of Shostakovich, Tchaikovsky, and Sergei Prokofiev, Tatyana said, "It was you and Papa who taught me to love the arts."

Galya smiled softly. "That is true. I wish we had more time for such things." She sighed. "But there is always work to be done. And right now, I need the eggs."

"Who cares about eggs when there are so many *real* treasures in the world waiting to be discovered? I am weary of thinking about the mundane."

"And how well will you be able to hear your 'literary music' if your stomach is grumbling?" Galya smiled. "Now go, and bring me some eggs. Your brother and Papa will be here soon, and they'll be hungry."

"All right." Tatyana frowned as she shuffled across the floor to the door. She lifted her boots from the wooden box, then sat down to pull them on. "At the end of this year's school term, I will be ready to go to the university in Moscow. It is incredible to think of myself sitting under the teaching of its distinguished professors." She yanked on her laces, then quickly tied them. "One day I will teach literature."

Galya's eyes saddened. "That is a very big dream for an eighteen-year-old commoner." She took a deep breath. "University is not for peasants. We till the earth and make things grow." A smile softened the lines etched in her face from years of toiling beneath summer suns and icy winter winds. "Our knowledge is limited to what we can glean from good books and music, and from each other." She gazed out the window for a moment. "We raise our families, and we love. It is a good life." She turned and looked at Tatyana. "God is not ashamed of this. You must continue to dream, but do not forget the reality of life."

"Yes, Mama." Tatyana rested her elbows on her knees and her face in her hands. "But, why does it have to be so? Why are we not allowed to do what we want?" She hesitated. "And the soldiers. Why do they come to the villages and hurt the people? Don't they care that we are fellow citizens?"

Galya's shoulders sagged a little and shadows darkened her eyes. "Life is as it is. We trust God will redeem us in this life or the next." She straightened her shoulders and said more brightly, "Now . . . the eggs."

Tatyana jumped to her feet, and just as she lay her hand on the latch, the door was pushed open.

"Galya, is our lunch ready? There are a couple of hungry men ready to eat," said Ivan Letinov as he filled the doorway.

Tatyana stepped back.

"It will be ready soon," Galya said. "I am waiting for the eggs." She raised one eyebrow and looked at her daughter.

"I'm going, I'm going," Tatyana said and slipped past her father.

Ivan tapped his boots on the step.

"Where is Yuri?" Galya asked.

"He's putting up the tools. He'll be here soon." Ivan took off his hat and wiped his brow with the back of his hand. "It felt like a cool day until I began haying."

"Sit. I'll get you some water." Galya filled a glass and handed it to her husband.

He drained it, then returned it to his wife. "Please, could I have another?"

Galya took the glass and refilled it. As she gave it to her husband, she glanced outside. In a whispered voice she asked, "Is it true? Did the soldiers come to the Ponomarev's last night?"

"Yes. Yes, they came." Ivan combed his heavy mustache with his fingers. "The Ponomarevs are gone. All their livestock, gone."

"Oh, no," Galya groaned. She sank into a chair. "When will it end? When will it all end?"

Ivan reached out and took his wife's hand but said nothing. He had no words of comfort. No one could stop Stalin's soldiers. They came and went as they pleased. If you resisted, you died. Many disappeared. Rumors of work camps and mass murders abounded, but common citizens could do nothing.

"Will they come here?" Galya asked.

"We are called Kulaks, so . . . probably they will come."

"It is so wrong—to label a person a Kulak just because they own a few animals and a little land. We have done nothing but live and feed our family."

Ivan patted Galya's hand. "I know. I know. This is the government's way of setting the people who own nothing against those who have a little. It is how they will control us.

They will keep us fighting among ourselves, and we will be defeated." He sipped his water. "It had to be someone we know."

"What?"

"The person who turned in the Ponomarevs had to be a neighbor or friend. No one from outside our township would know anything about them."

Galya stood up and smoothed her skirt. "Can we speak of something else?" She loosened her babushka, then replaced it over her hair and tightened it. "How is the haying going?"

"It's a good crop. We did several stacks this morning."

Galya glanced out the window. "The children are coming." She turned to the stove and, using the edge of her apron, opened the oven door and looked in, breathing deeply the sweet aroma of fresh bread.

"It smells good," Ivan said.

"And it's finished just in time. It will be perfect with some eggs and cheese."

The sounds of grinding gears and engines came from outside. Galya's stomach lurched. "What is that?" Her voice sounded sharp and tense.

Ivan went to the door. "Stay put." He stepped outside.

Galya quickly crossed to the window and looked out. "Oh, my God!" Her hand went to her mouth. "Soldiers!"

Several men jumped from the truck. Some stood with rifles ready and watched as a large imposing man, wearing the uniform of the Red Army, marched up to Ivan. He held a cigar between his teeth and didn't bother to remove it when he talked.

Unable to hear what was being said, Galya went to the door and opened it a little.

The soldier took the stogie from his mouth and tapped the end of it, dropping ashes on Ivan's shoes. He looked up and found Yuri and Tatyana approaching from the barn. "Who are they?"

"My children."

He glanced at Galya, then looked back at Ivan. "You're under arrest!"

"We have done nothing," Ivan said.

"You are Kulaks and enemies of the state."

"No! We are not!" Galya ran toward her husband. "That is not true."

Ivan reached for his wife, but the soldier closed his fist and back-handed him, knocking him to the ground. Hitting his head against a stone, he moaned, then lay still.

"Dear God!" Galya knelt beside her husband. "Ivan! Ivan!" He did not respond. She looked over her shoulder at their tormentor. "What have you done?" She turned back to her husband and wiped his bloodied cheek with her hand. "Please leave us alone. We have done nothing."

The officer studied the agitated woman, cocked one eyebrow, and returned his cigar to his mouth. "Internal Affairs will decide your guilt or innocence."

"Papa, are you all right?" Tatyana asked as she knelt in the dirt beside her father and took his hand.

Ivan pushed himself up on one elbow and put his hand to his head. "I . . . I think so."

Yuri stood squarely in front of the soldier, his fists rolled into tight balls. "Please go. We are good citizens and have done nothing wrong."

The man ignored Yuri and looked at Ivan and Galya. "You two, get your things. You will come with us."

Galya pushed herself to her feet. Her hand shook as she smoothed her hair back from her face. "But we have our children. What will they do without us?"

The soldier sized up Yuri and then Tatyana. "They look grown to me." He took one last puff on his cigar, tossed it to the ground, and crushed it beneath his heel. He looked back at Ivan and Galya and said coldly, "Move."

Tatyana and Yuri helped their father to his feet. Ivan leaned on them heavily and shuffled toward the cottage between his two children. Galya followed, and then the soldier.

Once inside the house, Ivan dropped into a chair while Galya gathered their belongings. Careful not to look at her children, she quietly bundled up warm clothing. She stopped at the shelf beside her bedroom door where a family photo rested. Gently she picked it up, running her hand over the images. Without a word, she slipped the photograph into her dress pocket.

"Kulaks are enemies of the state. Wealthy Kulaks will destroy the new plan," the officer said.

Wealthy? We have little. Tatyana chewed her lip.

The man folded his arms across his chest and glared at her.

Tatyana's stomach knotted. Could he know her thoughts? Without meaning to, she moved back one step.

The intruder stood away from the doorway. "Enough. It is time to go."

Tatyana reached out and took her mother's hand. "No, Mamochka! No!" She turned to their abductor. "Please. They have done nothing."

"Go to your Aunt Irina's. Tell her what has happened." Galya's eyes glistened with tears. "You will always be my *dochka,* my little daughter. I will not forget you. Do not forget me." She kissed her child.

Tears streamed down Tatyana's cheeks. Her throat ached, and she could say nothing.

Turning to Yuri, Galya said, "Take care of your sister, and trust the Lord. He is your only refuge."

Grimly, Yuri nodded.

Ivan looked at his son and daughter. "We will live."

The officer grabbed him by the collar and hefted him to his feet, then pushed him toward the door.

Tatyana dug her fingernails into her palms and watched helplessly as their mother and father were marched into the yard.

Some of the men led the livestock into the forest. Gun shots followed. Other soldiers stormed the house, pilfering anything that was small enough to carry.

"Hurry!" the commander ordered. "We have many *Kulaks* to deal with." He said the word as if it tasted bitter.

"We are not Kulaks!" Tatyana screamed. "We are only poor farmers."

The man turned on her and slapped her hard across the cheek. "There were three cows in your field and a set of mares to pull your plow. This is what you call poor? You have more than your neighbors. And you think this is right?" He leveled a venomous stare at the young Russian woman. "Stalin has a new plan. One that is fair to everyone. We will all be equal."

Tatyana fought rising nausea as she covered her stinging cheek with her hand. *This was fair?* She glared at the man.

The soldier ignored her and pushed Galya and Ivan toward the truck. As Galya stepped onto the back bumper, another prisoner reached out and took her hand and pulled her up beside him. The two then helped Ivan. Blood dripped from a wound on his forehead, but he paid no heed.

Tatyana could not bear it. "No! Do not do this!" She ran toward the truck, but Yuri caught her and held his sister in his arms.

She battled against him, trying to pull free. "Let me go! Let me go!"

"I am not the enemy. Be still," Yuri said sternly under his breath. "This is doing no good. Do you want them to take you, too?"

Yuri's words shattered her will. She stopped struggling. He was right. It was useless. The fight in her drained away. She dropped her arms to her sides and leaned against Yuri as tears spilled from her eyes and washed her cheeks. The truck's engine roared to life, and Tatyana thought she might faint.

"Mama, Papa," she said quietly. "Yuri, how can this be?"

Yuri clenched and unclenched his jaw, but said nothing.

The truck moved toward the road.

With one arm around his wife's shoulders, Ivan Letinov lifted his other hand and waved to his children.

The truck chugged down the road and out of sight.

A heavy quiet enveloped the farm.

For a long while Yuri and Tatyana leaned against each other and stared down the dirt road the way the truck had gone.

"They're not coming back," Yuri finally said. "We'd better go in."

Silently, Tatyana turned and walked back to their cottage.

Afternoon shadows fell over the house, and the sun no longer brightened the rooms. The cottage had been ransacked. Nothing was left intact. A chair lay on its side on the floor and, as Yuri righted it, a page from the book Tatyana had been reading slipped to the planking. She picked it up and stared at the blurred words through tears.

"They've taken everything, even our phonograph," Tatyana murmured, then hurried to a cabinet on the far side of the room. She pushed aside a damaged bureau and knelt in front of the cupboard. "Please be here," she whispered. "Please." She placed her hand on the latch but didn't open it for a moment, afraid of what she would find. Then, with her eyes closed, she slowly freed the lock and opened the cabinet door. Cautiously she opened her eyes. There they lay—the family's phonograph records. The soldiers had overlooked them. Gently she lifted one of the beloved discs and cradled it against her chest and wept, "Papa. Oh, Papa."

Maybe there would be music again.

CHAPTER 2

April 1933

TATYANA GENTLY WRAPPED THE last record between sheets of the *Pravda* newspaper and placed it in the box. She let her hand rest on the package. The music of Alexander Glazunov seemed to play through her fingers as she remembered evenings with her mother and father listening to his lush, colorful symphonies. Dmitry Shostokovich's less conservative rhythms marched through her mind. *What wonderful times,* she thought, blinking back tears. It had been so long ago, yet it seemed like yesterday. "And now I must leave Russia," she whispered, as she closed the carton.

Alexander's calloused hand covered his niece's hand. Gently he said, "Let me tie that for you."

Tatyana sat back. "Thank you, Uncle."

With a heavy piece of rope, he carefully tied the package, snugly cinching it off, then handed the package to his son, Lev. "This is the last box." Combing his graying beard with his fingers, he looked at Tatyana. "It's time to go."

Tatyana nodded. Slowly she walked to the door and took her heavy coat down from its hook.

Alexander held her coat while she slipped her arms into the sleeves. He let his arm rest across her shoulders and gave her a quick squeeze. Turning her to face him, he held her at arm's length. His usually bright blue eyes had lost their sparkle. Blinking back tears, he said, "We wish you happiness in your new home. You will be missed."

"Thank you for all you and Aunt Irina have done. You've been like parents to me and Yuri since Mama and Papa were taken. It is not an easy thing to say good-bye." She glanced at Yuri who stood at the door, his hand on the latch. "I wish I did not have to go—"

"There is nothing more to talk about," Yuri cut in. "It has been settled."

"Here is a blanket for you," Irina said, handing it to Tatyana. "I made it special for this trip. It is never warm enough on those trains." She forced a smile. "And it will keep the cold off your legs as you travel to Moscow."

Tatyana draped the plain-looking blanket over her arm. "Thank you." Emotion choked off her words, and she was unable to check her tears. "You have been so good to me." She swallowed hard, struggling to control her grief. "I love you."

Irina pulled her niece into her arms and held her close, then stepped back, keeping her hands on Tatyana's arms. Forcing a smile, she said, "Now you will have a great adventure. I wish I could have such an experience." Her eyes misted. "May God go with you."

Tatyana kissed her aunt on both cheeks, then hurried out the door without looking back.

With a quick wave, Yuri followed his sister.

The wagon pitched forward, then lurched back as the gray gelding tugged at its yoke. The spring thaw had turned the roads into mush, and passage was denied to all but the most determined.

Tatyana's stomach thudded as they dropped into another deep rut. She gripped the sides of the cart. "I think we should try another day. We'll never make it. It would be better to wait until summer."

The coffee-colored mud sucked at the wooden wheels and threatened to hold them fast as Yuri urged the animal on. Obediently the horse lunged forward, and the muddied road yielded to the travelers.

"We will make it," Yuri said decisively. "This is God's will for you. I know it."

"You have always been the strong one. Even when Mama and Papa were—" Tatyana stopped short.

"It's all right, Sister. Say it—even when they *were* alive." He paused. "They are dead. We must accept this."

"No. I cannot believe it. They must be working for the government somewhere. I've heard of camps where people work until they are released. Don't you remember Mr. Vikenti Grokholsky? He came back."

His voice sounding weary, Yuri said, "Yes. I remember. He was nearly dead from starvation." He flicked the reins. "But what about all the others?"

"The others?"

Yuri sighed out of frustration. "There are so many . . . gone forever."

Tatyana didn't argue. She knew what he said was true. Thousands of people had disappeared or had been taken by soldiers. Almost none returned. Fear prickled up her spine. The soldiers could come for anyone at any time. One minute a person could be enjoying his family or working the farm, and the next he was gone. She wondered what really happened to prisoners. She'd heard stories—tales of ghastly prisons with appalling conditions and labor camps where prisoners died from exposure and starvation.

She gazed at the fields of snow and mud, pushing the ugly thoughts aside. Soon the spring grasses and flowers would replace the muck left by the thaw. The birds would return, and her friends would celebrate the coming of summer. *And I will miss it,* Tatyana thought sadly. She couldn't bear the thought. If only her brother would let her stay.

She turned to Yuri. "I do not want to go to America! Why won't you listen to me? There must be another way."

Yuri kept his eyes straight ahead. "You will go. I have made the arrangements. And there is nothing else to be said."

"But, what if Mama and Papa *do* come back?"

"Do not be foolish. You know they will never return."

Tears stung Tatyana's eyes.

Yuri's look softened, and he patted his sister's hand. "I wish it could be different." He took a deep breath and turned back to guiding the horse. "But, things will not change. There will be no grain in the barns this year. As always, the soldiers will take it. They will not allow us to keep our crops. We might as well leave them in the ground to rot," he said venomously. "They have taken most of the livestock. It will not get better. They will do their best to destroy us or herd us all onto collective farms."

The horse whinnied and sidestepped to the left.

Tatyana eyes went to the ditch. "Dear Lord!"

The bodies of a woman and her child lay in the mud. Even in death, the woman had done her best to comfort the baby, holding the still, blue infant to her breast to shield him from the cold.

Tatyana turned away.

"No! Look at them! This is what you will know if you stay! This is what waits for you!"

"No. No. Life cannot be so monstrous." Tears washed Tatyana's cheeks. "How can God allow this?"

"It is not God." His voice turned harsh. "It is the evil one. He stalks the earth, and it is only with our permission that he has power over us."

Shocked at her brother's words, Tatyana turned a questioning look on Yuri.

"The enemy prowls around like a hungry lion, looking for anyone he can feast upon. When God's people refuse to look the enemy in the eye and stand against him, *he* prevails. We have allowed this by not standing up and fighting the evil that has overtaken our country."

Tatyana leaned against her brother. Despairing, she asked, "What could we have done?"

Yuri's jaw twitched, and he looked at the horizon. "We could have fought."

"And you would have died."

"There are things worse than death." He looked down at his sister and forced a smile. "Enough of this. Can we speak of something else?"

"What will I do without you? You have always been the strong one. Without you, I am nothing."

Yuri wrapped his arm about Tatyana's shoulder. "Without me, you will learn to look to God. You have depended on me too long." He paused. "Maybe I have loved you too well."

"You can never love too well. I thank God for you. I know Mama and Papa had peace because of your strength. They knew you would take good care of me." She snuggled closer. "Why must I go without you? There has to be a way you can come to America. We could start a new life together."

"It was not easy to get papers for even one." Yuri glanced at his sister, then let his eyes slide away and across the empty countryside. "We were only able to get the necessary documents with help from the underground," he whispered. "I thank God you have a chance for a new beginning."

"And what will happen to you?"

Yuri grinned his usual, easygoing smile. "You know me. I am very innovative. I will fight. Death will not get its ugly hands on me."

"And then what? Will you come for me?"

Moscow appeared through mists rising from the wet earth.

Yuri ignored Tatyana's question. "Look. We are almost there."

The Moscow skyline was dominated by the ponderous shadows of the newly constructed government offices. Twenty-six stories high, the building perched over the city like a malevolent monarch waiting to pounce upon its innocent subjects.

Tatyana couldn't subdue a shudder. "It looks frightening."

Yuri said nothing, but snapped the reins and hurried the gelding.

In the city, the roads were made of cobblestone and concrete, and the cart moved more easily.

Tatyana studied the people. Even here they carried the scars of hunger and hopelessness. Gaunt, suspicion-filled faces peered above colorless, heavy coats. Was it the same all over Russia? Was there no place to escape the hunger and the fear?

And yet, Tatyana did not want to leave. This was home. She had too many precious memories of her beloved Russia. Days of sunshine and plenty, winters filled with ice-skating and crackling fires, and nights of revelry with family and friends. Even the contrast between the warm, colorful summer months and the long, bleak winters brought a sense of energy. She took a deep breath; the cold air felt potent in her lungs. She belonged to Russia.

Tatyana pulled her coat tighter and glanced at her brother. "I have heard of hunger in America—that poverty plagues the country and evil lurks in the hearts of the people. There are stories of frightful murders and police who do not care."

Yuri pulled on the reins and slowed the wagon. When they stopped, he turned to his sister. "I already told you what cousin Lev said. Our government has lied to us. In America there is plenty for all. Everyone's larder is full, and there is more money than you can count. And our uncle has said the people are kind."

"If that is so, why doesn't Lev go to America to live with his uncle?"

Yuri shrugged his shoulders. "You know Lev is in love. He told me just this morning that he and Olya will marry."

"Why don't they go together?"

"She will not leave her family."

Tatyana folded her arms across her chest and sat back in her seat. "And I will not leave mine."

"You will." Yuri clicked his tongue and flicked the reins. The gelding pricked up his ears, blasted cold air from his nostrils, and moved forward.

She sat with her back stiff and stared straight ahead. Her heart ached. There would be no convincing Yuri. He had made up his mind. She would have to leave.

As they approached the railway station, street congestion increased. Everyone seemed in a hurry. City trams and buses moved along at a brisk pace, while horse-drawn carts plodded steadily through the rush. Unused to all the activity, their horse snorted and tossed his head, but Yuri kept him under tight rein. Tatyana couldn't understand why there was such a flurry of activity, but she welcomed the hurried pace, for it matched her own agitated mood.

At the train station, a sense of excitement and urgency filled the air. Delighted greetings and tearful farewells were exchanged. Tatyana wished she could feel anticipation. She tried to recapture her aunt's final words. She had told Tatyana to enjoy the adventure, but all she could feel was a deep sense of sorrow and loss.

Yuri pulled the horse to a stop. "The train should be here soon." He jumped down and took Tatyana's two bags and the small crate from the back of the cart. Glancing up at his sister, he struggled to keep his emotions under control. "I'll check on your ticket." He turned and walked into the terminal.

Tatyana folded her blanket back, laid it over her arm, then climbed down from her seat and followed her brother inside the station. Her natural sense of curiosity diverted Tatyana's thoughts from her grief. The room was alive with people and felt almost warm. She sat on a bench and, watching the travelers, wondered where they could all be going. Were they going on holiday, or had business drawn them away from home? She studied the anxious, distracted faces and tried to guess their destinations. People from every background filled the station. It was easy to determine whether someone was a peasant, *bourgeoi,* or a noble, simply by their clothing and the set of their shoulders. She looked down at her own garments and realized she wore her own label of peasant. Self-consciously she smoothed her skirt and sat a little straighter.

Finally, Tatyana turned her attention to a rail car filling with people. She'd traveled by train only once before when she was six years old. It was midwinter, and all she could remember was how cold it had been. Thankfully this time it was spring, and Aunt Irina had provided an extra blanket for her lap.

Yuri handed his sister her papers and ticket. "Everything is in order." He lowered his voice. "Now, don't worry about your identification papers. I was assured they are just as they should be."

Tucking them inside her satchel, she asked, "What will I do if someone asks me about them? What if something isn't right?"

Yuri thought a moment. "If someone asks, insist they are all in order. If you have to, become outraged and angry."

Tatyana's stomach churned. What if she was found out? "Do you think anything will happen?"

Yuri patted her arm. "No. Everything will be fine. Don't you worry."

Tatyana nodded and hoped she wouldn't have to show them to anyone.

A train crept toward the platform amidst the screech of brakes and blasting steam.

"This is your transport."

Tatyana slung her bag over her shoulder, plucked at a loose thread on the blanket, and studied the ground.

Yuri set her suitcase and the crate of records on the landing, then shoved his hands in his pockets. "I guess this is it."

Tatyana squared her jaw and, without looking up, nodded.

Yuri kissed her on each cheek and pulled her into his embrace. "Be cautious. Speak to no one."

Tatyana's resolve to remain emotionless melted, and she wrapped her free arm around her brother's neck and held him tight. "Please don't make me go," she whispered.

Yuri hesitated, then gently extracted her arm. Without releasing her hands, he stepped back. "I love you, Tatyana. I want something better for you." He lowered his eyes. "One day I will come to America."

She studied Yuri. He was tall like her, and although he was already twenty-three years old, he had not lost his boyish looks. His blue eyes glistened with unshed tears. She hugged him. "I will never see you again. I know it."

Yuri lifted her hands and kissed each one. "We are the same blood. We can never truly be parted." He took a deep breath.

"Remember, God loves us. He binds us together even if an ocean separates us."

Tatyana couldn't keep her chin from quivering as she nodded in agreement. "I know, but . . . it is . . . so hard." Unable to control her tears any longer, they filled her eyes and stained her cheeks. "Yuri, please pray with me."

He glanced around the platform. "We can't pray here, but know I am praying in my heart."

"I love you. Please join me soon."

"I will." Yuri pulled his sister back into his arms. He held her close for a moment, then released her and kissed her on each cheek again.

The train whistle shrieked.

Yuri handed the large bag and the box of records to the porter.

Tatyana turned and stepped onto the car's landing. She didn't move up the steps, but stood with her back to her brother as the train lunged forward. She longed to run back into his protective arms. He'd always been the steady one. What would she do without him?

Her shoes felt like lead as she forced her feet to climb the steps, walk down the aisle, and turn at the empty seat where the porter had stored her baggage. She sat down and scooted to the window. Wiping away the frost and moisture, she peered out.

Yuri stood on the platform, his shoulders thrown back and his jaw squared, as he searched the rows of windows. As the train moved away, he walked along the landing, seeking his sister. When he found her, he forced a smile and waved.

Tatyana placed her hand against the glass as the train picked up speed and the station disappeared. "Good-bye," she whispered through tears.

CHAPTER 3

TATYANA SETTLED INTO THE stiff, uncomfortable seat. She tucked her small satchel safely between herself and the wall and protectively rested her hand on it. The address of her uncle in America, what little money her family and friends had been able to pull together, some personal possessions, and, most importantly, her traveling papers were hidden inside.

A small coal stove at the back of the car did little to ward off the pervasive cold. Tatyana shivered, wishing she were sitting closer to the firebox. She spread the wool blanket Aunt Irina had given her over her lap and ran her hand across the rough wool. It still smelled of her aunt's house. Her heart ached at the reminder of home and the people she'd been forced to leave behind. She smoothed a pucker in the material. Irina had carded the wool, spun it, then weaved it herself. "Simple and plain is all we need," her aunt had said. Tatyana smiled as she remembered the woman's practical nature. She'd always been sensible and hardworking—so much like her own mother.

Blinking back tears, Tatyana rested her head against the window. Memories of her parents' arrest crowded her mind. She and Yuri had been shattered by the loss, but Uncle Alexander and Aunt Irina had tenderly reached out and taken them into their home. In the midst of sorrow, love grew; and before long Alexander and Irina's farm became home to the young Letinovs. Years had lessened the pain, but Tatyana had never given up hope of their returning. But now—

"I'll never see you again," she whispered to the empty plain outside her window.

She stared at the muddied snow. Solid slate-gray clouds stretched across the sky and looked ready to dump snow. She shivered in spite of her blanket. Spring storms could sometimes be the worst, laying down heavy, wet snow that piled up so deep the trains became entrenched in a sea of white. Her cousin had once been traveling when an unexpected storm forced his train to stop. Passengers had worked to clear the line. They shoveled and shoveled as the train followed them down the tracks. It had taken days to creep across the countryside. She hoped there would be no such problems on this trip.

Snow began to fall. As one icy crystal, then another and another, touched the earth, she thought, *At least it will cover the mud*. Tatyana hated the heavy, spring muck. Everyone did. It was trouble, sucking at boots as well as wagon wheels. The warmer weather urged farmers to their fields, but the mud made it impossible to till the soil and drove them back indoors.

The dreary landscape passed by, and Tatyana sighed. Sunshine would not accompany her across the plains. She longed to see a spring flower or two, although she knew it was too early. The delicate white blossoms of the wood sorrel that grew beneath the great spruce trees would be one of the first to push through the soil. As the days passed, the countryside would brighten with foliage. An image of a field ablaze with lavender, blue, and yellow blossoms filled her mind. She could almost smell the soft fragrance of wildflowers. *I wonder if there are such things in America. No, it is not possible. No place is as beautiful as Russia.*

The stink of cigarette smoke intruded upon Tatyana's daydreaming. She looked for the source. Across from her and one seat down, an old man slouched in his seat. Though his eyes were closed and he appeared to be sleeping, a cigarette rested on his lower lip. Each time he breathed out, ashes showered onto his dingy white shirt stretched across his rounded belly. Tatyana smiled and wondered if he'd ever caught himself on fire.

"Hello," came a small voice.

Tatyana looked down to find a little girl with huge brown eyes leaning against the frame of her seat. "Hello there." The little girl said nothing. "My name is Tatyana. What is yours?"

The child drew back a little, her dark eyes suspicious.

The fear has touched even the little ones, she thought sadly. Doing her best to disguise her own disenchantment with life, Tatyana smiled warmly.

The child relaxed a little. She reached out and touched the blanket. "This is nice. It will keep you very warm."

"My aunt made it for me."

Without looking up, the girl said, "My name is Galina Rukhamin. I am going to my cousin's house in Tikhvin. Mama says it is nice there, and we will live on a farm and grow food."

"I live on a farm, too."

"Is it a collective?"

"No. It belongs to my aunt and uncle."

The little girl nodded and smiled. Her pale yellow hair had been pulled into a tight ponytail that bounced when she moved.

"When I live on a farm my stomach won't hurt so much. We'll have lots to eat."

"Galina? Galina!" The voice sounded shrill and fearful.

"That is my mama. I must go." The little girl turned to leave, then stopped. "May I visit you again?"

"I would like that. We can talk about farming. It will be a long trip, and it will be good to have a friend to visit with."

A broad smile transformed Galina's solemn expression. She turned and bounded down the aisle, slowing at the sight of an NKVD official. With her hands tucked in close to her sides, she squeezed past the internal affairs police officer.

Tatyana's heart pounded. She hadn't noticed the man before. Had he gotten on at Moscow?

The officer made a slow perusal of the car. His eyes met Tatyana's. Like most policemen, his look was hard and detached. She quickly averted her gaze and instinctively placed her hand on her bag. The officer turned and strode out of the coach.

Tatyana's heart slowed, and she took a deep breath. She hoped she wouldn't see him again. *What will I do if he asks me for my papers? I'll face that if and when it happens,* she told herself and leaned her head back against the seat and tried to rest.

The hours passed slowly, and Tatyana's body grew weary. Her back and neck ached, and her legs had gone numb from sitting on the hard bench. *I must walk. I can't stand this another minute,* she decided, folding back her blanket and standing up. Careful to keep her satchel tucked beneath her arm, she sidestepped out of her seat. There was little space in the aisle, but it felt good to be on her feet. She stretched to one side then the other. With one hand braced against the small of her back, she arched backward, then bent forward.

She glanced at the seat behind her. An old woman, wearing a bright red and orange tunic with a scarf of the same material, nodded at her. Tatyana smiled in return, then strolled toward the back of the car. Near the rear of the coach, she found Galina sitting beside a solemn young woman. She smiled at the little girl and said, "Hello. It is good to see you again."

Galina grinned, but her mother remained somber, keeping a protective hold on her daughter. She didn't look much older than Tatyana and seemed frightened. She shared the same deep, brown eyes and flaxen hair of her daughter, but years of hardship had dimmed the light in her eyes.

"I'm sorry if I frightened you, but Galina and I have been visiting with each other." She hesitated. The woman barely inclined her head. "My name is Tatyana." She held out her hand.

The woman took it tentatively and shook it. "I am Ella Rukhamin. Galina told me about you."

Tatyana reached out and patted Galina's head. "She's a beautiful child."

The woman's eyes softened a little as she caressed her daughter's back. "She is, isn't she." She studied Tatyana for a moment. "I did not mean to be rude, but you . . ." she searched for the right word, "you surprised me."

"I am glad we met," Tatyana said. "I hope you and Galina will both have time for more visits."

Galina turned to her mother. "Will it be all right?"

Ella smiled slightly and nodded.

Galina grinned. "I will come later."

"Good." Tatyana tried to think of something else to say. "It is much warmer back here than up front." She nodded toward the stove. "You're lucky to be close to the heat."

Ella glanced at the firebox. "We are thankful." She gazed out the window and returned to her reserved manner.

"Well, it was good to speak with you," Tatyana finally said.

Ella nodded. "And you."

Tatyana tweaked Galina's nose. "I will see you soon."

After visiting the convenience, Tatyana reluctantly made her way back to her seat. The train lurched over the tracks, and she gripped the back of the benches to steady herself. When she reached her seat, she studied it for a moment. *Oh, I wish I had a bed or at least some cushions.* With a sigh, she dropped onto the bench and lay her head back. *I wonder how long before we stop,* she thought and closed her eyes. Soon her body gave in to fatigue, and she slept.

"Torzok. Torzok."

The words sounded muffled and far away as Tatyana struggled to drag herself from sleep. She blinked and looked about. Her neck had a crick, and she rubbed it, trying to relax the cramped muscles. She straightened her back and stretched her legs. Glancing around the car, everything looked the same, except the man with the cigarette was now sitting up and peering out his window. When the porter came by, Tatyana asked, "Did you say something a minute ago?"

"Torzok, ma'am. We're nearly to Torzok. You can disembark—you will find food and washing facilities there."

Tatyana brushed her hair off her face and tugged at her coat to smooth the wrinkles. Her empty stomach grumbled. Food sounded good. She stretched her arms overhead and tipped to the side a little, trying to work out her stiffness. It would feel wonderful to walk a bit. As the darkening landscape hurtled past, she searched for the depot. Homes and buildings swept by, and finally the train slowed as they rumbled into a small station.

Passengers stood up and filled the aisle, eager to leave their cramped quarters. Tatyana folded her blanket and set it on the seat beside her, then forced herself to remain seated until the walkway cleared. Taking her handbag and holding it close to her, she stood up and made her way to the aisle.

As she stepped off the train, a cold, sharp breeze carrying the aroma of hot food met her. Her mouth watered as she scanned the platform. Several merchants stood behind tables selling goods. The smell of sausages drew her to a bench laden with the hot, sizzling meats.

A short, stocky man with a woolen cap pulled over his ears tended the food. He peeked up from beneath heavy brows. "How many would you like?"

"How much do they cost?" Tatyana asked, studying the meaty morsels.

"One ruble."

"For how many?"

"One."

"That is robbery!"

"They are very good. I cannot give them away. You are lucky there is anything at all."

Tatyana wanted to throttle the man for his greediness, but she said nothing and studied the fare on the next table. There she found only black bread. It would fill her stomach but didn't look nearly as appetizing. She sighed and looked back at the peddler. "I can't pay what you ask." She folded her arms over her chest.

"All right. For you, seventy-five kopecks."

Tatyana considered the offer. "Fifty," she countered.

The man thought a moment, then slowly nodded in agreement.

It was still very extravagant, but Tatyana couldn't resist and dug in her satchel for the money. Taking out the exact change, she gave it to the vendor, who quickly handed her a sausage.

"Thank you," she said and took a small bite. The meat burned her tongue, but Tatyana didn't care. It tasted wonderful.

Nibbling on the succulent food, she moved to the table with the black bread. "How much for the bread?"

"Two slices, only thirty-five kopecks."

Tatyana calculated how much money she had. She would have to make it last until she reached America. "I will take two."

The woman sliced off two large chunks and handed them to a hungry Tatyana. "Enjoy," she said with a smile.

"Thank you." Tatyana took a taste of meat, then a bite of the hard bread. She chewed, closed her eyes, and savored the mingled flavors before moving to the next merchant.

Standing over a large pot, an old woman lifted the lid and swirled the contents. Steam rose from the kettle. She looked at the tall, young Russian girl. "You like some good, hot soup?"

Tatyana peered inside. "What kind is it?"

"Fish. It is very good. You would like some?"

Tatyana looked at the broth. Very little fish seemed to be floating amidst the greasy stew. She glanced down the platform and wished there were another choice. *I should be thankful there is anything at all,* she reminded herself. "How much is it?"

"Forty kopecks for one bowl."

"That seems like an awful lot for soup."

The woman clamped the lid back down on the pot. "You can go elsewhere."

Tatyana glanced at the coal-black engine of the train. It was quiet for now, but she knew it would be leaving soon and her stomach still felt empty. She dug into her bag and carefully counted out her money. "Here." She plunked several coins on the table.

The vendor dipped into the hot liquid and ladled some into a chipped mug. She handed it to Tatyana. "I want my cup back."

"Of course." Tatyana sipped the soup. It tasted better than it looked and felt warm in her empty belly. She quickly drained the mug and returned it. "Thank you."

The woman nodded.

The train's engines came to life, and a whistle blasted, signaling time to board. Dreading the hard seat that awaited her, Tatyana walked slowly. Reluctantly she boarded, found her place and, with a sigh, sank onto the unyielding bench. She pulled the blanket across her lap and nibbled on the hard bread, tucking the other piece into her bag.

As the train pulled away from the station, a young boy and a man wearing wire-rimmed glasses sat in the seat across the aisle from Tatyana. The boy stared at her while the man lifted his black, fur hat from his head and smiled in greeting. He set the cap on the shelf above his seat. "I don't suppose I'll need this in here."

"You may. It has been very cold." Tatyana liked the man immediately. He had a warm smile and friendly eyes.

"So, are you traveling far?"

"To Leningrad," she hesitated, remembering Yuri's warning not to speak to anyone, but unable to refrain from sharing, she added, "and then to America."

The stranger lifted his eyebrows. "America?"

"Yes. I have an uncle there."

A dreamy look came into the man's eyes. "One day I would like to visit America. I have heard it is a land of great freedom and wealth." He looked about the compartment. "Things I believe most of us will never know," he said a little sadly.

Tatyana managed a small smile. Under different circumstances, she too might be excited to explore the mystery of a new land, but right now all she wanted was to return home. She looked away and leaned her forehead against the window. Dusk lay over the snowy countryside.

What did her future hold? What would America really be like? *If only Yuri was with me.* Tatyana chewed her lip and tried to swallow the ache in her throat. She searched the horizon. *Mama, Papa, where are you? How can I leave home when I don't even know what has happened to you?*

"Why are you crying?" a small voice asked.

Tatyana wiped at her wet cheeks. "Oh, Galina, I didn't hear you."

"Are you sad?"

"I was just thinking about my family."

"Are they sick?"

"No." Tatyana gently blew into her handkerchief. "My brother lives near Moscow, but my parents . . . I . . . I don't know where they are."

"Did the soldiers take them?"

Tatyana nodded.

"My papa, too. They came and took him." Galina's eyes brimmed with tears. "Mama cries a lot."

Tatyana scooped the little girl up, set her on her lap, and hugged her. "I'm sorry. So sorry."

Galina buried her face against Tatyana's shoulder.

For a long while, the two held each other. They said nothing. No words were needed. They understood each other's pain, and sharing it felt good.

Tatyana smoothed the girl's hair and wondered how her own mother had felt when she'd tried to chase away little Tatyana's fears. The remnants of a bad dream amidst a stormy night reached out to her from the past. Her mother had come to her bedside when she'd cried out. She remembered the softness of her nightgown, the feel of her hand on her cheek, even the smell of soap, and then the memory slipped away like a mist, leaving Tatyana feeling empty and sad.

Galina sat up. "I'd better go now. Mama might wake up and worry." The little girl climbed down. "Please don't cry. I know they will be all right."

"Hey, what's your name?" came an animated voice from across the aisle. The sturdy-looking boy of about ten grinned at Galina.

Galina stared at him but didn't reply.

"Don't be scared. I won't hurt you." The boy smiled broadly.

"I'm not afraid," Galina said firmly.

"Do you want to play a game?"

"What kind of game?"

The youngster thought a moment. "How about a race. The first one to the end of the car wins."

Galina quickly caught his enthusiasm. "Catch me!" she cried, running down the aisle, bouncing from side to side with the sway of the train. The young boy hurried after her.

"To have such energy," the boy's father said with a shake of his head.

Tatyana nodded, noticing the frowns of disapproval on the faces of the closest passengers. She returned to staring out the window. In the near darkness, she could see a family moving along the roadway. Harnessed into a cart, a man strained to pull his wife and child and their meager belongings. A teenage boy trailed along behind. They looked gaunt and frail like those from home. Tatyana felt sick at the sight and leaned her head against the window. *God, where are you? Why has this happened? How could you allow it?*

Irina's voice echoed through her mind. Many times they had pondered the country's circumstances and personal tragedies. "This is not God's doing, but the enemy's," Irina had said more than once. "Remember, we do not fight against flesh and blood, but principalities and powers. This is a spiritual battle, and if God's people do not fight with the weapons he has given, we cannot win."

But we are flesh and blood, Tatyana thought. *How do we fight something we cannot see?* Almost immediately Ephesians 6 came to mind.

Therefore take up the whole armor of God, that you may be able to withstand in the evil day, and having done all, to stand. Stand therefore, having girded your waist with truth, having put on the breastplate of righteousness, and having shod your feet with the preparation of the gospel of peace; above all, taking the shield of faith with which you will be able to quench all the fiery darts of the wicked one. And take the helmet of salvation, and the sword of the Spirit, which is the word of God.

Father, I will try, but I'm weak. You must help me to stand.

A day, another night, and a morning passed. Just when Tatyana thought she would scream from the agony of sitting for so many hours, the porter announced Leningrad would be the next stop. At first relief flooded her, then uncertainty welled up. Soon she would board a ship to leave her homeland and begin life in a strange country across the sea.

As the train ground to a stop, the passengers stood, anxious to disembark. Tatyana hoisted her satchel over her shoulder, then drug the suitcase and box down from the upper shelf. She looked out the window and sat down, all the while staring at Leningrad Station. Momentarily forgetting her discomfort and desire to leave the train, she studied the immense white building. It looked grand, standing at least three stories high. Ornate arched windows adorned the front, giving the building an opulent appearance.

"Everyone halt," someone ordered.

Startled, Tatyana stood up and turned to see who had shouted the command. Several NKVD men marched into the car, including the man she'd seen the day before. Their eyes swept over the passengers—searching, searching for someone. The coach fell silent. No one breathed. Tatyana fingered her pouch. *Please, Father, not me.*

One man ordered two of the officers to move forward into the next car, and the three remaining checked the passengers and their belongings.

Tatyana's heart beat so hard it felt like it would burst. Her mouth went dry and her throat constricted as one of the men approached her. He stopped and studied her, looked at the luggage she carried, then stared at her face. After a very long moment, he moved on. Tatyana felt her legs go weak. She swayed and leaned against the window.

Another officer stopped in front of Galina's mother. He studied her, glanced at the papers in his hand, then looked back at the tiny woman. Ella blanched and looked at the floor.

No, God, no, Tatyana prayed.

"Your papers," the policeman snapped.

Her hands shaking, Ella looked through her bag. She searched for a very long time.

"Your papers!" the officer repeated.

Finally, she held up a crumpled piece of paper.

The man grabbed it. After glancing at the document, he asked, "This is what you call traveling papers?"

"It is all I have."

He grabbed her wrist and yanked her to her feet. "You will come with me." His voice reminded her of a killing frost.

Galina grabbed her mother's coat and clung to it. "No! No! Mama!"

With a look of contempt, the man stepped back and waited.

Ella bent and quickly hugged Galina. She whispered to her, straightened, and walked stiffly down the aisle. When she passed Tatyana, her eyes pleaded a silent message.

Tatyana understood Ella's heart and glanced back at where Galina had been. The little girl had disappeared. *Where is she?* Tatyana wondered, panic pulsing through her.

"Move along!" the officer ordered, shoving his prisoner.

As soon as the NKVD men had gone, the passengers began whispering among themselves, speculating over what had happened, some quick to condemn. One woman said, "Well, I suppose she gets what she deserves. Must have been a subversive."

The injustice was unendurable, and inwardly Tatyana fumed, but she remained silent. No good could be served by turning on each other. After all, isn't that what Stalin wanted? The man across the aisle held his son close, his outrage apparent.

"There is no justice anymore," Tatyana said just loud enough so he could hear.

"That is how it has always been for my people."

Tatyana wondered what he meant but didn't ask. All she could think of now was the abandoned little girl. *Dear Galina. What has become of you?* She hurried to the back of the car, stopping at Ella's seat. At first she couldn't see the child, but then she peered over the back of the bench and found her sitting on the floor with her legs tucked up close to her chest and pressed tightly against the wall. She had her eyes shut as if trying to close out the ugliness of the world.

"Galina?" Tatyana asked gently.

The youngster didn't respond.

"Galina, it's me. Tatyana. Please let me help you." She searched for the right words. "Little one, the bad men are gone. You don't have to be afraid."

The child looked up. "They are gone?"

Tatyana nodded. "We're comrades, you and I." She reached out.

Slowly, Galina unfolded her legs, took Tatyana's hand, and allowed her new friend to help her stand.

Tatyana pulled the little girl close and held her. Galina wrapped her arms around her neck and clung to her, but she didn't cry.

"We had better go," Tatyana said, lowering her to the floor and taking her hand. "Come on, we'll find your cousin."

Galina held back and stared at the floor.

"What is it?"

So quietly Tatyana could barely hear, the little girl said, "There is no cousin."

She placed her hands on Galina's shoulders and knelt in front of her. "Then who is it you are going to visit?"

"We are running away, and Mama just told me to say we were visiting my cousin. When they took my papa, Mama was afraid, and we left." Galina's eyes brimmed with tears. "What will they do to her? Will she be all right?"

Tatyana didn't know exactly what would happen to the young mother. Most of those detained went to prison or labor camps in Siberia where they died of hunger and cold.

Tatyana caressed the little girl's hair. "I'm sure she'll be fine. Are you hungry? Would you like something to eat?"

"No," she said in a small voice, gripping her friend's hand.

Doing her best to balance her small bag, her suitcase, and the carton of records, Tatyana led the girl from the railroad car and onto the station platform. *Lord, now what?* She looked down at Galina. How could she possibly care for this child? In just a few hours she would be on her way to America.

Galina sniffled and wiped at her nose.

"Well, we better find a place to stay tonight," Tatyana said. Gripping her suitcase in one hand and clutching her records under the other arm, she walked onto the platform and down the steps with Galina close beside her.

CHAPTER 4

Yuri sat at the kitchen table and watched the falling snow bury the recently exposed earth. "It will never end. This winter will never end."

Aunt Irina set a cup of tea in front of him. "What good is your anger? Winter will pass. It always does." She gazed out the window. "I remember your father sitting at this very table and saying the same thing. He would visit us and share a cup of tea, always anxious to get to his plow." She smiled softly. "He could barely contain himself. Sometimes I wondered if he might try plowing right through the last of the snow."

"He probably would have, too," Alexander said as he sat down across from Yuri, "if it hadn't been for the cursed mud." He patted Irina on her backside. "Woman, a cup of tea." He looked at Yuri and combed his beard with his fingers. "Do not look so worried. The snow will stop, and spring will come."

Yuri nodded absently. His mind returned to previous plantings and harvests shared with his father. Although the times had been uncertain, they had been good. *I wish it could be so again. Are you still alive, Papa, in a work camp somewhere? No,* he told himself. *I would have heard.* And what of Tatyana? Was she safe?

Irina handed each of the men a cup of hot tea. She glanced at her nephew. "It is not the weather that has you downcast is it, Yuri?"

Yuri looked at his aunt. "You know me too well."

"Tatyana will be fine. God will see to it."

"She is so young. She's never traveled this far from home. I mean, this is not just a holiday; she's crossing the ocean." He sipped his tea, then studied the cup's contents. "She didn't want to go. I forced her."

Alexander reached out and rested his hand on Yuri's forearm. "You did what was best." He lifted his cup and allowed the steam to warm his face. "Sometimes I think it would be good if we all left."

Irina placed her hand on her husband's shoulder. "You leave Russia? Never. You may speak of it, but you could not leave your home. Your roots go too deep and you know it."

"I think Tatyana had that same feeling of belonging to the land. I tore her from the only place she knew." Yuri turned his eyes back to the blowing snow. "Did I do the right thing?" he asked, not expecting an answer. He took another sip of tea. "What else could I do?" he said, his melancholy voice trailing off.

A government truck pulled into the yard. Yuri's heart thudded, and his stomach lurched. "Soldiers!" He stood up and inadvertently hit the table with his hip. The tea cup wobbled, rolled to the edge of the table, and fell to the floor without breaking. Yuri didn't notice.

"Remain calm. Trust in God," Alexander said as he stood and encircled Irina's shoulders with his arm. "We have done nothing wrong."

A canvas flap at the rear of the truck was pushed aside and a dozen soldiers leaped out. Orders were given, and the men scattered over the property. Several overran the barns, others searched the garden, and some disappeared in the storage shed.

Yuri clenched and unclenched his fists. If only he could stop them, but there was nothing he could do.

Her eyes filled with tears, Irina wrapped her arms around her husband's waist and leaned against him. Alexander's eyes burned with anger.

A soldier approached the door and pounded on it. Alexander let loose of Irina and strode across the room. Slowly he opened the door. An officer with close-cropped hair and a face that looked too young to have ever known the feel of a razor stood in the doorway. His jaw set, his eyes hard and emotionless, he barked, "You are hiding food!"

"No. We have nothing," Alexander said.

The soldier pushed past him. "We will see." He stomped into the kitchen and rifled through the cupboards.

"They will look and then leave," Alexander quietly reassured Irina.

Yuri could not remain so composed. "Why do you look?" he demanded. "Already the police have come and taken last year's harvest and left us to starve."

The man turned to Yuri and surveyed him slowly. "And still you refuse to move to a collective?"

"And be forced into slavery? Never." He looked out the window and gazed at the land. "This is good ground. Let us farm, and we will share with the government. There will be enough for all."

The officer returned to his task. He lifted the rug in the center of the room and pounded the floor with his booted foot, hoping to discover a hidden compartment. Disgusted, Yuri turned away. His words were wasted. The soldiers would do whatever they wanted.

When the intruder found no food or contraband, he went to the door and stepped outside. Another soldier marched up to the young commander. "We found nothing."

Yuri watched as one of the interlopers walked toward the field and the two piles of hay left from last year's harvest. His heart pounded wildly and his mouth went dry. The last of their stores were hidden beneath the moldy straw. He glanced at Alexander. "One of them is heading toward the field," he whispered.

Alexander closed his eyes, and Yuri knew he was praying.

A sharp blast from the commander's whistle split the air. All the men, including the one crossing their field, jogged back to the yard.

"There is nothing here," said the officer. Soldiers piled into the truck, and the vehicle rumbled out of the drive and down the road.

The two haystacks stood intact.

Yuri whispered thanks to God.

Alexander wiped the sweat from his brow. "I'm glad the younger children weren't here."

"They're at the Sedov's house. What if the soldiers go there?"

"We'll get them," Alexander said. "And warn our friends."

Irina kissed her husband's cheek. "Be careful. Go with God."

Yuri took his wool cap and coat from the hook, pulled the hat over his ears, and shrugged into his coat. He opened the door, then hesitated. "Thank God Tatyana is on her way to America."

* * * * *

The man from the train handed Tatyana and Galina each a bowl of cabbage soup and a slice of bread, then sat on the bench beside them. His son was already making slurping noises with his soup. "I suppose I should introduce myself. My name is Isaac Minls, and this is my son, Joseph." Joseph stopped slurping long enough to offer a friendly grin.

Tatyana nodded and said, "I am Tatyana Letinov, and you know Galina."

For a few minutes, they ate in silence.

Finally, Isaac asked, "Galina, do you have any other family?"

Galina shrugged. "I do not know. I think they are all dead." Tears filled her eyes. "Do you think my mama is dead?"

"No, of course not." Tatyana hugged her about the shoulders.

"Can we find her?"

We could go to the NKVD office, Tatyana thought, but quickly dismissed the notion; the police might send Galina along with her mother or to an orphanage. Both choices were unthinkable. She couldn't take her to America. She had only one ticket and no extra papers. Abandoning her to the streets was inconceivable. *Father, I need your help,* she prayed. *Tell me what to do.*

Isaac spoke. "I think we should ask God what to do."

Stunned, Tatyana could only stare. His words had been her exact thought; only she'd been too afraid to speak openly.

"Do you think he will hear us?" Galina asked.

"Of course. He hears our every prayer," Isaac assured the little girl.

"Then why did my mama and papa have to go away?"

"He knows where they are. And I'm sure he's taking good care of them." He patted the child's hand. "We don't always understand God's ways," he said solemnly, "but we can trust him."

Galina thought a moment, then asked in a small voice, "Will he take care of me? What am I going to do?"

Isaac's eyes met Tatyana's. "My wife and I are Jews, but we know Jesus Christ as Messiah. Quietly we spread the gospel and do all we can to help those in need." He patted Galina on the head. "This little one needs us." He paused and looked at his hands. "We lost our own little girl two years ago. I've been praying and thinking, and I would like it very much if Galina would come and live with my wife and me and Joseph." He quickly added, "Just until we find your parents, of course. We have a small apartment, but there is enough room for one more."

Galina's eyes brimmed with fresh tears, and her chin quivered. She turned to Tatyana. "What do you think?"

Tatyana considered Isaac. She barely knew him. How could she know if it was safe to leave Galina with this stranger? *Lord, how could you give me this burden? I barely know how to take care of myself.*

"We would take good care of her and love her as our own," Isaac pressed.

A strong sense of assurance about this man's goodness filled Tatyana. This must be God's answer. She smiled at Galina. "It is good for you to stay with Mr. Minls and Joseph."

Galina studied the man for a moment, then nodded.

Isaac stood up. "When does your ship leave?"

"Tomorrow morning."

"Do you have lodging?"

"No." She glanced around the station. "I thought I would stay here."

"Please, come with us. My wife will be happy to have a guest for supper." When Tatyana didn't answer right away, he continued. "And a bath would probably feel very good after being on the train for so long?" He smiled warmly.

Tatyana couldn't refuse. "I would like that. And a bath would be wonderful." She hesitated, afraid of her next question, but she needed to ask. "Also, I would like to hear more about how you share the Word of God." She looked at the ground. "I am afraid. It is very dangerous to admit to being a believer."

"You are right, but God is good. He goes with us through the fire." Isaac smiled and ushered Tatyana and Galina out of the terminal.

★ ★ ★ ★ ★

Tatyana stood at the curb and waited for the next bus. Her overnight stay with the Minls family had been strengthening. After a meal of soup and fresh bread, Isaac had led them in communion and prayer. He had prayed with a power and conviction Tatyana had rarely seen.

Later, in the warm light of the fireplace, Isaac leaned forward on his knees and looked at Tatyana. "I need to tell you about the service God has called us to." He glanced at Lenka.

She nodded.

"There are many who refuse to buckle beneath the tyranny of our present regime." He paused. "Some, in order to live, must go underground." He paused. "We help them."

Tatyana gasped, astounded that this quiet, gentle man would be involved in subversion. "How do you do that?"

Lenka reached out and touched Tatyana's hand. "Some need a place to stay for a few days; others just need a little food to see them on their way."

"But that is not all," Isaac said boldly. "There are those who need false papers for work or to emigrate. Sometimes we provide such things."

Tatyana slowly grasped the enormity of what the Minlses were saying. Their lives were literally in jeopardy. At any moment NKVD officers could knock at their door and seize them. "Why? Why do you do this?"

"It is what God has asked us to do," Lenka said quietly. "We have no choice but to obey him."

"He is our protection. We trust him," Isaac said, straightening in his chair. He smiled. "He keeps his hand on us and never takes his eyes from our work."

Tatyana had never seen such faith, and her own had been bolstered. She now felt some peace about her unwelcome emigration.

As they traveled to the port that morning, she'd been impressed with Leningrad. Channels and rivers crisscrossed the city, connecting elegant palaces, cathedrals, and gardens. Stopping long enough for a quick tour of the Winter Palace had been an unexpected pleasure. She'd only read of it but never thought it possible she would actually visit the home of the czars. Life-changing decisions had been made there and, although it was shelled during the Bolshevik Revolution, it remained glorious, wearing the golden dome of the czar's cloistered cathedral like a crown. She only wished she'd been able to share the experience with her family.

She looked at her hostess. "Thank you for showing me. I will never forget." Unexpected tears stung her eyes and she quickly blinked them away. "It will be a special memory I'll carry with me always."

"I am glad we could share it with you." Lenka smoothed her plain brown skirt and tugged at her coat, which gapped as it stretched over her rounded belly. She rested her hands on the small of her back. "I hope the bus comes soon. It will feel good to sit."

"How long before the baby?"

"About a month, but one never truly knows. Babies seem to have a mind of their own." She patted her stomach and smiled, her plain features brightening. "We're hoping for a girl."

Galina joined the women and leaned against Tatyana.

"If we have a girl, you will have someone to play with," Lenka said, resting her hand on the child's shoulder.

Galina tried to smile. "That would be nice, but if my mama . . ." Her voice broke and she stopped. "I miss Mama and Papa. Do you think they will come and find me?"

Lenka knelt down and pulled Galina into her arms. "I hope so."

A bus rounded the corner.

"Here it is," Lenka said, straightening. She took Galina's hand and called to Isaac and Joseph. "The bus!"

With Tatyana's suitcase thumping against his leg, Isaac hurried to join the women.

"Is it time to go to the boat and to America?" Joseph asked.

Tatyana's stomach lurched. Today she would leave Russia behind—perhaps forever.

The door of the bus whooshed open and Tatyana picked up her box of records and stood aside to allow Lenka to board first. Galina followed. Balancing her records on her hip, Tatyana stepped on, then Joseph and Isaac. The bus was crowded, forcing them to stand. A man offered Lenka his seat. Gratefully she sank onto the bench.

The odor of unwashed bodies, cigarettes, and cheap perfume seemed overpowering in the closeness of the bus. Although relishing the warmth, Tatyana longed for fresh air. A hodgepodge of activity—horse-drawn carts, buses, bicycles, and pedestrians —competed for space on the streets. Everyone seemed in a hurry. *It might be nice to live in a city one day,* she decided, shuffling her parcel to her other arm. *It feels alive.*

Galina took Tatyana's free hand. "How far to the boat?"

"Not far," Isaac said. "We should be there soon."

Galina tugged on Tatyana's shirt sleeve. "Please do not go. Stay."

Tatyana smiled reassuringly and caressed the little girl's hair. "I wish I could, but I must go. My uncle is expecting me, and my brother would be very angry if I disobeyed him."

Galina said nothing more as they continued through the city, but she tightened her grip on Tatyana's hand.

As they neared the docks, the scent of the sea mingled with the stench of the bus. A gull swooped down beside the window and, for a moment, matched their speed. Tatyana had seen these birds only once before. While still a child, her family had taken a holiday at the coast. The gray of its body looked muted, the white bright. With a quick flap of his wings, he soared from her sight.

She peered out the window, hoping to catch a final glimpse of the bird, but he was gone. Any view of the harbor was blocked by ancient-looking buildings and warehouses. She sighed. She would have to wait.

When the bus finally stopped, Tatyana placed her satchel on top of the record box and waited to disembark. Her stomach fluttered with butterflies. She couldn't believe she was actually about to board a ship bound for America.

As she stepped off the bus, Galina kept a tight grip on Tatyana's skirt. The little girl pointed toward a tall smokestack rising above the cranes and other buildings along the waterfront. "Is that your boat?"

Tatyana scanned the dock, looking for other steamers. It seemed to be the only passenger ship. "I think so, but it's awfully big." The butterflies took flight again.

Isaac plopped Tatyana's suitcase on the ground.

"Come on, Galina, let's look around," Joseph said and hustled his new friend off toward the pier.

"Children, wait," Lenka called.

Joseph stopped and faced his mother.

Galina did the same. "I have never seen the ocean before."

"I will keep her safe," Joseph promised.

Lenka looked at Isaac.

"They'll be all right," he said.

Grudgingly, Lenka nodded her assent, and the children scurried away. "Don't go far," she called after them.

Gripping her carton more tightly, Tatyana studied the pier. "Do you know where I should go to pay for my ticket?"

Isaac scanned the waterfront. "That looks like an office." He pointed at a small, plain building tucked between two large warehouses. A sign was posted in the window, but Tatyana couldn't read it from this distance.

Isaac picked up the suitcase and headed toward the building. The women followed.

"Do not be frightened," Lenka said. "God is with you."

"Until now I hadn't thought much about fear. All I could think of was leaving my family and my home," Tatyana said. "I don't want to go." The breeze snatched at her coat. With her free hand, she grabbed it and pulled it closed. "I am afraid." She studied the black waters of the bay. "When I think of traveling across the vast ocean . . ." She shuffled the box to her other arm and hooked her purse over her shoulder. "It just seems endless and sinister." Wrenching her eyes from the sea and looking at her friend, she said, "I do not know my uncle. Maybe he doesn't really want me to join him." She paused. "I have heard Americans are very strange."

"Anything new feels strange at first."

"What will they think of me?" Tears filled Tatyana's eyes, and she turned away. "I'm afraid I'll never return; that I will never see Russia or my family again."

Lenka gently took Tatyana's hand. "We do not always know the plans God has for us, but we must have confidence in him." She smiled. "I think he has great things waiting for you in America. Trust him. He will walk every step with you."

Tatyana dropped her eyes. "I can accept what you say here," she said, pointing to her head, "but my heart has trouble believing."

Lenka nodded. "I know. It is not always easy." A shadow crossed her face. "I believe we have only seen the beginning of Stalin's terror." Her gaze wandered over the city. "He is an evil man, and evil knows no bounds. Until God's people take up the battle, it will not stop." She looked at Tatyana. "Maybe it is God's will that you be spared from what is to come."

"That's what Yuri said. But he is staying. What will happen to him?"

"We each have our own path." She placed her arm around Tatyana's shoulders. "It won't be easy for you to write to us, but Isaac and I will try to keep in touch with your brother. We have the address you gave us. We'll write to him. And if he needs help, we'll be here."

Overwhelmed with gratitude, Tatyana hugged Lenka. "How can I thank you? You don't even know me and, yet, you have been a good friend. I wish we had more time."

"Maybe we will see each other again."

Tatyana nodded, but in her heart she knew this was the last time she would see these special people.

"Tatyana," Isaac called over his shoulder. "Do you have your traveling papers?"

Tatyana's stomach knotted as she remembered what lay ahead. "Yes. I have them." She set her box down and searched through her satchel for the precious documents. She came upon a family photo. Yuri, her mother and father, Aunt Irina, Uncle Alexander, Lev, and the two youngest children, Serge and Anna, stared back at her. She studied each face, then quickly tucked the photo back into her bag, exchanging it for her precious documents.

She stepped behind a partition. A puffy-faced man with pouting lips sat behind a large, wooden desk. Tatyana approached him and held out her traveling papers. Without a word, he took them. His expression stern and detached, he studied the documents.

Tatyana thought her heart would leap out of her chest.

After a few minutes, the man leaned back in his chair. It creaked beneath his weight. "Why are you going to America?"

"I have an uncle who is sick and needs someone to care for him," she said, exactly as she had been instructed.

"There is no one else who can do this?"

"No, sir."

"And what is wrong with your uncle?"

"He . . . he has tuberculosis."

The man looked back at the papers. "Everything seems in order," he said with a note of disappointment. Stamping the documents with a loud thump, he handed them back to Tatyana. "The man at the next desk will issue your ticket."

With a sense of elation, Tatyana forced herself to walk slowly to the ticket officer. Another hurdle crossed. She handed the paperwork to the man and paid the remainder owed on her fare. It took almost all the money she had left, but at least she had her ticket.

With her precious package of symphony records tucked under her arm, Tatyana walked along the pier toward the steamer, a shiver of fear surged through her as she studied the impressive ship. Longer than a city block and taller than most buildings, its rotund smokestack seemed to gaze down at her. "I've never been on a ship before," she said, her voice quivering a little.

Isaac kept his eyes on the boat. "I hear they are very comfortable these days. I'm sure you will have an uneventful crossing."

A soldier leaned against the railing, lit a cigarette, and studied the three.

"At least you'll be safe," Isaac remarked.

Galina and Joseph raced up to the adults, out of breath, their faces flushed. At the same time, they both began chattering about all they had seen. "Three men are unloading hundreds and hundreds of fish! And we saw a man who had only one leg and a beautiful woman who had on the prettiest dress I've ever seen!" Galina finished. "It actually sparkled in the sunlight!"

Tatyana did her best to be attentive, but her mind couldn't release thoughts of the ship that would carry her across the sea. She dragged her eyes away from the steamer and looked at the children. "It seems you had a real adventure."

Galina nodded. Joseph was busy studying the catwalk that bridged the ship and the dock and didn't seem to hear.

Tatyana slowed to a stroll. She tried to look calm, but her fingers worked a rough edge on the box. She could feel a nerve jump above her eye. She stopped a few steps from the gangplank. Taking a deep breath, she glanced up at the ship, then turned and looked at her friends and forced a smile. "Again, thank you. You have been so kind." She set the box of records on the ground.

"I'm glad I was on that train," Isaac said, taking her hand. "We are happy we could help." He glanced at the soldier who still watched them. "We must go." He set her suitcase beside her.

"Of course. Thank you. I will write."

Lenka stepped up and kissed Tatyana on each cheek. With one hand resting on the younger woman's shoulders, she said, "You are not saying good-bye as much as you are saying hello to a new life." She smiled warmly. "God has a plan. You will see."

"I know. I just wish I knew what it was."

"That is how we learn to trust him, by stepping out even when we don't know our destination. Remember what Proverbs says: 'In all your ways trust in the Lord, and he will make your paths straight.'"

"I'll remember."

Realizing the departure of her new friend was imminent, Galina clung to Tatyana's skirt.

Tatyana knelt in front of the child. "You and I have become real comrades. I will miss you. But, I'll write and tell you all about America. Maybe one day you can come and visit me there."

Galina's eyes brightened. "Do you think I could?"

Tatyana looked at Isaac and Lenka.

"Maybe one day," Isaac said quietly.

Tatyana kissed the little girl. "And when you do visit, we will have a grand party."

"With cake?" Galina said.

"Of course."

Joseph had held back but now stepped forward and extended his hand. "I wish you luck in your new life," he said in his most grown-up voice.

"Thank you, Joseph."

A deep blast came from the ship and echoed throughout the harbor.

"It is time." Tatyana kissed Galina again and held her tight. "I love you," she whispered. All of a sudden, she set her suitcase on its side, unfastened the buckles, and took out a lace handkerchief. "Please keep this. I made it. The material is not elegant, but my mama helped me embroider it." She touched the flowered design and handed it to the little girl. "Remember me."

Galina's eyes brimmed with tears. "Thank you. Thank you," she said, hugging the precious gift.

Tatyana closed and tied the strings securing her parcel, then stood up.

"We will meet again. My mama and papa and I will come to America."

"I will watch for you." Blinking back tears, she gazed at Isaac and Lenka, then with her box of records under one arm, her satchel balancing on it, she lifted her suitcase and walked up the gangplank.

CHAPTER 5

ONCE ON BOARD THE SHIP, A man in uniform greeted Tatyana with a smile. "May I please see your ticket?"

Without saying a word, she set her bags down. Her hands shaking, she searched her satchel for the receipt and handed it to him.

Taking it, the man studied the ticket, marked something in a notebook, then returned it. "You will be in cabin 314, forward."

Tatyana nodded. Careful to keep her bags with her, she went to the rail, joining several others who were waving to family and friends on the dock. She set the luggage down and, as she watched the strangers, loneliness settled over her. No one was there to see her off. Isaac and Lenka had disappeared into the city.

Shaking off her melancholy, she tried to focus on the activity below. Men carried boxes on their backs and stacked them onto pushcarts. Others positioned large crates in heavy netting, then stepped back as they were lifted by crane and loaded on board. Tearful farewells were still being said, and passengers continued to ascend the gangplank. Many faces were etched with uncertainty; some were crying. Tatyana wondered at their reasons for leaving Russia.

With a deep sigh, she slung her small bag over her shoulder, knelt and picked up her records and, while balancing them on her hip, hefted her suitcase. Careful with her heavy load, she headed for the companionway and made her way down the steps. On the next landing she stopped and studied her options, having no notion where her room was. Long, dimly lit corridors stretched out in either direction.

As she contemplated her choices, a steward swaggered down the corridor. "May I help you?"

"I am in room 314, forward?"

"Go straight, and it will be on your right," he said, pointing down a hallway.

"Thank you." Tatyana made her way down the narrow corridor leading toward the front of the ship. While still moored, the steamer tipped at an angle and that, coupled with the closeness of the walls, confused her sense of balance, and she felt unsteady and a little dizzy.

Tatyana stopped in front of a cabin with the number 314 posted above it. For a moment she stood and stared at the door. "This must be it." Taking a deep breath, she set her bag down and cautiously opened the door and peered inside. A frail-looking woman with graying hair sat on a narrow bunk. "Is this room 314?"

"Yes," the woman answered, her brown eyes crinkling as she smiled.

Still uncertain she belonged here, Tatyana hesitated.

"There is plenty of room," the woman said. "So far only four of us have been assigned to this room."

Lifting her suitcase, Tatyana stepped inside the small cabin. The door swung closed behind her. Three sets of three-tiered bunk beds lined the walls. A small cupboard, mirror, and a two-pronged hook filled the narrow space between each set. Each bunk had a bare, thin mattress, a wool blanket folded at the foot, and a small pillow.

"The two upper beds nearest the window are already taken. I like to be close to the door. And that one," she pointed toward a bunk opposite her, "has the top occupied." She shrugged. "You can choose from anything that's left."

"This will be fine," Tatyana said as she dropped her bag beside the bottom bunk opposite the stranger and set her package on the bed. She sat on the firm mattress. The tiny room pressed in, and a sudden longing for the openness of the upper decks overwhelmed her. It was all she could do to remain still.

The woman returned to her sewing.

Tatyana removed her scarf and folded it as casually as she could.

Without looking up, the stranger asked, "Are you traveling all the way to America?"

Tatyana nodded.

"Do you have family there?"

"My uncle."

"I'm going to see my sister, Augusta, and her family. It has been more than ten years since I've seen her."

Ten Years! Tatyana thought. *How can that be? I will certainly see Yuri sooner than that.* Aloud, she said, "That is a long time. You must be very excited."

The woman's face brightened. "Oh, yes. My sister is much younger than I, but we have always been close. She has a fine family—three children. Would you like to see a picture?"

The woman set her embroidery aside, rummaged through her purse, and pulled out a photograph. She handed it to Tatyana. "Here's Augusta and her older son, Dimitri; he's the tall, blonde standing on her right. He's very good looking. The little boy in the front is Samuel. He was twelve when this picture was taken. He looks so much like Dimitri. And the little girl is Ella. She should be nine now. The other man is Pavel, her husband."

Tatyana studied the photo. They looked friendly, and she had to admit that Dimitri was very handsome. His eyes were bright, and he seemed to possess some secret delight. "They look like good people," she said as she returned the picture.

"They are." With a sigh the woman added, "It will be good to be with family again."

Tatyana slid her suitcase and records beneath the bunk, then stood and studied the cabin. "This is a very small room for so many."

"Yes. I suppose by the time we dock in America, we will either be devoted friends or," she raised one eyebrow, "glad to be rid of each other."

Tatyana nodded, not knowing an appropriate reply.

The woman stood up and held out her hand. "I apologize. I haven't introduced myself. My name is Flora Leipman."

Tatyana shook her hand. "I'm Tatyana Letinov." Suddenly a blast came from the ship's horn, which made her jump. "Does that mean we're leaving?"

Flora shrugged. "I do not know. This is the first time I've traveled by sea."

"Me, too." Tatyana's earlier discomfort returned. She needed to get out! "I . . . I'm going up on deck." She threw her small bag over her shoulder and headed for the door.

Flora returned to her sewing.

I must see my homeland one last time, Tatyana thought as she stepped into the hallway and made her way back to the promenade.

Dusk had settled over the city with its blanket of cold. Relieved to be free of her close quarters, Tatyana headed for the railing. Leaning against the balustrade she breathed deeply, taking in as much of the sharp air as her lungs could hold.

Another blast came from the ship's horn. A flurry of activity broke out on the docks and on board ship as the dockhands made ready for departure.

Clutching the railing, Tatyana fought a rising surge of fear. *I need to get off! I can't do this!* She moved toward the gangplank, but already it was being withdrawn from the landing. She stopped, clutched her purse against her stomach, and struggled to regain reason. *I don't want to go! I don't want to go!* her mind cried. Blinking back tears, she closed her eyes and tried to pray.

It was then she heard the quiet voice of her heavenly Father. "I am with you even unto the ends of the earth." A sense of peace touched her, and she loosened her grip on her bag.

The ship pulled away from the dock, and the few remaining well-wishers standing on the pier waved and cheered to their friends. Tatyana took a long, steadying breath. The cold, moist air caressed her face, and the sound of the sea birds' lyrical cries offered another fragment of peace. She felt calmer.

As they moved further into the channel, the city lights glittered in the frosty air. Unexpected tears blurred Tatyana's vision. Her deep sorrow could no longer be put off as the finality of this good-bye set in. "Yuri, please come soon," she whispered.

The ship nosed into another wave, rolled over the top of it, then settled into the next trough. Tatyana groaned and struggled to keep her stomach steady. Three others were also confined to their beds, their moans mingling with Tatyana's and overridden only by the shrieking wind and pounding waves. The room reeked with the smell of unwashed bodies and vomit. The foul air was stifling.

Tatyana couldn't remember feeling so sick. Fighting to restrain her misery, she turned onto her side. Through heavy eyelids, she peered at the bunk in front of the tiny window. Tatyana thought, *If only I could get a breath of fresh air, I might feel better.* She pushed herself up on one elbow, but the room whirled, and, with a groan, she lay back down.

"Now, where do you think you're going?" Flora gently asked.

Tatyana closed her eyes. "I just want some air." Another wave lifted the ship. She laid her hand on her stomach. "Oh, I wish it would stop. When will it stop?"

Flora sponged the young woman's face with a cool, damp cloth. "It's just a spell of bad weather. It will pass."

Tatyana tried to focus on the woman's face. "You're not sick. Why?" she whispered, the effort to speak almost too much as she struggled to control her rising nausea.

As the steamer rolled over another wave and washed into a deep trench, Tatyana's stomach pitched, and she retched. Weak, she lay back on her pillows, tears trickling from the corners of her eyes and trailing into her hair.

"I'm so sorry. I wish I could help," Flora fretted.

"I'm sorry for being such a baby."

Gently the older woman tucked Tatyana's blanket under her chin. "You're not a baby. Sick is sick." With a maternal smile, she added, "Now, you try to sleep."

To everyone's relief, the storm finally passed. The sea quieted, and passengers were once more able to roam the upper decks.

Although weak, Tatyana was one of the first out of bed. She longed for the fresh breezes and insisted on spending time on the promenade, even if that meant nothing more than sitting on a deck chair. Bundled beneath a blanket, she enjoyed the feel of the cold air on her cheeks.

Small whitecaps crested now and then. They were all that was left of the storm. She breathed deeply, trying to soak in the fragrance of the salt sea. The distant horizon was silhouetted against the pale gray sky. The sea seemed endless, limitless—the vastness of the Atlantic incomprehensible. Tatyana felt small and insignificant against this boundless creation. *Yuri would love it,* she thought. He was always one for adventure. She felt the familiar ache of his absence.

Closing her eyes, Tatyana considered God and how pleased he must have been when he completed creating the universe. But in such a realm, how could her single life be worthy of his attention?

"It's remarkable, isn't it?" Flora asked as she joined Tatyana. Leaning on the railing, she gazed out over the sea.

"Yes." She sat up a little and tucked the blanket under her arms. "I was just thinking about how God must have felt when he created the earth. Do you think he really cares about each individual person? I mean the world is so huge."

"In the book of Matthew, it says that God knows the very number of hairs on our heads," Flora smiled. "It seems he must care very much."

Tatyana nodded. She hadn't thought of that. Feeling a little better, she leaned back and snuggled beneath her quilt.

Flora turned and, leaning against the railing, folded her arms over her chest. "You look better. You have a little color."

Tatyana placed her hand on her stomach. "I never knew how good it could feel not to be sick. Were many others ill?"

"From what the porter told me, yes, many."

"Thank you for taking care of me. I was awful."

"I was lucky not to be sick. So I'm glad I could help. And what kind of friend would have left you?" Flora's eyes flashed with mischief, and she gave a short laugh. "Maybe I should have been a sailor."

"I could never do that." Tatyana's gaze settled on the ocean. "The sea is beautiful, but I do not belong on it. I will be glad to have my feet on solid ground again."

"It won't be long. Soon we'll be in America."

"America. Just the word sends shivers down my spine. I cannot comprehend such a place. A country where there is no hunger and you can have anything you want." Tatyana gazed toward the west. "When my brother first told me I had to leave Russia, I was angry. I almost hated him." She folded the edge of her cover, then smoothed it with her hand. "But, of course, I could not. Now I must admit at being a little excited. I want to see this country I've heard so much about."

"Tatyana, you know some of what we've heard are just stories. It can't all be true. My sister has lived in New York City for many years, and she said that life is not perfect there, either. There is hunger and poverty." She smiled, and her face radiated hope. "But, there is freedom. People can travel anywhere they wish, go to church wherever they choose, even work for whomever they please. And Americans can own land if they want."

"Can you imagine?" Tatyana said. "To have such freedom! It is hard to comprehend." As she said the words, fear prodded her. Were the stories real or just fairy tales? "Do you really think it's true?"

"We will know soon."

The days blended one into another, the routine never changing. With too many idle hours, the immigrants' patience withered. Occasional fights broke out among the men, and sharp words were exchanged between some of the women.

Tatyana embroidered, reread Tolstoy's *Azure Cities* plus one of Pasternak's books of poetry, and visited with new friends, mostly Flora. In many ways she enjoyed the quiet hours but could feel her anxiety grow as the days passed.

One day, as she read a poem from Pasternak's collection, Tatyana was struck by the possibility of buying any book she wanted once she got to the United States. She let her volume of poetry rest in her lap and watched Flora work on a piece of needlework. "Flora," she said quietly.

The woman peered over her glasses.

"Do you think we will be able to buy books in America?"

Flora removed her glasses. "Oh, yes. My sister says there are many wonderful works. And she said there are lots of stores where you can buy books."

"Does the government control them? I mean do they keep out the treasonous ones?"

Flora thought a moment. "I do not know for certain. I think Augusta said the government doesn't dictate what books are written or sold."

"You mean *any* writings?"

"I guess so."

Tatyana cradled her book against her chest. "Maybe I can visit one of the stores." Remembering her cherished records she asked, "And what about music? Do you think there are places where you can buy a phonograph and records?"

"I'm sure there must be."

Unexpected tears filled Tatyana's eyes. "Do you really think so? I miss music. My family and I used to spend hours listening to symphonies by Shostakovich and Tchaikovsky. I so enjoyed his *Swan Lake!* Nothing is more wonderful than listening to his beautiful music while watching the ballet!"

"Beautiful, yes, but my favorite has always been Korsakov's folk music. Just thinking of it makes me want to prance around." Flora blushed. "Well, not exactly prance, but it has been a long time since I've danced." She paused, a shadow falling over her eyes. "Since before my husband, Slava, died."

The morning they approached New York harbor, Tatyana woke early. After dressing, she quickly packed her suitcase, pulled her case of records out from under the bed, and placed both on the bunk. She plopped down on the mattress but couldn't sit still and went to the mirror to tidy her hair. She gazed at her reflection. Although she'd had little sleep, her anticipation brightened her green eyes and tinged her skin a pale pink. Her hands shook a little as she pulled her hair into a tight bun and covered it with a dark blue bandanna. Would being an American make her look different? *You're being silly,* she chided herself. *Besides, I will never really be an American. I'll always be Russian.* She took her cloak from its hook on the wall and pulled it over her shoulders.

Flora sat on her bed watching her young roommate. "You are ready early." She glanced around the empty room. "It seems everyone else has also gone up already."

"Tonya and Katarina left over an hour ago, and Lyusya left even before that. She was gone when I woke this morning." Tying her cloak under her chin, Tatyana asked, "What do you really think it will be like?"

Flora shrugged her shoulders. "We cannot know. But soon our questions will be answered."

"Are you frightened?"

"Yes, a little. But I tell myself, 'What good will come from worrying?' And then I feel better."

"I wish I could do that. My stomach is filled with butterflies."

Flora stood up. "Maybe going on deck will help."

A wave of sadness swept over Tatyana as she realized this might be the last day she would spend with Flora. She looked at her friend. "I will miss my new friends but you the most."

"And I you," Flora said giving her a hug. "Now, you go on up. I will be there soon. Today is the day we look upon our new home."

Fog had settled on the surface of the sea, enveloping the ship. No matter how hard Tatyana stared into the mist, she couldn't see through it. "How will we ever be able to see New York?" she complained, continuing to peer into the dense haze. She shivered as the damp cold penetrated her clothing.

"Maybe we should go inside," Flora said. "A cup of hot tea would be good." She steered Tatyana toward the dining room.

After filling their cups, the two women sat across from each other and warmed their hands on the hot mugs.

Tatyana hadn't bothered to eat and, as she sipped her tea, enjoyed the sensation of the hot brew in her empty stomach. She tapped her fingers on the table. "Flora, I cannot stand this waiting. I need to know what is ahead of me." She paused. "I'm afraid." She glanced out the window at the mists swirling across the deck, caressing the passengers' legs, and floating over the balustrade. "For a long time I've wanted to leave this boat, but now I just want to stay, to hide." She studied the others lingering over meals and hot drinks, then looked back at Flora. "I have no one."

"What about your uncle?"

"I don't even know him. He may not want me."

With a steady gaze, Flora said, "I believe when God arranges something, he does it exactly right. Try not to worry."

"I cannot help it. I wish my brother were here."

As the hours dragged by, the sun gradually brightened the last remnants of fog. As they neared New York Harbor, the deep timbre of a fog horn echoed across the waters. Gulls skimmed the surface of the waves, then rising on the air currents, took a closer look at the ship and its occupants. Tatyana clung to the railing, holding her breath as she waited for her first view of the new land.

Flora kept her hand on Tatyana's arm. Neither said a word.

Tugboats joined them and deftly guided the ship into the harbor. A flotilla of fishing boats, steam ships, and freighters jammed the port. Tatyana had never seen such activity and wondered why there was so much congestion.

But there was little time to think on it, for out of the haze the new world emerged. A mountain of buildings rose from the harbor. They were clustered so closely that they reminded Tatyana of the great spruce forests of the Taiga. Some buildings were tall, slender towers with steep, turreted rooftops, while others looked more like squat boxes. All shared endless rows of windows. Tatyana wondered about the people who looked out at them through those clear panes. Seeming out of place, ugly, black smokestacks interrupted the skyline. The city stretched on as far as Tatyana could see. It was immense; a sight she knew she would never forget.

To their left, a small island with a statue of a woman holding a torch above her head claimed their attention. The lady seemed to stand guard over the bay. As Tatyana stared at the image, a gradual sense of understanding and a longing for something yet unknown stirred within her. "What do you think it is?"

"That is the Statue of Liberty," Flora answered confidently. "It stands for freedom for all who come to these shores."

"How do you know this?"

"My sister told me. I have been anxious to see it for myself." Flora wiped at her tears. "She's beautiful."

Tatyana nodded. "I wish Mama and Papa could see it. And my brother." Her voice trembled.

A blast came from the ship as they moved deeper into the harbor. A new life lay just beyond this bay. Tatyana gripped the railing and took a deep breath, hoping she would be ready for whatever awaited her.

CHAPTER 6

TATYANA TURNED TO HER friend. "I'm going to miss you, Flora."

"We do not have to say good-bye. New York is not so big that we cannot see each other." She paused, and when she smiled her eyes crinkled. "I'm certain my nephew would be happy to take me to visit you."

Tatyana studied Flora. "Are you matchmaking?"

Flora's eyes slid away. "Of course not."

"Good. Because I'm not interested in men right now." She squeezed her friend's hand. "But it would be wonderful if you came to see me." She gazed at the Statue of Liberty and felt a renewed sense of hope.

Guided by the tugs, the ship gradually turned toward an island overrun by a vast complex of red, brick buildings. The ornate turreted rooftops and white limestone arches framing rows of windows reminded Tatyana of a palace. She could not imagine why it was placed in the middle of the harbor. "What is this place?"

"All immigrants must go through Ellis Island before they can enter the United States. It is here we will be cleared to enter the country . . ." Flora hesitated, "or turned away."

Tatyana detected a note of anxiety in her friend's voice. Her stomach churned. There'd been talk about the physical examination, but until now, she'd forgotten. She felt strong and well. Did she have reason to fear? Was it possible the American doctors would discover some hidden malady that would keep her from entering the country? "Do you think very many are sent home?"

"I don't know," Flora said as she stared at the tiny island.

Tatyana glanced at the elderly woman. The journey had weakened her. As the possibility of Flora's rejection took hold, her apprehension grew. It would be a tragedy. Flora must be allowed to enter. *Father, please help her. She wants so much to be with family. Help her pass this test.* Then she added, much to her surprise, *and help me, too.*

They steamed past Ellis Island toward the towering city, maneuvering skillfully through the congestion, and gracefully floated parallel to a wharf. Men on shore worked with the ship's crew to secure the vessel.

Tatyana had studied the family photo of her uncle for weeks and now scanned the dock, seeking his face. All she found were anxious immigrants and longshoremen busily fulfilling their tasks. Guards yelled commands at the throng in a variety of languages. Tatyana did understand a Russian order to move along. She and Flora joined the crowd of newcomers filing into a roped-off area on the dock.

"Why are we here? Where is my uncle?" Tatyana asked, unable to quiet her apprehension.

"I think we must return to Ellis Island before we can enter the country," Flora said, pointing at a ferry loaded with immigrants, steaming back toward the island.

"And our families?"

She shrugged and looked around. "I do not know."

The new arrivals were jammed so closely together they were unable to sit and were forced to stand as they waited. Tatyana's legs and back ached, and a soft rain soaked through her clothing. Moisture dribbled down her face from beneath her brightly-colored babushka. She looked at Flora. Weariness lined her face. Protectively Tatyana circled her arm around her friend and wished she could help her in some way.

She looked down at the identification paper pinned to her coat. It seemed silly to wear such a thing. She knew who she was. She shifted her weight from one foot to the other. "It shouldn't be much longer," she stated, hoping that saying it would make it true.

"I'm sure you're right," Flora said as she leaned a little harder on Tatyana.

After two hours of waiting, a ferryboat powered toward the landing and docked. The guards herded people into lines, yelling at them in several languages. Occasionally Tatyana heard a Russian word, such as "hurry," or "line up." She did her best to do what they wanted.

Gratefully she and Flora were among the first to board the ferry. Standing shoulder to shoulder, immigrants filled the boat. Pressed in on all sides, it was difficult to move or even breathe. Tatyana felt a moment of panic, but Flora squeezed her hand and smiled reassuringly, and she relaxed. As they moved toward Ellis Island, she barely noticed the roll of the boat as they approached the immense compound that served as the reception center for the world's castoffs. Now, it seemed even larger and more intimidating than when she'd first seen it.

After mooring, passengers pushed their way onto the crowded dock. Some were so burdened with trunks and bags, they held their visas and passports between their teeth. Flora and Tatyana allowed themselves to be pushed along in the tide of people, then joined a long line trailing into the complex. Tatyana searched the mass of faces but still found no sign of her uncle. Her left arm ached from balancing her box of records on her hip. She switched arms, and a gust of wind nearly snatched her papers out of her hand. "Oh, dear Lord," she said and set her box and suitcase down. "What will I do with these? It would make more sense to keep them safely packed away."

"I agree, but we were told to have them ready," Flora said.

"They will be useless if they're blown into the water." She folded the documents and tucked them into her waistband.

Confusion pressed in. Babies cried while mothers shushed and cooed in a medley of languages. Some of the older children chased one another around the legs of strangers, while others clung to their parents' hands, eyes large and frightened. Some whimpered.

Tatyana had a sudden urge to be a child, to take refuge in her mother's skirts—to feel safe and protected. Right at that moment Flora took her hand and squeezed it.

The line inched forward. A man in a deep blue uniform took a quick look at Tatyana's identification papers, grabbed her arm, and grouped her with thirty people entering the massive brick building. Flora was forced to wait. Panic overwhelmed Tatyana, and she turned to go back, but the man pushed her forward, saying in Russian, "Move!" *I can't do this alone! What will I do without Flora? God, help me!*

Clutching her records beneath one arm and gripping her suitcase in the other hand, her mind whirled as she searched for solace. She looked over her shoulder at where Flora had been. The doors were closed. Yet, Tatyana could almost see Flora's heartening smile and, remembering her friend's courage and strength, she felt less alone.

Her hysteria eased, and she became more aware of her surroundings. She stood in a dark tiled corridor with a steep stairway in front of her. "Hurry up," she heard shouted in Russian. Three abreast, she and the others began their trek up the staircase. Many prayed.

Several officials met them at the top of the stairs, stamped their identification cards, and hurried them forward. The large doors opened, and Tatyana stepped into the largest room she'd ever seen. Blinking against the bright light pouring in through huge arched windows, she gazed at the domed ceiling more than fifty feet above. People leaned over a white railing on the upper floor and stared down at the rows of immigrants. For a fleeting moment, Tatyana wondered why they were there, then turned her attention to the room. It seemed alive with people. Some were wearing outlandish-looking clothing. One soldier was dressed in his uniform, including his sword, and many women wore brightly colored babushkas over their hair. Some were laughing, others cried, many simply stood in a stupor, overwhelmed by all they had been through. The noise reverberated off the expansive walls.

Rows and rows of benches filled the giant room. At the front a large flag hung from the upper balcony. Tatyana puzzled over the bright red, white, and blue flag with its bold stripes, so similar to Russia's. The cluster of stars was unlike her country's, and she pondered over what they represented.

Tatyana scanned the chamber, looking for Flora, but couldn't find her. *Where are you? What if she didn't make it? What if they decided to send her back? God, please help her.*

Interpreters shouted in several languages, "Move forward! Hurry up! The doctors are waiting."

Physicians dressed in dark blue uniforms watched everyone as they moved forward in single file. Nurses quickly examined their eyes and the skin on their hands and arms, then looked through their hair, before passing them on. Some of the immigrants had a large letter or symbol marked on their coats with a piece of chalk.

As they approached the "eye men," fear surged through the people. Tatyana had heard stories of individuals with an eye disorder called trachoma. Those with the disease were automatically deported. She'd also heard the examination was painful.

With her heart hammering, she stepped up to the doctor. Without a word, he used a small instrument to snap Tatyana's eyelid back. It did hurt, but not too much. After a quick glimpse at the under lid, he did the same to her other eye. It was over so quickly she didn't have time to respond before being propelled forward. Taking a deep breath, she did her best to prepare for the next test. The mingled odors of sweat, dirtied diapers, and cigarette smoke were suffocating, and she longed for a fresh breeze.

An old woman with a large chalk mark imprinted on the back of her coat stepped up to the next doctor. A nurse guided her behind a cloth screen. A few minutes later, Tatyana heard a pitiful cry from behind the shield. As gently as possible, a guard steered the sobbing woman to a large wire enclosure along the wall. Others already sat or paced within the pen, where they waited for further examinations and very possibly deportation. The woman staggered through the doorway, her face in her hands.

A young man pleaded with the physicians, gesturing his confusion when they didn't understand him. With the help of an interpreter, the debate continued, but the practitioners stood their ground and, finally, the bereaved man joined the woman. He stood outside the pen, his hands pressed against the wire. With their fingers intertwined through the mesh, they pressed their foreheads together and cried.

Everyone knew the son was saying good-bye to his mother. Sick at heart, the people stared, wondering if they would be next. Fear became a living entity and permeated the room. Tatyana looked away.

A hush settled over those nearby. No one wanted to be singled out.

Then it was Tatyana's turn. Her legs felt weak and her stomach knotted as she stepped up to the nurse. The woman smiled kindly and said something in English.

"I do not understand."

She repeated the words, then motioned for the Russian girl to roll up her sleeves.

Tatyana unbuttoned the cuffs, pushed the sleeves up to her elbows, and held out her arms. Quickly the nurse examined her skin, turned her hands over and scrutinized her nails, then searched through her hair and inspected her scalp before sending her on to the doctor.

Once behind the partition, the doctor looked at her mouth and throat, then peered in her ears. A nurse motioned for Tatyana to remove her blouse. Tatyana tightly clutched the neckline closed. The nurse smiled and gently unclenched the young woman's hand and unbuttoned the top clasp.

"No," Tatyana said and finished the buttons herself. She could feel her face flush in embarrassment. Careful to only let down one side at a time, she allowed the doctor to listen to her heart and lungs while he thumped on her back. Like the previous nurses, he gave her skin a quick examination, then motioned her forward. Relief flooded Tatyana as she rearranged her clothing, picked up her bags, and rejoined the line.

Feeling a little more confident, but exhausted, she sat at the end of the nearest bench and placed her bag on the floor between her legs. Leaning against the back of the bench, the young Russian carefully tucked the box of records beside her and held her satchel in her lap. She glanced down to the end of the aisle. Several men sat behind heavy desks with large ledgers propped in front of them. Each foreigner had to face one of these inspectors and answer his questions appropriately before being allowed in the country.

Many of the immigrants practiced what they would say. Some believed it best to tell all, while others thought the less said the better.

Tatyana didn't know what to say. She tried to imagine what she would do when it was her turn, but her head ached and her stomach felt painfully empty. She hadn't eaten since early that morning. She couldn't concentrate, so leaning against her box of records, she closed her eyes. *If only I could sleep,* she thought, then took a deep breath and stared straight ahead. Unconsciously she rubbed the smooth metal clasp on her bag over and over.

Time passed ever so slowly, but gradually the people edged down the row of benches toward the examiners. As each immigrant stood before an examiner, the examiner would ask the immigrant questions and write in his ledger. As Tatyana's turn approached, she felt her anxiety grow and repeatedly wiped her sweaty palms on her skirt.

When it was finally her turn, she gathered up her bags and stood in front of the official. Should she say something? Her mouth felt dry and her heart pounded.

The thin, tired-looking man studied her identification tag and wrote on the paper in front of him. He asked her something in English.

"I know only Russian," Tatyana said. "I do not understand."

He repeated the question and, again, Tatyana tried to explain she knew no English. Would he send her home for not knowing English? *If only I knew a little.* Panicked, she searched her mind for a solution.

Looking very bored, the man motioned to a woman who stood against the latticed wall behind him. Quickly she joined him and, standing behind the desk, asked in Russian, "Your name?"

"Tatyana Letinov."

"Please spell."

Tatyana rapidly spelled her name.

"Please say slowly."

Tatyana did as asked, and the woman repeated the spelling to the questioner.

He wrote it in his ledger and asked another question.

The interpreter asked, "How did you pay for your passage?"

"My family gave me the money." Tatyana's legs felt wobbly and she feared she might collapse.

Once more the official spoke to the interpreter.

"What kind of work do you do?"

Tatyana had never had a regular job. She'd always worked on the farm and didn't know how to answer. Finally she said, "I am a good cook, and I know how to clean house." She hesitated. "I also know how to care for farm animals and am educated. My mother was a teacher."

"How much money do you have? Show it to me."

Tatyana dug into her purse and pulled out her meager funds.

"Is anyone meeting you?"

The questions went on and on until the examiner asked for her papers.

With her hands shaking like leaves in a breeze, Tatyana dug into her waistband, unfolded the crumpled documents, and held them out. She willed her hands still, but they continued to tremble.

Without looking at Tatyana, the clerk took the papers and studied them, then staring at her, fired another question.

The interpreter asked, "Are you an anarchist?"

"No!" Tatyana answered, alarmed.

He stared at the Russian immigrant, as if trying to peer into her mind. Finally seeming satisfied, he stamped her papers, returned them, and handed her a landing card. "Stop at the money exchange at the end of the hall. They will trade your money for American currency."

"Yes. Thank you." Relieved, Tatyana lugged her bags to the end of the hall and changed her Russian currency for American dollars. She had no idea what the paper bills were worth, but she tucked them in her purse and made her way to the exit. Stepping out of the building and back onto the wharf, she breathed deeply of the fresh air. She had passed all the tests! She'd made it!

The morning rain had stopped, so she set her baggage down on the wooden planking and sat on it. Unexpectedly, emotional and physical exhaustion blanketed her. She was drained. Tears stung the back of her eyes. She needed to cry. Instead, she pushed herself to her feet and scanned the landing for Flora, but there was no sign of her. What if they had turned her away? She was Tatyana's only friend here. It was all she could do to keep her tears in check.

The door pushed open, and Flora stepped out into the sunlight, a smile on her face. Immediately her eyes found Tatyana's. "I made it! I made it! Now I will live in America!"

"Flora!" Tatyana called. With a quick step, she hurried to her friend and pulled her into her arms. As they held each other, tears wet their faces, washing away weeks of anxiety. Finally they took a step back and smiled at each other.

"What do we do now?" Tatyana asked.

Flora looked out across the bay and studied the imposing statue that graced the harbor. "We will live . . . free. We are free, Tatyana! Free!"

CHAPTER 7

O H, TO SEE MY AUGUSTA
again," Flora said, keeping her eyes trained on the distant pier as
they moved up the bay and into the river.

Cool spray splashed Tatyana as she leaned over the rail,
peering at the extraordinary city. Her mind was filled with so
many questions. Would she find a place for herself in this foreign
land? Would her uncle be glad to see her, or would he feel
burdened by unwelcome family? Would it be difficult to find
work? What kind of adventures awaited her?

The pier was a medley of faces, each anxiously searching for
loved ones on the approaching ferry. Some brightened and
shouted greetings; others creased in disappointment. None
looked familiar.

"Flora! Flora!" came a cry from the crowd. A vibrant, stocky
woman pushed through the throng.

Instantaneous tears brimmed in Flora's eyes. She put her hand to her mouth. "Augusta," she said in a whisper.

As the boat docked, immigrants pushed toward the exits and waiting relations. Flora held back until the crowd diminished. When she did finally step onto the wharf, she immediately dropped her bag and fell into Augusta's arms. Tears coursed down the women's cheeks as they clung to each other and repeated the other's name over and over.

Tatyana hung back, her own eyes burning with unshed tears. If only she were having such a reunion. She felt alone.

A large, blonde man stood beside Augusta. Tatyana recognized him as Dimitri from the photo Flora had shown her. He was even more handsome in person but almost seemed to swagger with self-assurance. The two youngsters she'd seen in the same photograph hung in close to their mother. The little girl's blue eyes sparkled with anticipation.

Finally the sisters stepped away from each other, keeping their hands clasped. "This must be Samuel," Flora said, bending and pinching the boy's cheek. He grinned and quickly stepped back. "And little Ella." She looked at Augusta and said, "She's beautiful." Flora patted the little girl's head, then looked at the big man beside Augusta. "Dimitri," she said, and smiled at the tall, powerfully-built Russian. "I have seen your photograph, but you are even more handsome in person."

Dimitri smiled warmly and bent to kiss his aunt, once on each cheek as was the custom. "I'm glad to meet you," he said in English.

Flora looked shocked. "Augusta, what did he say? Don't tell me you have forsaken our mother tongue?"

Dimitri shrugged. "It was ten years ago. I was only twelve when we left. I've forgotten." His blue eyes sparkled with mischief.

Augusta Broido playfully slapped her son across the arm. "He teases you. We would never abandon the beloved language of our fathers," she said in Russian.

Dimitri grinned. "It is very good to have you here, Aunt Flora," he said in perfect Russian, and hugged her again.

"So, you *are* teasing me."

Dimitri put his arm over the woman's shoulders. "A little teasing is not so bad."

He seems ill-mannered, Tatyana thought. In Russia one always treated the elderly with respect.

Augusta pushed her younger son and daughter toward her sister. "This is Samuel. He's thirteen."

The boy held out his hand politely. "It is good to meet you."

Flora took his hand and instead of shaking it, held it between both of hers. "I am so happy to be here and meet you."

Augusta placed her hand on her daughter's dark head. "And this is my Ella. She's just turned nine."

Ella flashed a bright smile. "Good to have you here, Aunt Flora."

Flora hugged her. "Oh, I am so glad to finally meet you. You were born after your mother left. All I've ever seen are photographs." She straightened. "Now, Augusta, where is your Pavel? It has been too many years since I've seen him."

"He wanted to be here, but they needed him at the bakery because of a mechanical breakdown. It is always something. But we are grateful for the work. It is not easy to find employment these days." Augusta laid her hand on Flora's arm. "You look tired, sister. Let's get you home." She circled her arm around Flora's waist. "It must have been an awful trip."

Flora laughed. "Awful? Ahh, maybe a little, but not all of it. I made a very good friend." She turned and looked for her cabin mate who stood next to the railing. "Tatyana, please, come meet my family."

Feeling a little shy, Tatyana joined Flora.

"Augusta, this is Tatyana Letinov. Tatyana, Augusta Broido, my sister."

"It is very good to meet you," Augusta said with a warm smile. She took the newcomer's hand and shook it. "Welcome to America."

"Thank you." Tatyana immediately liked this woman.

"We shared a room on the ship and have become very good friends." Flora turned to her nephew. "Dimitri, I would like you to—"

"I am so glad to meet you," the young man cut in. Taking Tatyana's hand, he was unable to hide his admiration.

Looking a little flustered, Flora finished, "Tatyana, this is Dimitri."

"And it is good to meet you," Tatyana said dryly. She couldn't understand such bold behavior, especially in a public place.

"I'm glad you have come to America. I'm certain you will like it very much."

Tatyana removed her hand. "I hope I will." She turned and scanned the station. "I do not see my uncle."

"Do you know where he lives?" Augusta asked.

"I have his address." Tatyana searched through her satchel. "Here it is." She held out the piece of paper.

Augusta took the address, studied it a moment, then handed it to her son. "Do you know where this is?"

Dimitri examined the note. "Yes, I know this area well. I have done some gardening there. It is not so far."

"Could you deliver Tatyana to her uncle's after taking Flora and me home?"

Tatyana bit back a protest. She didn't want to spend time with this man.

"Absolutely. It would be a pleasure." He winked at Tatyana.

Taken aback, Tatyana ignored the gesture and wondered at a man who would flirt so openly. *A true Russian would never do such a thing.* As casually as possible, she said, "Thank you for your help."

"It's a good thing Mr. Reynolds let me take the old Essex today."

"He doesn't use it anyway. Him and his fancy new car," Augusta said, unable to hide her dislike of the man.

Nothing could have prepared Tatyana for New York City. Already the adventure had begun. She'd never ridden in a car. It was strange how it glided so quickly and smoothly past the towering buildings hugging the streets. It almost felt like she was in a deep canyon. Her window was down, and Tatyana leaned out a little to look up at the distant rooftops, but it made her dizzy so she refocused her eyes on the roadway. A discordant clamor reverberated from all around. Buses, street cars, and automobiles congested the roadways, while people, their dogs, and vendors crowded the sidewalks.

"People must be very rich here. I have never seen so many cars."

Dimitri chuckled. "I guess it would seem so."

Hurt at his laughter, Tatyana wondered what she had said wrong.

"I know it looks like people are wealthy, but there are many here who struggle just to get enough to eat, like in Russia," Augusta said from the back seat.

Tatyana nodded but wasn't completely convinced this was the truth. After all, anyone who owned a car must be rich.

On many of the street corners men sold apples, a curious thing Tatyana thought. *Americans must like apples very much,* she decided, except that no one seemed to be buying any. Finally she asked, "Why do so many sell apples? Is it a favorite fruit?"

"Not exactly," Dimitri said. "We do like apples, but that's not why so many are selling them."

Confused, Tatyana said, "I do not understand."

"It's a way to make a little money. The orchards help people by selling the cold storage fruit from last fall at discounted prices."

"Times are hard," Augusta said. "There is a depression, and it's difficult to find a job. Sometimes selling apples is all a person can do."

"My brother and my cousin Lev said that in America no one is hungry. They said it is a land of plenty."

"That used to be true, but no more," Dimitri said. "The country has been facing hardship for several years. There are no jobs and people are hungry."

Fighting a growing alarm, Tatyana wondered, *What other lies have I been told?* Fear prodded her. Trying to calm herself, she sat a little taller and smoothed her skirt.

Dimitri pulled to the curb. They had stopped in front of a shabby-looking tenement. "It isn't much, but it's home." His voice held no apology. Actually, he sounded proud. Putting the car in gear and turning the engine off, he looked at Tatyana. "I'll take Flora's bag in and be right back." He stepped out of the car. His younger brother and sister scrambled out and, with a quick wave to Tatyana, hurried up the tenement steps. Dimitri grabbed the bag, then offered a hand to an unsteady Flora.

"I'm afraid I'm a little weak," she apologized.

"It's to be expected," Dimitri said as he looked at a boy leaning against the brick building. Setting the suitcase on the sidewalk, he dug into his pocket and tossed the lad a penny. "Watch the car for me? I don't want any hooligans bothering it."

After gaping at the money a moment, a grin lit the child's face. "Sure! Anything you want, Dimitri." He stuffed the coin in his pocket and quickly crossed to the car. Resting his hand on the hood, he proudly stood guarding it.

Augusta stepped out and turned to Tatyana. With a warm smile, she said, "It was very good to meet you. I hope we will see you again soon."

"You will come often?" Flora asked, squeezing Tatyana's hand.

"I will try," she answered, unable to promise anything at this point.

"Try not to be afraid. Different is not necessarily bad."

"Thank you for being such a good friend," Tatyana said, trying to keep her voice steady and her tears in check.

With a pat to the young woman's hand, Flora turned and joined her sister. With their arms linked, the two walked up the apartment steps.

Tatyana sat with her hands clasped in her lap. As soon as the tenement door closed, she turned her attention to the dashboard gadgets. She'd never seen anything like them and was momentarily overwhelmed by the many new sights and sounds she'd experienced just since arriving in New York. She longed for the familiarity of the farm back home.

Outside the car the young lad whipped off his cap and combed his hair back with his fingers. He peered through the front window at Tatyana. "Are you from around here?"

Tatyana couldn't understand what he had said and ignored him.

"Are you from around here?" the boy repeated.

Feeling she must respond, Tatyana answered in Russian, "I do not understand you."

"I am sorry," the boy said in Russian. "I should have . . . known. I heard family was coming."

"Are you Russian?" she asked, warming to the youngster.

"My . . . parents came . . . over when I was just a baby." He struggled with some of the words. "You will like it here."

Tatyana felt less a foreigner. "I hope so." To herself, she thought, *I do not think so.*

Dimitri bounded down the stoop. "Thanks for watching the car, Yuri."

Yuri! The name swept over Tatyana.

The boy tipped his hat and grinned. "Thank you."

"Is this boy named Yuri?" Tatyana asked.

"Yes. He's a good lad. He lives just one flight up from us," Dimitri said, studying her. "Is something wrong?"

"No, that's my brother's name. It just took me by surprise." She relaxed. "I suppose there are many Yuris here, also."

Dimitri pushed in the clutch and turned the key. The engine rumbled to life. "Not so many, but it's a good name."

Yuri grinned at Dimitri. "Is that your girlfriend?"

"No, I just met her," he shrugged and smiled. "But maybe not such a bad idea?" he laughed.

Yuri grinned. "See you," he called and ran up the sidewalk.

After Dimitri edged onto the road, Tatyana asked, "What did he say?"

"Who?"

"Yuri."

The big Russian grinned. "He wondered if you were my girlfriend."

Tatyana felt her skin flush. How should she respond to such an unbelievable remark? Sitting very straight, she searched her mind for a reply, but nothing came.

An awkward silence settled between them.

Gripping the steering wheel, Dimitri concentrated on the traffic. After a long silence, he asked, "Why didn't your family come to America with you?"

"They are only poor farmers, and there is very little money. It was decided that I would be the one to come and live with my uncle.

"Why?"

Tatyana took a deep breath and studied her hands. Should she tell a stranger about the afflictions of her homeland?

Glancing at her unwelcome driver, she decided it would be best to share a little or he would prod her for the information. "To be a Russian sometimes means only to endure, not to live. My brother wanted better for me."

Dimitri nodded. "I have heard about some of the trouble. The United States government should step in and do something."

The notion that help should come from an outside source galled Tatyana. She replied sharply, "We would never allow the Americans to interfere. Nor anyone else."

"But . . ." Dimitri began, then looking at Tatyana, ended lamely, "everyone needs help sometimes."

"We will solve our own problems," Tatyana said as she lifted her chin a little and glared at the road, clearly ending any further discussion on the matter.

Another long silence wedged itself between the pair. As Dimitri turned onto a less crowded street, he asked, "Do you know your uncle well?"

"No. We have never met."

Tatyana gazed at the medley of buildings and businesses lining the street. Many had brightly colored awnings shading their doorways. The signs in the windows made no sense to Tatyana, but she enjoyed the bright reds, blues, and greens used to paint them, although they did seem a little vulgar.

Not wanting to offend, she chose her words carefully. "This city is very different from Moscow or Leningrad. There are no cathedrals or dignified statues. And I have seen no soldiers."

"No. You will find no soldiers here. This is America. There is no place like it. I am honored to live here and to be a citizen of such a great country."

"You are a citizen? Does that mean you are no longer Russian?"

He thought a moment. "Well, I will always be Russian. That is my blood." He squared his shoulders. "But first I am an American."

Stunned, Tatyana could think of no courteous reply. A true Russian would never turn away from who he was. She could never do such a thing. She might live in this country, but she would forever be Russian.

As they rounded the corner, the city gave way to private homes, some with tiny lawns. They all looked neat and tidy. It felt neighborly.

"It's not much further now," Dimitri said. "It appears your uncle has done very well."

"That is what my cousin Lev told us."

Dimitri looked at the address on his paper and slowed as they passed the charred remains of a house on their right. He glanced around the neighborhood. "I need to check the address. What is your uncle's name?"

"Mikhail Vlasov."

He pulled to the curb. "Wait here." Stepping out of the car, he walked across the street and knocked on a door.

Tatyana could sense something was wrong. A sick feeling settled in her stomach. She turned and stared at the charred home. It looked hideous, its two fireplaces standing among the incinerated ruins like blackened ghosts.

She heard Dimitri's farewell. He tipped his hat to a woman and, with a sullen expression and a heavy step, walked back to the car. He didn't look at Tatyana as he slid onto the seat. For a long moment, he held the steering wheel but said nothing.

With her hands clutching her purse, Tatyana kept her eyes straight ahead.

"The house that is burned to the ground belonged to your uncle. It was destroyed a few weeks ago," Dimitri finally said.

Swallowing past a lump in her throat, she asked, "What about my uncle?"

"Well . . ." He cleared his throat. "It seems, according to that woman . . ." He paused.

"What? What is wrong?"

Dimitri turned and looked at Tatyana. "I'm sorry, but your uncle's dead."

Shock surged through her. "Dead? How can he be dead? He's the only family I have here."

Dimitri glanced down the street. "The neighbor said he was a Communist and that he'd been getting death threats." He fidgeted with the gearshift. "It seems someone burned him out."

Tatyana's eyes brimmed. Silently tears trickled down her cheeks. This is what Yuri had sent her to? She dug her nails into her palms and bit down on her lip.

"I'm sorry, Tatyana." Dimitri's voice sounded gentle.

She stared at the charred house and, in a hoarse whisper, asked, "What will I do now?"

CHAPTER 8

"Yuri!" Lev called as he strode across the field.

Yuri stopped his work, leaned on his hoe, and raised his hand in greeting. Taking a handkerchief from his hip pocket, he wiped sweat from his face and neck.

With a broad smile, Lev approached his cousin. "Why are you still in the fields? Have you forgotten my wedding?"

Yuri grinned. "Never, cousin. I just wanted to get this plot ready for the potato starts."

Lev kicked at the black soil with the toe of his boot, then gazed across the fields to the birch forests beyond. With a look of disdain, he asked, "And to what good? We labor, but the soldiers take our crops."

"Believe things will get better," Yuri said with a friendly pat on Lev's shoulder. He hesitated and, with less assurance, added, "Maybe this season will be different."

"Hah, not likely," the big man said.

"Many have already gone to work on the collectives. More than enough to feed our country. Maybe the government will leave us alone."

Lev folded his arms across his chest. "I do not believe they will stop until we're all working on collectives or dead."

Yuri removed his cap, smoothed back his hair, and gazed at his uncle's farmhouse in the distance. "Today is your wedding. It is not a time to be thinking about such things." He smiled and replaced his hat. "It is a new beginning for you and for Olya."

Lev's scowl was replaced with a look of expectancy. "Yes. Olya. She is a beauty and will make a fine wife and mother."

"What time is the wedding?"

"Six o'clock. After that we will celebrate. We will have food and drink, and dancing until morning."

Yuri cocked one eyebrow. "You and Olya will remain until the morning?"

Lev blushed. "Well, maybe not so late as some." He took a step toward the house. "I will see you at six."

"I will be there," Yuri promised.

That afternoon family and friends gathered at the Vlasov's home. Candlelight softened the interior of the room, and as Lev and Olya promised themselves to each other, thoughts of Stalin's tyrannical regime were pushed aside.

After the simple ceremony, the bride and groom were lavished with bear hugs, kisses, and good wishes. The guests cheered the bride and groom as they accompanied them to the Vlasov barn, where an evening of festivities awaited.

The barn had been cleared of its farm equipment, the cobwebs knocked from the rafters, the floors cleared of debris, and the windows scrubbed. Brightly colored draperies concealed dingy walls, and a long wooden bench, draped with a clean, white tablecloth, stood along one wall. The family heirloom, a crystal candelabrum, rested in the center of the table. Its candles burned brightly.

Although food was in short supply, the village had done its best to prepare a feast for the young couple. A hog had been butchered weeks before, and platters piled with sliced ham and sausages sat at each end of the table, tempting the guests. Fresh yeast breads, flat breads, and even sweet cakes filled the table. Someone had brought draniki, potato pancakes made from their few remaining potatoes. It seemed a real banquet.

Trying not to attract attention to herself, Irina quietly set a small ball of white cheese beside the other fare. Yuri smiled. She'd been saving the delicacy for something special. He only wished there were something he could offer the couple. But try as he might to come up with an idea, he'd been unable.

As the guests filled the barn, the feast was eyed by all, but no one ate. There would be time enough later. For now, it was best to savor the idea of the banquet to come.

There seemed no shortage of the homemade liquor, kvas, or vodka and stout ale. The glasses were filled, and a toast was made to the couple, then another, and another, until the final salute was given. After several rounds, the flushed guests grinned and laughed, and a call went up for the dance to begin.

Three musicians gathered at the end of the barn. One brought tambourines, another the mandolin, and another the balalaika. The man with the balalaika smiled as he readied the triangular, long-necked instrument. As he plucked the strings, a sweet, melodic song resonated from the walls and ceiling of the roomy barn. Then the clear, bright tones of the mandolin joined that of the balalaika, and the bells of the tambourine blended into the song.

Lev guided Olya to the center of the room. The bride and groom faced each other, their hands clasped behind their backs. With eyes of love, their feet beat out the rhythm of the folk dance. Guests watched and cheered as the couple moved in unison. Soon Lev and Olya twirled around and around each other, with their clapping hands raised above their heads. Olya's red and blue skirt swirled away from her legs, exposing slender, muscled calves. As the smiling couple came together, they pressed their hands against each other, then brushed lips in a whisper of a kiss.

Yuri grinned at this tender demonstration, acceptable only on special occasions, such as weddings. He reveled in the couple's happiness. One day he would have his dance.

Others joined the pair. Men and women leapt and pranced, forming a circle. Their steps matched the rhythm of the music while the clapping of hands beat out the cadence of the tambourines.

Yuri leaned against the wall, content to watch. Without warning, Lev left the dancers with Olya clinging to his hand. He bounced toward Yuri and grabbed his cousin's arm. "Come. Your turn," he said, as he dragged Yuri toward the circle.

Laughing, Yuri joined the swift-footed dancers. As he kicked and spun, sweat beaded up on his forehead. Happy faces swirled in and out of his vision. The sounds of the balalaika and tambourine seemed all that mattered. The men formed two lines, while the women fell back and clapped. One man did a handspring, then hooked a thumb into his belt loop, hefted himself off the floor with one arm, and kicked his legs straight out in time to the music. Cheers went up from the onlookers.

Another danced into the center of the room, raised his hands above his head, then dropped to a squat. He clapped his hands above his head, then slapped the floor while keeping rhythm with his feet and kicking his legs out in front of him.

Yuri couldn't resist. He moved forward and twirled, his feet performing intricate steps, while his hands clapped out the beat. With a shout, he bounced into a squat, folded his arms across his chest, and kicked his feet straight out in front of him, never losing the beat of the music. Lev joined his cousin, and the two danced side by side while the others shouted their approval.

One man after another came forward, each employing his own steps, each trying to best the one before. The music pulsated faster and faster until finally, with a shout from the musicians, the tambourine fell silent, the mandolin's clear tones ended, and the balalaika's sweet melody faded.

Gasping for breath and laughing, the guests collapsed against each other, onto chairs, and on the floor. Exhausted and spent, their euphoria crowded out anything but this moment of happiness. This was a time to consider family, love, and hope for a better future.

Yuri pulled Lev into a tight embrace. "I must go. It has been a wonderful party. Thank you."

"You are leaving?"

"I have work waiting for me tomorrow." He paused. "I wish I had something to give you and Olya," he apologized.

Lev clapped his cousin on the back. "You are enough." He thought a moment, then grinned. "Actually, I would like a gift from you."

Yuri eyed his cousin suspiciously.

"Sing us a song before you go." He raised his arms. "A song for the marriage couple." His voice rose so the guests could hear.

Soon other voices joined Lev's. "A song. A song. Yuri, sing to us."

Yuri lifted his hands as if to object, but shouts of approval drowned out his protest. Finally conceding, Yuri went to the balalaika player and, after speaking to the man, returned to the center of the room. As silvery notes rose from the delicate instrument, the people quieted. Yuri smiled at Lev and Olya. "This is for you. And for love."

He closed his eyes. A moment later his sweet tenor voice blended with the delicate tones of the ancient instrument. He sang of love and hope and peace. A hush settled over the room. Even the children grew still. Husbands and wives drew close, and tears brimmed in the eyes of many. With the final chords, Yuri's voice softened, and the song became a prayer.

For a long moment the room remained silent, then ardent cheers and clapping broke out. The guests convinced Yuri to sing several more tunes, until finally, with warm farewells, he went to his bed.

Yuri stretched out on his bunk and, smiling, studied the ceiling. It had been a good night. His smile remained until he fell asleep.

"Soldiers! Soldiers!"

The cries startled Yuri awake. He sat up and tried to clear his mind. *Soldiers?* He swung his legs over the bed, pulled on his pants, thrust his arms into the sleeves of a shirt and, still buttoning it, rushed into the living room. His uncle was already there. They pulled on their boots, threw their coats on, and strode out to the porch.

A neighbor boy sat astride a half-starved pony that panted from his effort of running from farm to farm.

Alexander and Yuri stepped into the yard. Yuri took the pony's halter and rubbed its face.

"What were you saying, lad?" Alexander asked.

Soldiers are coming!" The boy took a breath. "My father told me to warn you."

Lev joined Yuri and Alexander. Irina, Olya, and two younger children remained on the porch, still in their night dresses. Irina cradled her daughter against her.

The young neighbor glanced over his shoulder. "I have to go." He swung his pony around and trotted toward home.

Yuri grabbed his uncle's arm. "Was anything left out after the party?"

"Probably. It was late and better left until morning."

"If the soldiers find the food they'll think we have more. We must hide it!" Yuri hurried to the barn. The others followed.

The guests had been very generous and left everything that hadn't been eaten. A large portion of the pork remained, along with some bread, cheese, and liquor. And the candelabrum still adorned the table. Yuri was uncertain what to do.

The sound of a truck grinding through its gears came from the driveway.

Yuri looked at Irina and Olya. "You two go back to the house. Alexander, you and Lev meet the soldiers. I will find a place to hide this."

Mature for his years, Yuri had long been trusted and respected by those who knew him, and now everyone did as they were told without question.

Fighting a rising panic, Yuri searched the barn. Where? Where to hide the feast. His eyes probed the room and stopped at the loft. It was as good a place as any.

He shoved two loaves of bread and the cheese into a gunny sack and hoisted it over his shoulder. After dumping the few boiled potatoes into a bowl with the cabbage, he tucked them under his arm and hurried toward the ladder. He scrambled up the rickety steps and shoved the food into a back corner. As he turned, intending to make one last trip, the sound of the barn door opening stopped him.

Yuri froze. He held his breath and listened. At first, he heard nothing, then footsteps shuffled across the barn floor.

"Looks like you had a party," a voice snarled.

"Yes. My son Lev was married last night. We had guests. They were kind enough to leave these for our son and his wife."

"They would give away roasted pig and these vegetables?" the voice asked doubtfully.

"Our friends are very generous. We have little. I am only a poor farmer."

"Poor? Then what is this?" he said as he hefted up the candelabrum.

"It is nothing, only an inheritance from my grandparents. It is very old and has been in our family for years."

Yuri cringed as he listened to his uncle. It was humiliating.

Someone entered the barn. "Captain, they were hiding flour and oats in the hay stacks."

Yuri's stomach pitched. They were lost. Cautiously he peered over the edge of the loft.

A heavyset soldier with curly black hair escaping from beneath his hat grabbed Alexander by the collar. He pushed him against the wall. "Do you know what happens to subversives?" he asked through gritted teeth.

Alexander's eyes met the officer's, but he said nothing.

The man held the farmer a moment as he glared at him, then shoved him toward the door. "You are under arrest."

Straining to hear and longing to help, Yuri unknowingly moved forward. The boards creaked beneath him, sounding like a shot in the momentary quiet of the barn. Once found out, it was too late to pull back.

"Don't move!" the captain bellowed, pointing his rifle at Yuri.

He raised his arms.

The commander let loose of Alexander and walked to the bottom of the ladder. Sneering, he asked, "What would an innocent man be doing up there?"

Yuri said nothing.

"Come down!"

Slowly Yuri descended. When he reached the floor, he turned and met the man's cruel eyes.

"Step aside!" the officer bellowed and motioned a soldier up the ladder. "Let's see what is up there."

A few minutes later the man returned with the bag of hidden food.

"So, you have little. You're nothing but a farmer," the captain taunted Alexander. He tossed the candelabrum to the soldier, grabbed Yuri, and shoved him toward his uncle.

Both men were forced out of the barn at gunpoint.

Yuri squinted against the bright sunlight. He glanced at the house. The women and children huddled against the door.

Irina let loose of the youngsters, lifted her head, and marched up to the curly-haired soldier. She looked him in the eyes. "They have done nothing."

"Nothing? Do you call hiding food from the Soviet government nothing?"

"We only kept enough for ourselves. No more. We would have starved," she added lamely. It was clear these soldiers cared nothing about whether this family lived or died.

The soldier gave her a cold, measured look, then turned and pointed at Yuri and Alexander. "You, in the truck."

"No. Please no," Irina pleaded, but she stopped abruptly when Alexander gave her a warning glance.

Giving Alexander a look of apology, Irina stepped forward. "Please. We will join a collective. We will work to bring about a better Soviet Russia. We will do this gladly."

"I will not," Alexander said.

Irina's shoulders slumped forward, and she turned tormented eyes to her husband.

The commander chuckled. "It seems your husband is not so willing as you say."

"He will listen. If only you will let me speak to him."

The soldier hesitated, then abruptly turned and motioned for the soldiers to take the prisoners.

The color drained from Irina's face. She set her jaw but said nothing more as Alexander and Yuri were led away. She stared after them, wanting Alexander to know her thoughts—to know that any submission was worth his life.

Yuri glanced over his shoulder. "Don't tell Tatyana."

The two climbed into the back of the nearest truck, joining several other prisoners. The soldiers returned, the engines fired, and they pulled away.

Yuri stared at his family. Alexander placed his hand on his nephew's shoulder and gazed at his children, then fixed his eyes on Irina.

Lev stood in the drive between the two women, his arms around them both, while the children leaned against their mother. Ashen, wounded faces watched as the trucks drove away, but there were no tears.

A sudden breeze swirled up the dust around the house and engulfed it in a brown haze. It was the last thing Yuri saw as they drove away.

The trucks made several stops, and more prisoners were loaded. Each time, the cries of fear and outrage cut into Yuri's heart. But the soldiers didn't hear and savagely did their job.

With anguish, he turned his eyes heavenward and prayed. But he heard no answer; it seemed God did not hear. He asked, *Father, where are you?* Finally, he had no heart left for prayer.

Alexander sat on a bench, his head bowed, and his lips moving silently. Yuri knew his uncle was praying. *I should,* he thought, but he couldn't find the will. He felt empty. How could God allow this scourge on good people?

A young woman stood at the back of the truck. She didn't weep like many of the others. Instead, her dark and haunted eyes stared without seeing. She gave no impression of panic, only an angry resignation.

Yuri studied her. Although she was small, he could feel her strength and her rage. When she glanced at him, he smiled, hoping to penetrate her cold exterior. She ignored the gesture and stared at the canvas wall behind him.

At the end of the day, the trucks pulled onto a short lane leading into the woods and stopped. The soldiers piled out of the trucks, then forced the prisoners out. With feeble cries of protest the people climbed down and, waiting for instructions, huddled together.

Alexander and Yuri stood side-by-side. Yuri's eyes wandered over the birch forest. Why would they stop here? This is no prison.

Alexander seemed to understand. "God is with us," he whispered.

Yuri wished he possessed his uncle's faith, but God seemed very far away.

The soldiers sectioned off a group of prisoners and marched them into the forest. A hush fell over the woodland. Even the birds were still, and the wind refused to rustle the grasses and trees. Yuri felt a building sense of apprehension, not only within himself but also in those around him.

The sudden discharge of rifles pierced the silent forest. Gasps and cries of fear came from some of the prisoners. Yuri gave a reflexive jerk.

A woman moaned and cradled her nearly grown son. A child whimpered against her mother's skirts. Yuri's stomach lurched. He knew their fate. His eyes locked with his uncle's.

Sorrow emanated from the older man. "This is not the end," he said. "We will meet again."

The soldiers returned, and this time they sequestered Alexander into a group they herded away from the clearing. Screaming, the woman beside him broke away and fled toward the green haven of the forest. A soldier raised a rifle to his shoulder and fired. He never flinched but watched with indifference as the woman fell and lay still.

Cries and wails of horror came from the helpless onlookers. Yuri's mind shouted, *How can this be? God, how can this be?*

Using their rifles as prods, the soldiers forced the people into a march, and they headed into the forest.

Alexander stopped, looked over his shoulder, and gazed at his nephew. Yuri stared at the older man who projected a divine peace. Yuri breathed in the offered strength as a drowning man gulps at the air. *I can do this.* Alexander nodded slightly and turned away.

The last group of prisoners waited for the dreaded sound of shots. When they came, fresh shock raged through Yuri's body. He remembered his uncle's faith and lifted his chin and straightened his shoulders.

When the soldiers returned to take Yuri's group, the cries for mercy erupted immediately. They were ignored, and the group was herded through the tall, slender birch trees. Every nerve in Yuri's body felt alert and ready—ready for something. To meet death?

The spongy earth beneath Yuri's feet rebounded against his step. The pungent fragrance of spring grasses and moss smelled sharp and fresh. He ran his hand over the smooth, white bark of a tree. It felt cold. Peering through the treetops, he studied the deep blue of the sky. It seemed more vivid than he remembered.

After a short distance, the people were pushed toward a large pit and forced to stand in front of it. Yuri glanced down. Bloodied bodies lay in a senseless pile, their arms and legs intertwined. Blind, terrified eyes stared. Bile rose in Yuri's throat, and he turned away from the horrible sight. He even shut his eyes, but the gruesome picture remained.

The soldiers ordered the prisoners to stand single file in front of the open grave. A woman held her teenage daughter against her breast and wept. The girl clung to her mother. A man closed his eyes and recited the Torah. A young woman kneeled and begged for mercy. Her husband pulled her up, shushed her, and held her close.

The dark-eyed woman Yuri had noticed in the truck stood beside him. He glanced at her. She didn't seem to notice him. She stood with her body rigid, her shoulders thrust back, and her eyes trained straight ahead. Yuri felt a flush of pride for this stranger and wished they had known each other.

An order was given—the rifles raised. Yuri's legs shook, and his throat tightened, nearly cutting off his breath. He sought his Lord. *Father, help me to bear this. My life is yours.*

Shots splintered the air. A sharp burning pierced Yuri's right shoulder. Instinctively, he fell toward the mysterious woman, shielded her body with his, and thrust the two of them backward into the pit.

Keeping his eyes open, Yuri watched as others fell beside him. The Jewish man who had been praying lay with his eyes staring heavenward. A body on his left partially covered him. Blood surged from the man's wounds. Cries of the wounded came from all around.

The woman Yuri had shielded pushed against him. "Don't move!" Yuri whispered.

Immediately the woman stopped struggling.

Yuri could feel the blood from his wound dribble down his shoulder and across his chest. It hurt like fire. He stared as the others did and found himself looking into the dead eyes of an old woman. He wanted to shut out the horror but forced himself to hold his gaze.

Shots were discharged into bodies to finish the execution of the innocent. Muffled cries and groans came from the dying, but Yuri held still, praying for God's protection.

The gunfire finally stopped, and all was quiet. Yuri wondered where Uncle Alexander lay. Tears pressed against his eyes, but he willed them away. *Now, there is no time for such things.*

CHAPTER 9

As the military camp quieted, darkness blanketed the forest. The soldiers had not yet thrown dirt on the grisly grave, but Yuri knew that the soldiers would hide their atrocity at the break of dawn. He gritted his teeth and tried to swallow his rage, but it refused to be quieted and burned in his chest. *I hate them!*

The woman beneath Yuri pushed against him. "Move," she whispered. "I can't breathe."

As Yuri pressed his hand against the cold, sticky skin of a stranger and rolled to his right, his shoulder came alive with pain. Clenching his teeth, he stifled a cry. The body beneath him sank, and he forced back rising bile. Studying the night sky, he pushed the image of entangled, bloodied corpses from his mind. The moon hadn't yet risen. Now was their only chance to escape.

The brown-eyed stranger inched away from Yuri, her breath coming in small gasps. "How . . . how are we going to get out of here?" she asked, her voice laced with terror.

"I heard trucks moving out earlier. Probably the only soldiers left are the members of the burial crew." As he pushed up on his left elbow and edged toward the pit wall, his wound screamed at the movement, and bodies shifted beneath him. "The moon will be up soon. We've got to go now!"

As Yuri crawled forward, he placed his hand on a mass of sticky, damp hair. Quickly he snatched it back, then stared at his palm in the darkness before wiping it clean on his pants. He choked back rising nausea. "We'll hide in the forest," he managed to say and continued forward.

A sharp, piercing crack splintered the night. "Oh, my God!" the woman sobbed, then retched.

"Are you all right?"

"A baby! Her arm, her tiny arm . . . I . . . I broke it." Quiet sobs echoed across the open pit.

Yuri could hear the anguish in her voice and searched his mind for a way to calm her. "It's all right. She knows nothing now. We've got to keep going." Despite the evening chill, sweat dribbled into Yuri's eyes, and he wiped it away with the back of his hand before creeping forward.

He felt along the wall at the edge of the pit. It was too high and steep to climb out. "It's straight up. We'll have to dig handholds and footholds," Yuri said quietly, keeping his bad arm tucked in close to his body as he scooped away the dirt, making hollows in the damp earth.

His companion did the same.

Roots and sharp stones caught at his fingers. The smell of wet soil mingled with the stench of death. He kept his face close to the wall, trying to block out the fetid odor.

Their fingers bloodied, the two finally reached the crest of the open tomb. Yuri peeked out of the pit. Through the deep gloom, all he could make out were the last flickerings of a campfire. Someone coughed then cleared his throat. After that, all was quiet.

Yuri's heart pummeled against his chest. "We must go now!" he whispered. Careful to use his left arm, Yuri silently pulled himself over the edge. He ran away from the camp in a crouch, feeling a demon's pursuit as he raced for the protection of the woods. He heard the woman's footfalls behind him. *Please, Father, don't let the soldiers hear!*

A wall of underbrush slowed the fugitives as they scrambled for safety. Yuri barely noticed when a branch slapped him across the forehead.

Yuri and the woman kept running until they were certain they were a safe distance from camp. Gulping for air, Yuri leaned against a tree and stared back to where they had come from. Were they being followed? Quieting his breathing, he listened for sounds of a chase but heard nothing except the hammering of his own heart. His eyes tried to penetrate the darkness.

"Can you see anything?" came a whisper from beside him.

"No. Can you?"

"No. I wish the moon would come up."

Yuri continued to stare into the blackness, the ache in his shoulder throbbing in rhythm with his heartbeats. "If we can see, so can they. I guess it's good there's no moon." Gradually his pulse slowed and, hearing no signs of pursuit, he relaxed a little.

A sliver of light filtered through the trees as the moon climbed above the edge of the earth.

"It won't be long before the moon's full. We'd better move on."

"Please let me rest a little."

Yuri glanced back at the camp. "Okay. But not long." He folded his legs beneath him and leaned against a birch. Closing his eyes, he longed for sleep. *Just a few minutes rest,* he thought.

✳ ✳ ✳ ✳ ✳

"It's going to be light soon," a voice said, penetrating Yuri's slumber.

He jerked himself awake. Immediately, pictures of the hideous grave affronted him. Rubbing at his eyes and trying to blot out the image, he stood up, the sudden movement pulling at his injured shoulder. He gasped at the pain.

"Are you all right?" the woman asked.

"Yes." Yuri glanced at his bloodied shirt, then at the nearly full moon. He looked at his unexpected partner. She sat with her legs tucked close to her chest, staring in the direction of the pit and camp. Although he couldn't see clearly in the moonlight, he knew what he would find in the stranger's dark eyes and was glad he couldn't see it.

Yuri moved a little toward the woman. "My name is Yuri Letinov. What's yours?"

Keeping her eyes directed toward the encampment and their enemy, she said sadly, "What does a name matter now?"

"It matters." Yuri reached out, took her hand, and repeated, "My name is Yuri Letinov." He didn't release his hold and continued to look at her.

She sighed. "Elena. Elena Oleinik." She pulled her hand free and stood up. Grabbing hold of a tree branch, she stripped away its leaves, then bent it in the middle. "What do we do now?"

"I'm not sure. I can't return to my family." Despair swept over Yuri. "I'll probably never see them again. They won't know what has happened to me or Uncle Alexander . . . ," he faltered. "Uncle," he whispered, remembering how bravely the man had gone to his death. Tears burned his eyes, but Yuri quickly blinked them away.

"We could go to Moscow. Maybe find work." Elena stripped another branch of its leaves.

"Do you have friends there?"

"Friends? There is no such thing any more."

"There is work in the city."

Elena crushed a leaf. "I have no papers."

"Nor I, but I've heard of people who can help." Yuri plucked a slip of grass and chewed on it. His stomach rumbled with hunger. "Why were you arrested?"

Elena turned and glared at Yuri. "Why do you want to know?"

"I just wondered."

She pressed her foot against the tree's trunk and folded her arms. "I was hungry and stole a piece of bread. That is a crime worth death?"

"My uncle and I were caught hiding food on our farm."

Elena eyed him suspiciously. "Kulak? Are you a Kulak?"

"You accuse me? Why is it wrong to own a farm and a few animals? Should such a thing make a man an enemy of the state?"

The petite, young woman shrugged her shoulders. "They say Kulaks take from the poor."

"That's not true!"

"I know, but there are many who wish to believe it is so."

"We are only trying to live, as everyone else is." He spat out the piece of grass. "What has happened to our country? I thought Lenin and the Bolsheviks would bring peace and prosperity. But . . ."

"Stalin. He is what has happened to Russia. He will be the end of us."

"And, what can we do?"

"We can't do anything." She paused. "We will die. That is all."

Yuri swept his hair back off his forehead. "You act as if there is no hope."

"Is there?" Elena asked derisively.

"We're not alone. God will see us through."

Elena gave no reply but kicked at the tree.

"We'd better get moving. The nights are brief these days."

❋ ❋ ❋ ❋ ❋

The crash of a serving tray and breaking dishes made Tatyana jump and nearly drop the platter in her hands. Turning from the sink where she was up to her elbows in soapy water, she found Allison McCormack scrambling to pick up shattered pieces of china.

"Oh, dear! Oh, dear! Look what I've done!" Her hands shook as she picked up the fragments of fine glassware. She glanced at the house supervisor, Mrs. Wikstrom. "What will I do?"

"Now, Allison, calm yourself," Mrs. Wikstrom said as she dusted her hands free of flour.

"I will help." Tatyana towel-dried her hands, knelt beside the Irish house maid, and began picking up shards of glass.

"Ouch!" Allison dropped a piece of the delicate china. "Now I've cut meself." She pressed the wound to her mouth to stop the flow, wiped her finger on her apron, and returned to clearing away the mishap. With her apron full of broken dishes, she stood up and frantically looked about, undecided what to do.

"Just put it all in here," the housekeeper said as she opened a bin for trash.

Allison did as she was told. "Thank ye', Mrs. Wikstrom. I'm truly sorry."

The elderly domestic tucked a strand of graying hair back into place. "It was an accident. There's nothing more to be said."

Tatyana was intrigued by Mrs. Wikstrom. The matron rarely smiled and all too often seemed too concerned with what was proper and acceptable. It would be easy to believe she was severe and unkind, but Tatyana knew otherwise. Although she hadn't been in Mr. Meyers's employ long, she'd had enough time to know this woman wasn't all she appeared. Behind the stiff demeanor lived a merciful and generous human being.

After Dimitri had convinced his employer, Mr. Meyers, to hire Tatyana as a maid for his estate, it was Mrs. Wikstrom who had helped her settle in. She was the one who made certain Tatyana received her meals and took the time to make sure the young immigrant knew when and how to fulfill her duties. She was always patient, never bossy or harsh.

"Ooh, I'll be more careful, I promise," the young Irish maid fussed. "I always seem t' be doin' something wrong."

Tatyana glanced at the kitchen doorway, hoping Reynold Meyers hadn't heard the noise. Allison was always in some kind of trouble, and too often their employer was excessively harsh with the tiny, frail servant.

Mrs. Wikstrom took a broom and swept up the remaining glass fragments.

"I'm so sorry, ma'am," Allison repeated.

"You've got to learn to slow down. You were carrying too big a load."

"But Mr. Madison told me to, ma'am. He said if I did not start pulling me fair share around here, I'd be out on me ear." Tears filled the girl's eyes.

"Don't you fret about him. You do as I say." She dropped the glass in the dumpster. With a half smile, she continued, "Mr. Meyers has too many dishes anyway, if you ask me."

"Is that so?" Reynold Meyers asked.

Tatyana's heart skipped a beat. As she stood up, she hid a piece of broken glass behind her skirt and waited.

Mrs. Wikstrom's hand went to her throat as she turned to face the man.

With an arrogant air, the handsome aristocrat leaned against the doorway. He wore an insolent grin.

"Sir, I didn't know you were standing there."

"Obviously."

Mrs. Wikstrom met his gaze. "I'm very sorry if I offended you, sir."

He turned his attention to Tatyana, his eyes roving over her as he pulled on a pair of leather gloves.

Tatyana could feel her face redden under his visual assault.

He looked back at Mrs. Wikstrom. "No offense taken. I suppose we do have too much tableware." He placed his bowler on his head. "I'm on my way out. I'll be quite late." With a slight nod of his head and a scowl for Allison, he turned and walked out of the room.

"I thought me heart would jump out of me chest when I saw him standin' there."

"Enough nonsense," Mrs. Wikstrom said. "We've still got supper dishes to do, and I'll never get this bread baked and make it to bed at a reasonable hour at this rate."

Tatyana returned to her suds. A familiar sense of vulnerability settled over her. She didn't belong in this fine house so far from home. Unbidden tears stung her eyes, and she tried to blink them away. She'd only been in the household a few weeks and, although she was protected and well fed, she longed for home and family.

Life here was so different from Russia. She would never adjust. No one had roots. Everyone came from someplace else. People here had no tradition, no heritage to cling to. And people dreamed only of wealth; even her fellow servants talked of the riches they would have one day. Despite Tatyana's frustration, pictures of long soup lines in the city filled her mind, and she sighed. *At least here in America the government helps. In Russia people starve while the government builds more factories and bridges.*

Allison set a handful of glasses and silverware on the counter. "It seems Mr. Meyers takes a fancy to ye'," she said with a grin.

Tatyana lifted her chin. "I did . . . not . . . notice." She struggled with her English.

"Ah, come on now. Ye' can't tell me ye' 'aven't seen how he looks at ye'?"

Tatyana turned and faced the frail girl. In spite of her warm hazel eyes and gentle smile, she looked plain. Her hair was thin and wispy, and dark hollows lay beneath large cheekbones. Her starched collar couldn't conceal her bony neck and shoulders. "Please . . . do not speak so."

"All right, but that doesn't change the truth of it." She smiled and returned to the dining room to finish clearing the table.

Tatyana scrubbed at a roasting pan. As she considered the maid's words, her stomach tightened. What if Mr. Meyers wanted more from her than just cleaning and cooking?

"Tatyana, would you like to go for a walk after you're finished?" Dimitri asked as he breezed into the kitchen. "My mother said she'd love for you to come by for some tea and a listen to the radio."

Tatyana forced a smile. She did enjoy spending time with Dimitri's family, just not with him. He'd become far too comfortable about their relationship, always behaving as if she wanted his company. Too friendly and too kind, he made her uneasy.

She glanced around the room. It would be nice to spend time with friends away from dirty dishes and chopped vegetables. "I would like to go," she answered in Russian.

"No Russian. You must speak English. Otherwise, you will never learn." He smiled broadly, softening his reprimand.

Tatyana nodded and repeated, "I like go."

"Good, I'll wash some of this dirt off of me." He sauntered out to the back porch where he kept his street clothes.

"So, is it him you fancy?" Allison teased.

Tatyana hated the girl's teasing. "He has good family." She returned to her duties while Allison tramped up the back stairs. After she finished her work, Tatyana untied her apron and hung it on a hook.

Dimitri knocked at the kitchen door and peeked in.

"It seems your young man is here," Mrs. Wikstrom said.

"He not *my* man," Tatyana said, wishing she had never accepted the invitation.

The older woman lifted one eyebrow. "Oh? You might want to ask him about that," she said as she grinned. "He looks awfully eager to me."

Tatyana could feel the blood rush to her face. "What about how I feel?"

Mrs. Wikstrom made no comment but turned back to her kneading.

Tatyana went to get her sweater, then met Dimitri on the porch.

"Good thing you brought your wrap," he said. "It's a clear night, but you never know when it might get chilly, even in August. Let me help you." He took the sweater and slipped it over her shoulders.

Tatyana held very still, not wanting him to touch her. She hooked the top button. "It nice see your mother, your aunt Flora." She paused. "I not see too many weeks. Weeks? Is that right word?"

Dimitri smiled down at Tatyana. "Yes. You're getting much better."

"Thank you. I try . . . hard."

"Either you're a very good student or I'm a great teacher," Dimitri said with a smile, taking her arm and escorting her out of the house.

Tatyana stopped. "I able walk without help," she said.

Dimitri looked at his hand on her elbow. "Oh, I'm sorry." Looking a little wounded, he let go.

Immediately Tatyana felt bad and wished she hadn't said anything.

He stopped on the back porch. Taking a bouquet of sweet peas, carnations, and jasmine from the table, he said, "These are for you." Shyly he held them out to her.

Taken aback by his thoughtfulness, Tatyana didn't know how to respond. "Thank you. But, you should not have done."

"I grow them myself."

The flowers reminded her of the brightly colored blossoms scattered throughout the fields of her homeland. Her eyes teared at the memory. She breathed deeply of the fragrant blossoms. "Thank you," was all she could say.

Dimitri smiled. "I'm glad you like them." Reaching into his coat pocket, he took out a book. "I have something else. I remembered how you said you like books. I was at the bookstore and found this." He held out a copy of *Anna Karenina*. "It's written in Russian."

Tatyana looked at it, but didn't reach out.

He nudged it toward her. "I got it for you."

Taking the book, she gently ran her hand over the cover. "Tolstoy is an extraordinary writer," she said in Russian. "Thank you. I love it." Holding the book against her chest, she wished she hadn't promised to go with Dimitri. Now, all she wanted was to curl up in a quiet place and read.

Dimitri took her arm and led her down the porch steps. This time Tatyana didn't mind so much.

With evening, the traffic lessened and a "city" type of quiet had settled over the town. Fewer buses and cars filled the streets, and the sound of children playing echoed from a nearby street.

Tatyana's heart constricted as they approached a line of men, women, and children waiting for a free meal. "I feel . . ." She struggled to find the right word, "guilty when I see many . . . hungry. We have much . . ." she shrugged.

"Maybe Communism is not so bad. At least everybody eats."

Outraged at his ignorance, Tatyana stopped and stared at her young escort. "No. *Here,* everyone eats," she rattled off in Russian. "In Russia no one eats!" She gripped her fist with her left hand. "You say Communism is better? You do not know!" She stretched out her hand toward the line of people. "Here the government cares for the hungry, but in Russia the government turns its back. People, many people die every day. My eyes cry for them." Thoughts of Yuri and her aunt and uncle and cousins tumbled through her mind. Were they still alive? Or had they joined those who had already succumbed to tyranny and starvation? Unable to stop her tears, she continued, "My own brother . . . I do not know where he is or if he even lives."

"I'm sorry, Tatyana. I didn't mean to upset you. I thought you loved your country."

Embarrassed at her outburst, she stared at the ground. Quietly she said, "I do love my Russia, but it has a very bad government."

"The newspeople say the opposite. They're always writing articles about how good everything is over there. All I read says your government takes care of the people."

Tatyana's shoulders sagged. "It is a lie." She took a shaky breath. "I love my homeland. The people are very good, but Stalin is evil. He will destroy Soviet Russia." She looked at Dimitri. "Even so, one day I will return. It is my home. I cannot stay away." She turned and slowly moved down the street. Reverting to English, she continued quietly, "Maybe one day . . . government good."

"I hope so," Dimitri said as he took her arm protectively.

There was something in his voice Tatyana didn't understand. She glanced up at the young man. His brow was furrowed. "Something . . . wrong?"

"No." He paused. "Well, that's not completely true. I hate the thought of your returning to Russia." Uncharacteristically, he blushed and hastened his steps. "We better hurry. Mama is expecting us."

Tatyana didn't know what to think of Dimitri. Often he was pushy and overconfident, but there were times, like now, when he seemed uncertain and boyish, and she almost liked him.

They were welcomed into the sparse apartment by Dimitri's father, Pavel. "Come in! Come in!" The older man hugged Tatyana and pounded his son on the back. "Did you hear that some banks are reopening?"

"I heard. It is good news."

"The best. Maybe soon there will be money to spend. You think?"

"I hope so."

"Come sit," Flora said in Russian. "Tell me about your life at the big house."

Tatyana took the old woman's hands and sat beside her on the threadbare couch. She'd only spent a few weeks in this apartment, but it felt like home.

Ella, her big blue eyes bright with interest, sat on the other side of Tatyana and cuddled up close. "Please tell us what it is like at the big house."

"Hush, Ella," Augusta said.

Flora smiled at the child. "Now, what do we care about banks and such? It has nothing to do with us. I'm much more interested in what has been happening with Tatyana."

"I don't understand all the bank talk, but it seems important to them," Tatyana said.

"Would you like tea?" Augusta asked.

"Yes, thank you." Tatyana accepted a delicate saucer and cup filled with steaming, golden liquid. She studied the china. "This is lovely."

"Speak English, speak English," Dimitri said.

Ignoring her son, Augusta sat beside Ella and continued in Russian. "Thank you. I'm sorry to say it is one of the few pieces I was able to save when we came over." She folded her hands in her lap. "Now, tell us about your life at Mr. Meyers's."

"I like my work. I clean the house and help cook and do dishes, lots of dishes. Sometimes I iron. It is not difficult, but it is a very large house and takes many hours." She frowned slightly. "Sometimes it seems such a shame."

"What is a shame?" Flora asked.

"It is such a big house for only one man. I do not understand."

"Oh, that is the way of the wealthy. And one I'm sure we'll never understand," Augusta said as she clicked her tongue disapprovingly. "That Mr. Meyers is a spoiled child. Dimitri said he inherited all his money. And he doesn't treat his employees well, either."

"He is not so bad," Tatyana said. "I guess when people are used to being in charge of everything, they just forget to appreciate those who serve them." Remembering her employer's earlier bold perusal, she hoped he wanted nothing more from her but chose not to mention it to her friends. *Allison is probably imagining things,* she told herself.

"And he expects everything to be done perfectly," Dimitri interjected.

"I think you're being too hard on him," Tatyana said.

"How do *you* feel about him?" Augusta asked Tatyana.

"He has always been kind to me, although I have to admit he has been cruel to some of the others. Poor Allison. She tries so hard."

"You should watch out for that man. He is a fox," Flora added. "Be wise. The Scriptures teach us to be gentle as a dove and wise as a serpent."

"I think I've heard that somewhere," Dimitri interjected.

Flora gave the young man a disdainful look. "And so you should read the Word of God. Then you would know where it comes from." She turned back to Tatyana. "Well, that is what you must do, dear. God wants us to be kind but not foolish."

Augusta patted Tatyana's hand. "It is right that you are good-hearted," she said gently.

"All right you women, quiet down," Pavel said good naturedly and turned up the volume on the radio. "All you do is gossip. *Amos and Andy* is coming on."

Augusta Broido waved her hand at her husband. "Shame on you, Pavel. All you can think about is fun. There is so much more going on in the world."

His blue eyes sparkling, the jovial man said, "Shush, woman." He planted a kiss on his wife's cheek, wrapped his arm about her shoulders, and scrunched down beside her on the couch. "There is plenty of time to think about life and its grief. Now it is time for fun."

As Tatyana prepared for bed that night, a soft smile remained on her face. As usual, her evening at the Broido home had brought light into her life. Pavel's tunes on the mouth organ still played through her mind. She forced herself to keep from humming so as not to waken her roommate, Allison.

Laughter, fun, and good food always accompanied her visits to the Broido home. She could still taste the succulent sausages they had served with draniki. Always a favorite at home, the fried potato pancakes had been a treat. Tatyana knew the evening fare was an indulgence and that the Broidos would have to cut back on their food allowance the rest of the week to make up for their generosity. She wished they wouldn't sacrifice so much for her.

Tatyana lay back on her pillow and stared at the dark ceiling. Dimitri's friendly face intruded on her thoughts. What would she do about him? He was a good man but definitely not the kind she could ever be interested in. She mulled over Mrs. Wikstrom's earlier comments about him being "her young man." Did he want more than friendship from her? She knew the answer. He wasn't good at all about concealing his feelings. If only life weren't so complicated. She didn't want to hurt him, but romance could never be a part of their relationship. He was far too ill-mannered.

She picked up the photograph of her family and gazed at it. Her heart constricted as she studied the faces. *Mama, Papa. What has happened to you?* Gently she touched the glass, and tears fell. *Yuri. Oh, Yuri.*

Angrily she wiped away the salty droplets. *I will write him,* she decided. She lay back down. *I will tell him of America and how he must come and get me and take me home.*

She set the picture back on the bureau and lay down. Scenes of Yuri and cousin Lev played through her mind. She could see them stacking hay beneath the hot summer sun, their shirts soaked with sweat. How she missed them.

Yes, one day Yuri will come, she thought as sleep finally blanketed her.

CHAPTER *10*

TATYANA SET HER PEN ON THE oak desk and peered out the tiny third-floor window. The world looked very different from this viewpoint. Cars seemed small, their noise muted. The young maple with broad leaves seemed scrawny. She smiled as a young boy wobbled down the sidewalk on his bicycle. Obviously he'd just recently learned to ride.

Studying this new domain, she felt a sense of peace. *What an extraordinary place,* she thought. Although people have troubles, they live lives of hope, knowing that tomorrow can be better. They do not dread the intrusion of soldiers and unjustified imprisonment. I doubt they have ever considered such things. A sense of wonder welled up in Tatyana. *They truly are free.* An ache settled in her chest as she thought of Yuri and how she wished he could experience this newfound freedom she was still learning to savor.

Dimitri stepped around the corner of the house and bent over a rose bush. With unexpected gentleness, he inspected the plant, then plucked off the withered blossoms. He did the same with all the rosebushes. Kneeling in the lush grass, he deftly pulled the newly sprouted weeds, leaving only the unblemished, dark loam.

Tatyana had noticed how immaculate the grounds were kept and knew Dimitri worked hard to maintain them. She still didn't know what to make of the young Russian. Although a hard worker, he seemed very brash and unruly. However, she had to admit she'd seen a tenderness in the man that intrigued her.

He glanced up. When he saw Tatyana watching him from the window, he smiled and raised his hand in greeting.

Taken off guard, Tatyana jerked back then edged forward and gave him a half-hearted wave. He'd seen her spying on him; now what would he think?

She picked up her pen, stared at the half-written letter, and tried to concentrate. Although she'd written Yuri before, he hadn't replied. She wasn't surprised. Mail service in Russia had long been unreliable, and now, under the new regime, it was even worse. She doubted he actually received her letters. Still, she could hope.

She reread the words. "On my last day off, I had the most exciting time. Pavel and Augusta took Flora and me to the Empire State Building. It is a remarkable place. Did you know it's the world's tallest building? When we got there, we entered a lobby that is three stories high! The floors were made of colored stones, and the walls had lighted panels. Of course it didn't compare to the grandeur of the Winter Palace, but it was lovely.

"After that we took an elevator to the eighty-sixth floor. At first I thought I might lose my breakfast, but I felt better after a moment. We were there so quickly. Visitors can look out from a walled-in observatory. I wanted to see, but I was frightened.

113

When I first stood at the barrier and looked down, I felt dizzy. We were so high that the huge city of New York looked small. The wind was blowing, so I held onto the guard rail to make sure I kept my feet.

"It was wonderful! You would have loved it, Yuri. I could see for miles and miles. Looking down on the city was like looking at a map. In the distance I could see Upper New York Bay sparkling beneath the sun and Ellis Island. It looked tiny. And just beyond that stood the Statue of Liberty. Again I was moved, remembering how she looked when we entered the harbor and how I felt when I realized that freedom was within my grasp.

"So much has happened in such a short time. When I first discovered our uncle's death, I felt so alone, but then my new friends took me in and cared for me. Dimitri helped me get a job here where he works, and now I'm living in a luxurious mansion on Fifth Avenue." Tatyana thought a moment, then wrote, "I guess anything can happen in America. Please come soon, Yuri.

"My employer, Mr. Meyers, isn't a bad sort," she continued, "but he has little understanding of what it means to live with hardship. He's had everything he ever wanted and is very spoiled. He's a lawyer and works a lot of hours at the courthouse. I don't know just exactly what he does there."

Tatyana chewed on her pen. What else could she tell Yuri about Mr. Meyers? She didn't dare mention his amorous looks, especially since she wasn't certain that's what they were.

She decided to move on to a safer topic and chatted about the street vendors and the interesting wares they sold, items she'd never seen before. She couldn't fathom why people bought some of the products, although with the tough times most people were buying only necessities.

She went on to tell Yuri about the different foods she'd tried since arriving and especially about one of the most interesting she'd purchased from a street vendor. "Americans especially like a food called a hot dog. It is a strange-looking sausage wrapped in a long roll. Mr. Broido insisted I try one. So I did. It tasted very good. When you come, you will have to eat one."

Sadness settled over her. She let her pen rest on the stationery and returned to staring out the window. Dimitri was gone. Dark clouds had gathered along the horizon, and the wind beat a sprinkle of rain drops against the window. Afternoon storms were common, and Tatyana had grown used to them. She sighed. This place, as interesting and exciting as it was, simply was not home. Memories of her family filled her mind, and her eyes brimmed with tears. She longed for them and her friends. She missed the pastures dotted with bright flowers, the dark green potato patches, and the pungent aroma of freshly cut hay drying beneath the hot sun.

Allison breezed into the room. "How are ye' doing?" Before Tatyana could reply, the young maid continued. "Guess what? Dimitri and Johnny have invited us to the movies! The Marx Brothers are playin'." She barely paused long enough to take a breath. "They're so funny. Harpo is me favorite."

Tatyana didn't know what she was talking about. She put her pen down and stared at her tiny roommate. "What you saying?"

"Ye' know, the movies. Talking pictures? The boys invited us. And ye' won't need to worry about money. They'll be payin' for it."

Tatyana didn't feel like going, especially not with Johnny and Dimitri. Johnny could be so obnoxious and Dimitri—well, she didn't want to give him any ideas about the two of them. She glanced down at her letter. "I have to finish."

"I'll not be goin' with the two fellows alone," Allison said, taking Tatyana by the hand and pulling her to her feet. "That can wait." When Tatyana sat back down, Allison placed her hands on her hips and said, "Now, ye' know this is me only day of rest this week. And I do believe in havin' some fun. Now, come on."

"But, I not know about movie."

Allison's face brightened. "Ye'll love it! Ye'll see."

Tatyana sighed. "Let me finish, then I go."

"Okay, I'll tell them." She nearly danced out of the room, her skirt swirling away from her tiny ankles.

Tatyana returned to her letter and explained her movie invitation to Yuri, promising to tell him all about it.

Two sharp raps rattled the door.

Wondering why Allison would knock, Tatyana said testily, "I nearly done." She didn't bother to look up.

"Is that so?" a man's voice asked.

Tatyana dropped her pen and turned to find Reynold Meyers standing in the doorway wearing an amused smile. "Mr. Meyers, sir." Tatyana stood. "I . . . I not know it you."

Her employer said nothing, only leaned against the door frame and stared at her.

Tatyana felt her face redden and wished he would say something. "Sir?" she finally asked.

"I have a dinner engagement downtown." He paused, looked at his neatly manicured hands, then said casually, "I'm looking for some company."

Tatyana didn't understand and waited for further explanation. When none came, she asked, "Yes? What want?"

Reynold laughed, showing perfectly straight, white teeth. He pushed his brown hair off his brow. "I forget you foreigners don't know anything about our ways." In a mock bow, he said, "I was asking if you would like to accompany me. I would enjoy your company."

Stunned, Tatyana's mind went blank. "Oh," is all she said.

Mr. Meyers continued to stare at her and waited.

Finally she asked, "Me, sir? Why me? I am only servant."

Reynold stepped into the room. Tatyana wished he had remained outside.

He glanced around, quickly taking in the scarcity of the quarters. "I'll have to remember to get you girls some new draperies for the window and . . . maybe some pictures for the walls. This is absolutely dreary."

"No, that is . . . " Tatyana sought the right word, "un . . . necessary." How could she go with this man? He was her employer. Grateful for Allison's invitation, she said, "Thank you, sir, for asking, but I already go with friends." Under his piercing look, her thoughts were a muddle. "We go to movies."

Mr. Meyers straightened and pulled at his shirt waist. Clearing his throat, he said brusquely, "Very well. Maybe another time." Without another word, he turned and walked out the door.

Tatyana could hear his footfalls on the carpet as he tramped down the hallway. She knew he was angry. Staring at the door, she asked, "Now what I do?"

She placed her unfinished letter on the desk shelf, set her pen in its cubicle, and closed up the writing board. She glanced in the mirror. Her pale blonde hair had fallen out of its pins, and tendrils fell onto her face. It needed recombing, and because she hadn't planned on leaving the premises she was dressed in her practical brown skirt and white blouse. "I can't go looking like this."

Rifling through her meager wardrobe, she chose the pale yellow, flowered cotton dress Mrs. Wikstrom had given her when she first arrived. It fell mid-calf and had short, puffed sleeves with dainty, cotton edging around a squared neckline. The empire waist allowed the dress to fall loosely over her hips, giving Tatyana freedom of movement. She liked the simple gown. It looked colorful and lively. She quickly put it on in place of her drab attire.

After splashing her face with water, she studied her reflection in the mirror. Many American women painted color on their lips and cheeks. *I look drab,* she thought, and wondered if she ought to do the same. "But, I have no colors," she said ruefully and quickly brushed her hair into a tight bun. She started to pin it up, then let some fall onto her shoulders. The women here didn't wear their hair severely like the Russians. Many had lovely pins that held their hair off their face but allowed it to cascade onto their shoulders. She thought it pretty. *Maybe I will buy some hair clips,* she thought, then said to her image, "You're much too vain. If you are not careful, you will become a spoiled American." She finished pinning her hair, grabbed her sweater, and hurried out of the room.

Allison, her friend Johnny, and Dimitri were sitting around the table talking when Tatyana pushed the kitchen door open. They all stood.

"I was beginnin' to think ye were never comin' down," Allison said as she smoothed her dress and linked arms with Johnny.

Johnny's dark eyes flashed with humor. "Yeah, we were wondering if you'd gotten lost." He glanced around the room. "It wouldn't be hard to get lost in this place. One day I'm going to live in a mansion even bigger than this."

"Oh, Johnny, don't ye be wastin' so much time on impossible dreams." Allison nudged him. "I like ye' just the way ye' are."

"No reason a man can't dream," Johnny said with a smile, but his eyes looked hurt. "Let's go."

Dimitri joined Tatyana but refrained from putting his arm through hers. "If we don't, we'll be late. Have you ever seen the Marx Brothers?"

"I not know these men. Who they are?"

"It's 'Who are they?'" Dimitri corrected.

"Who are they?" Tatyana repeated.

"They're really funny guys who act in comedy movies." Johnny leaned on the counter. "Have you ever been to a moving picture?"

"I never see."

"This ought to be fun," he said sarcastically.

Tatyana felt dim-witted. Evidently everyone knew about movies except her. "Maybe I stay here. I . . . I do not know these things. I not belong."

Dimitri shot Johnny an exasperated glance, then looked at Tatyana. "No. You'll like it. Please come."

Tatyana did want to see a real movie. In fact, after giving it some time, she had become excited about the prospect. She studied her friends.

"Please say ye'll go," Allison pleaded.

She took a deep breath. "All right, I go."

"Good," Dimitri said with a grin and held out his arm to her.

Tatyana took it and allowed him to guide her out the door.

It was a long walk to the theater, but Tatyana didn't mind. Still amazed at the sights and sounds of the city, she enjoyed every excursion.

When they reached the movie house, Tatyana stared at a large billboard with flashing lights framing the title. "What does say?"

"It's advertising the movie *Duck Soup*," Allison explained. "Wi' the Marx Brothers it canna' be anything but funny." She waited by the doorway while Johnny walked to a window and placed several coins on the counter. "Ten cents seems like an awful lot for a movie," he complained to the ticket clerk.

The perfectly coifed woman only shrugged and pushed two tickets through an opening below the window.

"Johnny, I can pay me own."

"No way. When I take a girl out, I pay the bill."

"I just thought—"

"I'm no heel."

"We know. Calm down," Dimitri said. He strolled up to the ticket window and plunked down twenty cents. "Two, please." Taking the tickets and holding them up, he said, "Let's go in."

Tatyana's feet sank into deep carpeting as the door closed behind her. The city noise faded. She looked around, taking in the heavy brocade wallpaper and trying to place the interesting smells. *So this is a movie house,* she thought.

"D'ye want something to eat?" Allison asked, walking up to a booth laden with brightly wrapped candies. "The smell of popcorn makes me mouth water." She looked at Tatyana. "Ha' ye' ever had popcorn?"

"No. Is that what I smell?"

"Uh huh. Ye've got to ha' some." She turned to a friendly looking woman behind the counter. "Is the popcorn still a nickel?"

"Uh huh."

"I would like one bag." She dug into her purse.

"I'll get it," Johnny said.

"No, I've got me own money, and I'll pay. I'm the one who wants it." Taking the popcorn, she smiled and said, "I'll share of course."

"This way," Dimitri said as he steered Tatyana toward a doorway. He pulled the door open and ushered her inside.

It took a moment for Tatyana's eyes to adjust to the dim room. She stood in the back of a large chamber with a domed ceiling arched two stories above and filled with rows and rows of cushioned seats. Two long aisles separated the seating into sections. A stage draped with burgundy curtains filled the front of the theater. On the right, a woman at an upright piano played a lively tune, seemingly unaware of the influx of people.

"I don't like sitting down in front much. Do ye' mind if we sit somewhere's in the middle?"

"I don't," Johnny said, taking hold of Allison's hand and leading her down the walkway. When he stood in what seemed to be the middle of the theater, he asked, "This all right?"

"Just right," Allison said and followed him as he sidestepped between the seats.

"After you," Dimitri said with a small bow.

Tatyana followed Allison and sat beside her friend. Watching the pianist, she asked, "Is she part of movie?"

"No, she just entertains us until it starts," Dimitri explained, leaning back in his seat.

"Oh. Well, good she is."

"Tatyana, you say, 'she is good.'"

Tatyana sighed in frustration. "Sometimes I think I never learn English."

"You're doing very well." Dimitri smiled and patted her hand.

Tatyana nearly jerked her hand away, but she constrained herself and settled back into her chair and stared at the stage. All too aware of Dimitri's nearness, she tucked her elbows in close to her body and clasped her hands in her lap.

The pianist lifted her hands from the keys, pushed the bench back, and left the stage. The lights dimmed, then the room went dark. Tatyana could hear the curtains being pulled back. She stared at the darkened stage in anticipation.

A shaft of light cut through the blackness and dust particles danced in the beam. A strange clicking sound came from the back of the theater, and large numbers flashed on the screen. Tatyana turned to find the source of the queer noise and the light. Both emanated from a small, square window above the balcony. *That must be where the movie is coming from,* she decided.

Loud music filled the theater, and Tatyana turned to find images of soldiers with rifles strapped over their shoulders marching down an unfamiliar city street, then a restless-looking man with a tiny mustache stood before cheering crowds raising arms in salute and yelling "Heil Hitler." As the footage was being shown, a newsman talked about the fear rippling throughout Europe at this man's rise to power.

"Would ye' like some?" Allison whispered, bumping Tatyana's elbow and holding out her bag of popcorn.

"Yes. Thank you." Tatyana took a piece and gingerly put it in her mouth. It tasted salty and buttery. She chewed. It felt like biting down on air but tasted good. "I like it," she said and took another piece. "I thought you say this funny. This is not."

"No, silly. This isn't the movie. It's a newsreel."

"Oh."

Another headline filled the screen. Tatyana couldn't read, but she understood the pictures of men standing in soup lines and of others putting up tin shacks. She didn't want to look at the tired faces lined with despair, but she couldn't take her eyes from them.

After that, a story about a new actress named Katherine Hepburn flickered to life. A confident reporter narrated his predictions of her certain stardom. Tatyana immediately liked the freckled, guileless-looking woman and hoped that one day she would have the chance to see her in a movie.

Next, a Flash Gordon adventure filled the screen. Tatyana sat on the edge of her seat as the champion of justice battled repulsive-looking villains. The close-fitting space suits intrigued her, and she wondered if that was how real space explorers would dress. Just as the heroine was about to lose her life at the enemy's hands, the picture ended.

"Why? Why they stop?" Tatyana asked.

"They will continue it next week," Allison explained.

"Yeah, that way they get us to come back and pay again," Johnny said dryly.

"I not know if I can."

"Do you want to?" Dimitri asked.

She glanced at the big man. She didn't feel good about keeping company with him, but she did want to see the end of the film. "I will think on it," she finally answered.

After a short intermission, the screen came to life with the feature film, *Duck Soup*. Tatyana found the four clownish men only slightly entertaining. She didn't understand most of what they said. The jokes made no sense, and when the man with the heavy eyebrows and a cigar made lewd gestures about his buxomy costar, she thought it in very poor taste.

While her friends hung on every word and roared with laughter, she could feel her cheeks flame in embarrassment. Dimitri glanced her way more than once. Not wanting to offend him, she did her best to look interested.

When the film ended the lights were turned up. Relieved, Tatyana stood. "Over, yes?"

"Yes," Dimitri said and stood up.

"Say, how would you like to go for a soda?" Johnny asked.

Dimitri looked at Tatyana. "Do you want to?"

"What mean? Go for soda?"

"They serve drinks and food at the soda fountain at the drug store." He stepped into the aisle. "Sometimes we stop and get something to eat or drink after a movie."

Tatyana felt tired and would have preferred going straight home, but the others seemed eager to stop, and if this were customary she didn't want to infringe on their plans. "All right," she said. "We go."

As the sun set, the foursome walked the two blocks to the store. A bell jingled as Johnny opened the door. He stood aside and allowed Allison and Tatyana to enter. Dimitri followed.

Tatyana had never before been in such a place. A large, wooden bar with stools standing all along the front of it occupied one end of the store. A mirror graced the wall behind it. A young man behind the bar filled a glass with a drink. He looked up and smiled at the newcomers. "I'll be with you in a minute."

Allison led the way past aisles of sewing supplies, books, magazines, hair clips, and other necessities. She sat at a table beside the picture window. "This looks like a good spot." With her elbows resting on the table, she placed her chin in her hands and looked up at Johnny, smiling sweetly. "This way we kin watch the people as they go by."

"Perfect," Johnny said and sat beside her.

Dimitri pulled out a chair for Tatyana.

"Thank you," she said, wondering what to expect next.

Sitting beside Tatyana, Dimitri asked, "Are you hungry?"

"Maybe a little."

"How about you?" Johnny asked Allison.

"No. I ate all that popcorn. I'll just ha' a soda."

"Would you like something, Tatyana?" Dimitri asked.

The young man from behind the bar stepped up to the table. "So, what'll you have?"

"We'll have one soda and a Coca-Cola," Johnny said.

"Tatyana?" Dimitri prodded.

"I am thirsty, but I never taste these things."

"How about if I buy a malt and you have a Coke and we'll share."

Tatyana shrugged. "Okay."

"So, what did you think of the show?" Johnny asked.

"It was funny," Allison said. "Especially that Harpo. He's cute. The way he goes around honkin' that horn and never sayin' a word."

"I thought I'd die laughing when Mrs. Teasdale said, 'she stayed with her husband until he passed away' and Groucho said 'No wonder he passed away.'" Johnny laughed. "He's the funniest man I've ever seen."

"And what about when the lemonade seller and Harpo ran into each other and their hats fell off, then they switched 'em. I canna' remember seeing anythin' so funny."

The waiter brought their sodas and ice cream. Allison took a long drink. "That's so good."

"What did you think of it?" Dimitri asked Tatyana.

"The movie?"

Dimitri nodded.

Not wanting to offend anyone, she chose her words carefully. "I like first movie very much. The man was brave." She took a sip of her drink and wrinkled up her nose in distaste.

Allison laughed. "You look so funny, Tatyana. It does take a wee bit of gettin' used to."

"I never taste before."

"When you were in Russia, what did you do for fun?" Johnny asked.

"Fun?" Tatyana thought. "Sometimes we sing, and at special times we dance."

Allison emptied her glass. "Didn't you ever go out?"

"Yes. Sometimes. We go to ballet. Beautiful ballet."

"You like that stuff, huh," Johnny said with a smirk.

"Yes. Very much. You see ballet?"

"Can't say that I have, and I don't think I want to."

"I've heard of it, but I've never been." Allison put her elbow on the table and rested her chin on one palm. "I'd like to though."

Dimitri leaned forward. "I've been a few times. My mother loves the ballet."

"What you think?"

Dimitri shrugged. "Oh, I liked it. The music was beautiful and the dancing kind of elegant."

Johnny laughed. "Not you, Dimitri. Please don't tell me you're a ballet nut." He drained his glass. "I could sure go for something a little stronger. It gripes me, no liquor."

Dimitri glared at Johnny.

"Why you not drink liquor?"

"Prohibition," Johnny said scornfully.

"I never hear this word. What prohibition mean?"

Dimitri sipped his milkshake, then explained, "The government decided that drinking alcohol was dangerous and outlawed it." He stirred his malt. "This is good. Would you like some?" He handed the spoon to Tatyana.

She dipped in and took a bite, then smiled. "Very good. I like." She took another taste. "Now, how you mean dangerous? Is it bad drink vodka and kvas?"

"Uh huh."

Tatyana had to smile. Oh, how her uncle Alexander would have hollered over such a law.

Johnny stood up. "Yeah, well, I heard they're thinking of repealing it, so it probably won't be long before we can get a real drink." He wiped his mouth with his napkin. "I'm sorry, but I got to go. I have to work in the morning." He wadded the napkin into a ball and tossed it toward the trash can. When it missed, he didn't bother to pick it up.

"Me, too," Allison said.

"Why you work on Sunday?" Tatyana asked.

"I guess because I donna' go to church, and most the rest of the household does."

"Oh."

"Would you like me to accompany you Sunday?" Dimitri asked Tatyana.

"No. I not need. I know way." Taking one more sip of her drink, Tatyana remembered she didn't like it and set it down. "Why you not go to church most times?"

Dimitri tipped his glass and looked at the bottom. "I've got one more bite. Do you want it?"

Tatyana shook her head no and stood.

Scooping it out, he looked at Tatyana as she waited for his answer. "Oh, uh, church. Well, I used to go, but it never really interested me much." He set his glass on the table and pushed his chair back. "Don't misunderstand. I believe in God. I just don't believe I have to go to church."

"But church is good."

"Maybe for some, but not me."

Tatyana would have liked to tell him all the reasons God wanted believers to go, but she bit her tongue. It probably wouldn't make a difference, and besides, Dimitri's faith or lack of it really didn't concern her. He wasn't her responsibility.

CHAPTER 11

TATYANA PLACED THE LAST cooking pot in the cupboard. With the back of her sleeve, she wiped the sweat from her forehead and turned to study the kitchen. All she had left to do was to clean the sink and wipe down the cupboards. "It is hot."

"Aye, that it is," Allison agreed. "'Tis no wonder we're all a bit done in. And some say tis s'posed to go on."

"I certainly hope not," Mrs. Wikstrom interjected. "I've got too many years on me to endure much more of this."

Taking a deep breath, Tatyana thought of the cold lemonade in the refrigerator, and her mouth watered in anticipation. "Rest and cool drink be good," she said, returning to the sink. She scrubbed the porcelain until it sparkled.

Mrs. Wikstrom tucked a damp strand of hair back into place. "I'll be glad when this day is over. Ahh," she groaned. "I've still got baking to do this evening. The master wants fresh bread for his toast in the morning."

"He's cracked. Ye'd think he'd know better than to make ye' do extra baking in this heat."

All Tatyana could think about was her need for fresh air. "Is door open?" she asked. "I feel no wind."

"Yes, but there doesn't seem to be a breeze this evening. It's still as a morgue out there." The housekeeper mopped her neck. "Tatyana, I'm sorry, but when you're finished here you won't have time to rest on the porch with a cool drink. You've got to pack your things."

Tatyana whirled around. Bewildered and thinking she'd been dismissed, she asked, "Why? I do something wrong?"

"No, no. Nothing like that." Unable to meet Tatyana's gaze, Mrs. Wikstrom glanced at the floor. "It's just that Mr. Meyers is taking a trip to the Chicago Exposition." She looked squarely at Tatyana. "He said you're to accompany him."

Tatyana's stomach dropped. "What you saying?" she asked, hoping she'd misunderstood.

"You're to accompany Mr. Meyers to the Exposition." The older woman turned and rewashed the already clean stove. Her voice strained, she added, "You better get to packing."

A knot anchored itself in Tatyana's stomach. "Why he ask me?"

"Canna' ye' see the way he looks at ye'?"

Tatyana's hand automatically went to her collar, and she fumbled with the button. "What you meaning?"

"Ach, are ye' daft?"

"Allison." Mrs. Wikstrom gave the impulsive girl a sharp look. She crossed to Tatyana and stood directly in front of her. Placing her hands on her shoulders and looking her in the eye, she said, "He does seem taken with you, but I know him to be a gentleman. He needs someone to see after his things. You know, to keep his clothes laundered and pressed and to fetch things. Try not to worry."

The housekeeper didn't sound at all convinced of her own words, and Tatyana's mind whirled with questions. *I don't want to go. Can I refuse? Is anyone coming with us? Why doesn't he ask someone else?* "Do I have to go?" she asked.

"I wouldna' have the courage to say no," Allison burst out. "I'd be afraid of bein' dismissed. And then what would a person do? Ye'd be out on the streets."

"Allison, enough!" Mrs. Wikstrom snapped. She stepped back. "This is a special opportunity, Tatyana. Most of us will never see a World's Fair. You should be grateful."

"Is other person going?"

Mrs. Wikstrom folded her arms beneath her small bosom. "I'm certain it will all be very proper and that someone will be traveling with you. It wouldn't be suitable for you to make the trip alone and, knowing Mr. Meyers as I do, he's always careful to observe proprieties. I'm sure you'll be perfectly safe."

"He'll be needin' someone to carry his luggage and such. If I were ye' I'd ask Dimitri to go along. It canna' hurt. He'll keep an eye out for ye.'"

"Mr. Meyers will decide who goes and who doesn't," Mrs. Wikstrom said, frowning at Allison.

With a disgusted exhalation, Allison returned to polishing a large serving spoon.

"Are you finished here, Tatyana?"

"Yes, ma'am."

"Then you'd best go up and pack. You'll be leaving on the morning train."

Tatyana folded her towel, draped it over the stand, and left the room. She couldn't quiet the fear growing inside and searched her mind for a way out. But it seemed as if there were nothing she could do. Allison was right. If she refused, she could be dismissed. Then what would she do? Her step heavy, she made her way up the staircase to her room. *Maybe Mrs. Wikstrom is right. Maybe there's nothing to worry about.* No matter how hard she tried to convince herself of this, she couldn't forget the way Reynold Meyers looked at her.

❧ ❧ ❧ ❧ ❧

The following morning, with her stomach in her throat, Tatyana ascended the stairway. Clutching her handbag against her abdomen, she stood in the foyer and waited. She glanced at her reflection in the glass panel beside the doorway. She'd purposely worn her plain, dark blue traveling suit and pinned her hair severely beneath a matching felt hat.

The sun hadn't yet brightened the morning gloom. In spite of a restless night, Tatyana didn't feel a bit sleepy. Her insides felt jittery, her stomach queasy. She transferred her weight from one foot to the other while fidgeting with the clasp on her handbag.

Mrs. Wikstrom primly marched into the foyer. "So, do you have everything?"

"Yes, ma'am. I pack with care."

"Now, just do as Mr. Meyers tells you. This will be a wonderful trip."

"I hope so." She paused. "Mrs. Wikstrom, what is Exposition?"

"Why, it's a World's Fair. There will be exhibits from all over the world, new inventions, and wonderful food and games."

"I never see fair before."

Her eyes crinkled as she smiled. "I think you'll like it."

"I hope."

Dimitri came in the front door. "Good morning." He tipped his hat. "Seems we'll both be traveling to Chicago."

"You going?" Tatyana asked, a sudden sense of relief flooding her.

"Yes. I'll be the fetch-and-carry man this trip." Nodding toward Tatyana's suitcase sitting just inside the door, he asked, "This is yours?"

"Yes."

Without another word, he picked it up and carried it outside.

Tatyana followed him through the door and stood on the porch and watched as he added it to the luggage already in the trunk of the traveling car. Heartened, she said to no one in particular, "He is going."

"Yes, God watches over his children," Mrs. Wikstrom said, glancing back toward the entryway. Looking troubled, she reached into the large apron pocket and withdrew a slip of paper. She pressed it into Tatyana's hand. "This is the address of a friend of mine in Chicago. If . . ." she hesitated, cleared her throat, then continued, "If you need anything, she will help."

Tatyana didn't understand what she was implying. "Why I need?"

The housekeeper straightened her shoulders. "Well, you never know when you'll need a helping hand."

"Madison!" bellowed Reynold Meyers. "Madison!" He stepped into the foyer. "Where is that man?"

"I'm sure he's on his way, sir."

Tatyana heard the hasty click of heels and tucked the note into her purse.

"Oh, there you are. Do you have my briefcase?"

"Yes, sir. Right here, sir."

Mr. Meyers took the case and turned, his eyes meeting Tatyana's. "Oh, good morning. We'd better hurry or we'll miss our train," he said curtly, striding through the door, down the porch, and to the car. The chauffeur opened the door for him, and he slid in.

Tatyana followed, uncertain where she should sit. The chauffeur stepped around the automobile and opened the back door. Standing aside, he held it for Tatyana. She took the seat beside her employer and, with an uncertain smile, sat back. She'd ridden in a car only once before, the day she arrived in America. This one was much nicer than the first. She ran her hand over the soft upholstery, enjoying the feel of it. The car had an unusual odor, a pleasant blend of leather and pipe smoke.

The chauffeur climbed behind the wheel and waited while Dimitri closed the trunk and joined him up front. He turned the key, and the engine flared to life, vibrating as it idled.

A jolt of adrenaline surged through Tatyana, and she gripped the armrest.

Dimitri twisted around and looked at Tatyana. "Are you feeling all right?"

"Yes," Tatyana answered, trying to quiet her agitation.

"You look a little pale."

"I am good."

"Michael, I suggest you put your foot on it. The train leaves in less than an hour."

"Yes, sir," the man said and eased out of the drive into the early-morning traffic.

Tatyana swallowed hard, certain everyone could hear her pounding heart. So much was happening all at once. *Lord, I need your help,* she prayed. The city swept by the car window, its noise shut out by glass panes. The quiet, smooth ride through town seemed strange, and Tatyana felt detached from the outside world.

An armrest divided the back seat into two halves. Mr. Meyers rested his right arm on it. Tatyana was thankful for the partition. He lit a pipe and took a long drag. Slowly allowing the smoke to escape his lips, he watched indifferently as it curled into the air.

As inconspicuously as possible, Tatyana studied her employer. His thick, brown hair curled onto his forehead. His eyes, the pale blue of an autumn sky, looked cool and detached. He glanced at Tatyana, offered a weak smile, and opened the daily news. With his broad brow furrowed, he read the paper.

Tatyana turned and stared outside. *Can I trust him?* she wondered as she watched the hurried people crowding the sidewalk.

After a short time, the driver pulled to the side of the road. "We're here, sir." Briskly he vacated the automobile and opened the door for Mr. Meyers.

Folding his paper and tucking it beneath his arm, the handsome businessman stepped out. He glanced at the large clock on the terminal wall. "It's 6:45. We'd better get moving."

Dimitri unloaded the baggage. "This way, sir?" He motioned toward the terminal entrance.

"Yes. Go ahead and take them down."

Tatyana stood on the sidewalk, gazing at three huge windows on one wall.

"Come along, Tatyana," Mr. Meyers said as he entered the station.

"Yes, sir. I am sorry, sir." She followed him inside. A cascade of noise echoed from several flights below. Gingerly she stood beside the landing balustrade and stared down into a cavernous room.

"Impressive, isn't it?" Mr. Meyers said as he stepped onto the broad stairway.

Tatyana didn't answer. She followed, careful to watch her footing and yet sneaking quick glances at the immense room.

A medley of voices reverberated throughout the congested station. Overwhelmed by the immensity of the terminal, Tatyana gaped at towering pillars and statues and took delight in the lofty walls painted with colorful murals. A huge ledger, with a collection of numbers, covered one wall.

"What is that?" Tatyana asked.

"That's the schedule of arrivals and departures," Mr. Meyers said. "Come along, now," he added, a hint of amusement in his voice. "This is not the Sistine Chapel, for heaven's sake."

Tatyana hurried after him.

Mr. Meyers stopped beneath an arched entryway.

"Here, sir," Michael said, holding out three tickets.

Mr. Meyers studied them a moment, tucked them into his coat pocket, and hurried through the entrance. "This is it," he said and stopped at a landing with a waiting train idling its engines. He turned to Dimitri. "You did check my luggage in?"

"Yes, sir. It should already be on board." He tightened his grip on his and Tatyana's bags.

Tatyana stared at the train and could feel her earlier fear return, only now more intensely. Glancing up, she found Dimitri staring at her. Although she'd never wanted to connect with him, she now felt a bond with the big, friendly man. Having him nearby made her feel safer. She offered him a tremulous smile.

"Everything will be fine," he said quietly.

"I . . . I know." She glanced at the floor. "I am glad you here."

"All aboard!"

Mr. Meyers quickly boarded.

Dimitri handed one suitcase to an attendant and offered Tatyana a hand up the steps.

She took it and followed her employer.

Mr. Meyers had already headed down a corridor.

"Where will we find you, sir?" Dimitri asked.

Glancing over his shoulder, he answered, "I have a sleeping compartment. I'll be in room 310." He turned and continued on.

Tatyana and Dimitri entered the next car.

Balancing the two suitcases, Dimitri sidestepped down the narrow walkway. Stopping midway, he said, "How about right here?"

"That is good."

After hefting their bags onto an overhead shelf, he stepped back and allowed Tatyana to sit down, then took the seat facing hers.

The train jolted forward, and Tatyana felt a stir of excitement. Maybe this would be fun. So far Mr. Meyers had behaved properly. She'd probably been worrying about nothing.

As they left the station, she watched people on the platform wave to loved ones. A sudden pang of loneliness settled over her as she remembered her farewell to Yuri. Gradually the train picked up speed and moved through a darkened passageway. Bright light greeted the travelers as they left the terminal behind. The sun had risen and its early morning glow cast a soft golden hue over the city.

The train made its way through the metropolis. The crowded streets and skyscrapers gradually gave way to scattered collections of houses and finally to open countryside where farms freckled the landscape. Tatyana gazed at the passing scenery, trying to soak it in. She had missed the country but only now understood how much.

As they moved on, miles and miles of open land flashed by. Golden fields bordered by trees, green patches of produce, and dark, tilled earth ready for next year's harvest refreshed Tatyana. She thought of home and could see Uncle Alexander handing the hay to Yuri and Lev, who made certain the hay was stacked evenly. Taking a deep breath, she swallowed past the lump in her throat and blinked away tears.

"Do you miss the country?" Dimitri asked.

"Yes, very much."

"I've always lived in the city, so I don't know how you feel."

"This look much like home."

"I suppose you miss it a lot."

Tatyana only nodded, not trusting herself to speak.

A companionable silence fell between the two immigrants. Tatyana watched the changing landscape, gazing at the varied automobiles and farm equipment parked at railroad crossings and the people operating them. She wondered what their lives were like. She hadn't thought much about life outside the city until now. A fresh longing for home and its ordinary existence settled over her.

The passing hours gave Tatyana an opportunity to read her book, *Anna Karenina*. Since Dimitri had given her the gift, she'd had little time to read. But even with its vivid descriptions and intriguing characters, the rhythmic sway of the train finally lulled her to sleep.

"Tatyana, wake up," came a whispered command.

She tried to open her eyes, but sleep summoned her back to its peaceful void.

Someone nudged her shoulder.

"Wake up. Mr. Meyers wants you."

Tatyana forced her eyes open. "What you say?"

"Mr. Meyers wants you," Dimitri said.

Sitting up, she tried to focus. "He want me?"

"Uh huh."

Still feeling the remnants of her nap, she tidied her mussed hair, stood up, retucked her blouse, and smoothed her skirt. Her heart hammered as she made her way back to his compartment. Why did he want her? She glanced at the number Dimitri had written, then looked at the numbers over the doors. When she found a match, she stopped. After rechecking her clothes, she knocked.

"Come in," came a reply from inside.

Hesitantly, Tatyana opened the door but didn't step inside. "Sir, you needed me?"

"Oh, yes, I want you to press my clothing for dinner," he said as he nodded toward a suit thrown across a chair beside the doorway. "It's over there. Ask the steward, and he'll show you what to do."

"Yes, sir." Tatyana glanced around the tiny compartment. It consisted of a small divan, a sink with a mirror, and a bed. A large window looked out on the passing world. She picked up the clothes and turned to leave.

"Oh, Tatyana, would you accompany me to dinner?"

"Me, sir?"

"Is there anyone else here?" He smiled. "Yes, of course you."

She searched her mind for a way out of the invitation. "But, sir . . ."

"Is there a problem?" he asked, the pitch of his voice a notch higher than normal.

There was nothing she could say. "Yes, sir," she finally answered meekly.

"Oh," he said as he stood up and took a box from the shelf and handed it to her. "You'll need something more appropriate to wear. Those things you've got on are dreadful."

Confused, Tatyana stared at the box.

"I hope I got the right size." He looked at her. "It's a dress."

As understanding dawned, Tatyana pushed the package back into Mr. Meyers's hands. "I cannot take."

"You must. It's for you." He refused to accept the box, and in a dismissive tone, said, "I'll see you at seven." He held the door open.

"Seven," Tatyana said, feeling defeated.

An hour and a half later, she found herself seated in the dining car across from Mr. Meyers, wearing the deep green, silk frock he'd purchased. She'd never owned anything so elegant. Although at first she'd chafed at wearing the dress, she couldn't pretend she didn't like wearing the exquisite gown.

White linens, polished silver, and crystal goblets covered the table. Tatyana placed her hands in her lap and fidgeted with the button at her waistline.

"You should have more beautiful things. You are stunning," Mr. Meyers said, his admiration obvious.

"Thank you for dress."

"You're welcome." He leaned back. "Now, what would you like for dinner? The food here is actually very good."

"I not know what to eat."

"Let me order for you." He studied the menu a moment, then gestured for the waiter.

"May I help you?" asked a slender young man dressed in a white uniform.

"We'll have your filet mignon, baby boiled potatoes with baby onions, and asparagus, lightly buttered."

"Yes, sir, right away." The waiter bowed slightly.

"Oh, and bring us a bottle of your best cabernet."

"I'm sorry, sir, but we don't serve alcohol."

"Haven't they repealed that silly law yet?"

The waiter smiled. "Soon. I hear Congress is working on it."

"Well, just bring us water then."

With a smart bow, the young man left.

Tatyana tried to concentrate on the passing countryside, but it was difficult to see. The sun had settled behind a distant hill, and dusk blanketed the land.

"So, how do you like the trip so far?"

"It very nice. Much better than train in Russia."

"So, you traveled by train in Russia?"

"Yes. When I leave home. It very cold and sitting not soft."

"You're lucky to be in America."

"America is good place, but I miss homeland."

"I'm sure you'll adjust."

"My family there. I never stop missing."

Reynold leaned forward and folded his hands on the table. "I know it must be difficult for you, but to be free of such an oppressed country must be a relief."

"What you mean 'oppressed'?"

"Well, trampled on by cruel leaders."

Tatyana could feel her frustration rise. Couldn't people understand there was more to Russia than its politics. "Russia have many good things. It very beautiful country."

Mr. Meyers took a sip of water. "Why are you here?"

"Because brother say I must come. One day I return."

"I'd say your brother's a smart man. It would be foolish to waste beauty like yours in a place like Russia."

Tatyana recoiled inwardly at his brazenness. Before she could respond, the waiter returned with a pitcher of water and refilled their goblets.

At the end of the meal, Reynold raised his glass, "To friendship."

Tatyana sipped her water and returned the glass to the table.

Myers escourted Tatyana back to the car in which she and Dimitri were traveling.

"Thank you for the company," Mr. Meyers said. "I'm looking forward to spending more time together in the coming days."

Tatyana thought she caught a hint of something more in his words but only said, "Thank you for dinner." Then she sat down in her seat.

Reynold turned to Dimitri. "So, did you get something to eat?"

"I did, sir," the gardener answered stiffly.

"Good." Reynold tipped his hat. "I'll say goodnight then."

"Good night, sir," Tatyana and Dimitri replied in unison.

Dimitri said nothing for a long while. He stared into the blackness. "So, did you have a good time?" he finally asked testily.

"Food very good."

He glared down the passageway the way his boss had gone. "That's a beautiful dress. Did he give it to you?"

"Yes," Tatyana answered, embarrassed that she'd accepted such a personal gift.

"Was he a gentleman?" Dimitri's voice grated with hostility.
"Yes."

"Would you tell me if he wasn't?"

Irked at his domineering tone, Tatyana asked, "Why you angry?"

Dimitri glared at the floor with his arms folded over his chest.

"What I do?"

The big Russian didn't look up. "Nothing."

"I thought we are friends."

"Me, too. So, why did you have dinner with him?"

"You think I could say no?"

"Did you have to wear the dress?" He kicked the heel of one boot with the toe of the other.

Tatyana couldn't deny the guilt she felt at accepting the gift and didn't have a good answer. "I never have nice dress like this," she said, smoothing the satin fabric.

Dimitri looked at Tatyana. "Would you have dinner with me if I asked?"

Inwardly Tatyana winced. *So, this is why he's angry. He's jealous.* She didn't want to be close to this man. One day she hoped to return to Russia, and he was too much an American. "Dimitri, we share many meals."

"No. I'm not talking about with other people. I'm talking about a special, sit-down dinner, just the two of us." He grinned nervously. "You know, a night out." Dimitri sat up a little straighter. "Maybe when we get to Chicago?"

Tatyana studied the young Russian. He was handsome and kind, but she couldn't allow herself to care.

"So, do you think we could?"

"We good friends," Tatyana said as she glanced out the window. "Maybe we have dinner."

CHAPTER 12

DIMITRI KNOCKED. "TATYANA, ARE you ready?"

She finished pulling the brush through her hair and hurried to the door. With her hand resting on the knob, she asked, "Dimitri?"

"Yes."

She opened the door a bit and peeked out.

"Good morning," Dimitri said, smiling.

"Good morning."

"Mr. Meyers is ready to leave. He's waiting in the lobby."

"I'll hurry."

"Good. I'll tell him." He nodded and walked down the hall.

Closing the door, Tatyana returned to the mirror. Studying her reflection, she considered what to do with her hair. "Maybe I should wear it more like the American women." She swept the brush through it and loosely fastened a clasp on one side, then did the same on the other, allowing blonde waves to fall over her shoulders. She stepped back and gazed at the new hairstyle. It looked pretty. Pinching her cheeks, she wished she had color for her lips and face, like other women.

She smiled at herself and did a half twirl. Her dress swished away from her. Its princess neckline was flattering, and the soft yellow material intensified the green of her eyes. Or maybe it was just the excitement that made them glisten.

So much had happened. First, the train trip, then Mr. Meyers had treated her and Dimitri to dinner at an elegant restaurant with fine linens and delicate crystal. A small orchestra played while they feasted on roasted lamb with sweet peas and creamed baby potatoes. For dessert they ate cheesecake topped with strawberries. Tatyana couldn't remember ever tasting anything so heavenly. And now, they were off to the Exposition.

Mr. Meyers had remained a perfect gentleman all the way from New York, and Tatyana decided she must have misjudged him. "You always worry too much," she said aloud.

She considered her hair. Maybe it was too provocative. It would never be considered proper in Russia. She undid the clips and, with a quick sweep of her brush, twisted it into a bun and pinned it.

With one leg casually thrown over the other, Mr. Meyers sat in a wingback chair reading a newspaper. When Tatyana entered the lobby, he stood up, folded the paper, and tucked it under his arm. "Good morning." He quickly surveyed Tatyana's attire. "You look charming."

"Thank you." She scanned the room. "Where is Dimitri?"

"He went to get his travel guide. He should be back any minute." He glanced down the hallway. "Ah, here he is." Without waiting for his gardener to join them, Reynold Meyers took Tatyana's arm and guided her out the front door. "So, are you ready for the day of your life?"

Tatyana flinched inwardly when Mr. Meyers touched her. She looked at her arm and wished he would remove his hand, then glanced over her shoulder at Dimitri who glowered after them.

"It should be exciting," he continued.

"Yes, very exciting," she said, remembering with anticipation the adventure awaiting her and forgetting, for the moment, that she walked arm in arm with her employer.

The doorman flagged a taxi, and the three tourists climbed into the car, Reynold Meyers and Tatyana in the back, Dimitri up front.

Dimitri looked at Tatyana. "I've heard the Exposition is beyond belief. Everyone is talking about it. Do you know what you want to see first?" He pulled a pamphlet from his pocket and held it up. "I have a visitor's guide. It tells all about the fair." He opened the brochure and scanned it. "It says here that there are exhibits from all over the world."

"That's right," Mr. Meyers cut in. "I think one of the most intriguing is the Industrial Hall. All the latest technologies are on display."

"That sounds fine," Dimitri said, "but, I thought it would be fun to visit the Ford display. The company actually has an assembly line set up. You can watch a car go from sheet metal to a working automobile." He looked at Tatyana. "What do you think?"

Both men waited for an answer.

Tatyana didn't understand all they were saying but knew not to pit the two against each other. They had been in a restrained sparring match since the first day on the train. "I think both are good," she answered tactfully. "We see both?"

After a short drive, the taxi stopped at the park's terminal. Long lines of people crowded the sidewalk. Tatyana gazed up at bullet-shaped cars dangling overhead and moving toward the fairgrounds. Passengers peered down at the visitors. "What is that?"

"The 'Sky Ride.' It takes people to and from the fair," Dimitri explained, clearly pleased with himself at knowing the answer. "According to the brochure, it's two hundred feet above the ground."

"We must ride in this?" Apprehension swept over Tatyana. "It is safe?"

Mr. Meyers rested his hand on Tatyana's back. "Yes, absolutely safe. Otherwise they wouldn't allow people to ride in it. There's no need to worry."

Tatyana stepped away. She watched the cars swing as they ascended and found little comfort in her employer's assurances.

When it was their turn to board, Tatyana cautiously stepped inside the car and sat down. Gripping the handrail, she offered a friendly looking woman a half-hearted smile.

As they left the platform, the car swung free and pitched forward. Tatyana's stomach lurched. She tightened her hold on the rail, careful to keep her eyes on her feet. A gust of wind caught at her hair, and the gondola swayed.

Dimitri leaned close to Tatyana. "Are you all right?"

She looked up and, careful to keep her eyes on his face, answered, "Yes, I am fine."

He smiled and looked out at the world. "Good. You looked a little pale." He laughed. "It's wonderful! Everything looks so different from here. But, Tatyana, you can't see much staring at the floor. You're missing it all."

"I . . . I feel better if I look at floor."

"Please, just take a peek."

Slowly she tipped her head up and sought the horizon. At first her stomach quailed, but as she became accustomed to the view it quieted. She pointed at a massive body of water that met the skyline. "What is that?"

"Lake Michigan," Reynold Meyers said. "It's one of the Great Lakes."

Tatyana loosened her grip. "It is beautiful." Feeling braver, she looked below. A huge park bordered by the lake on one side sprawled across a huge expanse of land. Buildings with spires and steep-pitched rooftops dotted the grounds. As they passed over a pavilion with tall towers reaching toward the sky, she asked, "Is that Ripley's Believe It or Not?"

Both men gave her a curious look.

"How do you know about that?" Dimitri asked.

"I hear maid at hotel talk about. She say it is very interesting. Say there is two-headed snake and mummy."

"Well, maybe we ought to stop at the 'Odditorium' first," Reynold said jovially.

Tatyana studied the man. She'd rarely seen this light-hearted side of him. Maybe he wasn't as stuffy as she'd thought. He caught her gaze and smiled. Tatyana quickly looked away and, pointing at another building, asked, "Is that it?"

Dimitri took off his hat and combed his hair with his fingers as he peered down at the structure. "I don't know. You can't tell what's what from up here." He placed his hat back on his head.

A few minutes later they docked, and passengers crowded onto the landing. Possessively, Mr. Meyers took Tatyana's arm and steered her toward the walkway. Crowds streamed past, intent on adventure. Unusual sounds and smells bombarded the visitors, and brightly colored displays lined the concourse where vendors hocked their wares. Some sold tiny lapel pins, others miniature flags, balloons, inexpensive jewelry, or tantalizing foods.

Tatyana's heart beat a little harder, and she hurried her steps, impatient to see it all. She did her best to soak it all in, thinking how she would tell Allison and Mrs. Wikstrom about the sights.

A display of large, national flags fluttered in the breeze. Tatyana searched for the one from her homeland but didn't find it. Squelching her disappointment, she moved through the throng.

An exhibition hall with pictures of midgets depicted in different costumes caught her eye. She couldn't read the poster and asked, "What it say?"

"Midget Village," Mr. Meyers said.

"What this is?"

"Midgets portray different roles in plays. It sounds boring to me." He moved on.

When the threesome came to a huge building titled "Ford," Dimitri said, "This is what I've been wanting to see." Without waiting for his companions, he went in.

"Well, we might as well join him," Mr. Meyers said, guiding Tatyana into the nine-hundred-foot-long assembly plant.

Captivated, she watched the incredible process of transforming metal, glass, and fabric into a working automobile. After they'd been through the assembly line, they took in the exhibit demonstrating methods of highway construction. It was nearly as fascinating.

Carefully guarding his place beside Tatyana as they left the building, Reynold Meyers said, "Sometimes it seems there is nothing man and technology cannot do."

Trailing behind, Dimitri added, "You're absolutely right. There's no telling where we'll be in ten or twenty years." His comment went unnoticed.

After that they visited Ripley's Believe It or Not. Amazed, Tatyana gaped at a two-headed snake, shrunken heads, photos of a two-headed calf and a man with two pupils in each eye, as well as a myriad of other marvels. They also explored the "Hall of the World a Million Years Ago." Mechanical dinosaurs stomped and roared, and Dimitri laughed at Tatyana's apprehension over the animated beasts.

By early afternoon, Tatyana was exhausted. "Can we sit?" she asked.

"By all means," Mr. Meyers said. "Why don't we get something to eat?" He hesitated, then looked at Dimitri. "Perhaps there is something else you would like to do?"

As Dimitri grasped Mr. Meyers's meaning, anger flickered across his face. "Yes, sir. I'll see you at the hotel."

"Well, I didn't mean—"

"No, sir. I'm tired anyway." With a nod at Tatyana, he walked away.

Tatyana didn't have a chance to say a thing. Clutching a dinosaur replica in one hand and a miniature American flag in the other, she felt abandoned as she watched his receding back disappear into the crowd. She glanced at her escort. How could he be so ill-mannered? He'd been charming, and she'd nearly forgotten who he was.

"Well, what would you like to eat?" he asked. "We've seen a lot of fascinating choices. Was there anything in particular that interested you?"

All Tatyana could think about was the hurt she'd seen in Dimitri's eyes. She glanced at Mr. Meyers and wanted to tell him how rude he was.

"How about Chinese?" he suggested. "I've had it before, and it's very tasty. I think you'll like it."

Tatyana held her utensils and studied them, wondering how they worked. They were sticks. How could a person eat with sticks? Glancing at a nearby table, she watched as a man deftly held the implements between his fingers, then picked up a chunk of meat and pushed it into his mouth.

"These are called chopsticks," Mr. Meyers explained as he tasted his rice. "It's not difficult once you get the technique."

She held her chopsticks awkwardly in one hand. She poked at the peculiar-looking pile of noodles and tried to entrap them between the utensils. Each time she lifted them toward her mouth, they slipped off. She tried again and again. With each failure, she could feel her face flush with embarrassment. Was she the only one unable to master the skill?

With a sympathetic smile, Mr. Meyers finally reached across the table, unrolled a fork from inside a napkin, and held it out. "Try this."

Gratefully Tatyana set her chopsticks aside and took the fork. "Thank you." She speared her noodles and pushed them into her mouth. She hadn't realized how hungry she was. As she chewed, sweet and tangy flavors merged. She decided she liked the new food and took another bite.

"So, how are they?"

"Good."

She sampled unfamiliar vegetables, rice, sliced pork, and prawns. She liked it all, except the prawns, which tasted too peculiar.

The crowded restaurant provided an abundance of distractions, and Tatyana felt more at ease. She studied the other patrons. Many were dressed in the latest fashions, while some wore obvious hand-me-downs. She wondered what kind of sacrifices the poor had made in order to be here.

A variety of languages resonated throughout the room. A dark-skinned man, wearing what looked like a scarf around his head, happily conversed with a female companion who was dressed in a colorful, flowing silk gown. A woman and two children wearing berets and plaid kilts with matching knee-high stockings ate at a nearby table. Wide-eyed, the children seemed more interested in the people than in their food.

"So, are you having a good time?" Mr. Meyers asked.

"Yes, sir. This is very nice."

"Tatyana, call me Reynold. There's no need for proprieties here."

"Yes, sir, I mean, Reynold." It felt improper calling him by his first name. She preferred the more formal title.

"Is there anything you would like to see this afternoon?"

Tatyana thought a moment. "There is music?"

"Yes, in fact, there's an orchestra playing this evening in the open air theater." He gazed intently at Tatyana.

Wishing he wouldn't look at her that way, she reached for her water.

Reynold caught her hand in his.

A shock surged through Tatyana. She looked at her hand as if it were detached. Reynold's palm felt smooth and uncalloused. *How strange,* she thought.

"Tatyana, you must know how I feel about you."

"Sir?" She wanted her hand back.

"When Dimitri asked if a friend of his could come to work as a maid, I had no idea my decision would bring you into my life. I remember the first day you came into my office. You looked so proud, standing tall and doing your best to hide your fear." He caressed the top of her fingers. "But it's your eyes that really captured me. They're like emeralds." He tightened his hold. "I've been smitten ever since."

Tatyana felt trapped. What could she say?

"Do you know how beautiful you are?"

Unable to find her voice, she simply shook her head no.

"You're exquisite. Sometimes I think I can feel you in my soul." He reached up and touched a strand of hair that had come loose.

Tatyana leaned away from his caress.

"Have you ever thought of letting it down?"

Remembering how she'd almost worn it loose, Tatyana was thankful she'd changed her mind. She swallowed hard. Her mouth tasted like cardboard, and her throat felt like she'd swallowed dirt. "I . . . I am thirsty," she finally said, wrenching her hand free. Picking up her water, she took a sip and looked out the window, wishing she could escape into the crowd.

Nothing was said for a few moments. "You're very quiet."

Tatyana cleared her throat and took another drink. Setting her glass on the table, she folded her hands in her lap. "I . . . cannot feel for you this way. I am a servant."

"That's not a problem. I'm very progressive. When people care about each other, class shouldn't matter."

He believes I feel the same as he? Oh, Lord, what do I do? "Sir, it matters. I cannot work for someone . . ."

"If that's the only problem, you can live in the house, but you don't have to work."

Tatyana sat up very straight and opened her eyes wide. "Sir? You want me to be fancy woman? I can never do!"

With a laugh, he said, "No. No. It wouldn't be like that at all."

Tatyana stood up. "I am sorry, sir, but I go to hotel." Throwing her shoulders back and holding her spine very straight, she walked to the door.

Reynold caught up to her and grabbed her arm. "Tatyana, wait. Let's talk about this."

"There no talk." She looked at his hand on her arm. "Please, let go."

A man dressed in a white apron yelled, "Your bill. Sir, your bill!"

Reynold glanced at the man, then at Tatyana. "Wait." Irritably he strode back to the man, took out several paper bills, and threw them on the table, then hurried after Tatyana, who had already stepped outside.

Mutely they walked to the Skyride. As they traveled above the park, silence hung between them. It grew as they motored to the hotel and clung to them as they took the elevator to Tatyana's floor. Reynold stepped out of the lift.

"You not come," Tatyana said and walked down the hall. Needing to be alone, she fought her tears. She hadn't wanted anything like this to happen. *This is what I was afraid of. I forgot my place. I should have kept my distance.*

151

"Tatyana, wait. Can we talk?"

"What talk about? You employer, I am a servant. We not—" She searched for the right word, "keep company."

Reynold grabbed her wrist and turned her to face him. Her flag fell to the floor. Pinning her arms against her sides, he said, "You don't understand. I need you." He moved closer. "You work for me. I can make you do as I say."

Tatyana felt the wall against her back, and panic pressed down on her. *Help me, Father, help me!* she prayed. Anger welled up, overpowering her fear. She jerked her arms free. "You cannot!"

"You won't like it on the streets," he said through gritted teeth, his facade of decency gone.

"What's going on?" Dimitri asked, disbelief on his face. He stepped into the hallway. "Tatyana? Mr. Meyers?"

Immediately Reynold Meyers stepped away from Tatyana.

"What's going on?"

"Nothing. Nothing at all," Mr. Meyers said as he smoothed his jacket.

Dimitri eyed Tatyana. "Is that true?"

Tatyana glanced at her employer, then looked at Dimitri and shook her head no.

He dropped all pretense and said, "A kiss. All I wanted was a little kiss."

Dimitri's face reddened, and he balled his hands into fists. Glaring at the man, he stepped up to him and, with his chest only inches away, shouted, "How dare you treat her this way!"

Tatyana had never seen Dimitri so angry. She was scared for him. "Please. I am fine," she said, but Dimitri didn't hear.

"You will apologize to her," he demanded.

"Apologize? To a servant?"

Dimitri clamped one hand on Mr. Meyers's shoulder.

He glowered back but kept his mouth firmly shut.

Tightening his grip, Dimitri repeated, "Apologize."

Unable to keep from wincing, Mr. Meyers glanced at Tatyana, then back at Dimitri. "There's no need for violence."

Dimitri's hand squeezed.

"Okay. I'm sorry. I didn't mean to mistreat you."

Slowly Dimitri relaxed his hold.

Reynold Meyers stepped back. He glared at his attacker and pulled at his jacket sleeves. He looked at Tatyana, then at Dimitri. "You're fired, both of you." Without another word, he stormed down the corridor.

Tatyana slumped against the wall, and the tears she'd fought brimmed. In Russian she said, "I should never have come to America. I want to go home."

"I'm sorry, Tatyana. I shouldn't have left you," Dimitri replied, speaking in Russian as well. "I meant to take better care of you. This is my fault." He moved as if to put his arm around her, but he didn't.

"No, you are not to blame." She looked up at her friend, and unexpected admiration welled up. "I'm grateful for you. Thank you. You stood up for me. It was a very brave thing you did."

Dimitri took a slow, deep breath. "I really fixed everything. Now we're both unemployed."

Tatyana felt drained. "What will we do?"

He shrugged.

Remembering the address the housekeeper had given her, she said, "Mrs. Wikstrom knew. She gave me the address of friends here in Chicago. She said if I needed help I should contact them."

"She knew?" He thought a moment. "Well, if they're friends of Mrs. Wikstrom, I know they'll help. We'll go to them."

"And then?"

"We will return to New York. You can stay with my family."

"Dimitri, your family is very kind but you don't have enough for an extra person."

"There's always enough for you." He gazed down at the Russian girl. Placing his hand on his chest, he said, "I think you know my heart, Tatyana. But please understand this, I will never *take* anything from you."

An unfamiliar flutter touched Tatyana's stomach as she met his tender look. He had never asked her for friendship; he'd only offered it. And she had not even been willing to give him that. Gently she covered his hand with hers. "You are a true comrade. Thank you."

CHAPTER *13*

Yuri gritted his teeth as the jackhammer bit into rock. Pain shot up his arms, into his shoulders, and down his back. A familiar ache settled in the right shoulder, a reminder of his near execution. If not for the help of Mrs. Shabashova, he might have become a cripple. The weathered face of the kindly peasant warmed him. She'd taken in the refugees and nursed Yuri's wound, in spite of the danger to herself.

He straightened. The long days were taking their toll, but he couldn't let up. He closed his eyes and willed his body to obey. If he didn't meet the daily quota, his ration cards would be reduced, or even eliminated, and his stomach already felt hollow.

Sweat dripped into his eyes, but under the overseer's brutal gaze, he dared not stop to wipe it away. Always seeking compensation from the political leadership, supervisors readily turned in anyone who might be considered an "enemy" of the state. Those shirking their responsibilities were quickly singled out.

The frozen ground beneath Yuri's feet seemed to move as he struggled to keep his footing. He could barely feel his gloveless hands in the cold.

Pushing a wooden cart, Elena stopped at the pile of rock and dirt building up alongside the wall. She glanced at Yuri but didn't speak; no one dared to speak beneath the foreman's watchful eyes. Even during breaks, the workers spoke only in hushed tones. Everyone was suspect and lived in fear of arrest.

Elena shoveled rock into her cart.

Yuri wished she didn't have to work so hard. He knew how her body ached, but she rarely complained. After watching her steadfastness for weeks, his admiration for this unexpected comrade had grown, although there was still so much he didn't know about her. She guarded her past and had made it clear there could be nothing between them beyond friendship. Something haunted her. In time, he hoped she would tell him what it was.

After filling the wagon, Elena gave Yuri a fleeting smile as she wheeled the wagon to the lift where she loaded the debris into a basket that hauled it to the surface. Her feet shifting on the slime of the cavern floor, she returned for more rock.

Elena glanced furtively down the tunnel. The supervisor had disappeared into the darkness. She nudged Yuri.

He stopped his drill. "Do you want us reprimanded?"

Elena smiled as she bent, cupped her hand close to his ear, and whispered, "He's out of sight. I think I know what it feels like to be a mole."

Yuri almost laughed. "Me, too." He studied his friend. The dimness left much of her face in shadow. Electric bulbs dangling from the ceiling provided little illumination, and the life in her eyes was hidden by the gloom.

He looked down the long tunnel and watched as a worker made her way up the rickety ladder to the street. Shaking his head, he thought: *So, this will be Russia's great accomplishment, showing the industrialized world we are as good as they are. How many must die so Stalin can feel like a big man?*

The supervisor stepped into the light and headed down the tunnel toward Yuri and Elena. They both quickly returned to work.

After escaping the soldiers, Yuri and Elena had made their way to Moscow. The days passed in a blur of hunger and fear as they hid in the shadows, seeking a way to live without disclosing their fugitive status. If not for the kindness of Mrs. Shabashova, Yuri didn't know what would have happened to them. No one could be completely trusted due to government-fed hostilities and suspicions.

Moscow held the promise of work. The exiles hoped to disappear within its enormous population, but the tight government controls made disappearance difficult to achieve, even in the largest city. Only after putting their trust in a man who worked for the underground, did they secure false identification papers and permission to rent a room in a Moscow apartment building.

In recent weeks the NKVD had made night visits to their building. Many of the residents had disappeared. Yuri knew he and Elena were at great risk and feared arrest and exposure of their false papers. His stomach quaked as he thought of what awaited them if they were ever found out.

Tightening his grip on the jackhammer, Yuri's body vibrated as the machinery bit into rock. What lay ahead of him? What could life offer a fugitive in a totalitarian country? *Maybe I should just stop putting off the inevitable and turn myself in,* he thought. *I have no future.*

His mind turned to Tatyana. *Thank God she's in America. At least she's safe.* A lump formed in his throat. He'd never see her again. His mind filled with memories of long talks they'd had and evenings of shared stories or classical music.

"Go faster! Faster!" barked the director. "Stalin rewards hard work. If you do not make your quota, you will bring shame to us all."

As the man passed, Yuri glared after him. He drove the workers too hard, implementing tougher and tougher quotas. Although orders came down from the higher authorities, Yuri thought this coward did their bidding with too much delight.

The government was like a hungry beast devouring its young, never satiated and always looking for more victims. Keeping his drill pounding against the wall, he peered at the other workers. They reminded Yuri of cattle being driven to slaughter, oblivious of what lay ahead. He shuddered at the mental image. *We must do something. What? What can we do?*

A whistle blasted, and gratefully Yuri turned off his machine and leaned it against the wall. His arms felt heavy as he straightened. Pressing his hands against the small of his back, he arched, then stretched to the side. Holding his arms over his head, he bent straight over at the waist and touched his toes. Slowly he straightened. "I feel like an old man," he said.

Elena stuck her shovel into the pile of rock, removed her hat, and tousled her flattened hair. Sneaking a glance at the supervisor standing several yards away, she half whispered, "We all feel old. But what is our alternative? If we don't work, we don't get ration cards, and without food we die."

Yuri nodded and hunkered down against the rock wall. He pulled a paper sack from his coat pocket. Opening it, he removed a piece of dark bread and a small hunk of cheese. He tore the bread in half and handed Elena her portion, then did the same with the cheese. He stared at his share disdainfully. "This isn't enough to feed a rat." He took a small bite of cheese. "I guess I should be grateful. There are many who have nothing."

"Thankful for crumbs?" Elena said derisively. "Never. To think I must spend twelve hours a day working in a hole then try to fill my empty belly with a gram of cheese and some stale bread!" She nibbled on the cheese.

Yuri reached for the water bottle sitting next to the wall, uncapped the lid, and gulped down the liquid. "We could be buried with the others back in the forest."

Elena kept on chewing and said nothing.

Yuri swallowed a bite of bread and leaned forward, resting his arms on his knees. "Elena, we have to make a decision."

"About what?"

"The soldiers have been to the apartments three times in the past week. We're going to have to move."

Elena stared at Yuri for a long moment. "Where? Where can we go? You know there are no apartments available. We might wait for years."

"We found the one we're in, didn't we? Just like before, we can find someone willing to take in boarders."

"If we move we'll have to get permission, and we'll have to show our identification papers." She brushed a dark strand of hair off her forehead. "It is too great a risk."

"I agree it's dangerous, but if they come to the apartment and force us to show our papers, it will be worse."

"Worse, how?"

"We're not married," he whispered. "You know it's against the law for us to live in the same house without a marriage license. If they come to the apartment, they'll ask for one."

The supervisor approached.

Yuri swilled down the last of his water.

The man scrutinized the pair as he strolled by, hands clasped behind his back. He nodded slightly and moved down the tunnel.

"Why does he care?" Elena said as she nodded toward the guard. "He's like the rest of us. We're all like mice trapped in a cage with the cat ready to pounce."

Yuri stood up and brushed the dirt from his wool pants. "He's hoping he'll be rewarded for his commitment to the party. He imagines his name on the list of faithful Stalinists." Yuri eyed the man. "But he's being naive. Stalin has no favorites; he loves no one."

"But this man is treading on the backs of his own countrymen."

"He's afraid, Elena, just as we are."

"How can he be so stupid? Stalin has even his closest associates executed. How can anyone believe in him?"

"Fear does strange things."

Elena leaned against the wall. "That's no excuse for stupidity." She shoved the last of her bread into her mouth, chewed, and swallowed. "Oh, for a piece of fruit or a slice of pork." She closed her eyes. "Sometimes I lie in bed at night and imagine I am at a feast." She looked up at Yuri and forced a smile. "I think I've forgotten what meat tastes like."

A man approached.

"He's new, isn't he?" Elena whispered.

The stranger transferred his lunch sack to his left hand and held out his right. "Hello. I'm Daniel Belov."

Yuri shook his hand. "I am Yuri."

Elena eyed the dark-haired stranger warily and, with her arms at her sides, merely nodded.

Daniel smiled at her, then turned to Yuri. "It is good to meet you. I haven't been working down here for many weeks. He looked at the ceiling, then down the tunnel. "They say the Moscow Metro will be an unrivaled accomplishment."

"They say that, yes."

"Do you mind if I sit?" Daniel asked. "I'm weary."

"Please," Yuri said and held out his arm as if offering him a chair.

Daniel turned, folded his legs beneath him, and leaned against the wall. "That feels better." He took two apples out of his bag. "My sweet Tanya. What a special woman. She's packed me an extra apple." He held up the badly bruised fruit. "Would you like one?"

Elena stared.

"Please, take it."

She looked at Daniel, her eyes asking if he was sure. When he motioned again for her to take it, she snatched the gift like gold coins from a banker's hands. At first she only gazed at it, then caressed the skin. Her eyes closed, she pressed it to her nose and breathed deeply. She took a bite, then another, and another. Only when her mouth was full, did she stop and chew, juice dribbling down her chin.

Yuri chuckled. "I'm glad you're enjoying it."

Wiping her mouth, she mumbled, "Thank you. It is wonderful. It reminds me of summer visits to my grandfather's farm." Her eyes glistened with tears. "We picked apples and ate and ate." She held the fruit out to Yuri. "Please, have some."

Yuri accepted the offering and quickly bit into it. Sweet juice filled his mouth as he chewed. He closed his eyes and savored the flavor, wishing there were some way to make it last. He licked the juice trailing down the side of the apple. Looking at Daniel, he said, "Thank you. Where did you get this?"

"My wife got them. She went to a farm and gleaned the last of the crop."

Yuri took another bite, handed the fruit back to Elena, and sat beside the newcomer. "So, how long have you worked on the transit?"

"Only a couple of weeks. How about you?"

"We've been here two months."

"It's tough work. All of Russia watches and waits while the metro is built. They glorify the workers who produce record quotas, but no one understands what it is like to climb down into this pit every day. Each morning I stand at the top of the ladder and gaze down into the darkness, afraid."

Yuri knew few who would speak so honestly with good friends, let alone strangers. He didn't know quite what to think of this man, but his honesty felt refreshing.

Daniel gazed up at the dark ceiling. "This is a dream for the Russian people, but for the workers it's a nightmare we face each day." He sat up a little straighter and glanced at the supervisor who was involved in his own meal. He looked at Yuri a moment, then at Elena. His voice quiet, he said, "If not for my faith, I don't think I could make myself climb down the ladder each morning."

"Your faith?" Elena asked, standing and leaning against a pile of rubble.

"I mean, my trust in God." Daniel stood up. "It is only because of his strength that I can endure." He glanced down at the others along the tunnel. "I don't know any other way. How do people make it without the Lord?"

"Lower your voice. Someone might hear you," Elena said as she straightened.

"Either I trust in God completely or not at all. Either he's in control or he isn't." He threw back his shoulders a little. "I will not betray God by pretending I don't know him." He looked at Yuri. "Do you believe?"

The young Russian was ataken back by the question. How should he answer? Of course he believed, but could he trust this man? His eyes looked honest, his face sincere. Meeting the stranger's eyes, he said, "Yes, I do."

Daniel smiled. "I thought you were a countryman when I first saw you." He patted him on the shoulder. "It's always good to meet fellow believers."

"What do you two think you're doing?" Elena whispered. "Enough of this. You'll get us all arrested."

"God takes care of his own," Daniel said confidently.

With her arms folded over her chest, Elena glared at him. "You believe that?"

He nodded.

Her voice venomous, she asked, "What kind of God allows families to be torn apart and then arrested? What kind of God allows the executions of innocent people? And what kind of God leaves a person in the streets to starve? And, and . . ." she looked around the chamber. "I work in this cave all day, sleep on a floor at night, I'm always hungry, and my country is disintegrating." She stopped and turned away for a moment, then whirled around and faced him. "This is what you call the work of a good God?"

Daniel met her gaze. "No, I don't." He didn't flinch but continued to meet her piercing stare. "This is the work of the enemy."

Elena and Yuri said nothing, waiting for Daniel to explain.

"The Bible says, 'Our adversary, the Devil, walks about like a roaring lion, seeking whom he may devour.' We need to be vigilant, to resist him; only then will we be able to live triumphant lives."

"You believe that?"

Daniel measured Elena carefully. "The lie is not believing. And Satan uses our unbelief to keep us powerless. It is one of his principal tools. If we don't believe, we will not fight. God says we must stand against the enemy if we are to win the battle."

"How do you fight an enemy you cannot see and you're not even certain exists?" she asked.

"Do you not see him in those who persecute innocent people?"

"Evil has always been here. It isn't something new," Elena said, grasping the shovel handle.

"Yes," Yuri said. "It has, but only since Satan came to rule on earth." Hope stirred in him. He looked at Daniel. "How do we fight him?"

"We use the weapons God gives us."

"I remember my Aunt Irina talking about God's armor."

"Yes. Anything else is useless."

"What are you doing?" the supervisor demanded.

The three whirled around and faced him.

He stood only a few yards from them, his feet slightly parted, his hands clasped behind his back, and a scowl on his face. "What is it you are speaking of?"

Yuri searched for an acceptable answer. "Just how we can destroy our enemies by working for the party and working harder." He shot a desperate glance at Daniel, willing him to keep his faith to himself.

The supervisor studied him suspiciously. "I hope that's all it is," he finally said and moved on.

Daniel carefully folded his lunch sack and tucked it into his pocket. "You two are married?"

Yuri grinned. "No, just comrades."

"Have you known each other long?"

"Many, many years," Elena lied.

Yuri gave her a questioning look but said nothing.

"Where are your families?" Daniel asked.

Yuri answered first. "Mine were taken by the soldiers three years ago; I have only an aunt and a cousin left. My sister lives in America."

"My family is dead." Elena's eyes turned hard, her mouth set in a grim line.

Yuri could feel Elena's bitterness like something physical. He knew her parents had been dead a long while and had seen this festering anger before, but he couldn't understand the depth of it and wondered what horrible thing had happened to her.

"Back to work," Daniel said, pushing himself to his feet. He dusted his pants, then chuckled. "Why do I bother?" He looked at Yuri. "Would you like to join my family for dinner?"

"Are you sure? Do you have enough?"

"Always. Our home is open to visitors."

Yuri wondered if Daniel could be trusted. He studied the man. He sensed nothing dishonest about him. "I would like that. What do you think, Elena?"

Elena scrutinized the stranger. Warily she said, "I suppose it would be all right."

"Good. I'll look forward to seeing you tonight about seven o'clock? We live on Babel Street just outside the city. Our apartment is just across the river and on the right. We are on the first floor, second door from the left."

※ ※ ※ ※ ※

"We should not have come," Elena said, pulling her coat more closely about her. "We know nothing about this man. It could be a trick. What if he works for the NKVD?" She shivered. "It is so cold. Too early for winter."

Yuri looked skyward. Stars were already blinking in the blue-black of early evening. "It will not be the first time winter has visited in September."

Elena stopped and folded her arms across her chest. "I don't feel good about this." She stared at Yuri. "I'm not going."

Yuri looked at the diminutive woman. In the fading light she looked beautiful, her brown eyes defiant. She could be formidable, but now he saw fear in her. He wanted to comfort her, to replace trepidation with peace. He smiled. "Why are you so reluctant? It's just dinner."

She nearly grinned but didn't move.

"I don't believe he works for the Secret Police. But until we know, we'll be very careful." He blew on his gloveless hands and tucked them into his pockets. "I want to go. There's something about Daniel, and I feel it's important we know him."

Elena still didn't move.

"Please, Elena."

She let her arms drop. "All right, but I join you under protest. I will leave if I decide it is best."

"Of course."

They turned onto Babel Street. "This must be it," he said as they approached a shabby apartment building. Lights glowed from inside.

They followed the walkway to a small wooden porch. The boards creaked beneath their feet.

Elena fidgeted with her gloves, and Yuri raised his hand to knock.

CHAPTER *14*

A PLAIN WOMAN WITH PALE
blue eyes and brown hair opened the door. She peered out.
"Hello? You must be Yuri?" She glanced over his shoulder. "And
Elena?"

"Yes," Yuri said.

The woman smiled and opened the door wide. "Please,
come in. I'm Tanya Belov."

Yuri stepped aside and allowed Elena to enter first. The
aroma of fresh bread and boiled meat welcomed the visitors.
Yuri's mouth watered, and his gnawing hunger grew more
intense.

"Daniel is out but will be back soon. Please, sit." She
motioned toward a threadbare settee, partially hidden beneath a
colorful afghan. Turning to the stove, she lifted the lid of the pot.
Steam rose into the air, and the wonderful odor of cooked meat

filled the small apartment. She stirred the contents, then settled the cover back in place.

Elena and Yuri both sat stiff-backed with their hands folded on their laps. Yuri could feel springs pressing against his backside. He looked around the tidy room. It was much cheerier than he'd expected. A vivid blue afghan draped the back of a cushioned chair. A russet throw rug lay in front of the firebox, which radiated warmth throughout the room. Two wooden shelves on either side of the hearth were adorned with knickknacks and photographs. What caught Yuri's eye most, though, were the beautiful paintings on the walls. He stood and crossed to one illustrating a field of wildflowers in full bloom. "Where did you get this? It's wonderful." He touched the canvas. "They look real. I can smell the fragrance."

"I'm glad you like it," Tanya said, a soft blush rising in her cheeks. She joined Yuri and gazed at the scene. "It was one of those perfect days, the perfume of flowers in the air and the sun beating down, hot."

"You painted this?"

"Yes. Art is one of my joys."

"You're very gifted."

Elena joined Yuri and studied the picture. Her voice laced with suspicion, she asked, "Where do you get the paints?"

"It is very difficult, but each time my jars are empty, more is provided."

"Provided, how?"

"When I need paint, it's just . . ." she sought an explanation, and finally said simply, "here. I find some that's been cast aside, or someone offers it as a gift, or there is money to buy more." She grinned. "Although, when the paint is available, it sometimes means waiting in a line extra hours that week. I don't mind." She paused and studied Elena. Quietly, she added, "God provides."

The door opened, and Daniel breezed in. A little girl with curly blonde hair sat on his shoulders, and a dark-haired youngster held his hand. "Ah, you are here. I'm glad you made it." He smiled and, taking two long strides, gripped Yuri's hand in a friendly handshake.

The older child ran to her mother and held out a sprig of flowers. "Mama, we found these for you."

With a look of devotion, Tanya bent and accepted the gift. "Thank you. You are always my sweet *dochka*." She held the blossoms to her nose. "They smell wonderful, like summer."

The little girl grinned.

Daniel swung his daughter to the floor, then hung his coat and hat on a hook just inside the door. He hugged Tanya and kissed her cheek. "Something smells good."

"It's stew."

Turning to Yuri and Elena, Daniel said, "I'm sorry to be late, but there was a small crisis, and I was needed."

Yuri wondered what kind of emergency Daniel could have been involved in but said nothing. "I was admiring your wife's art work. She's very talented."

Winking at Tanya, Daniel said, "Her paintings make our lives richer." The younger child clung shyly to her mother's skirts and stared at the strangers.

Tanya tenderly placed her hand on her daughter's shoulder. "Girls, we have guests for dinner. I would like you to meet Yuri Letinov and Elena Oleinik."

Yuri and Elena smiled at the children. "We are so happy to be here," Yuri said.

"Sasha is our oldest," Tanya said and, gently squeezing the younger one's shoulder, added, "and this is Valya."

Sasha grinned and stepped up to Yuri. "It is good to meet you. I am seven," she said, proudly holding up seven fingers. "I am going to the school this year. I passed my examinations, and one day I will go to the university."

"That is a good plan." Yuri liked the spunky youngster. He glanced at Elena, thinking she must have been much like Sasha as a child.

Daniel eyed the pot on the stove. "Will dinner be long?"

"We've just been waiting for you," Tanya said. "Please, everyone, sit."

Crowding the small house, a battered wooden table with four chairs stood between the tiny front room and the kitchen area. Tanya set the stew pot in the center and a wooden platter with bread beside it. Returning to the stove, she took the kettle and set it beside the other food.

Daniel's wooden chair scraped the floor as he pulled it away from the table and sat down. He motioned for Yuri and Elena to join him. "Please, we will break bread together." After everyone was seated, Valya on her mother's lap and Sasha on Daniel's, he said, "We will pray." He bowed his head, and the others did the same. "Merciful Father, we come to you with grateful hearts. We thank you for being a God of love, one who watches over us as well as walks beside us. We pray our lives will bring honor to you. Help us to be strong. Help us to be faithful." He paused, "I thank you for bringing new friends to us. May you bless them. And," his voice turned gentle, "we thank you for this remarkable food and ask that you would bless the hands that made it. We pray these things in your Son's name. Amen."

Daniel's prayer reminded Yuri of how home used to be. A lump formed in his throat. God had always been the core of his family and, after his parents had been arrested, Uncle Alexander and Aunt Irina had embraced their niece and nephew with the same faith. Until now he hadn't realized he'd been starving for more than food. He yearned for the fellowship of other believers. He looked at Elena. She was a true comrade, but seemingly nothing he could say would dispel her ambivalence toward God. They'd never been able to share the spiritual parts of themselves.

Shame welled up in him as he recalled his infrequent communion with God these past months; he had seemed so distant. Yuri knew it was his fault; he'd not taken the time for prayer and meditation. Sitting at this table with a fellow believer felt good. He looked at his host and said solemnly, "Thank you."

Tanya lifted the lid off the tureen and stirred the contents. Setting the lid aside, she took Elena's bowl and scooped out a large portion of stew. She did the same for Yuri while Daniel sawed through a loaf of bread.

Yuri stared in disbelief. How could they have so much? Had he misplaced his trust? He glanced at Daniel, who handed him a slice of bread. He fingered it and stared at his meaty stew. Such a feast for a humble family seemed strange. Eyeing Daniel, he wondered, *Is he really who he seems?* He spooned a bite of stew into his mouth and chewed. The flavors of meat, carrot, and rutabaga tantalized his taste buds. "Am I dreaming?" he asked with a smile.

"No," Tanya laughed. "The meat was a gift. It's reindeer. And the vegetables were gleaned from a nearby farm. I had a few left. We also have tea," she said, lifting the kettle and filling the cups.

Daniel smelled his stew. "God has been good to us. His Word tells us, 'For everyone who asks receives. And what man is there among you who if his son asks for bread will give him a stone, or if he asks for a fish will he give him a serpent? If you, then, being evil know how to give good gifts to your children, how much more will your Father who is in heaven give good things to those who ask him.'" He leaned forward on his elbows and looked intently at Yuri. "Are you a man of faith?"

Taken off guard by the question, Yuri didn't know how to answer. He wanted to speak the truth, but how could he tell this man, who seemed to live a life of exceptional faith, that he'd barely spent a moment with God in recent months? He felt a poke in the ribs. Elena mutely willed him to silence. He met Daniel's gaze. "I believe in God."

"Even the demons believe," Daniel said and didn't take his eyes from Yuri.

The young Russian's discomfort grew. "I guess I would have to say, I *used* to be a man of faith."

Keeping her eyes on the table, Elena tapped her spoon against the side of her bowl.

Yuri had never easily escaped the truth. He'd always been compelled to speak honestly. This time was no different, even if it painted him in a poor light or jeopardized his freedom. He wrapped his hands around his mug of tea. "What I mean is, I would like to be a man of faith. All my life I've followed Christ, but recently he seems far away."

"God never removes himself from us; we are the ones who stray. Can you think of what has caused the gap?"

Yuri looked at Elena, who was clearly agitated. "I must tell him."

She shook her head no.

"I must."

Elena stared into her cup.

Tanya reached out and patted her arm. "Do not be afraid," she said softly.

Yuri gathered his thoughts, then looked squarely at the man across from him. *Can I trust him?* The moment his mind asked the question, a powerful sense of assurance enveloped him. He took a deep breath. "Daniel, I believe you are a righteous man, and so I will tell you what has brought us to this place." He gave Elena one last look, hoping for her approval, but she wouldn't meet his eyes. "Three years ago soldiers came to my home and arrested my parents. My sister and I never saw them again."

"Many have disappeared," Daniel said sadly.

Yuri swallowed and continued. "Tatyana and I lived with our aunt and uncle after that. We always hoped Mama and Papa would return, but they never did. A few months ago, soldiers came again and arrested my uncle and me."

"What was their reason?"

Elena sat up very straight in her chair, seemingly ready to flee.

"My family was labeled Kulaks because we owned our own farm. When my cousin married, we had a celebration. Many of our neighbors kindly left their gifts of food, and the following morning, when the soldiers came, they found the food and assumed we'd been stockpiling." Yuri took a sip of tea. "My uncle and I were arrested. But they didn't take us to prison. Instead they drove us and the other prisoners into the forest." As he spoke, the scene replayed in his mind. Adrenaline surged through his body, and he tried to swallow away the fear. His eyes brimmed with tears. "They shot everyone, my uncle included. I lived and escaped." He glanced around the table. "Now I am here."

Smoothing the hair of her oldest daughter, Tanya said, "God has spared you for a reason, Yuri."

Yuri said nothing.

She placed her arms around both of her children and drew them close. Her voice soft and gentle, she said, "Even when death touches those we love, we can trust God. We are only pilgrims on this earth. Our true home is in heaven. We are forever the Lord's, forever in his presence, whether in this body or our heavenly bodies. Your loved ones are with him. He has not deserted them."

"I believe that, but still my heart is heavy."

"Walking in faith is different than just believing in God. And sometimes it hurts."

"Your sister? Where is she?" Daniel asked.

"She's living in America with an uncle. I sent her there. She was angry with me, but it is best."

Daniel reached out and patted Yuri's back. "I thank you for trusting me. We will talk more."

Dipping her bread into her stew, Sasha said, "I love God. He is good to us."

The little girl's sincere adoration touched Yuri, and he remembered God's admonishment to all believers to have faith as little children. He wished he possessed such faith. *How does a person acquire it?* he wondered. He'd seen it in his uncle the day the man died. The picture of Alexander's confidence still haunted him. He glanced around the table. Peace pervaded the room and the people. Hope was alive here.

Daniel let his spoon slip into his bowl and leaned forward. Staring at Yuri, he said, "As Tanya has said, I also believe God has a plan for you—and Elena." He waited as his words sunk in. "We would like to help."

"I wish I was so sure," Yuri said.

✹ ✹ ✹ ✹ ✹

Weeks passed, and the friendship between the Belovs and Yuri and Elena grew. In the beginning Elena visited rarely, but gradually her need for the kind woman's companionship grew, and she could often be found in the tiny apartment.

One afternoon Sasha charged through the door. "Mamochka, guess what?"

"Sasha, you're being rude," Tanya gently reproached. She set the socks she'd been darning in her lap. "Do you not see we have a guest?"

The little girl looked at Elena. Clasping her hands behind her back, she said, "Oh, I'm sorry." She waited for permission to speak.

"What is it, little one?" Tanya finally asked.

"A circus is coming to Moscow! It is wonderful! I saw a poster! There are clowns and tigers and acrobats! Can we go?"

"It sounds exciting, but did the advertisement say how much it would cost?"

"I don't know. I didn't see anything." The little girl's voice held an edge of disappointment.

"We will see. If it is something God wants, he will provide a way."

Sasha offered only a small smile as she walked outside.

"I haven't been to a circus since I was a child," Elena said wistfully. "It seems so long ago."

"I love the music and silly clowns." Tanya looked at the door Sasha had just stepped through. "It would be a special treat for the children. They would love it." She returned to her mending. "I remember when sewing meant embroidering delicate designs in fine linen rather than darning old socks." She glanced up at Elena. "There are some things I will always miss."

"Me, too." Elena said as she offered a half smile.

"Did you live in Moscow when you were a child?"

Elena set her sewing aside and stood up. Walking to the shelf containing Tanya's scant collection of teacups and saucers, she lifted a delicate hand-painted cup. "This is so beautiful but fragile. It would take little to destroy it."

"You don't have to tell me."

Elena turned and faced her friend. "Yes, I lived here in the city." She wished she could turn off the pictures that played through her mind. It was another time and place. And the child she had been no longer existed. She'd had a wonderful childhood, one filled with the pleasures afforded only to the affluent. Her family members had been devoted to their children. They'd shared beloved literature, played games, and sung together. The notes of a concerto she'd played at the last family gathering flitted through her thoughts. If only she could return to that time. Without warning, screams replaced the music. She dropped the cup, clamping her hands over her ears.

Hiding in the darkened alcove beneath the stairway, she'd watched as her mother, clutching baby Anna and begging for mercy, was dragged through the front foyer and out the door by soldiers. She could hear her screams. Elena squeezed her eyes shut, trying to close out the images. Her father, so stoic, had followed. They pushed him through the door, and he tripped and fell. His hands chained behind him, he stumbled to his feet in the cold night. And she, Elena, frozen by fear, had remained hidden. The intruders had come and gone, while she did nothing. She'd done nothing!

"Elena. Elena, are you all right?"

Tanya's words cut into the nightmare, and Elena looked at her. The horror was still so close. Gradually she recaptured the present reality. Returning her hands to her side, she said, "I'm sorry. I was just . . . thinking." Her voice sounded foreign to her.

"You look terrified." She wrapped her arm around Elena's shoulders.

She pushed the memories into a corner of her mind, wishing she could keep them trapped there, but she knew there was no escape. They never ceased tormenting her.

Tanya knelt and picked up the cup Elena had dropped. It was intact. Holding the dainty cup to the light, she said, "Some things are stronger than we think."

* * * * *

Daniel managed to acquire tickets for the circus. Another gift, he explained. He had enough tickets to include Yuri and Elena. They stepped off the bus and walked toward the circus grounds. Sasha skipped ahead, a smile plastered on her face.

Once inside the huge tent, the Belovs sat with their girls between them. Elena settled beside Tanya, and Yuri sat next to Elena. Three-year-old Valya squirmed on her mother's lap, craning to see the crowds of people. When the lights were lowered, she cuddled against Tanya's chest.

A spotlight traveled through the huge tent, illuminating even the corners. It finally stopped at center stage. The ringmaster stepped into the spotlight, and the music swelled while drums rolled. Then all fell quiet as the ringmaster raised his hands. His voice booming, he announced the first act. Sitting on the edge of her seat, Elena momentarily forgot life's circumstances.

Three clowns rolled into the ring, two of them riding the same bicycle. As they tousled with each other, Elena laughed. Following the clowns, her favorite act, the ponies, pranced into the ring. Flamboyantly dressed Cossacks balanced on their backs. They swung from one side of the horse to the other, did handstands, and skipped rope while the animals galloped around and around. Finally they cantered out of the circle and disappeared through the doorway.

When a man entered a cage with fierce-looking tigers, Yuri said, "Sometimes I feel like him." He chuckled.

Elena watched the man. He seemed fearless. She wondered if he really was, or only pretending.

The evening passed in a blur of bright colors and music. They saw trapeze artists, a dancing bear, trained elephants, and well-trained dogs dressed in silly costumes. Daniel even managed to buy the children a candied apple, which they shared.

It was over too soon. After the lights had been turned up and the people began to file out, Elena remained sitting and staring at the stage. She felt Yuri's hand on her arm and looked up at him.

"I'm glad we came. It's nice to see you laugh."

"I wish we could come again. It feels good to close out the world for a little while."

A thin layer of frost covered the ground and an occasional frozen puddle crunched beneath Yuri's step. Daniel walked beside him, Sasha sitting on his shoulders, her body draped across his head in slumber. Tanya and Elena strolled ahead, taking turns carrying a sleeping Valya.

Yuri studied Sasha's precarious position. "It seems the evening was too much for the little ones. Would you like me to carry her now?"

"No. She's fine. So, what are your plans? Will you be moving?"

"We must. The soldiers come more and more often. If we stay, we will be found out. I just don't know where we can go. There are no apartments available."

"Tanya and I have talked. We agree it would be good if you and Elena stay with us."

"That is very kind of you, but I don't want to put you in danger."

Daniel laughed. "I haven't told you everything about myself. We don't exactly live a sedentary life."

A sick feeling settled in Yuri's stomach.

Daniel grinned. "Don't worry. I'm not the Secret Police, and I'm doing no evil." He shifted his daughter a little. "Bibles are confiscated, churches raided. There are many who have no Bibles or any spiritual teachings. They are left with only their memories to rely on and are starving for God's Word." He paused and lowered his voice. "I'm part of an underground organization that supplies Bibles and Christian pamphlets to those who need them."

Yuri stopped and stared at his friend. "You're making a joke?"

Daniel turned a somber look on the young Russian. "No, I am not."

"But, they will kill you," Yuri whispered.

"I know the danger, but I cannot live in fear. I must do as God asks. Even if the law forbids my sharing the gospel, I'm compelled to do it." He continued walking. "God is with us always. But *if* he allows imprisonment, or even torture or death, I'm in good company. For centuries God's people have died for

Christ. I, like them, must trust my life to God." He cleared his throat. "There is more."

"More?" Yuri braced himself, unable to imagine what Daniel could be doing.

"We also provide false identification and work papers for those who need them. Many wish to leave the country, and we help them."

Yuri couldn't believe what he was hearing.

"You probably went to someone in our organization when you returned to Moscow. You have falsified documents, don't you?"

Yuri hadn't told anyone about his papers. He took a deep breath. "Yes. I never thought much about the people who provided them." He pulled his hat down a little. "I guess I should have." He looked at Daniel. "It's difficult to believe you are so deeply involved in the underground."

"Not so difficult. I could see no other course." Daniel laid his hand on Yuri's shoulder. "Brother, maybe it is time you asked God what it is he wants for your life."

CHAPTER 15

ELENA, IT'S GOOD TO SEE YOU Please, come in." Tanya smiled and opened the door wide. "I'll make us a cup of tea."

Elena didn't know why she'd come. Something about the Belovs drew her. Their home felt like a refuge, and she wanted that, needed it. Peace dwelled here. She stepped inside.

"It will only take a few minutes," Tanya said, shoving kindling and a piece of old newspaper into the stove.

"Tea would be nice." Elena started to remove her coat, but the outside chill had moved inside so she left it on. A new painting hung on the wall. Something about it felt familiar.

"What do you think?" Tanya asked. "I just finished it a couple of days ago. The paint is barely dry."

Elena didn't hear. All she knew was the painting. Drawn as if by a magnet, she walked on stiff legs across the room until she stood right in front of the image. Her mouth had gone dry, and her heart pounded erratically. The home she'd known since childhood stared back at her. Shaded by a large spruce, the house looked serene. Its steep-pitched roof sheltered the large front porch, and the carved birch trim around the windows still gleamed white. The deserted street in front looked much like it always had, except for additional uncleared brush. She'd learned to ride her bike there.

Tanya's voice came from close behind Elena. "It's a beautiful home. When I saw it, I had to paint it."

Elena struggled to find her voice. "You have done well." She continued to stare, unwilling to release the memories. She could smell the scent of spruce and hear the wind as it swirled through the tree boughs and whipped beneath the eaves. The rat-a-tat-tat of woodpeckers echoed from the tree, and the sounds of gleeful children danced through her mind. She tenderly touched the picture.

"You can have it if you like," Tanya said, reaching out to remove it.

Her words penetrated Elena's reverie. "No. Please leave it."

"It's my gift." Tanya said as she looked more closely at Elena. "Are you all right?"

The reality of all she'd lost enveloped Elena. It twisted in her chest like a knife. Her throat closed, and she struggled to hold back her tears. "It belongs here," she managed to say.

Tanya gently placed her hand on her friend's shoulder. "Please, may I help?"

The loving touch broke through Elena's barrier, and she could no longer fight off her grief. Tears brimmed and trickled down her cheeks. She buried her face against her friend's shoulder and wept.

Tanya said nothing, only wrapped her arms around the diminutive woman and pulled her close, tenderly stroking her hair.

Elena sobbed as years of rage and anguish freed themselves. Even when her crying quieted, she remained in Tanya's embrace, unwilling to relinquish the sense of protection. Finally, wiping at her eyes, she stepped back. "I'm sorry. I didn't mean—"

"Hush. There is no shame in sorrow. Crying is good for the soul." She studied Elena a moment. "I only wish I could help."

Elena took a handkerchief from her dress pocket and wiped her nose. "There is nothing to be done."

"Maybe if you tell me we can find a way."

"I . . . I don't know how to tell you." She looked at the kind woman, then at the picture. "You have painted my home," she said, her voice a whisper.

Tanya looked at the image and touched the frame. "I didn't know. I'm sorry I hurt you." She ran her hand over it, then stepped back. "It's a lovely home."

All Elena could do was nod and choke back fresh tears.

"Would you like me to take it down?"

Ignoring the question, she studied the picture and took a shaky breath. "It was lovely, once . . . until the soldiers came." Her voice hard, she continued, "I can never forgive them. They took everything from me." The familiar hatred and accompanying guilt twisted in her gut. *I should have done something.* She said nothing about her own offense. How could she admit to anyone what she'd done?

"God will help you, if you allow him. He loves you and will enable you to forgive."

Elena felt like she'd been slapped. She looked at the woman who had become her unexpected confidant. "God? He never cared about me."

Before Tanya could respond, Daniel tramped through the door. "We're needed at Klin. Joseph asked if we could come up and help with a typhus outbreak." He pulled off his hat. "He says many are ill and there's no one to nurse the sick."

"I'll pack," Tanya said, already in motion. "I'm sure the Rykovahs will take care of the girls."

"Yuri said he'd help."

"What about work?" Elena asked. "What about our jobs?" Her voice sounded panicked and shrill.

"I don't know." Daniel shrugged. "I can't turn my back on these people, but I can't speak for Yuri. You'll have to ask him. He's packing and will be here soon."

★ ★ ★ ★ ★

Yuri transferred the heavy bag to his other shoulder. "What am I doing?" he asked himself, knowing that to leave with Daniel would be sacrificing his job and probably Elena's, too. His mind returned to the confrontation he'd had with his supervisor. "Why couldn't he give me leave?"

Elena's face flashed in his mind. *She'll be furious,* he thought, wishing there were a way to avoid a confrontation with her. He knew he couldn't escape. He'd have to face her. And how could he make her understand his reckless decision? He didn't understand it himself. All he knew was that when Daniel asked, he felt compelled to help. With a quick glance at his apartment, he thought, *I'll never see this place again.* He closed the door and, with his bag balanced on one shoulder, he hurried down the hallway.

Arriving at the Belov's, he dropped the pack at the door. Taking a deep breath, he gathered his thoughts and his courage and knocked.

Daniel opened the door. Swinging it wide, he said, "It's good to have you here, Brother. Come in. Come in." He bent and lifted Daniel's bundle. "What do you have in here? It feels heavy as bricks."

Yuri looked at Elena, then back at Daniel. "Everything we own."

Elena pursed her lips and glared at Yuri. With her arms folded over her chest, she asked, "Everything *we* own? What have you done?"

"I . . . I'm sorry, but you weren't around to ask, and I had to make a decision. I didn't think you'd want me to leave your things." He gave her a pleading look. "Elena, I know it's hard for you to understand, but I believe God wants more from me than to toil in the earth like a mole enslaved by the government."

"What about me? I've not heard from this God of yours. When the NKVD comes for you, they'll find me. And what about our jobs and our apartment? You throw them away as if they mean nothing!"

"I'm sorry. I really am. I know none of this makes sense, but . . ."

"You aren't sorry! You did what you wanted. You didn't think of me! What about the consequences? Who will pay for your actions? Me?"

He took a tentative step closer. "I did think about you, Elena. I did. Please try to understand. I'm compelled to do this. To refuse would have been disobedience to God."

"That's foolishness. You've done a very stupid thing." She stopped and thought. "It's not too late to fix. Did anyone see you leave the apartment?"

Yuri shook his head no.

"We can move back and be at work in the morning."

Yuri gazed at the floor, then looked at Elena. His voice quiet, he said, "I can't. I have to go. You do what you have to. I'm not forcing you to come."

Her face etched with panic, Elena looked from Daniel to Tanya, then back to Yuri. "Where can I go? When you don't go to work, the police will investigate. They will find me! You will be gone, and I will pay the price for your stupidity!"

Yuri didn't speak.

Elena stomped to the door and grabbed the handle, but instead of opening it, she stood there.

"Elena, please, come with us. You will see. God will take care of us."

With her hand still on the knob, she stared at the dilapidated wood. "How can you say that? I haven't seen his hand in anything. He's deserted us."

"That's not true. Have you forgotten how he saved us from execution? And provided a home and work when there was none?" Yuri crossed to the door and placed his hand on Elena's. "If you look for his guardianship you will find it. It is those who refuse to look who never see." He gently loosened her hand and turned her to face him. "This is the right thing to do. I know it."

Keeping her eyes averted, Elena took a slow deep breath. "I really have no choice." She looked at him. "I will go."

Yuri grinned. "Thank you! You'll be glad of it! You'll see!" He wrapped his arms around the tiny woman and lifted her off the floor, hugging her tightly.

"It will be good to have you with us," Daniel said.

Elena placed her hands against Yuri's shoulders. "Put me down." Her voice sounded cold. She looked at Daniel. "I am still not certain I agree with you."

The foursome traveled three days by wagon across the rutted, half-frozen roads that led from Moscow to Klin. Elena fretted about how they would make it through the checkpoints and where they would find shelter and food, but she needn't have. They were well cared for. Friends welcomed the travelers into their homes and shared what little they had, and miraculously their false papers satisfied the authorities.

When they finally approached a small cluster of homes outside the town, Elena was relieved to have the journey behind her. The constant jarring of the wagon had set every muscle to aching, and she was glad to be done with the dreaded checkpoints. However, placing herself in the midst of a typhus outbreak sent shivers of fear through her.

Daniel slowed the horses. "I'll see if I can find someone who can tell us where we're needed." He handed the reins to Yuri and climbed down. "Wait here." He smiled at his wife, then walked toward the village, his boots sinking in the snow-covered mud.

A short time later he returned, and, as he approached the wagon, he said, "We're expected and greatly needed." He climbed back into the seat. "It's bad," he said, taking the reins. "We're going to need God's help." His voice sounded heavy as he turned the horses toward the cottages.

"Tanya, you and Elena can start here. Yuri and I will begin at the other end of the street, and we will work toward the center." He cupped his wife's face in one large hand and kissed her tenderly on the lips. "God be with you."

Elena's stomach knotted. Why had she allowed Yuri to talk her into this? She didn't want to be here. She knew nothing about nursing, and what if she got sick?

With a soft knock on the door, Tanya stepped into the closest cottage. Elena followed. The smell of vomit, sweat, and human waste washed over her. Trying not to gag, she fought the urge to run. She pulled the door closed and stepped inside the dark home. They waited a moment, allowing their eyes to adjust.

The house was small, only one room. The window shutters were closed, and the only light emanated from a single bulb hanging from the ceiling.

"Elena, please go out and open the shutters. We need air and light."

Elena gladly obeyed and stepped back outside. She pulled the window covers open, latched them, and, wishing she could remain outdoors, took a deep breath and returned to the dank house.

"That's better," Tanya said, bending over a woman with a tiny infant at her breast. She placed her hand on the mother's forehead, then the child's. A little girl with fiery red skin looked at Elena from beneath a tattered quilt. "Water. Please, water." The child closed her eyes.

Compassion welled up in Elena, and she forgot her own fears. Crossing the room, she sat on the edge of the bed and gently brushed matted hair off the girl's face, shocked at the heat emanating from her skin. She couldn't be more than seven or eight, but her eyes were sunken and empty. She looked old.

"I'm thirsty," the child croaked. "Water, please."

"I'll get you some," Elena said, her eyes searching the room for something, any kind of liquid.

"There's nothing here," Tanya said. "You'll have to get it from the outdoor pump."

Elena spotted a bucket on the counter. Taking long strides, she crossed the room and picked it up. It was empty. "I'll be right back." She hurried out to fill it.

When Elena returned, Tanya sat at the side of an old man. Glancing up, she said, "We need that really badly. These people are very dehydrated."

Tanya and Elena did their best to make the family comfortable, helping them sip small amounts of water and sponging their hot bodies.

"Bless you, bless you," the woman said as Elena pressed a teaspoon of water to her lips.

She didn't know what to say. The woman was emaciated and the fretful infant suckled at her empty breast. She doubted they'd live.

Tanya gazed around the room. "This needs cleaning. And some broth would be good." Taking an empty pot off the stove, she said, "I'll get more water and heat it."

The door thudded closed. Alone with the sick, Elena's fear crept back. The old man's breathing sounded raspy and shallow;

the infant whimpered, and his mother did her best to comfort him.

Elena moved to the little girl. Sitting on the side of her bed, she stroked her hot forehead. The child seemed unaware of her. Elena scanned the house. The room was bare. In the center stood a wooden table and one chair. There was nothing else, except the beds. Three small windows were framed by threadbare curtains, their once bright patterns now only faded images. A piece of molded bread tipped off the edge of a plate on the counter. She saw no other food and wondered what Tanya would use to make the broth.

The door swung open, and Tanya backed in, carrying a full pot of water. She poured some into a large wooden bowl. "This will be for drinking," she said. The rest is for cleaning and cooking. She looked at Elena. "Try to get them to drink a little more while I start a fire."

The sounds of crackling wood gave the home a sense of warmth, although heat hadn't actually reached into the house. Tanya searched for something she could use in the soup. All she found were shriveled potato peelings and a small wedge of cabbage. "These will have to do." She dropped the bits of potato into the water, then sliced the cabbage and added it.

Elena held cups of water to parched lips and sponged hot faces and necks. It seemed so little for such a devastating disease. They needed more. "Is there anything else we can do?" she asked, feeling desperate.

"They need a doctor," Tanya said, ladling thin broth into a mug. She handed it to Elena. "Try to get the child to take some." Carrying another mug of soup, she moved to the mother and infant.

Elena did as she was told, but clearly, it wasn't enough. Only a miracle could save these people. She wondered if God would grant one. The child sipped the broth, then fell back into a fitful sleep.

CHAPTER *15*

After doing their best to wash away the filth, the two women moved on to the next home, and the next, and the next.

In the days that followed, the pattern of care continued. With little sleep, the caretakers did all they could. Still, too many died. But it was the hope of life that kept them laboring. Elena had never known such weariness. Her days and nights became a haze of sweaty brows, frightened faces, and the smell of death. Sometimes she was uncertain if she was awake or asleep. It seemed that overheated bodies, cries of pain, and fear were everywhere, even in her dreams. The endless suffering tormented her, and she wanted to quit, to walk away, but she couldn't allow herself to stop. Somehow she found the strength to continue.

None of those who had come to help, including two from a nearby village, had fallen ill. This amazed Elena, and she wondered what could be protecting them. Each time Yuri's words about God's guardianship came to mind, she would push them aside, unwilling to accept his beliefs.

Finally several days passed without any new cases. People began to recover, and the burden lightened. Elena felt hopeful.

Her day nearly done, the sun low in the sky, she decided to check on the girl she'd tended first. Natalia hadn't been able to free herself from the disease, and Elena had taken to spending part of each day with her. When she approached the cottage, the mother staggered into the yard, carrying her daughter's lifeless body. She bathed the child in her tears. When she saw Elena, she lifted her a little as if offering her to the one who had come to help. Elena stepped back, unable to offer comfort. Everything she'd experienced in the past weeks crashed down on her. This was too much. Tears filled her eyes and brimmed over as she turned and ran. *How could this happen? It is so unjust.* She bumped into Yuri; if he hadn't caught her, she would have fallen.

He held her at arm's length. "Elena? What is it?"

"She fought so hard," she sobbed. "She wanted to live." She wiped at her tears.

"Who?"

"Natalia." She looked at Yuri. "Why? Why didn't God help her? Where is he now?"

A gust of wind swirled rain droplets through the air, splattering them against Elena's face. The cool shower mixed with her tears. "I don't believe there is a God," she said, her voice hard. Taking quick, short steps, she walked away.

"Elena, Elena," Yuri called, running after her and matching her steps.

She didn't look at him.

"A storm is coming. You'll end up sick if you persist." Another gust of wind drove a blast of heavy rain. He grabbed her arm, forcing her to stop. "Please."

The clouds opened and dumped their moisture. Rain soaked Elena's hair and washed into her eyes. She stared at Yuri. "I don't understand," she said, her voice empty.

Gently Yuri placed one arm about her shoulders, and holding her against him, guided her back toward the house where they had been staying. Elena shivered. "We better get you dried off," Yuri said.

She nodded and wiped at her nose.

* * * * *

Natalia was the last to die. The others gradually recovered. One afternoon Elena and Tanya nursed an elderly couple, two of the few still needing help. Fall sunshine warmed the cottage as Elena bent over the old woman and held a cup of broth to her lips.

The woman swallowed and smiled. Laying her hand on Elena's arm, she said, "May God bless you. I don't know what would have happened if you hadn't come to us." Her eyes filled with tears. "God is good."

Elena didn't know how to respond. How could this woman believe God was good? She managed a small smile and pulled the blanket up under her patient's chin. "You need to rest now. I'll be back to check on you later."

The woman settled back and, with a look of contentment, closed her eyes.

Tanya stood in the kitchen. She washed the last dish and set it on the counter, then dumped the water out of the basin.

Elena watched her. She felt weary and wondered if she would ever regain her energy. These weeks had been cruel and taken her strength. Why did Tanya give so much of herself to people she didn't know? "Tanya," she finally asked, "Why do you do this?"

Her friend stopped her work and looked at Elena. "What?"

"This." Elena lifted her arms up away from her sides.

"You mean help the sick?"

"Yes. I wouldn't have done it. Never. And I don't ever want to do it again. All I can think about is returning to Moscow. These past weeks I've watched you and never heard you complain or saw you frightened."

Wiping her hands on a towel, Tanya turned and faced Elena. "I'm no saint," she said as she smiled. "But thank you." She folded the towel and placed it on the counter. "I'm no different from you. Sometimes I'm frightened, and sometimes I want to be doing anything except nursing a sick child. But I am always reminded of what my Lord did for me, and I can't complain."

"What do you mean?"

"He chose to suffer for us. He didn't have to, but because he loved us, he allowed himself to be beaten, nailed to a cross, and then he died. But even more than that, he took on the sin of the entire world so we could be free of it. I cannot imagine his torment." Her eyes filled with tears. "And he did it because he loves us."

"It makes no sense to me."

Tanya put her arm around Elena's waist. "Come, we will sit in the sun and talk. Soon winter will be here to stay, and there will be no warm afternoons."

The two sat on an overturned tree and gazed out at empty fields. A bird flitted to earth, searching for seeds. It darted from one patch of ground to another.

"Where do the birds go in winter?" Elena asked.

"I don't know exactly where, but south." Tanya stretched her arms above her head and yawned. "I wish I could go along. To always live in the summer warmth would be wonderful." The bird hopped onto a branch of the tree, leaped into the air, and flew away. Placing her hand on Elena's, Tanya said, "I want to speak to you about something."

Elena waited, fairly certain she didn't want to hear what her friend had to say.

"I heard what Mrs. Kravchenko said to you in there. Did you?"

"I heard her. But I don't understand how she can say God is good when she's suffered so much."

"I cannot know everything in Mrs. Kravchenko's mind, but I know this—suffering helps us grow strong. We are taught to believe that all hardship is evil, but God lets nothing go to waste in our lives, even the difficult and hurtful things. This is what he uses to help us grow and mature. Something you must remember is that death is not the end for believers; it is only the beginning."

"I don't understand how you can accept such things so easily."

"I try to see with God's eyes. He knows what awaits us after death, and he doesn't fear it. It is his reality. We are often afraid of what we don't know."

"I still don't understand why he allows evil. People die from disease, they are murdered by their own government, and many starve because of government interference."

"Do you know the story of Adam and Eve?"

"Yes. When I was a child I attended church with my parents."

"God offered humankind paradise, but we chose to submit to the serpent and sought knowledge instead. It was our own frailty that brought about the world we live in. It's not what God wanted. We live with the consequences of sin."

"But, why doesn't he intervene?"

"He made it very clear what the consequences would be. Does he dare lie? He is God."

"But evil people go unharmed. Why?"

Tanya smiled. "This life is short. In light of eternity, it is only the blink of an eye. If one prospers here on earth, it matters little, for true reality is life everlasting. Stalin and people like him will pay a hideous price for their tyranny. There is nothing worse than eternal punishment." She peered at the bare limbs of the tree. "I feel sorry for him. He will not be able to hide from God."

Elena squirmed. She'd often wondered if God knew her heart.

Tanya looked squarely at Elena. "The most wondrous thing is that God would forgive even Stalin if he believed. He never forsakes us and he never stops loving us."

Elena studied the ring on her finger and rotated it a half turn. It was her mother's. She'd taken it from the nightstand and worn it since *that* night. It sounded wonderful, a God of love who would never forsake you, but she knew it was only a fairy tale. She looked at Tanya. "I wish I could believe you."

CHAPTER 16

THE FRONT WHEEL OF THE wagon dropped into a hole and jolted Elena out of her drowsiness. Gazing at the surrounding fields, she took a deep breath of cold air and pulled her coat tighter. Winter had made its first true assault on the Moscow countryside. Snow blanketed the barren land and clung to scrawny tree limbs. "How much further?"

Yuri turned and looked back at Elena. "Hopefully no more than two hours." He glanced at Daniel. "What do you think, comrade?"

"It shouldn't be too long if the road doesn't get any worse." He flicked the reins. "Seems the government hasn't been able to spare workers to fix the roads. They've been too busy building factories and bridges."

"And tunnels," Elena added, folding her legs and tucking them close to her chest. Resting her chin on her knees, she thought about what might lay ahead for her and Yuri. Her stomach quaked. They had abandoned their jobs and home. *How foolish.* "Yuri, have you decided what we will do when we get back?"

Tanya placed her hand on Elena's arm. "Please, would you both stay with Daniel and me? You will be safe."

Elena studied her friend. She liked Daniel and Tanya, but could she live with them? Although she hated what the government stood for and the evil it brought to the people, she couldn't understand the Belovs's subversive life. And their religious beliefs made her uneasy. "I don't think it would work out."

"What alternative do we have?" Yuri asked.

Elena searched her mind for an answer. She'd considered the dilemma for days and could come up with no solution. She shrugged her shoulders. "I don't know."

"What alternatives do either of you have?" Daniel asked. "You made a real sacrifice for those people, and you can feel good about it, but now your choices are limited."

"We would like it very much if you lived with us," Tanya said. "And the girls love you both."

Elena looked at the plain woman who sat beside her and wondered what life would be like with the Belovs. Would they push her to believe as they did? And what if their underground activities were discovered? Everyone associated with them would be suspect and arrested. Yet, what choice *did* she have? She glanced at Yuri. "I guess we could try it," she finally conceded.

Tanya smiled. "Good. It is done, then. You will become a part of our family."

Elena looked Tanya squarely in the eyes and said, "You need to know, I don't feel good about what you and Daniel are doing.

One day you will be caught. It will happen. It always does. The NKVD will eventually corner you. No one is safe."

After returning home, Daniel's supervisor questioned him about his absence from work. Although it was illegal for anyone to leave a job without official consent, his explanation of aid to friends was accepted, and he was allowed to return without discipline.

Afraid their false papers would be too closely examined, Yuri and Elena didn't return to their jobs or their home. Elena chafed at Tanya's glowing claim of "God's miraculous protection." After all, she didn't have a job or an apartment, but she was grateful they hadn't been confronted by the authorities.

The weeks passed, and gradually Elena and Yuri blended into the household. But as Yuri became more and more involved in the underground, distributing flyers and sheets of copied Scripture, Elena's anxiety grew. Nothing she said deterred him. He relished the work. She wondered if his service was truly from the heart or something he did to please Daniel. The man had become Yuri's champion.

Purposely she remained ignorant about their activities, wanting nothing to do with the secret life. She kept busy helping with the children and the household. The arrangement worked out perfectly, providing Tanya with more time to mimeograph Scriptures and occasionally help Yuri and Daniel distribute the literature.

One day Yuri burst through the front door. Wearing a grin, he held tickets and waved them over his head. "You will not believe what I was given today."

"What do you have?" Elena grabbed for the passes, but Yuri deftly moved them out of her reach.

He held them out for a moment, then shielded them with his other hand. "Guess."

"I will not guess! Tell me!" She returned to kneading the heavy black bread and ignored him.

CHAPTER *16*

Yuri leaned on the counter. "Ah, so you don't care about a night at the Bolshoi?"

Elena's hands stopped their work. She looked at Yuri, then eyed the tickets. "Are you teasing?" She dusted her hands on her apron.

Yuri smiled triumphantly and handed her the passes.

She studied them, and her mouth fell open. "These are for the *Nutcracker!* How did you get them?"

"You are always talking about how dangerous our work is. You forget that many people appreciate what we do." He pinched off a piece of bread dough and ate it. "A minister who is grateful for the copies of Scripture we provide gave them to me. We can all go."

Still in shock, she asked, "How did he get them?"

"I don't know. It's not my business," he smiled smugly. "Of course, if you're worried about their source, you don't have to go."

"Of course I want to." She leaned her elbow on the counter, rested her cheek in her hand, and closed her eyes. "It has been years. There was a time when my family and I used to go to the ballet and to the symphony."

Yuri had been to the ballet only once. The memory was vivid. It had been Tatyana's fourteenth birthday, and it was her wish to visit the Bolshoi. The family had combined their funds and purchased the tickets. When Tatyana opened the envelope containing the gift, her face lit up. The expense had been worth that single expression of joy.

They traveled to Moscow and stayed with friends. The night of the ballet, dressed in a beautiful hand-sewn gown, her hair piled on her head, Tatyana looked very grown up. All through the evening, she wore a look of delight.

For weeks she talked about the ballet and spent hours listening to the music of the *Nutcracker,* reliving the adventure.

"Yuri. Yuri."

He pulled himself back to the present, wishing he could linger a little longer in the memory.

"What are you thinking about? You had such a faraway look on your face."

"Just about my sister," he said, struggling to speak through the lump in his throat.

✳ ✳ ✳ ✳ ✳

Carriages and fine automobiles pulled up outside the entrance of the Bolshoi Theater. Elena watched a parade of women wearing lush furs and long gowns enter the front doors on the arms of tuxedoed men. She looked down at her simple skirt and wet boots. "I'm not dressed properly for the ballet," she whispered. "This is not suitable."

"No one cares what you're wearing," Yuri said.

"That's not true. They pay attention. I remember."

"Difficult times affect everyone, not only you," Yuri chided. "And once the lights are down, no one will notice anyway." He studied her. "And, if what I think counts, you are beautiful."

"Thank you," she said, unconvinced. She straightened her scarf and glanced up at a row of arched windows overlooking the square. Stepping onto the stone stairway, she remembered the years when a visit to the Bolshoi was customary, although it had always been a delight.

Immense columns reached several floors above to the lower rooftop. Balanced on the peak was a statue of a warrior standing in a chariot and reigning in four lunging horses. Just beneath that, two elegant angels were carved into the stone where they looked down on the theater's guests. *Such a contrast between the two,* Elena thought. *Control rather than guardianship, and power instead of love.*

Daniel, with Tanya on his arm, led the way up the broad steps. "I don't know if I'm up for this," he said over his shoulder, then straightened his tie. He watched a man who was dressed in a tuxedo carelessly flick his cigarette aside. "I really don't fit in."

"You'll love it," Tanya said. "There's nothing more beautiful." She held his hand.

He took a deep breath and moved up the stairway.

A distinguished-looking usher took their coats; another checked their tickets. "Your seats are right through there," he said, pointing at a nearby entrance.

Daniel steered Tanya toward the doorway. Yuri and Elena followed.

As Daniel stepped through the entry, he stopped and gaped at the immense room. "I had no idea. It's huge, like a cathedral." His voice sounded hushed.

"Very impressive, isn't it?" Yuri asked.

Although they had entered on the third level, they still looked up another four stories, where much of the audience was already seated. The socially elite were on the floor and the lower levels. The women there were dressed in elegant gowns, their jewels sparkling beneath the lights, and the men were wearing tuxedos. An enormous, crystal chandelier hung in the middle of the seven-story chamber. The entire theater was a wash of plush red carpet and draperies. Broad, ornate bands of gold belted each level and shimmered in the light of countless chandeliers.

Daniel still gawked. "This is unbelievable. I've never seen anything like it."

"Please, move on," a man just behind them said irritably.

Daniel looked back. "I'm sorry." Quickly he stepped down the aisle, still gazing at the immense oval chamber with the stage at one end.

"Daniel, you can close your mouth now," Tanya teased. She took his arm. "I think our seats are this way." She guided him to their numbered places and settled into cushioned chairs. Yuri and Elena sat beside them.

Yuri ran his hand over the velvety material. "I'd forgotten how extraordinary this place is." He looked at Elena. "You don't seem very impressed. Have you been here many times?"

Elena gazed at the stage. "Yes." She didn't elaborate, still not ready to share her past.

"I thought so. You seemed comfortable from the moment you stepped inside. You look like you belong. And you may not be dressed as elegantly as some of these people, but you are still the loveliest woman here."

Elena looked at Yuri. Unnerved by his devoted expression, she didn't know how to respond and offered him a half smile before turning her eyes back to the stage. Yuri was a fine person, but loving hurt too much. She wasn't about to allow herself to care for anyone too deeply.

Yuri leaned forward and ran his hand over the carved wooden banister in front of him. It was polished to a glossy shine. "This is an incredible place."

"It is the splendor of Imperial Russia, the way it was," Elena said. She looked at Daniel. "You have never been here before?"

"No," Daniel answered. "And this will probably be my only visit. I don't feel like I belong."

Tanya patted his hand. "You belong anywhere you decide you want to be. These people are just like us."

With a wry grin, Daniel said, "I don't think so."

Listening to the hum of conversation, Yuri settled back in his seat. *Tatyana would love this,* he thought. *I wish she were here.*

The lights dimmed, and the people hushed. As the curtain opened, the stage came alive with ballerinas dressed in lavish gowns and male dancers wearing tuxedos. They moved gracefully, mingling as if at a party. A sweet-looking, young woman took center stage.

Yuri was struck by her resemblance to Tatyana. She was very tall and slender, with long blonde hair and a fair complexion. Many times his young sister had twirled and leaped across their front room, imagining she was a prima ballerina. Forcing back a rush of emotion, he focused on the stage.

He was quickly drawn into the tale of young Claire, who on Christmas Eve was given two gifts, one a nutcracker, the other a dream. Yuri glanced at Elena and wondered if she was still able to dream. She seemed tormented.

In Claire's dream the nutcracker came to life and, with the flash of his sword, battled a wicked mouse king. After being wounded, he was magically restored and transformed into a handsome prince. While the flutes and oboes mingled in a lyrical blend and the trumpets rejoiced, the couple leaped, spun, and waltzed, unaware of anything outside themselves.

The violins sang a lament, and the mouse king appeared once more. A battle ensued, but this time the prince thwarted the attack.

Wrapped in their own happiness, the prince and maiden danced to the soft tones of French horns, only to be frightened once more by the evil mouse king who, always watchful, lurked in the darkness, waiting for an opportunity to steal their happiness.

How like Stalin's regime, Yuri thought, a deep sorrow settling over him. *Can any of us dream any more?*

With one long embrace, the magic on stage came to an end. Claire struggled to hang on to the dream, but reality could not be held back. Gradually morning came, and she was forced to wake and face the truth.

The stage turned dark, and Yuri stared at the blackness. For a long moment the theater was still, then exploded with applause as people stood and displayed their approval.

Yuri joined in the applause, but as he looked around the room he understood this was not reality. It was a fantasy, and he knew not to hang on to it too tightly, for in the "New Russia" there was no room for such things.

Elena leaned close to him. "Thank you, Yuri." Tears misted her eyes.

"I wish I could have found a way to bring you sooner."

"When something is uncommon, it is cherished all the more," she said softly, touching his arm.

Yuri laid his hand over hers, a rush of devotion welling up in him.

Too quickly she turned and followed the others down the aisle.

As the foursome stepped into the cold December air, they followed the crowd down the steps. Once in the square, Tanya stopped. With people streaming past, she lifted her face and closed her eyes. "The cold air feels good. The theater beginning to get a little stuffy."

Yuri's melancholy lingered. He took a deep breath and stared at the sky. The stars looked dim against the brightness of the full moon.

"It was wonderful!" Tanya said, rising on her toes and allowing Daniel to twirl her away from him.

"I didn't know you were a ballerina as well as an artist," Elena quipped.

Tanya bowed. "I am a person of many talents."

"I feel like a walk along the river," Yuri said.

Daniel pulled his hat down snug. "That sounds nice, but I have to be up early."

"Me, too," Tanya said.

Yuri looked at Elena. "And you?"

"I would like to walk. It is a beautiful night, and maybe I can hang onto the magic a little longer."

"We'll see you at home, then." Daniel linked arms with Tanya and walked away.

"I like how the fresh snow crunches beneath my feet. I've always liked walking in it just after it has fallen." Elena stooped and picked up a handful, tossed it into the air, and watched as the crystals fell to the ground. "Do you believe dreams can really come true?"

"Yes, of course." Yuri studied a leafless tree, its branches twisted and piled with snow. "But sometimes it's difficult—like that tree. Right now we don't see the life within, but we know it's there. Until spring it will look dead. When it begins to blossom, it will be like a dream come true."

"So, you believe spring will always come?"

"In nature yes, but in our lives . . . I don't know."

Snow began to fall. Elena looked up and peered at the flakes, blinking as they touched her eyes.

In the moonlight, her face was rose-tinted. *She is beautiful,* Yuri thought and gently reached out and brushed a delicate flake from her cheek.

She opened her eyes and looked at him, a startled expression on her face. Yuri wanted to wrap her in his arms and pull her close, but instead, he stepped back. She'd been clear from the beginning that there could be no more than friendship between them. He knew she carried deep scars from her past and instinctively understood she was too vulnerable to allow herself to love right now.

"Yuri, is something wrong?"

"No." He gazed up at the falling snow. It was coming down harder. "I think we need to hurry. It looks like a real storm is setting in."

CHAPTER *17*

THE RADIATOR CLANKED AND groaned, echoing in the quiet room. Veikko tapped his pipe against his teeth, and the clicking sound nettled Yuri as he studied his playing cards. A single bulb screwed into the ceiling was the only light, forcing the four men around the table to squint as they contemplated their hands. The radiator rumbled again.

"I wish that racket meant it was putting off heat," Oleg said, as he pulled his jacket closed and nudged his small round glasses.

Two jacks, not bad. Not good, either, Yuri thought. He looked at Oleg. Did he have a good hand? He'd already laid his cards face down and, now, looking very relaxed, rested his chin in his hands as he watched the others. He looked too confident. *He's bluffing,* Yuri decided.

Veikko stroked his heavy mustache and grimaced. Tossing his cards aside, he said, "I have nothing. I would have done better to stay at home. At least my Zoya would have kept me warm." The men chuckled. "And what of Elena, eh, Yuri?"

"What about her?" he challenged.

"She is very beautiful. You cannot tell us you do not think about—"

"I've told you, we are good friends, nothing more."

Veikko scrutinized Yuri. "I cannot understand why a man would choose to remain distant from someone like her."

Yuri stared at his cards, then glanced at Veikko. "As comrades we have no worries the way lovers do."

"And no love," Oleg jested.

Yuri shuffled his cards. "Some relationships are not meant for passion."

"Well, I don't understand it," Oleg said, peering over his glasses.

Saodat had been silent throughout the conversation. The thin man with pale blue eyes scratched his scrawny goatee and stared at his cards. He glanced at the others with a detached expression.

Yuri didn't like the newcomer. He seemed cold and indifferent. He reminded him of a Doberman pinscher, always watching with a steady eye, ready to strike if provoked. He sniffed around like a dog, as if hunting for a bone. Yuri wondered what kind of bone he searched for. *You're being paranoid. Oleg said he was a good man.* He'd met Oleg months ago and knew him to be trustworthy. *If he has confidence in him, that's enough.* Yuri looked at Saodat. "Are you going to play that hand?"

He turned his pale eyes on Yuri. "Give me a moment," he said in a cool voice. He gazed at his cards, then placed one kopeck in the center of the table. "I'm in." Leaning on his elbows, he looked at Yuri and Oleg. "Show me what you have."

With a grunt of disgust, Oleg lay out his hand. "Nothing. I have nothing."

Saodat grinned. "And you? Are you bluffing also?"

Yuri grudgingly spread his cards face up in front of him. He knew it wouldn't take much to beat him. "A pair of jacks."

Saodat laughed and laid his cards down, his queen covering another face card. "Queens over threes." He quickly scooped them back up and reached for the coins.

Veikko placed his hand on top of the stranger's. "Wait a minute. Show your cards again. I didn't see them all."

"What, you do not believe me? I am offended."

"Be offended, but show us the cards." Veikko sat back and stroked his mustache. When Saodat didn't respond, he repeated, "Show us the cards."

Sweat broke out on the man's forehead. He laid out his hand—a pair of threes, one queen, a jack, and a nine. He stared at them as in disbelief. "I'm sorry. I thought my jack was a queen." He glanced at the three men. "I was certain I had two queens." He shrugged and gave Yuri a crooked grin. "I made a mistake. It was a jack. I'm sorry."

Veikko chewed on his pipe and eyed the newcomer, then placing his big hands on the table, he stood and leaned toward the cheat. "You thought?"

Gathering up his cards, Saodat brushed a strand of blonde hair off his forehead. "It was a mistake. Anyone can make a mistake."

"Make no more *mistakes*."

"I . . . I won't. I'll be more careful."

Yuri scrutinized the man. In his gut he knew he was lying, but he had no reason to doubt him. He'd simply made a blunder. "The lighting is bad," Yuri said, scooping up the scant coins. The wind gusted against the window, and the radiator continued to complain as he shoved the money into his coat pocket. He shivered. "Oh, for more heat. Sometimes it seems I'll never be warm again." He closed his eyes. "I remember days on the farm. They were good. When Mama baked bread the heat from the stove and the smell of bread filled every corner of the house." He opened his eyes and forced a smile. "To have those days back."

"Do you think it will happen?" Oleg asked, his voice heavy.

Veikko shuffled the cards. "I would like to see it, but I have little hope. My babies are hungry. They grow weaker every day." He held the deck out for Yuri to cut. "Maybe when summer arrives, we will have more to eat—a little beef and some fruit."

"To have a little meat again—the thought makes my mouth water," said Yuri.

"But we have meat," Saodat said.

"You call the rotting allotment of fish we get meat? There is barely enough for a meal, let alone a month," Yuri said. "And while our stomachs rumble with hunger, the government tells us to work faster, work harder. How can the government expect so much from starving citizens?" He looked hard at the stranger and continued, "Drive through the country and you will see the government's generosity." He sounded bitter. "What you will find is death—the starved bodies of women and children."

Saodat said nothing; he only glared at Yuri.

"Oh, what I would give for just a little chicken," Veikko said as he dealt the cards. "My mama used to make the most delicious chicken stew. She would add fresh vegetables from the garden and serve it with hot biscuits and butter. Those biscuits were so light. We needed to keep one hand beneath them to catch the crumbs that flaked off when we'd bite into them." His eyes turned sad, and his voice quieted. "My job was to butcher the rooster for dinner." He cleared his throat and tipped his chin up a little. "That was a long time ago. Things are different now."

Yuri put his cards down, incensed at the reminder of everything the people had lost. "Different is not the right word for what has happened to us. The Russian people have been robbed of what God has supplied. Stalin has stripped away the blessings. He stole them from each of us." His anger grew, and he pounded the table. "We should not tolerate the evil that stalks the land!"

Saodat leaned forward on his elbows. "You believe personal happiness is more important than the good of the people?"

Oleg and Veikko glanced at each other, but neither spoke.

Yuri met Saodat's gaze. "I believe both are important, but it's wrong to care for the "people" at the expense of individuals. After all, individuals make up the multitude."

The newcomer tapped a cigarette on the table and lit it. Taking a deep drag, he studied the glowing ashes, then looked at Yuri. "Can you explain this concept of God's blessings? I don't understand." He leaned back in his chair and took another puff on his cigarette.

Yuri knew if he met this man's challenge he would be placing himself in danger, but he couldn't keep silent. "God blesses those who love him and serve him."

"By blesses, do you mean he gives you *things*?"

"Yes. But not necessarily things. It can be peace, or a warm bed, or something like food or clothing."

"And, what do you mean when you say *serve* God? Are you talking about being a good citizen or working hard? And what about the collective good?"

Yuri searched his mind and his heart. He knew if he spoke the truth he could face frightening consequences, but to remain quiet would be cowardly. Daniel wouldn't be afraid. He stood up, crossed to the window, and stared down on the empty snow-covered street. A wisp of heat drifted up from the radiator.

"Why don't we play cards?" Oleg suggested.

"Yes, that's why we came here," Veikko added.

Yuri ignored the distraction and turned to look at Saodat. He studied the man a moment, then began, "Serving God *is* being a good citizen and working hard, but it is more. It's seeking his will above your own and doing it. It may mean loving someone you want to hate, taking good care of your family, or—"

"Or tearing down your own government?" Saodat interrupted.

Yuri ignored the question and continued, "What matters is trusting in Christ. It's an individual decision, not something people do as a group." Yuri knew he was going against the Communist belief that the collective good always outweighed individual needs, but he refused to be cowed by this man.

"So, explain this *individual* blessing."

Yuri didn't answer.

Saodat softened his expression and his voice. "I'm truly interested."

Yuri knew his sincerity was probably a ruse, but could he ignore an open opportunity to share his faith? If he couldn't trust God to protect him when asked to share the gospel, when could he trust him? He took a deep breath. "What I mean is, if a person believes in God and trusts in his Son for salvation he will receive God's blessing of eternal life in heaven. But, it's something each person must decide."

Saodat took a drag of his cigarette, then tapped the ashes into a tin lid. All pretense gone, he glared at Yuri. "The law states clearly that religion is a threat to the people and it's illegal to speak of it. Aren't you afraid of arrest?"

Yuri looked straight into the man's eyes. What he saw there made him quake. He was a predator. Yuri sat down, picked up the deck of cards, and tapped them against the table. "We came to play cards. We should play."

* * * * *

They came for Yuri three days later.

Late in the afternoon, he left a friend's apartment and headed toward home. With his Bible carefully concealed under his jacket, Yuri made his way down the icy sidewalk. He heard an automobile pull to a stop behind him. He looked over his shoulder, and his stomach dropped. A dark green van, the kind he'd seen the police use for arrests, had pulled to the side of the street. He hurried his steps.

"You! Stop!"

Knowing they were calling him, but hoping some other unlucky individual was their target, he continued.

"Halt or I'll fire!" The voice was sharp and compelling.

Yuri stopped and faced an NKVD officer. The man held a gun, and it was aimed at him.

"Yuri Letinov?"

His heart pounding, Yuri pressed his elbow against his Bible. He met the man's eyes. "Yes."

"Come with us."

Yuri didn't move. "Where? Where are you taking me?" His voice shook.

"We ask the questions."

Another man opened the back of the van. The door squeaked on rusted hinges.

The officer waved the gun at Yuri. "Get in."

"What about my family?"

"They will be notified."

Yuri knew better. People disappeared all the time, and no one ever knew what happened to them. He swallowed hard and tried to keep from trembling as he realized he was about to become one of the missing. His friends would search for him, but he'd simply be gone and would never return.

He looked up and down the street seeking a familiar face—someone he could tell. He found no one. Where was Daniel? He needed him. "I . . . I must tell my family."

"They will be notified," the officer repeated in a harsh monotone. This time he marched up to Yuri and jammed his gun against the young man's chest. "In the van. Now."

With one last glance down the empty street, Yuri walked toward the transport. His legs felt like lead, and his mind was a jumble of confused thoughts. Although he'd feared this, now that it had happened it didn't seem possible. He had trusted God. What had happened to his guardianship?

Standing at the rear of the vehicle, he gazed inside. Two rows of what looked like lockers lined the sides of the van. There was no room for passengers.

"Get in," the policeman barked.

"Where? There's no place to sit." The man pushed him, and Yuri stumbled inside.

The officer followed him in. Taking a set of keys from his coat pocket, he jammed one into the rusted latch of one of the heavy metal lockers and turned it. The door creaked open. "Get in!"

Yuri stared at the tiny space. He couldn't be serious. There was no possible way he could fit his six-foot frame in the small compartment. He looked at the guard. "I can't fit."

"Get in," the man said and pressed the gun against Yuri's side.

Yuri put one foot on the edge of the locker. It stank of sweat and urine. The two officers shoved him, abruptly forcing him into the cramped box. They pushed hard against the door, jamming Yuri inside, and latched the bolt.

Yuri's head was wedged against the top of the cell, forcing his chin onto his chest. With his right shoulder jammed into a corner, his old injury ached. The other shoulder was flattened against the metal wall, and he could barely expand his lungs enough to take a breath.

The van door slammed, and the engine revved. Yuri could feel the vehicle move away from the curb and head down the street.

A vivid picture of his near execution filled his mind. Remembering his uncle's uncompromising faith, he knew he didn't possess such assurance. And, in spite of his work with Daniel, his faith was feeble. Tears mingled with his sweat and dripped off his chin. He knew escape could not come to one man twice.

The van made many stops to load prisoners. The shouts and cries for mercy tore at Yuri's soul. A woman in the cage next to him sobbed. There was nothing he could do for her. There were no words for such a time.

Faces of heartless soldiers and images of dead bodies lying in the pit continued to play through his mind. Was that what awaited him? Dread and despair overwhelmed the young Russian. Ashamed, he squeezed his eyes shut. *Where is my faith?* he anguished. *I thought I was strong, but I'm weak. I'm a fake. I'll never be like Uncle Alexander or Daniel or any of the others.*

The afternoon seemed to go on and on. The air became stale, and the aching parts of his body numbed. He needed to be freed. At one stop he cried, "Let me out! Please let me out!" Yuri felt he'd been closed in his own coffin.

The van stopped, and he heard the familiar squeak of the door. This time no one was loaded. Footfalls approached his locker. Although his body screamed for freedom, dread bore into his soul. He heard the latch release, and the door fell open. Two men grabbed him and wrenched him out of his tiny prison. He couldn't feel his legs, and they buckled beneath him. Linking their arms under his, the officers dragged Yuri out of the van and into an empty yard. The door slammed shut, leaving the others locked in their boxes.

He looked up at a familiar three-story stone building. *Prison!* His mind screamed. He'd heard horror stories about what went on behind the granite walls. There would be no merciful death for him.

As the feeling returned to his limbs, he tried to stand, but pain burned through his legs and into his feet. He took a step and stumbled, falling flat out.

"Get up!"

Yuri pushed himself to his hands and knees, then slowly straightened. He stared at the ugly building and whispered, "God, help me."

A blow to the side of his head sent colors spiraling through his mind. His ears rang, and pain roared behind his eyes.

"Head down, hands behind back!"

Yuri looked at the ground and clasped his hands behind his back. He walked several yards to an iron gate. The guard opened it and shoved Yuri through. After walking several more yards, he was steered through another gate. It clanged shut behind him, and the bolt was slammed into place. Yuri thought he might vomit. He swallowed hard as he moved deeper into the compound, panic seizing him. He knew he would never leave.

When they reached a flight of stairs, Yuri was half carried, half dragged up the stairway, then propelled down a dimly lit corridor. The guards stopped in front of a small door and knocked.

A man's voice from inside called, "Enter."

One guard opened the door and pushed Yuri inside. The lights were bright, and Yuri blinked, trying to clear his vision. He stood in front of a large wooden desk where a gaunt man with greenish, golden eyes and black hair studied him. Yuri had never seen eyes that color.

One of the guards handed the man Yuri's paperwork. The man scanned the report. Setting the papers aside and wearing a half smile, he scrutinized the young Russian. If not for a weak chin the man might have been considered good-looking. He sucked on a cigarette that had nearly burned down to his nicotine-stained fingers. Silently he stared, his golden eyes boring into his young prisoner.

Yuri could smell the odor of garlic and wondered if the man ever blinked. He started to shake and, although he willed himself still, it only grew worse.

"Strip him," the man finally said, his monotone voice cutting the silence. He took a disinterested drag of his cigarette.

The guards obeyed immediately. One held up Yuri's leg, while the other pulled off a shoe and sock. They did the same with the other foot. Seeming to take pleasure in the humiliation, they pulled Yuri's pants and shirt off. His Bible plunked to the floor. For a moment, stillness filled the room as all eyes gazed at the book. One of the guards picked it up and handed it to the man at the desk. Then he returned and stripped away Yuri's underwear.

The garlic-smelling man examined the Bible. He opened the pages and leafed through it, then slammed it shut and eased it from one hand to the other. With a smile playing on his lips, he watched the continued degradation of his captive.

His clothing in a pile next to him, Yuri stood, covering his nakedness with his hands. His body trembled uncontrollably.

The interrogator at the desk motioned to the guards. One moved quickly and pried open Yuri's mouth, ran a finger over his teeth and under his tongue, then roughly moved his hands all over his body, including his most private places, completing Yuri's shame.

After that they went through his clothing, checking the pockets and removing the buttons from his pants and the laces from his shoes. His papers and a letter he'd intended to post to Tatyana was handed to the inquisitor. He glanced at the documents, then tore open the letter and read it. Laying the letter aside, he took the Bible and turned it over. Balancing it in one hand, he asked, "What is this?"

"It is only a Bible."

"These are outlawed!"

"It belonged to my mother. It has sentimental value only," Yuri lied to protect himself. Feeling like a coward, he wanted to crawl into a hole.

CHAPTER 17

Setting the Bible aside, the man picked up the letter. "And this?"

Why would they not leave him alone? "You have seen it. It is only a letter."

A kick to his kidneys sent him sprawling on the floor. Yuri sucked at the air, his back on fire.

The man pushed his chair back and stood over the young man. He grinned. "Now, would you like to answer my question?"

Yuri forced himself to his feet. "It is only a letter."

"It is addressed to someone in the United States of America! What connections do you have with the Americans?"

"It's my sister. She lives there. It means nothing."

He glared at him. "I will decide what is nothing." Softening his expression, he partially turned his body away from Yuri. His voice quieter but firm, he said, "You will tell me about your counterrevolutionary activities."

"I am not a counterrevolutionary. You have seen my work and living permits. Everything is in order."

"Maybe they are in order, maybe not."

Yuri's fears grew.

"Who was working with you?"

Elena's face flashed through Yuri's mind. Had she been picked up, too? And what about Daniel and Tanya? "No one. I did nothing wrong."

The man kicked his garments toward him. "Get dressed."

Yuri quickly pulled on his clothing. They had taken his belt and ripped two of the buttons off his pants, so he was forced to hold his pants to keep them from falling off. Still, he felt less vulnerable dressed. Gathering his courage, he asked, "Am I not allowed to know what I've been accused of? Will I get a trial?" His voice sounded strange, like it belonged to someone else.

In a voice as sweet as syrup, the examiner said, "In time you will confess your crimes. If you admit to your subversive activities now, you will save yourself a great deal of suffering." He ground out his already dead cigarette in an ashtray. Sitting on the corner of his desk, his sick smile returned, and he studied his prisoner.

He reminded Yuri of a hungry cat. "I've done nothing. Please let me contact my family."

His voice turning hard, the inquisitor said, "Stop lying. You are an enemy of the state." He held up the letter and the Bible. "What other proof do we need?"

Yuri wondered why, if they had enough evidence, did they need his confession? Had they discovered his underground activities? No. It must be what he'd told Saodat, and he'd revealed nothing about his work with Daniel. He looked at the man. "I have done nothing."

The interrogator's smile disappeared. He wrote something on a piece of paper. "You will confess," he said as he nodded toward the guards. "Take him to his cell."

"Head down, arms behind your back, no talking!" the guard shouted as he shoved Yuri toward the door.

CHAPTER *18*

WITH A GUARD ON EACH SIDE
and one leading the way, Yuri trudged down a dark, wide
corridor. The only sound was the men's boots as they rapped
against the concrete. Yuri wondered why it was so silent. Where
were the voices, the clearing of a throat, or a cry of despair? Yuri
listened hard but heard nothing.

With one thumb hooked through the loop of his pants, he
kept his hands clasped behind his back as ordered and was
careful not to look up. On both sides of the passageway he
caught glimpses of heavy, steel doors. He knew the hopeless
huddled behind them. The doors went on endlessly. Could there
be a reason for so many?

Trying not to lift his head, he glanced at the walls. Seeing
that there were no windows, he understood the reason for the
damp, fetid odor that permeated the place. No air passed

through these chambers. He shuddered. Soon he would be caged along with the others, concealed from the world, maybe forever. Panic welled up within him, and he wanted to run. This couldn't be happening! He closed his eyes, hoping to drive away his terror. He looked at the guards. There was no escape.

"Head down!"

Yuri fixed his eyes on the floor, his mind a jumble of questions. Would anyone come for him? How long would he be locked up? Why had God abandoned him? He set his jaw. *I trusted you,* he thought. *Is this my reward?* Immediate guilt over his irreverence pressed down on him.

The guards stopped in front of a steel door. The two at Yuri's side grabbed hold of his arms, while the other removed a huge key from his belt. He fit the key into the lock, then using both hands, grimaced as he forced it to the left. With a loud clink the door fell free. The guard pushed it open with his foot and stepped back. The two holding Yuri shoved him forward.

"In!" the lead guard ordered.

Yuri stumbled into the dimness. Like a wave, a vile stink of unwashed bodies and human waste swept over him, and he sprang backward into the hallway.

With one hand over his nose, the guard jabbed Yuri in the back with the key, forcing the young Russian into the cell. The door slammed shut, and the lock clinked into place.

Yuri gagged and nearly retched. The foulness of a pigpen smelled sweet in comparison to the stench permeating this hole. He felt weak. As the room tipped, Yuri reached out to steady himself, then quickly jerked his hand back. A sticky dampness covered the wall. He breathed shallowly through his mouth. There was no way to escape the fetor. He could even taste it.

Panicked, he backed into the door, then turned and pushed against it. It didn't budge. He knew it wouldn't, but he had to try. Glancing up at a dim light burning beside the door, Yuri faced the small room.

As his eyes adjusted to the gloom, he realized his new home was a tiny cell about five feet by ten feet. A boarded window on the opposite wall shut out any hope of fresh air or daylight. The chamber was lined on two sides by benches set a foot away from the walls. More than a dozen men sat on them, their backs straight and their hands on their knees. They only glanced at Yuri, then stared at something just beyond him. No one spoke.

Yuri turned sideways and shuffled between the men's knees to an empty spot on the bench. He sat down. No one moved; no one spoke. Everyone watched a peephole in the door.

The wall was too far from the bench to allow Yuri to rest against it. He sat with his back straight like the others. The cell felt like a tomb; the only sound was the occasional drip of water. Yuri studied the men, but they seemed not to notice him. Finally he said, "My name is Yuri." His voice echoed in the silence.

The only response was a sensation of movement and a nervous twitch of a man's finger.

The prisoners continued to stare at the door.

"I said my name is Yuri."

Without taking his eyes off the peephole, the man next to Yuri held his finger to his lips.

Swallowing hard, Yuri forced down his rising terror. So this is where those who disappeared from the streets of Moscow ended up. And like them, his fate was to sit on a bench in a foul hole and stare at a door. It was impossible. No one could endure this.

A man sitting opposite the newcomer stood up and hobbled across the tiny cell, his legs brushing against another's bony knees. A large metal pot with a wooden lid sat on the floor to the left of the door. When he lifted the lid putrid gases swept over the room. The man dropped his pants and gingerly lowered himself over the makeshift toilet. He was careful not to look at his prison mates. No one moved his eyes from the peephole.

Yuri closed his. *This is a nightmare,* he thought. *Soon I will wake up.* He pinched his arm. Nothing changed. He pinched himself harder, but, still, the cell and the men remained. "Wake up! Wake up!" he screamed. The small room seemed to swallow the words.

The quick footfall of hard-soled boots came from outside. A shadow covered the peephole. Someone pounded on the door. "No talking! You'll be disciplined!"

The man on the *parasha* quickly pulled up his pants and scurried back to his place on the bench. Without a word, he straightened his back, fixed his gaze on the door, and placed his hands on his knees.

The guard moved away. The prisoner on Yuri's opposite side gently touched the newcomer's hand. In the quietest whisper, he said, "Do not speak. They will come."

The man never took his eyes from the door, and Yuri wondered if he'd imagined the words.

The following day Yuri was still too sickened and too scared to eat. When the guards passed in wooden bowls containing a hard, round ball of porridge, he let the man beside him have it. When molded, black bread and thin, foul-smelling soup was brought at midday, he passed again. And, although his stomach gnawed with hunger, when another ball of porridge was passed through the tiny window that night, he couldn't eat.

Yuri did this for two days. The morning of the third his hunger had become a beast, and when his tiny ball of porridge was handed to him he devoured it. His stomach still felt empty. After that he ate every bit of nourishment offered, but the pain in his stomach never left. The gnawing emptiness became a steady companion.

One desolate day followed another. At first Yuri tried to keep track of the passing time, but there was no variance of light, no change in the daily routine, only the endless monotony.

When he counted the tenth day, he was uncertain if it was really nine days or maybe eleven. Finally he gave up trying to count.

Although the men never spoke, Yuri came to know his cell mates. All had shaven heads, all were emaciated, and all suffered varying degrees of dysentery. Though they rarely moved, except when called out by the guards or to use the dreaded parasha, each man's personality gradually emerged. Some remained stoic no matter what was inflicted upon them; others couldn't suppress soft whimpers of pain or despair; and, some shared their meager food rations with the more feeble. All were subjected to repeated interrogations. Night after night men were taken. When they returned they were bleeding and sometimes unconscious.

There were rules: no talking; keep your hands clearly in sight on your knees; keep your back straight; and, watch the door. If anyone broke a rule, all paid the consequence of no food for three days. Sometimes, if a guard was in a particularly foul mood and discovered a discrepancy, he would wrench a prisoner off the bench, beating him with his fists. When the prisoner laid on the floor, the guard would kick the offender, using the toes of his boots as instruments of torture. When one prisoner was being beaten, the others remained motionless and silent. Yet, all knew they shared the same torment as they witnessed the violence.

The days passed, and Yuri sat staring at the peephole. In the beginning he prayed, but gradually his supplications ceased, and he began to feel God didn't care or maybe didn't exist. Had he believed a fairy tale? He remembered Daniel's words about the martyrdom of the early believers and the stories he'd read in the Bible over the years. Could he expect more? Living with the consequences of one's devotion was much different than reading about it. Yuri wondered if he had the strength to hang on to his feeble faith.

One night the cell door opened, and a guard called Yuri's name. At first he thought he'd heard wrong, but when it was repeated, he stood up. For a moment he wondered if he were being released, but he quickly remembered the interrogations, and his legs nearly buckled.

He looked at the guard and stumbled toward the door. The man grabbed him and, without a word, steered him down the corridor.

As Yuri stepped out of the main prison compound, a scream cut through the stillness. The hair on his neck stiffened, and terror enveloped him. It came again. Yuri stopped, paralyzed.

"Move!" The guard shoved him toward a flight of stairs.

Forcing one foot to follow the other, he made his way up the stairway. When they reached the door, Yuri threw back his shoulders and tried to look detached. Then it opened, and he was pushed inside. He swallowed hard and faced the man with the gold-colored eyes. The smell of garlic still clung to him.

Placing his elbows on the desk and staring at Yuri, the interrogator leaned forward and carefully peeled a large orange.

Unable to help himself, Yuri gaped at the fruit. His mouth watered. Even the peel would be treasured.

The man grinned as he split the orange in half and pulled a slice away. He bit off a chunk, then popped the remaining half into his mouth. Holding it up, he asked, "You would like some?"

The citrus smell was almost too much for Yuri. His aching stomach complained more fiercely, but he said nothing.

"You tell me what I want to know, and I'll make sure you get some of this." He stripped away another section and pushed it into his mouth. As he chewed, juice dribbled down his chin. For a moment the man left it there, before carefully wiping it away. Leaning back in his chair, he placed his polished boots on the desk and casually crossed his ankles.

Yuri forced his eyes to the floor.

Taking two more quick bites, the interrogator stood up. He chewed and swallowed. "Now, you will tell me what I want to know about your counterrevolutionary activities." He held up a piece of paper. "And you will sign this confession." A phony smile played across his lips. "If you tell me what I need to know, you will go free."

Yuri looked more closely at the paper, but the writing blurred. He rubbed his eyes but still couldn't read it. "What does it say?"

"Only that you have been led astray by your friends, and it is because of their influence that you were forced to take part in a plot to overthrow the government."

"That's not true."

"Your punishment will be light compared to what awaits you if you do not confess." His tone was cruel.

"I haven't done anything."

The man's smile disappeared, and his eyes turned hard, the gold color intensifying. Pounding the table with his fist, he shouted, "You are subversive scum, and you will tell me what I want to know! Now! What was the plan to overthrow the government, and who was working with you? Where were you meeting?"

Yuri stared at the window. "I did nothing."

The blow came so quickly he was unprepared. His head felt like it exploded as it snapped backward. Staggering, he grabbed for the wall. The heel of the man's boot hammered him in the kidneys. As Yuri turned, the man's toe caught him in the stomach.

Yuri gasped, then crumpled to the floor clutching his abdomen. Pain seared his back.

"Get up!"

When Yuri lay there, the guards grabbed his arms and dragged him to his feet. He hung limply between the two.

Tasting blood, he blinked and tried to clear his vision. The room spun.

"Now, will you admit your treason?"

Yuri shook his head no.

Enraged, the interrogator screamed, "Turn him around!"

Clearly knowing the drill, the guards rotated Yuri, pressed him against the wall, waited for him to get his feet, then quickly stepped away.

The inquisitor pounded his fists into the small of Yuri's back. "You will confess! Confess!"

Blinded by pain, Yuri couldn't have answered even if he'd wanted to. He pressed against the wall, wishing that somehow he could disappear into it. Sucking in oxygen, his fingers clutched a warp in the paint. His legs felt like jelly.

The pummeling continued, but Yuri didn't answer the man's accusations. Spinning him around, the interrogator's enraged face was only inches from Yuri's. Spittle clung to his lips, and excitement lit his eyes. "You will tell me what I want to know."

Yuri could smell garlic and wanted to vomit. He didn't answer.

This time the punches tortured his belly, but Yuri kept quiet. His legs nearly folded, and the room blurred.

Waving the paper in front of Yuri's face, the man screamed, "Sign!"

Yuri shook his head. Death would be better than giving in to this man. He would never concede.

The interrogator gripped Yuri's throat in his long bony fingers. His face contorted, he asked, "Do you want to die?"

Yes, Yuri thought, but it didn't matter. The pressure on his larynx cut off his speech.

"Tell me what I want to know, and you will live." He loosened his hold.

"I . . . I can't. I know nothing."

He cuffed Yuri with the back of his hand. "Tell me!"

"I know nothing. Nothing."

The man's eyes glowed like fire as he grabbed Yuri's hair and repeatedly beat his head against the wall.

Pain thundered through Yuri's head, then he went numb, and the room spun wildly as he fell forward. As if in a dark cocoon, he slipped into welcomed blackness.

Cold water splashed over Yuri's face, and he forced his eyes open. Seeing through a haze, he looked at the man who'd rendered his agony, then allowed his lids to close. More freezing water forced him awake. He stared into the evil, contorted face of his tormentor, and hate welled up. All he could think was how good it would feel to kill the man who stood sneering at him.

"You fool." He walked to his desk and gazed at his prisoner. "Take him back."

The two guards dragged Yuri out of the room and back to his cell. Opening the door, they shoved him inside. Yuri sprawled across the floor and landed beside the vile *parasha,* but he didn't care. Nothing mattered. He heard the cell door slam. It sounded far away. Then he felt gentle hands lifting him. Tenderly, the way his mother had done when he was a child, he was carried back to his place on the bench and wedged between two men. The men pressed their bodies against his and held him there. After that Yuri lost consciousness. When the guards brought the porridge in the morning, his cell mates woke him and helped him to eat.

After that the guards came for Yuri often. Each time the vicious interrogator demanded a confession. When Yuri refused, he beat him, clearly taking pleasure in the task. Yuri knew in his heart to confess meant execution. And he refused to give this demon the satisfaction of conceding, even if it meant dying beneath his punishing hands.

One day the cell door was swung open, and all the men were herded out. *Now what?* Yuri wondered, pushing himself up from the bench. He hobbled toward the door. No one seemed frightened or agitated. Careful to keep his head down and his hands behind his back as required, he followed the others through the compound. They shuffled to an outside courtyard. Yuri blinked, nearly blinded by the brightness of the sun. The cold air hit his lungs. Still, he took deep breaths, sucking in all he could. After being locked in the filth for so many days, the fresh air felt like food for his soul, and he couldn't consume enough.

"Heads down, hands behind backs!" came the orders as they were lined up outside a wooden structure. Yuri's anxiety grew. The door opened, and they were driven into another room single file. Yuri's cell mates began to strip off their clothes, including their shoes. He did the same. They hung them on a rack. A few minutes later, a guard came in and rolled the rack away. Yuri wondered what was happening but didn't dare ask.

Another guard entered, carrying a pair of hair clippers. "Line up!"

The prisoners silently complied and, one by one, the man worked his way down the line, clipping hair. He not only shaved the hair from their heads, but all over their bodies, including their underarms, legs, and chest. Yuri recoiled at the invasion. He closed his eyes as the man snipped him all over. Soon the room was a sea of hair. Feeling bare and exposed, Yuri shivered.

"Line up!"

Again the men did as they were told. After entering a bath house, the door slammed shut behind them. Water spouts dotted the ceiling, and the men stood beneath them. When streams of water poured from the spigots, they were either hot or cold, never warm. The men moved from one to the other. Yuri did the same, shivering beneath one, then being scalded under the next. Blood ran down his body and colored the water. His wounds burned.

The men began to talk. And they did so with relish, trying to make up for the endless hours of silence. The man who'd been sitting on Yuri's right for days held out his dripping wet hand. "My name is Vikenti Bondarenko."

Taken off guard, Yuri didn't know how to respond. Finally he smiled, took his hand, and shook it. "Yuri Letinov." He thought it strange how the introduction sounded so "normal." He almost laughed when he considered how it would have looked to an outsider, naked men standing in the showers greeting one another and chatting.

"We have only a few minutes. So far you have withstood the interrogations. To confess means death. They will execute you if they think they have a reason."

Yuri nodded. "I know." He scrubbed his head, then looked at the man. "Does it ever stop?"

"Sometimes, but then they always begin again." He shrugged. "I have not been interrogated for many days. Maybe if I am lucky, they will leave me alone."

"How long have you been here?"

"How does one know? Weeks, months, maybe years." He closed his eyes and turned his face into the water, letting it wash over him. Goose bumps raised on his pallid skin. He scrubbed his face with his hands, then looked back at Yuri, his eyes cold. "I will die before I confess anything to them." His loathing was clear.

Yuri understood. He'd struggled against his own hatred. Sometimes it felt good to hate, but he knew it would destroy him. Clinging to his faith, he'd refused to allow hate to rule.

The water stopped, and the guard returned. The men were marched out. Their steaming clothes waited, but no one moved toward them.

"Dress!" the jailer shouted.

Quickly the men pulled on their pants.

Yuri grabbed his but nearly dropped them. They were so hot they burned his hands. Gingerly he slipped his wet legs in, the material roasting his newly shaved skin. His shirt was the same, and his shoes even worse. His toes cooked inside the leather.

Hanging onto his pants to keep from losing them, Yuri followed the others back to their dark cell. There he sat on the bench beside his comrades and resumed his silence.

CHAPTER 19

Dimitri shifted his weight from one foot to the other. He looked at the large clock on the wall. *Four-thirty! I've been waiting eight hours! And nothing!*

A burly man pushed his way to the front and leaned on the counter.

"Hey! Get back in line," another man yelled. Others joined in. "What d'ya think you're doing? Wait your turn."

Ignoring the clamor of disapproval, he bellowed, "The paper said you had jobs! I've been here since eight o'clock this morning, and you haven't handed out one single work slip."

The gray-haired receptionist looked up and peered at the big man over small round glasses. "I'm sorry, sir, but we have no control over what comes in," she said in a snippy tone. She went back to typing. A moment later, seeming to regret her harsh manner, she looked up and said more kindly, "Sometimes the orders come late in the day." She glanced at the clock. "There's still time."

Looking dejected, the man returned to his place.

When the telephone jingled a moment later, the room quieted, and people leaned forward a little to listen. Those just outside the door crowded in.

The woman picked up the black receiver. "New York State Employment Department. May I help you?" She listened and wrote down notes, then hung up the receiver. "I need a typist," she called out.

Several women scrambled to the partition. Quickly filling out work orders, the secretary handed them to the five closest women. "Wagner's needs a temporary typist. All the information is on the slip."

Heels clicking against the tiled floor, the women rushed out of the office. Those not chosen watched them leave, despair etched on their faces.

Dimitri sighed as he took two steps closer to the counter. He needed work, any work. Since losing his position with Mr. Meyers, he'd found infrequent, one-day jobs. Sometimes he shined shoes for a few cents a day. Even his father, Pavel, was working fewer hours. The bakery had cut back because of lack of business. Like many shops the bakery faced the possibility of having to close its doors. If that happened Dimitri didn't know what his family would do. As it was, little work was available for young men. His father, at forty-three, faced an even tougher challenge if he lost his present job.

Dimitri combed his hair back with his fingers. The family was barely hanging on. That morning, when he scooped out coal to feed the fire, he discovered the bin was nearly empty. *There might be enough for another week or two. After that we'll have to scour the railroad yard for pieces dropped from the coal cars.* The thought sickened him.

Last month his family had struggled to come up with the rent, and he didn't know what they would do about this month's payment. *We could end up on the street like so many others,* he thought. The cupboards were empty more and more of the time. He shook his head. The last of the mush had been doled out at breakfast. There was nothing left except a few condiments. Dread filled Dimitri as he realized he and his family would have to face the humiliation of standing in a soup line that night if they wanted to eat.

He glanced out the front window. A light drizzle fell. *If only the warm weather would come. Then I could start my rooftop garden.* Winter lingered, and the warmth of summer days was still far away. Nighttime freezes blanketed the city; if Dimitri put out plants now they would die. He would have to wait.

The shrill ring of the telephone reverberated through the office and pulled Dimitri from his thoughts. The secretary snatched up the telephone. With the receiver cradled between her chin and shoulder, she wrote something on a notepad. With a crisp, "Thank you," she replaced the phone in its cradle. Peering over the counter, she looked at the anxious unemployed. "I need two men for bricklaying."

Dimitri stepped forward with several others.

The woman pointed at the two in front of him. "You and you." She held out work papers.

Greedily the men grabbed the papers and hurried out the door.

The woman glanced at the clock. "I'm sorry. That's all today. It's closing time."

Grumbling, the crowd quickly dissipated. Heavyhearted, Dimitri ambled outside. He looked up at the dark sky. Heavy clouds blanketed the tallest rooftops. He pulled his hat down tighter and tucked his hands inside his coat pockets. *Now what?* Shoulders hunched, his eyes on the sidewalk, Dimitri headed toward home. There was nothing more he could do today. He passed a boy hawking newspapers. *I don't even have enough to buy a paper,* he thought, his dignity smarting.

When he reached his tenement, he sat on the stoop. He wasn't ready to tell his family he'd failed again and that they would be standing in a soup line for their evening meal. With his elbows braced against his knees, he rested his chin in his hands and watched the people passing by. Now and again a friend waved and said hello. Dimitri tried to smile and wave back.

"Hi," called Samuel as he climbed the steps. The boy grinned. "Guess what?"

Dimitri forced a smile. "What?"

Samuel held out his hand, palm up, and displayed a nickel and one penny. "Bottle money. The man paid me two and a half cents each for the jumbos and one cent for the stubby."

"You did well, little brother." Dimitri tousled the boy's blonde hair.

"Me, too," said Ella as she sat beside Dimitri and showed him a penny. "I found one, too."

Placing his arm around the girl's shoulders, he said, "You two did much better than I."

Samuel sat on the other side of Dimitri. "Tomorrow's another day. You'll find work."

"I hope you're right."

"What is all this?" Augusta asked, standing at the bottom of the steps.

"Hi, Mama," Samuel said. "We sold some bottles!"

"What kind of bottles? Have you been selling to the bootleggers again? I told you never to have anything to do with those men."

"Mama, prohibition was repealed in December," Dimitri said.

"Oh, that's right. I forgot." She looked at the children. "So, what kind of bottles did you sell?"

Samuel looked at his feet and said quietly, "Beer bottles."

A cloud passed over Augusta's face. "Who did you sell them to?"

Samuel glanced at his mother, then at Ella. "The only man who wanted them is the one who owns the tavern. We sold them to him."

"You went into the tavern?" Augusta's voice sounded shrill.

"We had no choice."

"You took your sister into a bar?"

"No. She waited outside while I went in."

"You know you're not to go into those places. You purposely disobeyed."

"I'm sorry. I just wanted to help."

"Up to your room right now. I'll hear no more."

Looking dejected, Samuel stood and walked down the steps. Holding out the coins, he said, "Here. They're for the money jar."

Looking contrite, Augusta took the change. "Thank you." Ella skipped down the steps and gave her mother the penny, then followed her brother inside the building.

Dimitri stood and waited for his mother, a half grin on his lips. When she reached him, he affectionately rested his arm across her shoulders. "Samuel and Ella did nothing wrong. They're just trying to help."

"I know. I was too harsh, but I don't want them spending time at the tavern. There are all sorts down there." She trudged up the steps and stopped at the landing. "I'll talk to them." Looking at Dimitri, she asked, "Any work?"

"No. Nothing."

With a soft smile she patted his hand. "You'll find something. Be patient."

"I can't be patient. Soon we'll be out on the street. We have no food, we're out of coal, the——"

Augusta raised her hand. "Enough, Dimitri. We must trust God. Worrying will accomplish nothing." She opened the door. "Maybe Tatyana found something today. She's a fine seamstress and an even better cook." She smiled up at Dimitri. "She'd make a good wife."

"I know that very well. But I don't think she's interested in being *my* wife."

"Now, what makes you say that? I think she likes you very much."

"She likes me, but like a brother, I think."

"I would not be so sure. Flora says she can always tell when someone's heart is turned toward another, and she says you two are meant for each other."

"You make her sound like a soothsayer. I didn't think you believed in such things."

"Just because someone is wise and has a good eye doesn't make her a fortune teller. And from what I hear, she's been right many times."

When they arrived at the apartment, the aroma of baking greeted them. "What is that smell?" Dimitri asked.

Wearing a bright smile and wiping her hands on her apron, Flora walked into the front room. "The most remarkable thing happened today!" she said in Russian.

Dimitri bent and kissed the older woman. "And what is that?"

"When I went for a walk earlier today I passed by the bakery, and a man inside was giving away food! Imagine offering food to strangers. He gave me a bag of flour and sugar, and half a pound of butter!"

"Praise God," Augusta said. She looked at Dimitri. "Didn't I say we needed to trust him?"

"And that is not all," Flora continued. "He also gave us a ham!"

"Who was he?" Dimitri asked.

"I do not know. But he said he wanted to share his bounty with others."

Pavel walked in. "What is that wonderful smell?"

"Dinner," Augusta said, planting a kiss on her husband's cheek. "It is a gift from a stranger and from God. What a blessing!"

Whimpering came from beneath her husband's coat.

Augusta stepped back and eyed a suspicious bulge. "What is that?"

Pavel smiled sheepishly. "It is nothing, only a little dog." He reached in and pulled out a tiny puppy with big brown eyes, a bristled tail and fur to match.

"Pavel, not again." She studied the small creature. "What are we going to do with a dog? We can barely feed ourselves."

"He is starving. I found him in the alley. I couldn't leave him." He gently stroked the animal's head. "If we don't take him in, he will die."

Samuel and Ella peeked out of their room. "What is it, Papa? What do you have?"

"Come. Come and see."

They glanced at their mother, who nodded consent, then bounded across the room to their father.

"He's cute!" Ella squealed, letting the puppy lick her fingers. "Can I hold him?"

"No, I was here first," insisted Samuel. He took the pup and cuddled him against his chest. The whelp wiggled and licked, wagging his spindly tail as fast as he could.

"See, the children love him, and he loves them," Pavel said.

Augusta sighed. "Pavel, we can't feed him. And do you remember what happened last time?"

"We'll keep him indoors and always use a rope when we take him outside. And this time, we won't let him near the street," Samuel pleaded. "Please, can we keep him?"

"We cannot have a dog." Augusta folded her arms across her chest, then made the mistake of watching the ecstatic animal. "He's not even cute," she said, her voice softening.

"He is too." Ella snatched the puppy away from her brother. "Look at his sweet brown eyes. I'm sure he'll be very goodlooking when he grows up."

"And when he grows, he'll eat even more."

"He's never going to be very big," Pavel assured Augusta. "I'll share my portion with him. And, you always say we need to trust God for everything. Don't you think he cares about this young creature? He won't let us starve, and there will be enough for him, too."

"He's not our responsibility," Augusta said, but her voice had lost its determination.

Pavel patted the puppy's head. "He won't be any trouble; I will see to it."

"Pavel, sometimes you are more child than man." Augusta smiled tenderly. "You would take in a hungry vulture if you thought he needed help."

Pavel circled his arms around his wife and grinned. "And you love me for it."

She stood on tiptoe and kissed his cheek. "All right. You may keep him, but I won't feed him if it means taking food away from my own family."

Pavel hugged Augusta.

Ella jumped up and down, the puppy's head bobbing with each leap. "Thank you, Mama, thank you!" She looked at the wiggling creature. "What should we call him?"

"He should have a good name, one that means something special," Flora said. "I was just hearing about a man named Theodore Roosevelt. He used to be a president? He sounded like a fine man."

"Theodore?" Samuel asked, curling his lip in distaste. What kind of name is that for a dog?"

Ella stroked the pup's head. "What about Teddy? I think he looks like a Teddy."

"That is a fine name," Pavel said. He took the puppy and held him at arm's length. "So, Teddy it is. Hello, Teddy."

What is this?" Tatyana asked as she walked in the door. "It sounds like a party."

"We have a new family member," Dimitri said. "Tatyana, meet Teddy."

Pavel held up the dog for her to see.

"He is so little. Where did you get him?"

"You know Papa. He found him in the alley," Dimitri explained.

That evening the Broidos gathered around the table and thanked God for his blessings. They dined on savory ham and fresh bread with melted butter. It was a feast.

Teddy lay beneath Pavel's feet, where the family passed tidbits to him.

The following morning Tatyana was the first one up. The room felt cold, and she pulled her quilt around her as she shuffled to the coal bin. She scooped out a few pieces, dropped them into the stove and, using wadded paper, lit them.

Lying on the couch, Dimitri pushed himself up on one elbow. "We're almost out."

"Why did Augusta not say so?"

"I think she's waiting for one of her miracles," he said as he struggled into his pants, taking care to keep himself covered with his blanket. Flinging the quilt back, he grabbed his shirt off the back of the davenport, pulled it on, and buttoned it.

Tatyana shivered. "It is cold." She went to the window and peered out. "Snow! It is snowing!" She turned and looked at Dimitri. "Does this happen often in March?"

"It's not exactly common."

"In Russia snow in spring is normal." She pulled her wrap tighter. Dimitri tromped to the kitchen. He peered into the percolator. Soggy grounds from the past two days remained. "We can reuse these. The coffee will be weak but drinkable." He ran water into the pot and set it on the stove. "It'll take a few minutes." Heading for the door he said, "One day, I swear, I'll live in a house that has its own privy." Stepping out into the hallway, he was careful to close the door quietly so as not to awaken the others.

Bundled in her blanket, Tatyana sat at the window and watched the white flakes float past. Snow probably still covered the ground at home. She knew the farmers would be watching anxiously, waiting for the melt so they could begin their planting. Since she hadn't heard from her family, she had written to the Milns, hoping they would be able to contact her relations, but still nothing. What was happening? Something was wrong; she knew it. Lately her mind had been troubled by thoughts of her brother. Each time she thought of him, fear knotted her stomach. *Oh, dear Yuri, I pray you are well.*

The splutter of the percolator was the only sound in the tiny apartment. The aroma of coffee filled the room.

"Smells good," Dimitri said when he returned. He lifted the lid of the coffee pot. "Looks done enough. Would you like some?"

"Yes. Thank you."

He poured them each a cup and handed one to Tatyana, then sat at the table. "Sometimes, it seems winter will never let go." He sipped the weak brew and wrinkled his nose. "I think this is the last time we can use these grounds."

Tatyana sampled hers. "It is not so bad." She looked at Dimitri. "You look sad. Is something troubling you?"

"You have to ask? I can't find a job, we barely have enough coal to keep us warm another week. We have no food, and I can't even have a decent cup of coffee. I think that's enough."

Setting her cup on the table, Tatyana pulled her knees up close to her chest and snuggled beneath her blanket. "We have food."

"For the next few days. Then what?"

Tatyana shrugged. "I do not know, but something will happen. And you are not the only one who has no job. I am looking and not finding. It is not so bad as you think." She sighed. "Life could be worse. At least we can hope for better days. Some people do not have even that."

Dimitri took a deep breath. "I guess you're right." He gazed out at the falling snow. "I just feel useless. I don't know what else to do. I wait in the lines at the employment office day after day and nothing. What little work there is always goes to someone else."

"It will happen. You will see." She stuck one hand out of her blanket and picked up her cup. Taking a sip, she said, "We have not gone hungry yet, and summer is almost here. The farms will have crops soon."

"I don't know; the draught in the Midwest continues. There will be shortages."

"But you will have your garden."

Dimitri didn't answer. He just glowered at his cup.

"Dimitri, what is it? Always, you are the one who finds happiness."

He tasted his lukewarm drink. Taking a deep breath, he said, "I want more than this." Sweeping his arm in a half circle, indicating the apartment, he continued, "I want my own home and family." He looked at Tatyana. "I have nothing to give the . . . the woman I love."

Tatyana didn't like where this was leading and didn't want to hear it. She turned her eyes to the falling snow.

Dimitri drained his cup. "This week you, Mama, and the children will have to scavenge coal from the railroad yard just so we don't freeze. When last night's food is gone, we'll stand in soup lines again. It's not fair." His eyes turned tender. "I want more for you, Tatyana, for us."

Tatyana stood up. "I do not complain."

He took her hand. "You know how I feel."

Tatyana felt a shiver at his touch but quickly pushed aside her rush of emotions. She couldn't love Dimitri. One day she would return to Russia. That is where her future lay. Dimitri's was here. He would never leave. She couldn't let go of her dreams for his.

"Please, say no more." Gently she removed her hand from his. "One day, you will have a family. When times are better, you will find someone. I cannot love you, I will—"

Before she could explain, Dimitri stood up, his jaw set. Stiffly he walked to the door and took his coat from its peg. Shrugging into it, he grabbed the knob. Without looking at Tatyana, he jerked open the door. "I can't believe you don't feel something for me." Saying no more, he stepped into the hallway and slammed it behind him.

"I do care," Tatyana said to the empty room.

CHAPTER 20

TATYANA SLID THE BLUE RIBBON beneath the box, wrapped it around the sides, and tied it in a bow at the top. She patted it gently. Holding the package at arm's length, she studied it. "This is plain," she told Flora. "I wish I had special paper. "Does it look all right?"

"It is beautiful," the older woman answered in Russian.

"You are sure?"

"Your bow is perfect. And what really matters is what is inside. You have made a feast for the lucky man who bids highest." She glanced at Dimitri. "Maybe someone we know very well will share lunch with you?" Her eyes sparkled.

Dimitri acted as if he didn't hear and continued reading the paper.

"It might not go to him. Maybe someone else will bid." Tatyana felt a momentary discomfort. In the days after expressing his feelings for her, Dimitri kept to himself and was quieter than usual. Tatyana wanted to help, but there was nothing she could do. She considered trying again to explain why she felt as she did but decided it was finished and best left alone. Any more explanations would probably only heighten his distress. And she doubted there was anything she could say that would help him understand. So she waited, careful to remain friendly and approachable.

After finding work as a warehouseman at the wharf, Dimitri seemed to brighten, and gradually their friendship had warmed with the passing weeks. The encounter was not mentioned again.

She looked back at the box. "It is not a special lunch."

"That is not true," Flora said indignantly. "You are a wonderful cook."

Tatyana smiled. "Thank you. We did have corn beef and bread for sandwiches. And Mrs. Wikstrom gave me fresh strawberries for a pie, but it's not very big." Lapsing into Russian, she closed her eyes and said, "One day I will have a garden full of strawberries. And I will pick all I want."

"Didn't you get some peas from Dimitri's garden?"

"Yes."

"They will be a special treat—so sweet."

"I hope whoever buys this lunch likes them."

Flora patted her hand. "Don't worry. I'm sure he'll like it all. The most important thing is that we will be helping the church and community with the money that's raised."

Augusta breezed through the room to the stove. She pulled the oven door open and bent to remove a casserole she'd been warming. "Is everyone ready to leave?" She wrapped the dish in a heavy towel. "I hope this stays hot."

Tatyana smoothed her cotton dress.

Augusta looked at the young woman. "You are lovely. I think the lavender in that frock brings out the green in your eyes."

"Thank you for the fabric."

"You should thank Mrs. Clarno. When she offered it to me, I knew it was perfect for you."

"When I see her, I will tell her. A dress should not be so important, but it is good to have something new."

Careful to protect her hands with the towel, Augusta grasped each end of the casserole dish. "She has been very good to us. I was hired only as a housekeeper, but all the time she is giving me something.

"This family owes her a great deal," Flora said, insisting on speaking in Russian.

Dimitri looked at the woman, his arms folded and a grin on his face. "I thought you were supposed to speak English."

"I am too old to learn."

"You'll never make it here if you don't."

"I am doing just fine so far."

Enough, enough," Augusta said. "You leave your aunt alone. She will speak English if she wants to. Now, it is time to go." She nodded toward the chair in the front room. "Could you carry those two quilts?"

Dimitri picked up the blankets and laid them over his arm. "I'm looking forward to this. I've been saving my appetite." Eyeing Tatyana's box, he patted his belly.

Augusta circled her arm around Tatyana's shoulders. "She has made a special meal for *whoever* bids highest." With a knowing smile, she added, "Did you bring your money?"

"I've been saving. And it is a real sacrifice," he added with a grin. "My job could end any day." He opened the door, holding it for the women. "Where are Papa and the children?"

"They went ahead to help set up chairs and tables."

"I told Allison we would meet her there," Tatyana said.

Dimitri followed Tatyana into the hallway and closed the door. "Allison is amusing. It will be good to see her. How did she know about this? She rarely goes to church."

"I asked Mrs. Wikstrom to invite her."

"Is she coming too?"

"No, she said she is too old for such things. I think she would have fun, but work is all she knows."

When they arrived at the church, Allison was waiting for them outside the front entrance. "Good day to ye'," she called and waved. She stepped off the brick porch and tumbled forward, only keeping her chin from meeting the concrete by throwing her hands in front of her face. She pushed herself upright and brushed the dirt from her scuffed palms.

Dimitri hurried to her. "Are you all right?" He reached down and took her hand.

"Aye. Oh, dear, I'm so clumsy." She stood, brushed her skirt, and straightened her hat. "Thank ye', Dimitri. It seems I canna' learn to keep me feet under me. I'm always dropping something. I'll be lucky to hang on to me job at the manor."

"Are you still having trouble?" Tatyana asked.

"Aye, sometimes I think Mrs. Wikstrom believes I'm cracked."

"No. I do not believe that."

"If I was her, I would."

Dimitri looked at his mother. "Would you like me to carry that?" He nodded at the casserole.

"No. I'm fine."

"What did you make?"

"Oh, it is just the recipe I got from my mother—cabbage with beef."

"Mmm, one of my favorites."

"Mrs. Clarno gave us the roast. She's a blessing."

"Well, you are a good worker. I am certain she appreciates you," Flora said.

Dimitri looked up at Tatyana. "Do you think after I eat your lunch I'll have room left for some of Mama's casserole?"

Tatyana smiled smugly. "Maybe that is all you will have."

Flora laughed. "You will have to pay dearly for Tatyana's lunch."

Dimitri looked at the older woman. "Aunt, English, please, English."

"I am Russian," is all she said as she hurried toward the church entrance accompanied by Augusta.

"One day I will convince you that speaking English is good," Dimitri called after her.

"It's not so easy to learn a new language," Allison said.

"Difficult, yes, but not impossible." Dimitri turned and looked at Tatyana, a mischievous gleam in his eye. "So, did you pack my favorite foods?"

"Why do you . . ." Tatyana searched for the right word, "persist? Someone else might be the one who eats it."

"It will be me," he countered with a grin and held out his arm.

Tatyana took it without a word.

A fancy automobile pulled up to the curb. Tatyana's breath stopped for a moment. It looked like Reynold Meyers's car. *Don't be silly. Why would he be here?* She exhaled in a rush.

A chauffeur who looked very much like the one who worked for Mr. Meyers stepped out. With a snappy stride to the back door, he opened it.

Tatyana gripped Dimitri's arm.

Looking as arrogant as she remembered, Reynold Meyers stepped out. He straightened his jacket and looked about. When he found Tatyana, he leveled a steady gaze on her, then smiled boldly. He merely glanced at Dimitri. With a nod of his head, he turned and walked into the church.

"I didna' believe he would do it."

"Do what?"

"Come here. He said he would, but I canna' believe me eyes."

"How did he know about this?" Dimitri asked, irritation in his voice.

Tatyana grabbed her friend's hands. "You knew?"

Allison nodded.

"Why? Why would he come here?"

"All I know is he overheard me talkin' to Mrs. Wikstrom, and he said he'd be joinin' us, but I never really thought he would."

Tatyana looked up at Dimitri. "What do you think he wants?"

"I don't know, but don't worry about him. There's nothing he can do to us now. We don't work for him anymore." Dimitri glared at the door where Reynold Meyers had just entered.

Although Tatyana knew he couldn't harm her, she still felt uneasy. *He must have a reason for being here.* She stared at the church, her anticipation gone. She'd just as soon board the next bus and return home.

"Let's go in," Dimitri said resolutely.

Taking a deep breath, Tatyana straightened, threw her shoulders back, and walked toward the church. Allison did the same.

Dimitri smiled down at the ladies. "So Allison, is your friend, uh . . . Johnny going to be here?"

"Yes, but he had some business this morning and said he might be a wee bit late." She smiled brightly. Lowering her voice nearly to a whisper, she said, "I think he wants me to marry him. Anyway, he's hinted at it." She lifted her basket. "I made all his favorites."

"Hello there!" came a shout from across the street.

"Hello, Johnny," Allison said, wearing a bright smile as she turned to face him.

The wiry young man loped across the street and joined the threesome. "Boy, this is weird, me going to church. Religious pursuits have never been my cup of tea." He grinned and took Allison's arm. "Hope you made something good."

Allison blushed. "And how d' ye' know ye're the one who's going t' share me lunch?"

He patted the bulge in his back pocket. "I came prepared. No one will outbid me." He took his wallet out, opened it, and flashed several bills.

"Where did ye' get all that money?"

"I've been saving." He stuffed the cash back in the billfold and, with a snap, closed it. Tucking it in his pocket, he grinned. "Like I said, I plan to make it big one of these days. Soon I'll be rolling in the dough."

"And what happens if you're wrong?"

"I'm not."

"A little cocky aren't you?"

"No. Just sure of myself." He squinted at the sun. "I'm thirsty. Let's see if there's something to drink inside."

For the next hour, Tatyana, with Dimitri close beside her, visited friends. Mrs. Hazeldon, a sweet but very chatty spinster, talked endlessly about her family, some of whom still lived in Russia. Tatyana tried to look interested. The woman always prattled on about the same things, plus she shot the words out of her mouth like bullets from a gun, making it difficult to understand her. Tatyana caught only some of what she said but smiled and nodded politely whenever she thought it was appropriate.

She made certain to keep a safe distance from Reynold Meyers. She found him watching her more than once. Each time she acted as if she hadn't noticed and continued to visit with those around her. But she found her anger growing as he moved about the room. He wore a smile and visited openly, clearly making a good impression on the parishioners. Tatyana wanted to tell them what he was "really" like.

"That Mr. Meyers has a lot of gall showing up here," Augusta said as she sipped her punch. "I can't believe his nerve. After what he did?"

"Now, Augusta," Pavel said, "you have told me many times that God loves us all. And we're to be charitable even to those we think don't deserve it."

Augusta folded her arms over her chest. "Well, it tries the soul. Sometimes I am not as strong as I should be. And I think God understands." Saying no more, she continued to watch the man.

The weather was unseasonably warm for June, and soon the hall was stifling. Tatyana decided that some fresh air would be rejuvenating, so she stepped outside. A short, brick wall ran between the sidewalk and a tiny lawn alongside the church. The building protected the area from the sun. Tatyana sat on the wall, thankful for the shade. There was little traffic in this area of town, and the clamor of the city seemed far away. A soft breeze washed over Tatyana's bare arms, cooling her. Enjoying the quiet and feeling refreshed, she took a deep breath and closed her eyes.

"Do you mind if I join you?" Reynold Meyers asked, sitting beside her.

Startled, Tatyana looked at the man, uncertain what to say. She glanced back at the church and wished Dimitri would come looking for her. She scooted a few inches away from the interloper. "You may sit. This is free country."

"Hey, I like that—free country. I never thought of it quite like that."

Tatyana didn't respond; she just stared at the empty street. For a long while, neither spoke.

Unable to stand the silence any longer and angry at him for intruding, Tatyana finally asked, "Why are you here?"

"Well, when I heard about this it seemed like a good thing to do on a Saturday afternoon. I had some free time and—"

Tatyana turned and met his eyes. "That is not a true reason."

"No, I guess it isn't." He plucked a blade of grass and twirled it between his fingers. "Actually, I wanted to speak to you." Stripping away a section of the grass, he continued, "The house has been empty without you. I was wondering—"

"What is it you've been wondering?" Dimitri interrupted, his voice hard.

Reynold glared at Dimitri as he stood up. "If I wanted to talk with you, I would have asked you to join us."

Dimitri ignored the comment. "What concerns her concerns me."

Nearly as tall as Dimitri, Reynold squared his shoulders and glared at the big Russian. Ignoring the question, he grinned insolently and said, "I heard Tatyana is a fine cook. I plan to find out for myself."

Dimitri's face reddened, and he set his jaw. Glaring at his former employer, he said in a slow, decisive voice, "She'll be sharing lunch with me."

"Is that right? I heard the meal and the lady's company went to the highest bidder." Reynold looked Dimitri up and down. "It doesn't appear your station in life has improved. So I wouldn't count on the pleasure if I were you."

Inwardly Tatyana cringed at Dimitri's pained expression. Quickly retrieving his composure, he met Reynold's gaze. "I told you she's having lunch with me."

Tatyana stood up. "Stop. Both of you, stop. You act like spoiled children." Without another word, she hurried back inside the church, wishing she'd stayed home.

Augusta grabbed Tatyana's hand. "Oh, I'm glad you're here. They're ready to start bidding. I was beginning to worry you would miss the auction." She glanced around the room. "Where is Dimitri?"

"Outside," she said, her voice shaking a little.

Augusta looked more closely at Tatyana. "What is wrong?"

Keeping her eyes on the auctioneer, Tatyana said, "Nothing."

"You are not telling me the truth."

"I do not want to talk of it," she said as she glanced at the door. What would she do if Reynold Meyers did buy her lunch? She couldn't bear the idea of sharing another meal with the man.

The auctioneer held up the first lunch. It was a lovely box with delicate flowered paper and a matching bow. After reading the owner's name from a label, the bidding began and two men vied for the privilege of sharing the meal with the woman who had prepared it. When the bidding rose to $2.50, one of the suitors dejectedly sat down, and the box was handed to the higher bidder. He accepted the package with a smile and left with a pretty, dark-haired woman Tatyana barely knew.

When Allison's box was held up, the young Irish woman stood close to Tatyana. Gripping her friend's hand, she said, "Mine isn't nearly as pretty as the first one. It's so plain. Do ye' think anyone besides Johnny will bid on it? And I canna' cook very well. Plus, I'm as plain as my package."

Tatyana looked at the nervous girl. "You are not plain. Your eyes are very pretty."

The auctioneer began the bidding at twenty-five cents. Allison's attention was riveted on him. Johnny was the first to bid. Then a man Tatyana didn't recognize countered.

"Who is he?" Allison asked, gazing at the pudgy man dressed in an expensive suit.

"An admirer?"

"I don't know him."

A bidding war began, and the tension mounted between the two men. Clearly more was going on between the two than a simple rivalry over lunch. When the stranger finally bid $11.50, Johnny faltered. He glanced at Allison, raised his hand, and called out twelve dollars."

"Do I have another bid?" The stranger fidgeted but kept his hands stuffed in his pockets.

Slamming his gavel on the bench, the auctioneer called the bidding closed and awarded Allison's lunch to Johnny. With a broad grin, he took the lunch and held it above his head. He glanced at the man who had bid against him and nodded slightly. Striding up to Allison, he said, "It took nearly every penny I've got, but I did it."

"Oh, Johnny, you spent so much. You shouldn't ha'."

He placed his arm around her shoulders. "Anything for you." He held out his arm for her.

Blushing and smiling demurely, Allison took it and allowed him to escort her outside.

The bidding continued, and Tatyana felt sick to her stomach. What if Mr. Meyers bid on hers like he'd said? *Maybe I should leave,* she thought. *No, that would be cowardly.*

The auctioneer sold four more lunches before he came to Tatyana's. He held up the white box with the blue ribbon and read her name from the label. "And how much am I bid for this meal? I hear Tatyana is a fine cook." He winked at the young woman.

She could feel her face redden. Her fingers intertwined, and she forced herself to remain still.

"Anyone would be lucky to share this meal," the auctioneer continued.

Augusta nudged her in the ribs and grinned.

"So, I'll start the bidding at—"

"Twenty-five dollars," Reynold Meyers said, raising his hand. An audible gasp went up.

For a moment the auctioneer looked befuddled; then he smiled. "That's very generous, sir." He held up the box half-heartedly and scanned the crowd, stopping at Dimitri. "Are there any other bids?"

Dimitri glared at Reynold Meyers, then gave Tatyana a helpless look.

"Going once, going twice . . . sold to the gentleman in back."

Reynold quickly walked to the front and retrieved his prize. Holding it close to his chest, he crossed the room to Tatyana.

She wanted to run away but managed to remain still.

He approached her and bowed slightly. "So, I am to have the pleasure. Where would you like to eat?"

Dimitri joined them and stood beside Tatyana.

"I tried to tell you how it would be," Reynold said with a smirk.

The big Russian looked as if he might hit the man.

"Please, Dimitri, go with your family."

With one last hateful glance, he walked away.

Fuming, Tatyana looked at her unwanted companion. He didn't care a whit that his behavior hurt others. How could she tolerate him through an entire meal?

"So, where do we go?"

"In back, there is grass and trees."

Possessively he took her arm and steered her outdoors.

"I . . . I brought a blanket," Tatyana said, crossing to the table where Augusta had left it. She glanced at Allison and Johnny who sat beneath a tree, oblivious to the other picnickers.

She rejoined Reynold after retrieving the quilt.

He stood in the center of a grassy area. "Is this all right?"

"Yes," Tatyana said as she spread the blanket on the ground.

Reynold waited patiently while she straightened the corners, then set their lunch in the center. "I'll get us some punch," he said and headed back inside.

Disappointed and angry, Tatyana sat down. This was not what she'd had in mind. She glanced up to find Dimitri staring at her. Wearing a scowl, he sat with his parents, brother, sister, and Flora at a table several yards away. Augusta seemed more animated than usual and flashed Tatyana a quick smile. *I wish I were sharing lunch with them,* she thought.

"Here you go," Reynold said, handing a glass to Tatyana.

She took the drink. "Thank you."

He folded his legs and sat down. "So, what did you make me?"

Tatyana gritted her teeth. "I did not make for you."

"So, who did you have in mind?"

"I . . . I do not know, but not you."

He picked up the box and fiddled with the bow. "When you prepared this, you understood the rules. It would go to the highest bidder."

Tatyana looked squarely at the contemptuous man. "Yes, but you do not play fair. You have more money than these people."

"You are saying it is wrong to have money?"

"No. But you use your money to control people and get your way. You know Dimitri cannot bid against you."

"So, that is who you made it for."

Tatyana could feel her anger grow. Taking a deep breath, she tried to calm herself. She glanced at her unwanted companion. "Why did you bid on mine?"

"I wanted to have lunch with you," he said casually.

"That is not the truth."

Reynold studied another couple, then looked at Tatyana. "As I began to tell you earlier, I want you to come back to work for me." He set the box lunch down and straightened his tie.

Tatyana's anger overflowed. "You attack me, then fire me and Dimitri, and you want me to return?"

"I'm sorry for the way I behaved in Chicago. I was a rogue, I admit it. I'll not push myself on you again, if that's what you're worried about." He reached out and took her hand.

Tatyana wiggled it free of his grasp.

"The house is not the same without you."

"I cannot."

"Please reconsider. Times are hard, and I know you must need the money."

"We are fine."

"Oh, yes, I can see that," he said sarcastically. "It seems you are all doing very well. You work yourselves into the ground and never have enough to eat."

"Why do you care about such things now?"

He glanced at the ground. "When I fired you I was angry. In spite of what you think, I'm not heartless." He looked at Dimitri. "He seems very taken with you."

"We are friends." Tatyana untied the ribbon around the boxed lunch. Carefully she opened it and took out a half sandwich. Handing it to Reynold, she said, "You must be hungry."

He took the sandwich, but instead of eating it, he asked, "What is it you want, Tatyana?"

"What do you mean?"

"What do you want out of life?"

"You want to know?"

"Yes, I do."

She thought a moment, surprised at the question. "I would like to go back to Russia and rejoin my family."

"What if it doesn't happen?"

Tatyana thought a moment. "Then, I pray God will change my heart."

He bit into the sandwich and chewed slowly. "You believe he cares?"

Tatyana looked straight at Reynold. "Yes, I do."

"I've been in church all my life, and I've seen that those who take care of themselves are the ones who make it, not the ones who stay on their knees praying."

"It is not always what you see on the outside that matters, but what is in a person's heart."

"Sounds like foolishness to me."

"Maybe one day you will understand."

Reynold stood up. "I doubt it." Taking his pocket watch out and glancing at it, he said, "I have a meeting I need to go to." He tucked the timepiece back in place. "Why don't you donate the rest of my lunch to your friend?" He looked at Dimitri. "I'm sure it will cheer him up." He tipped his hat and walked away.

Tatyana watched him go, wondering what had just transpired. What did Reynold Meyers want?

CHAPTER 21

PAVEL TURNED THE KNOB ON the radio. "I hope it comes in clear today." The receiver crackled, and a man's voice came across the wireless. He was selling soap. Pavel smiled. "Ah, there it is." He looked around the room. "Where are Samuel and Ella?"

"They've gone out to play," Augusta said. She shook her head. "Children are more interested in hopscotch and stickball than music."

Pavel straightened and crossed to the sideboard in the kitchen. He took down his pipe and a tobacco pouch. Carefully measuring out a pinch of the crushed leaves, he dropped them into the bowl and tapped them down. "There is nothing like a good smoke while listening to Guy Lombardo or Rudy Vallee." He smiled as he took a match from its tin and struck it against the side of the container. Holding it over the pipe bowl, he sucked hard, then took two quick successive puffs. A plume of smoke drifted toward the ceiling. Shaking the match out, he dropped it into an ashtray, returned the tobacco and matches to the shelf, and strolled back out to the small front room. Settling into his overstuffed chair, he clenched the pipe between his teeth and rested his head against the cushioned back.

A harmony of women's voices brought the soap commercial to an end, and the announcer said, "Good evening, ladies and gentlemen. Welcome to this evening's 'Hour of Music.' Tonight's broadcast is sponsored by Spring Breeze, the fragrant soap for the entire family. I hope you're ready for the sweetest music this side of heaven, because tonight we bring you melodies from Guy Lombardo and his band, the Royal Canadians."

As the theme song played, the mellow voice of Mr. Lombardo came across the radio. "Thank you for that kind introduction. Good evening, ladies and gentlemen. This is Guy Lombardo coming to you from New York City. We hope you like our selections this evening. Please, just sit back and enjoy."

"He sounds like such a nice man," Augusta said as she slipped her embroidery needle through ivory-colored material.

The exaggerated vibrato of saxophones blended with the clipped tones of brass, and sweet, rhythmical notes spilled out into the airways. Teddy climbed onto Pavel's lap and snuggled against his slightly paunchy stomach. "See, even the pup is soothed by the music," he said.

Augusta rocked her chair in unison with the beat. "I love his style. One day we should go dancing."

"In Russia we have nothing like this," Flora said, her knitting needles flying. "We have only the symphonies to listen to on the phonograph. They are lovely, but this, this is special. I like it very much."

Tatyana struggled with the intricate pattern on a slipcover. "I cannot do this right," she said, plunging her needle through the material. She held it up to the light and studied it. "Oh dear, it looks terrible. Now it will have to be redone." She let the sewing rest in her lap.

Augusta offered her an encouraging smile. "Don't give up, dear. You'll get it. We all struggle sometimes."

"My mother was a very good . . . sewer? Is that the right word?"

"Seamstress is correct," Dimitri explained.

"Oh, seamstress, then. Mama teach me, but I did not have so much trouble before." She rested her head against the high back of the rocker. The melodic sounds of "Star Dust" swept over her in a calming wave. "My mamochka would like this very much, I think."

"Maybe one day she will come to America," Pavel said.

Tatyana looked at the man who had taken on the role of father to her. "I do not think she lives. After the soldiers took her, she never returned."

He nodded sadly, leaned forward on his knees, and puffed on his pipe.

"There is always hope," Flora said with an encouraging smile.

Augusta set her embroidery aside and stood up. "I think a cup of tea would be nice."

"I'll help," Dimitri said.

"Thank you. Would anyone else like some?"

Everyone nodded.

With the rich sounds of the band playing, Tatyana returned to her sewing. As the soothing tones of a trombone came from the radio, she looked up and asked, "What is that?"

"A trombone," Pavel explained.

"It sounds different than I have heard before. One day I would like to watch a band, to see the music."

Pavel laughed. "You cannot see music."

"I mean watch the music players."

"There are clubs here in the city," Dimitri said from the kitchen. "Bands play there. Maybe we could go."

"I would like that." Tatyana looked at her surrogate family. "And maybe you would like to also?"

Augusta dumped tea into a piece of cheesecloth. "That would be fun." Looking at Pavel, she smiled. His eyes were drooping. "But, I think he will not stay awake long enough."

After the radio program ended with "Goodnight Sweetheart," Tatyana excused herself to escape the heat of the apartment. She took the stairs to the rooftop. As she opened the door, she immediately felt the refreshing early evening breeze. It was always cooler here late in the day. The garden greenery kept the rooftop shaded, and the lush plants gave it a tranquil feel, a stark contrast to the indifferent steel gray of the city's concrete. The roof had no barriers, and the wind moved freely. A gust caught Tatyana's hair and swept it across her face. She brushed a strand out of her eyes.

Sitting on the edge of a planter box, she was surrounded by the smell of damp earth and living things. The city seemed far away. Tatyana loved spending time here. Under Dimitri's tender care the garden had flourished, and although it was a far cry from her farm at home, it still reminded her of where she had come from and where she planned, one day, to return.

The last of the peas still clung to the vines. Tatyana plucked a plump pod and, running her thumb down the center vein, popped it open. Green orbs spilled into her hand, and she tossed the sweet meats into her mouth and chewed.

She pitched the empty pod back into the soil, and her eyes followed the sprawling string bean tendrils inching up guide wires. In the next box, small green tomatoes hung from sturdy plants, promising an abundant harvest of juicy fruit later in the summer. Carrot tops had sprouted in a nearby box, but it would be many weeks before they would be ready to eat.

Tatyana remembered how many of the tenement residents had worked alongside Dimitri when the seeds and tiny plants had been placed in the soil. Like so many others in the city, the people in this building lived with hunger, yet remarkably, no one filched any of the fruits or vegetables. In many ways the garden had become a community project. The tenants respected Dimitri and his efforts, and his reputation for generosity. He often shared the yield with his fellow lodgers. Those living in the building frequently helped Dimitri tend the plants.

Tatyana took a deep breath and walked between the carefully cultivated planter boxes. *God blesses hard work and generosity,* she thought, wondering if Dimitri really understood how his behavior had brought God's blessings to them all. Turnip greens rustled in the breeze. Tatyana reached down and brushed dirt from the root. Grasping the stem, she gently wiggled it back and forth, then pulled it from its earthen bed. She wiped away the dirt, exposing white skin. Its musky smell greeted her, and her mind carried her home. She closed her eyes, trying to bring the farm into focus—the weather-worn barn, stacks of hay in the field, and Yuri and her parents digging in the soil. The image seemed so close. Suddenly a siren screamed, pulling her back to the present.

She walked to the edge of the roof and gazed out at the city. The sun lay low in the sky, its light shattered by haze. Six floors below, a woman walked her dog, unaware of Tatyana's scrutiny. Yanking on the animal's leash, she moved with short, brisk steps. Tatyana was struck by how everyone always seemed in a hurry. *Why are we in such a rush?*

"It's nice up here, isn't it?" came Dimitri's strong voice.

Tatyana jumped. "Oh, you scared me. I did not know you were here."

Taking long strides, he joined Tatyana and leaned on the roof wall. They gazed silently at the city for a long while.

His voice quiet, Dimitri said, "Sometimes, I wonder what is happening out there. I think about the people and what they might be facing—their joys, hardships, new babies, deaths . . ." His voice trailed off. He glanced at her, then turned his eyes back to the city. "Sorry, I didn't mean to get so morbid."

"Morbid? This means what?"

"Oh, you know, sad, gloomy."

"Oh." She looked at Dimitri. "You are the least *morbid* person I know. You help us all feel happy." She followed his gaze. "Sometimes I think about what is happening out there, but always my mind wanders across the sea to Yuri." She propped her elbow on the brick wall and rested her chin in her hand. "I think of Uncle Alexander, Aunt Irina, and my cousins Lev and Olya, and . . ." She shook her head. "There are so many, I cannot name them all. I do not even know if they live."

She turned and looked back toward the garden. Reverting to Russian, she said, "Americans think life is hard, but they do not know true suffering. In Russia there is unimaginable affliction. Most here have not known real hunger. In Russia I have seen starved bodies lying dead beside the road or in yards. I have known mothers who have mourned the loss of not just one child but all of their children." Her eyes brimmed with tears. "I saw my own mother and father ripped from our home." She wiped her tears. "Here there is hope, but in Russia," she hesitated, "I do not know." She sniffled and forced a smile. "And yet I love my homeland. There is so much beauty there."

Gently Dimitri put his arm around Tatyana's shoulders. "I'm sorry life has brought so much sorrow to you. It makes my own grumbling sound trivial."

"That is the way of humankind."

Dimitri straightened and smiled. "You said you would like to see a band. Why don't we go and listen to one?"

"Now?"

"Uh huh."

"But it is late."

"It's still early. I know of a club not too far from here. It's not a fancy place, but it has good music."

Tatyana smiled. "All right. We will go."

Dimitri walked protectively beside Tatyana. His arm brushed hers, and she wished he would give her more space. She knew it was only because he cared about her, but it still made her own resolve not to care for him more difficult. She moved over and walked close to the building fronts.

The traffic had quieted by the time they crossed the street to the club. Dimitri led her down a stairway that led to a scarred door below street level. A small neon sign, announcing the existence of the nightclub, flashed above it. He opened the door and allowed Tatyana to enter ahead of him. A man stood just inside the door. He studied the newcomers, then nodded for them to enter.

The smoke-filled room was already crowded with patrons. Most were talking loudly or laughing. A bar on the far wall with a mirror behind it and a row of stools in front was jammed with people. Small, round tables were scattered haphazardly, and Dimitri steered Tatyana toward one just left of the stage.

"This is a good spot," he said and pulled out a chair for her.

Tatyana quickly sat down. Feeling her excitement rise, she scanned the room. "Everyone seems very happy."

"That's probably the liquor."

Tatyana gave him a puzzled look.

"Some people drink a lot when they come to these places."

"Oh." She smiled. "My Uncle Alexander would like this place."

A man with a small white apron tied around his waist stood at their table. "Is there anything I can get you?"

Dimitri looked at Tatyana. "Would you like a drink?"

"Yes. A lemonade?"

"We don't serve lemonade, ma'am."

"It's a little different here," Dimitri explained.

"She'll have a root beer?" He looked at Tatyana and she nodded. "I'll have a beer."

"I did not know you drink liquor. That is right? Beer is liquor?"

"Yes. But it's not as strong as some of the drinks and not something I do very often."

The band members began to assemble on stage and pick up their instruments. Some musicians blew into their horns; the drummer gently tapped his drums; and, a man with a string bass plucked the strings. The combination of sounds made a terrible racket.

"Looks like they'll be starting soon," Dimitri said, leaning back in his chair.

A man dressed in a pin-striped suit stepped onto the stage. He stood in front of the microphone and thumped it, sending a squealing sound echoing around the room. Seeming satisfied, he said, "Ladies and gentlemen, it is good to have you here tonight. We have a special treat for you." He made a half turn so that he was partially facing the performers. "All the way from Saint Louis, please welcome the Calloway Brothers!"

Applause broke out, and the announcer stepped off stage. The men readied themselves. The bass player leaned over his instrument, the drummer held his sticks over the drums, and the others put their woodwinds to their lips. On cue they began to play, tapping their feet to the beat. The sounds of trumpets, saxophones, and clarinets mingled with the soft thumping of the cello and the beat of drums. Tatyana could feel the gooseflesh rise on her arms and couldn't keep her toe from tapping. Unable to contain her smile, she leaned close to Dimitri. "They are wonderful. Are they really brothers?"

Dimitri laughed. "I don't think so; it's probably just a stage name."

"Oh," Tatyana said and returned to watching them. A minute later she leaned toward Dimitri again. "Thank you for bringing me."

Dimitri smiled broadly and nodded.

The band played one song, then another and another. The dance floor filled with patrons. Tatyana watched, enthralled. This was nothing like watching a ballet or the symphony. And the dancing was not at all like the folk dances she'd done back home. It looked fun. She wished Dimitri would ask her. He didn't move but sat watching and smiling. *It would be rude to ask him,* Tatyana decided, so she forced herself to remain still and enjoy being a spectator only.

A tall, slender man approached their table. He bowed slightly toward Tatyana and asked, "Would you care to dance?"

She looked at Dimitri. "Is it all right?"

Dimitri's mouth was set in a line and, after taking a good look at the intruder, he turned his eyes back toward the stage. "If you want to dance, you should."

The man held out his hand.

"I do not know how," Tatyana said.

"I'll teach you," the stranger said with a warm smile.

Feeling unsure, she took his hand and followed him onto the polished floor. "I cannot," she said and turned to retreat.

The man tightened his grip. "It's not hard. Just follow me." He circled one arm around her waist, took her right hand in his and, swaying to the music, moved across the dance floor.

At first Tatyana felt awkward and clumsy. She didn't know any of the steps. But her partner was a good dancer, and gradually she caught on simply by following his lead. As she gained more confidence, he became bolder in his moves and soon they twirled around the room. Tatyana laughed when he dipped her, then flung her back into his arms. Abruptly the song ended.

They stood side-by-side and clapped along with the others. Another song began, and before she knew it, Tatyana was again swinging into step with his arms around her. She glanced at Dimitri and felt a pang of uneasiness at his gloomy expression. *Maybe I should stop,* she thought, but the music seized her, and she ended up sharing one more dance with the stranger before insisting he return her to her table.

Sitting across from Dimitri, she felt guilty for leaving him alone so long.

"You looked like you were having fun," he said.

"It is fun. Why do you not dance?"

"I don't know how."

"You should learn." She took a long drink of her root beer.

"Ah, it's not something I really want to do."

"I feel bad dancing so long. I should have—"

"No, you did nothing wrong. I'm glad you're having fun." He drained his second beer. "Are you ready to go?"

Tatyana nodded.

Dimitri took her hand and led her outside. Night had fallen over the city, and the cool evening air felt good.

Tatyana took a deep breath. "The smoke inside was bad. This is better."

"It's getting late," Dimitri said and, taking her arm, turned toward home. With a contemplative expression, he walked silently beside her.

"What are you thinking?"

"Nothing special." He turned onto an unfamiliar street. "Let's take another way home." He continued on, still unusually quiet.

Finally, Tatyana asked, "Is something wrong?"

"No. Well, yes. I don't know. I . . . I need to talk to you." He continued walking. When they came to a bench, he stopped. "Let's sit here a while." He sat down, and Tatyana joined him.

"What is it?" she asked, afraid to hear what might be bothering him, but unable to leave him so troubled. She studied a trickle of water running along the edge of the curb. It swirled into a pool just before disappearing down a grate.

Dimitri rested his arms on his legs and, with his hands clasped, stared across the street at a sign posted over a pharmacy, blinking the word *closed*. He straightened, cleared his throat, and turned to Tatyana. Taking her hands in his, he looked straight into her eyes. "Under the street lights your eyes sparkle like emeralds."

"Please . . ." Tatyana moved to stand up, but Dimitri gripped her hands tighter, holding her there. Tatyana forced herself to relax her muscles and sat back.

"Don't speak until I'm finished, please," said Dimitri. He cleared his throat. "Tonight as you danced, you looked so beautiful and happy. My love for you welled up, and I wanted to tell you. I can't hide how I feel anymore. I can't pretend you're only my friend. I've tried, but it does no good. Do you have any idea how strong my love is? I want to spend my life with you. To take care of you. To have children with you." He swallowed. "If I can't have that, I don't think I want to live."

"Dimitri . . ."

"Wait, I'm not finished. You say you don't love me, but I've seen it in your eyes, heard it in your voice. You can't deny it."

Tatyana watched a piece of crumpled paper tumble down the street, carried by the wind. What he said was true, but she couldn't admit that to him. It would only make everything worse. How could they have a life together? They were on completely different paths. How could she make him understand?

"I'll find a better job, and we'll make a home together. My family already loves you." He waited for a man to pass. "I want to marry you. Will you marry me? Please say you will."

Tatyana's heart felt like it would break as she looked at the handsome Russian, his face etched with pain. She didn't want to hurt him and wished she could say yes. Blinking back a rush of tears, she swallowed past the lump in her throat. "Dimitri, please don't ask me."

"What is it you want me to do?" he said as he wrapped his arms around her, pulling her close. "Tatyana, we are a perfect pair. I know we are meant to be. I've known it since the first time I saw you at the wharf."

His arms felt good. She wanted to cuddle against him, to allow him to love her and take care of her, but it would only intensify the hurt that would inevitably come. Gently she pushed against him. "Dimitri, I cannot lie. I do have feelings for you."

Dimitri brightened.

"But, we cannot marry."

"Why? If you love me and I love you, why not?"

"We cannot love. It is impossible. I am Russian. You are American. I cannot change who I am, and you cannot change who you are."

"But I am Russian."

"You came from Russia, but you have forgotten your homeland."

"I can change. I'll be anything you want."

Tatyana shook her head. "No. It is impossible." She looked at the thread of water and wished it were a river that could carry her away. Anything would be better than looking upon Dimitri's anguish. "One day I must return to my Russia." Her hand shaking, she wiped away her tears. "I do not fit here. Americans are very different. Sometimes they are rude and silly, and they spend too much time thinking about money." She reached out and touched his hand. "Even you sometimes," she added with a smile. "But you are also kind and gentle and loyal. I do not want you to change."

Dimitri looked stricken. "What can I do to make you change your mind? I will do anything."

"You are a good man," she said, then looked down the street. "But you know I do not belong here." She met his eyes. "One day I *will* leave."

"How can you go back to that place?" He spat out the words as if they were bitter.

"It is not easy to understand even for me, but I am tied there. I am . . . incomplete here. I love my country. I honor it. And my family is there. When the ship left Leningrad, I stood on deck and watched my homeland disappear. My heart began to ache. It has not stopped." Tears flowed. "The only way to end the pain is to return." She stood up. "I cannot say yes."

"People only remember the good about the past. They forget how bad things were. Home won't be the same. What you see in your mind isn't there any more. Until you let go of what was, you will never be able to live today."

"No. My answer is no," she cried. Pressing her hands over her ears, she ran toward home.

CHAPTER 22

YURI FORCED HIS EYES OPEN. THE cell floor pressed against his cheek. *I confessed,* he thought, and shame welled up. He'd given in and done as they demanded. But he wanted to live. Last night's beating had been the worst. He knew he would die if he didn't do as they asked. Sweat mixed with blood stung his eyes.

He rolled partially onto his back, his body screaming at the small movement. Gritting his teeth, he bent his legs and tried to roll over and push himself to his knees. He needed to get up and sit on the bench or face another beating.

Viktor, the man who'd sat beside him for months, stood over him. Gently he took Yuri's hands and pulled him to his feet. Biting back a scream of pain, Yuri tried to help, then slumped against his friend. Viktor slowly edged back to their place on the bench, allowing the young Russian to lean against him.

When the porridge was poked through the small window that morning, each man shaved off a piece of his own and added it to Yuri's bowl. Gratefully he shoved the food into his mouth, but the image of his shaking, bloodied hand scribbling his name across the bottom of the confession plagued him. He'd probably be executed. His weakness had won him nothing but an extra day in this hole.

Maybe I am guilty, he thought. *Maybe I am a counterrevolutionary.* He wasn't sure anymore. The life he'd left behind seemed like a dream—events, places, and friends, a muddled memory. Elena's elegant face haunted him. Was she still living, or was she on the edge of life in a cell like this one? *Oh, I want you to be alive,* he thought.

Bruised and battered, his eyes were slits, and he struggled to keep his place on the bench. As he'd done for months, he stared at the spot on the door. He avoided the *parasha* as long as he could, knowing his water was blood. He didn't want to face the truth. He would probably die no matter what they did to him.

Months before, when he'd taken his place on this bench, he'd shivered with the cold. Winter raged outside, but the radiators gave no warmth. Now with the summer heat pressing down on the city, they put off heat day and night—another cruel game the administrators played.

With the warmth, the damp fur covering the walls became denser and so did the horrid pests. They were relentless, never giving rest to the afflicted. Sleep became additional torture as tiny creatures scrambled over their victims, feasting and leaving painful, itchy welts. Yuri did his best to keep his mouth clamped shut while sleeping. Occasionally an inmate would cry in anguish as he worked to dislodge an insect that had found its way inside an ear. Yuri was spared this agony.

Even after the beatings stopped, Yuri still fought his demons. He wondered when the guards would come for him and when his execution would take place. Some days his confusion was so profound that he wondered if he'd gone mad from the endless silent hours in the dark. On these days death seemed to be the only reasonable escape.

One day the door opened, and a guard pointed at him. "You. Come."

This was his time. He knew it. Fear swept over him. He stood on weak, shaking legs and hobbled to the door. He knew he would never return to this place. With a look at his cellmates, he said a silent farewell. Many of the faces had changed since his first day. Some had died and been replaced by others. And there were those who had been taken away to a fate one could only guess at. He wanted to thank them for their kindness toward him but, without a word, he stepped into the corridor, and the door slammed shut.

The guard shoved a grimy, typewritten document into his hands. Yuri stared at the paper, his vision blurred. He held it up toward the feeble light. It read, "The Special Board of the NKVD has reviewed your case and, for your counterrevolutionary crimes, you have been sentenced to ten years hard labor."

His arms fell to his sides, and the paper drifted to the floor. Ten years. *How could he survive ten more years?* What kind of man would he have to be to endure?

The guard shackled his hands and jabbed his shoulder with the cell key. "Move! Head down, hands behind your back."

Yuri forced his legs to carry him forward. They felt detached. He stumbled and fell.

"Get up!" came the order.

Yuri pushed himself to his feet and moved on. The transport waited outside. He was crammed inside a tiny locker and could hear the whimpers and groans of others. The sounds seemed distant and unreal. All he could think about were the words he'd just read: "You have been sentenced to ten years hard labor." The back door slammed shut, and the vehicle moved away from the prison. There was no escape.

His body crushed inside the small locker, his mind whirled with questions. Would the camp be better or worse than prison? He'd known only one man who'd survived and returned home. His eyes had always looked haunted, and he'd never talked about what had happened to him. Yuri's empty stomach cramped with hunger. Would there be more food in camp? And where was he assigned?

Elena's face filled his thoughts unexpectedly. He wished he'd told her how he felt. Now she would never know. "Elena, Elena," he whispered. He squeezed his eyes closed. "I pray your fate is not this." A deep ache burrowed into his chest. Trying to force it away, he opened his eyes and stared at the metal wall. Tears dribbled down his cheeks, onto his chin, and fell at his feet. "God, where are you?" he cried.

The van stopped, and Yuri could hear as one by one the prisoners were yanked out of their cells. Standing at the railroad station, the men and women huddled together. Yuri looked at the scorching sun, then closed his eyes, still seeing a yellow ball behind his lids.

With shouts of, "Head down, hands behind backs, no talking!" the guards yanked the prisoners apart and forced them into a line. They were marched through Moscow Station.

Yuri glanced up. The last time he'd been here was when he'd sent Tatyana to America. It had been a lifetime ago. As he walked past the platform where they'd embraced, an irrepressible moan escaped his lips.

The guard hit him across the back with his rifle. "Head down! No talking!"

Yuri lurched forward but kept his feet. He glared at the ground, hating the guard.

The prisoners filed past waiting trains. When they reached the outskirts of the station, Yuri saw the prison car, a *Stolypin wagon.* It would transport them to a labor camp. The side facing Yuri had steel-meshed windows running the entire length. Soldiers walked back and forth, their rifles ready to squelch any rebellion.

"Halt!"

Yuri and the others stopped. The women were separated and herded to another car.

A guard unlocked the door and jerked it open. "Line up!" Everyone did as told. They were shoved into the wagon one at a time. Yuri struggled up the catwalk and stumbled into the overcrowded car. The windows lined one side only, allowing little light to penetrate the transport. They were sealed shut. Thus there was no movement of air, and a foul smell permeated the room.

A row of cells crammed with prisoners lined the other side. Each compartment had four bunks, two lowers and two uppers. Obviously the pen had been built for four men, but at least fifty were packed into each, and the new prisoners were to be added.

Panic welled up in Yuri. They would be crushed. How could any man survive in the horde of people without being trampled or suffocated? He studied the top bunks. They were the safest and probably provided a little more air. Prisoners already claimed them and were clearly ready to defend their positions.

The emaciated face of a man with compassion-filled eyes floated into view in the sea of faces. Yuri stared at him, drawn by his benevolence. The man smiled kindly. Yuri didn't know what to do, so he looked away. But something about the stranger pulled at him, like an anchor of sanity amidst the madness. He looked again and found the calm eyes. His own terror lessened.

The man spoke. "Don't lose hope. Just believe."

Someone grabbed Yuri's arm and shoved him into a cell. When he looked, the man was gone. As Yuri was propelled forward he was nearly knocked off his feet. He struggled to breathe as bodies pressed against him and pushed him deeper into the enclosure.

Yuri found himself next to the wall and gratefully leaned against it. Men crowded in. Yuri couldn't move, and his panic grew. He would suffocate! Taking a deep breath, he told himself, *No, you can breathe. Be calm.* He looked about him and wondered what would happen if someone died. There was not even enough room for him to fall. *Maybe some are already dead,* he thought.

For hours the captives stood, crushed against each other. The train remained at the station, and the sun beat down on the car. "Please open the windows!" someone cried. "Yes. Open the windows!" another added.

No one listened. The heat built up, and sweat drenched the prisoners. The air was heavy, and Yuri found it hard to breathe. His legs and back ached, and he longed to sit, to rest his head on his hands and sleep.

Yuri gradually made his way to one set of bunks and leaned against the metal post. It felt cool. A pair of legs dangled beside him. Before he knew what had happened, he grabbed the legs and jerked on them as hard as he could. A prisoner fell on the floor in front of him. Without thinking, and ignoring the oaths screamed at him, he scrambled up and took the man's place. Huddling next to the wall with his legs tucked against his chest and his arms wrapped around them, he couldn't believe what he had done. Stunned by his actions, he felt disgust at himself. *What have I become?* he wondered, but he didn't move. With sweat trickling into his eyes, he leaned his head against the wall. *I'll just rest a little while; then I'll let someone else have my place,* he thought.

The man yelled more profanities at Yuri. Then he glared at him and blended into the crowd. Yuri felt sick at himself, but he didn't yield his place. He wanted to live. Afraid someone would yank *him* down, he watched the people around him, wary of a surprise assault.

As he studied the crowded cell, he could see some had already succumbed to their prison deprivation and the heat. Bodies lay beneath the feet of those who still lived.

The car jolted and lurched forward. The clanking sound of couplings stretching then collapsing startled Yuri as the train eased forward. Gradually they picked up speed and rolled out of the station. Yuri pressed himself tighter against the wall, squeezing his emaciated body between two others. He laid his head back and closed his eyes. He dozed for a moment, but jolted himself awake, afraid of what would happen if he were to sleep. He blinked hard and forced his eyes open. *I must stay awake or I will never make it.*

"We're going east!" a man yelled.

"East! East!" the word spread through the car. Like a deadly virus, the men recoiled from the truth, their eyes filled with fear. Some knew where they were heading, but the fear of many simply fed on that of their prison mates.

Yuri knew Siberia would be their destination, but which camp he could only guess. He shuddered. The compounds were located at the outer edges of the world.

Many hours later, the train stopped. Yuri rested his chin on his knees, struggling to remain alert. The bodies of the dead were removed, carelessly handled like baggage. Some prisoners were taken off, others added. Bread was brought on board and distributed. Yuri grabbed his portion and shoved it into his mouth. The only water for the day was passed around in a tin.

After that they continued east.

As the hours passed, Yuri slept off and on and was surprised to find himself still intact on the bunk each time he woke. Realizing he would have to make a trip to the "toilet," he resigned himself to relinquishing his place. He climbed down and made his way to a hole cut in the floor of the car. Somehow the men managed to keep a clear space around the convenience.

The hours and days passed. Some prisoners visited quietly among themselves; others entertained themselves with games; and, some spoke to no one. Yuri kept to himself.

More died. Their bodies were thrown off at periodic stops, their deaths seen by the guards as no more than an inconvenience. Gradually the deceased gave the living more room, and Yuri was able to find a place against the wall to rest. Leaning there, he slept much of the time.

One day Yuri awoke to the sounds of a brawl. Immediately alert, he watched as two men attacked another. He recognized the men as the two criminals who had been harassing other prisoners since being loaded at the first stop. The bigger man, Ilya, held the victim's arms while Rufus, the smaller but meaner of the two, stripped off the man's coat. He shrugged into it with a grin. Gloating, he strutted in front of the onlookers. "When you bet and lose, you pay." Casually he removed the coat and held it up. "When winter comes, I will remember your generosity." He sat down and took a stone from his pocket. After a quick shuffle of the stone from hand to hand, he held out closed fists. "Now, which hand is it in? Make a bet."

No one moved. He focused on a prisoner already without a shirt. "Bet."

Grudgingly the man removed his shoe and set it in front of the trickster. He studied the closed hands.

"Hurry up. Hurry up. Pick one!"

The prisoner pointed at one closed fist.

With a grin, Rufus turned his hand over and opened his fingers. It was empty. "Better luck next time," he said gleefully and snatched the shoe. He tossed the stone back and forth between his hands. "All right, who is next?" He focused on a small man with hollow cheeks. "You."

The man stood up and started to walk away.

"Where are you going?" He shuffled the stone again and held out his clenched hands. "Bet."

"I'm not playing." The man turned away.

With unexpected speed, Rufus jumped up and grabbed him by the back of his collar, pulling it tight. "I say you'll play."

No one stepped in to help. The guards gathered outside the cell and watched but did nothing.

The man wrenched away from his attacker and turned to face him.

"Do you want to die?" Rufus asked.

The prisoner met his gaze but said nothing.

All of a sudden, Rufus grabbed a thatch of the man's hair, pulled his face down, and kneed it. The man fell, and Rufus jumped on him. He wrapped his hands around the man's throat and squeezed. His face turned red, and hate filled his eyes. His victim grabbed at his hands, but he couldn't dislodge them. He kicked and pulled, but in the end, he fell still, his lifeless eyes staring at the ceiling.

Rufus let him go and turned to look at the others. "Now, we will play." He glanced around at the onlookers. "You," he said, pulling another man to his feet. "You will bet."

Shaking, his eyes filled with fear, he quietly submitted. He sat and removed one sock, placing it in front of Rufus. The dead challenger lay where he had fallen. Rufus looked at his partner and, with a grin, tossed the stone from one hand to the other.

Yuri pressed against the wall. This was a deadly game, even without Rufus's cruelty. A man without clothing would die during a Siberian winter. He leaned his head back and closed his eyes. *God, if you are real, help us.*

All his life Yuri had believed in a Savior. He understood that knowing Christ didn't mean you were spared hardship. In fact, he understood that God used struggles to strengthen men's faith, but this suffering was beyond his endurance. The words, "When you are weak, that is when you are strong" played through his mind, but he couldn't hold on to their truth. He only knew he was weak and frightened. *I need strength,* he thought as the rocking of the train lulled him into a fitful sleep.

There was no real rest. Yuri's mind filled with frightening images—a man staring through dead eyes, a massive grave filled with bodies, the shadow of a guard behind a peephole. The loathsome images floated aimlessly. Out of the shadows his parents beckoned to him. He approached them, but no matter how hard he tried, he couldn't reach them. Each time he drew near they would move away. Again and again he tried to touch them, longing for their embrace, but he could never get close enough. Each unsuccessful attempt left him grieving. In his dream he cried, "Mama, Papa, I need you."

The shrill blast of the train's whistle cut into the illusion. The train braked and jerked as it slowed. Yuri tumbled sideways. It took a few moments for him to pull himself from the fantasy. He longed to return to it.

The cell doors were thrown open, and the car's gate slid aside. "Out! Everyone out!"

The prisoners climbed down and shuffled into a tiny station. Yuri didn't know where he was. He only knew that Moscow was many miles away, and Siberia, with it's yawning expanses, waited for him. He gazed at the flat tundra, bordered in the distance by an immense forest.

The guards divided the men into two groups, herded them into lines, then marched them toward the forest. Too quickly the station was swallowed up in the massive flat plain.

The prisoners were forced to walk hour after hour beneath the relentless summer sun. They were given no rest and no water. Yuri wondered if a giant pit waited for them in the forest, like the one he had faced near his home. Sweat ran in rivulets down his back and soaked the lining of his coat. But he dare not remove it or risk having it stolen. He longed for the shade of the trees.

As they came closer to the forest, Yuri could make out huge stands of pine and spruce. The evergreen giants offered welcomed shade, their heavy aroma sweet. Yuri breathed deeply, forcing one foot to follow the other as the guards pushed them on along the front edge of the timber.

One man fell.

"Get up!" a soldier yelled.

"I can't. Please, let me rest."

"Get up!"

The wasted prisoner lay with his face against the dry grasses. "I cannot."

Without warning, the guard leveled his rifle at the man and fired. Without even looking at the dead man, he moved on.

The men filed past the prisoner. Most averted their eyes. No one slowed his pace.

As they entered the shadow of the trees, Yuri looked for the place of execution. It didn't come. Instead, after only a short distance, a broad clearing emerged. In it stood a compound of squat barracks and other buildings. The entire complex was surrounded by a tall fence with barbwire across the top. As Yuri staggered through the gate, he left all hope behind.

The prisoners filed into a bath house much like the one at the prison. After removing their clothing, their body hair was shaved, and they were herded into showers. The water was ice cold. It splayed over the men who shuffled back and forth beneath the water spouts, unable to stand the cold for more than a few moments at a time.

Yuri rubbed his skin hard, doing the best he could to remove the filth. Still naked, he was forced into a line where a man grabbed each finger, pressed it against an ink pad, and then onto identification papers. He was handed prison clothing—a pair of heavy quilted pants and jacket, both black, and a pair of *leptis* or grass boots made from the underbark of trees. His coat had disappeared.

The men were divided into work crews and assigned to barracks. Yuri followed his workmates to their quarters. As he passed row upon row of squat, wooden barracks, he realized how large a complex this was. Each set of quarters must hold at least fifty men or more. He also noticed guards in high towers carrying machine guns.

Their escort stopped abruptly. "Inside. Find a bunk." The men filed past.

Yuri noticed a firebox and quickly took a bed close to it. Winter would descend soon, and being close to the heat would be important. He sat on a hard wooden bunk with a single thin blanket and a straw cushion. It was a place off the ground where he could actually lay down to sleep.

The man he'd seen on the train the first day took the bed next to his. He sat down and closed his eyes. His lips moved silently.

Yuri watched him and wondered if he was praying. *What do I care?* he thought and lay down, turning his back to the stranger. What good had religion done him? God had deserted him.

"So, do you know why you have been sent here?" the man asked, his voice surprisingly calm and gentle.

Yuri ignored the question.

"You are young. This must be very difficult for you."

Still, Yuri said nothing.

"I'm from Leningrad. You are from?"

Aggravated, Yuri finally rolled over and looked at the man. For a long moment, he said nothing. The stranger looked gaunt with deep-set, sorrow-filled eyes, but Yuri could detect no bitterness. Instead he found compassion.

The man reached out a large hand in greeting. It looked out of place against his starved body. "My name's Alexander."

The name stirred memories of Yuri's Uncle Alexander. He took the offered hand and shook it half-heartedly. "I am Yuri Letinov."

"It is good to meet you, Yuri."

The man swung his bony legs up onto the hard bunk and laid down. He was incredibly skinny. Yuri wondered how long he would live, then realized he hadn't seen himself in many months. He probably looked as bad. Sadly he thought, *If I returned home, no one would recognize me.*

"I saw you get on in Moscow. Are you from there?"

Yuri looked at Alexander. "Yes."

"You were in prison there?"

"Yes. Why do you care?"

"I just thought that if we will be doing hard labor together, we should know each other. Maybe we can help one another."

"There is no help for us," Yuri said bitterly, studying the man. "Why are you here?"

"I am a political. I was caught teaching a religious class."

Yuri sat up. "This is what I do not understand. If God cares, why doesn't he help his people? He's able to do all things. Why would he allow someone like you to be thrown away like this?"

"God never throws away his children. I am here for a reason. Everything is used for good for those who love God. If I trust and obey him, I will still have purpose wherever I am."

"I used to believe that."

"And now you do not?"

Yuri didn't answer. He didn't want to talk about it.

"We must remember the battle we fight is not against flesh and blood, but against principalities and powers."

Yuri felt like he'd been hit. How many times had he heard his mother and aunt quote that passage? Once he'd believed them, but now . . . now he didn't know what he believed. He felt forsaken, alone. How could he fight a battle that seemed impossible to win? The enemy was too powerful. "I don't believe God is real. If he is, he's deserted you and me. You are wasting your time believing he will help you."

His voice steady and strong, Alexander said, "It is you who have been deceived. The enemy has convinced you God does not exist. It is a powerful weapon. He uses it often. He has your ear, but you must not listen or he will destroy you."

Yuri laid back down and faced the opposite direction. Who was this man? He felt uneasy around him. Yuri decided he'd avoid the stranger. But he couldn't ignore the glimmer of hope that stirred in his heart at Alexander's words. He possessed so much peace amidst this hopelessness. *He still has his faith.* Yuri closed his eyes. *I wish I had mine.*

CHAPTER 23

DIMITRI RESTED HIS ARMS on his thighs and looked at his shoes. Holes ventilated the leather. He'd have to come up with some money soon. With a heavy sigh, he settled against the back of the bench and gazed at a flock of pigeons pecking at tidbits on the ground. Abruptly they lifted off the earth, their feathers beating the air, then soared in unison to a new patch. Dimitri thought it odd, the way they moved in one accord.

A pudgy little boy carrying a paper bag skipped toward the birds. They fluttered into the air, but as soon as the child reached into his sack, they settled back to the ground, just out of his reach. He tossed bits of stale bread, and the pigeons crowded closer, gobbling them up. He giggled and dropped more. When the bread was gone, the birds continued searching for crumbs, cooing and strutting, their heads bobbing back and forth. The child ran at them, and they opened their wings and sailed above the square. Circling a few moments, they landed several yards away, still hoping for a handout.

The boy's mother took his hand and led him to the nearby playground. He immediately found a friend, and the boys raced toward the big slide.

Dimitri smiled as they clambered up the ladder. The boy who'd been feeding the birds stood at the top, then sat down and pushed off. Lifting his hands, he glided to the bottom. Grinning and flushed, he quickly stood up and ran back to the ladder, intent on repeating the feat. Two girls squealed with joy as they pumped their legs hard, forcing their swings to soar. They relaxed and leaned back, allowing themselves to sway easily back and forth. Other youngsters balanced on a teeter-totter, laughing as they rocked up and down.

One day, I'll bring my own children here, Dimitri decided. He studied the mothers and fathers watching their little ones. They smiled proudly, their eyes rarely leaving the children, even as they visited with one another. *I will watch over mine that way,* Dimitri thought, a pang of sorrow settling in his chest as he realized it wouldn't be Tatyana who stood beside him.

Pushing the dismal feeling aside, he told himself, *I shouldn't be sitting here. I need to find work.* His job at the wharf had been a good position but temporary. He'd hoped it would last longer. Now, unemployed again, the household money dwindled as he searched for a job. Work was difficult to find. Even Pavel worked less than a day a week. If not for his mother's position at Mrs. Clarno's and Tatyana's occasional sewing jobs, no money would be coming into the house.

I have to find something, he thought, staring at his ragged shoes. *I should have bought myself a new pair while I was working.*

Two men sat on the other end of the bench. They nodded at Dimitri, then leaned back and watched the activity in the park. The larger and older of the two puffed on a cigar. It smelled good. Dimitri thought, *When times are better, I'll smoke a cigar whenever I want.*

"So, what do you hear from Al?" the older man asked.

"I guess he's still looking for work. But there just isn't any." The man shook his head. "He's willing to do almost anything. I checked, but there are no openings at the plant. In fact, they're talking about laying off more workers. There's nothing for decent folks to do, and more and more banks are closing their doors."

"I've taken to keeping my money in my mattress," the older man said as he chewed on the end of his cigar.

The younger man leaned forward and studied his hands. "Seems to me a big part of the trouble are all the immigrants. They're taking jobs away from us Americans. Why do they have to come here anyway? Mr. Roosevelt ought to close Ellis Island or at least deport some of them."

Taking a hard puff on his cigar, the other man said, "I think they should send them all back where they came from. Don't get me wrong. I've met some who are good people, but there's just no place for them here these days."

Dimitri clenched his jaw and closed his hands into fists. He stood up, ready to give them a piece of his mind, when a ball rolled between him and the men. A child ran after it. Dimitri bent, picked it up, and held it out to the youngster.

"Thanks, mister," the boy said and ran back to his playmates.

Dimitri glanced at the strangers. *They probably cherish their ignorance.* "Idiots," he muttered and headed toward the employment office. Standing there would probably be a waste of time, but what else did he have to do?

When Dimitri approached the office, he sensed excitement among the waiting people. They pressed close to the door and talked among themselves. He took his place, wishing he'd come sooner. "What is happening?" he asked a short, pudgy man in front of him.

"The CCC has openings. They're paying thirty dollars a month! And they're looking for strong, healthy men." He sized up Dimitri, and a look of discouragement crossed his face.

A secretary wearing a dark blue business suit stepped out the door. Pad and pen in hand, she looked down the line. "You, you, you, and you," she said, pointing at several men. They quickly left their spots and hurried inside.

She hadn't even looked at Dimitri. His frustration and discouragement grew. *Please, God. My mother is always telling me how you watch over us. If you are, I need you now.* The woman glanced down at her pad, then back at the unemployed. The man in front of Dimitri straightened, threw his shoulders back, and expanded his chest. She looked past him. "And you," she said, pointing at Dimitri.

Unable to believe his luck, he asked, "Me?"

The woman smiled. "You're certainly big enough, and you look sturdy. There's work for you with the CCC."

Work slip in hand, Dimitri strode toward home. He looked at the instructions again. In two days he was to take the bus to Grand Island, Nebraska, and report to the CCC camp there. He hated the thought of leaving home, especially Tatyana, but this was a good job. He would be making thirty dollars a month, and a mandatory twenty-five dollars would be sent to the family. The government provided room and board, so he'd have no worries.

Dimitri stopped at the front stoop of his apartment house and looked up at the building. In two days he'd be leaving the only home he'd known since immigrating. His mother would be hurt when she heard the news. "It's something I must do," he told himself and climbed the steps.

Flora stood at the stove stirring something in a pot. The smell of chicken soup filled the apartment. As Dimitri stepped inside, the dog vaulted around his feet, yipping excitedly and demanding to be picked up.

"Hello, Teddy," Dimitri said as he scooped the animal into his arms. He patted his head and stroked his fur while trying to avoid the dog's lapping tongue. Pinning him beneath his left arm, he crossed to the kitchen and wrapped his other arm around Flora. "Hello, Auntie." He planted a kiss on her cheek.

Flora smiled. "You certainly look cheerful," she said in Russian.

"I am. I have good news." He scanned the apartment. "Where is everyone?"

"Everyone is on the roof picking vegetables for our dinner." She reached out and caressed his cheek. "Bless you for the garden."

"It's nothing. I love working with the soil and plants. I wish I could do more."

"You do your best. Who could ask more?" Flora said gently and patted his cheek. "Now, what has happened?"

He glanced toward the door. "I have good news, but I want to tell everyone at once." He peeked inside the pot. "Mmm, smells good. Chicken?"

"Yes, I had some broth, and the family is bringing the vegetables."

"My mouth is already watering." He walked to the window and stared down the crowded street. Leaving his family would be painful, but such a good job couldn't be passed up. He'd have to make certain to tell his family all the good points about it.

"What has happened to your smile? You look worried," Flora said, setting her wooden spoon on the stove and placing a lid on the pot.

Dimitri gave Teddy one more pat, then set him on the floor. He looked at his aunt. She'd been a part of the family for only a little over a year, but it seemed she'd always been there. "Everything is fine. I'm just thinking."

The door flew open, and Samuel tramped in wearing a grin, his arms loaded with carrots and onions. "Look what we have for dinner." He held up the vegetables. "And we have a little corn, too!" He licked his lips in an exaggerated way. "I love corn. I wish we could have a great big garden with lots of it." He looked up at his father, who followed him through the door. "Papa, do you think one day we can live on a farm?"

Pavel's eyes looked a little sad. "We will wait and see. It is in God's hands," he said as he patted the young man's back.

Ella held three ears of corn by their husks as she stepped inside. Tatyana and Augusta followed close behind. One ear slipped out of Ella's hand and dropped to the floor. Augusta picked it up and carried it to the sink. Turning to her son, she studied him a moment. "What is it? What has happened?" Her voice sounded strained.

Dimitri grinned. "Good news, Mama. Please, everyone sit down, and I will tell you." He stepped into the center of the front room and waited for his family to gather.

Samuel set his vegetables in the sink. "What do you have to tell us?"

Dimitri motioned for him to join them. "Just come. Sit and you will find out."

Samuel plopped down on the floor beside his father's chair. Clutching the last two ears of corn, Ella took a place on the edge of the davenport. Augusta sat next to her and wrapped an arm around the youngster. She stared at her son, her eyes lit with apprehension.

Watching Dimitri closely, Tatyana sat beside Augusta, while Flora stood in the kitchen doorway.

Pavel perched on the edge of his chair. "So, what is it you have to say?"

Dimitri took a deep breath. "I got a permanent job today!"

His father jumped up and pounded Dimitri on the back. "Wonderful! Wonderful! I knew you would find something!"

Augusta smiled. "I am so happy for you! What kind of work is it?"

"I'll be working on bridges and highways."

"That sounds very important," Pavel said, beaming and obviously proud of his son.

"Who will you be working for?" Augusta asked.

"Dimitri scanned the faces, hesitating at Tatyana's. "The CCC."

"Where?"

"In Nebraska."

Stunned silence followed.

Dimitri rushed on. "It's a good job, and it pays thirty dollars a month!"

Looking stricken, Augusta quietly said, "Nebraska?"

"What is the CCC?" Tatyana asked, her hands clasped tightly in her lap.

"It stands for Civilian Conservation Corps. The government runs it and hires people to work in different parts of the country. You're given a place to sleep, and all your food is provided, too. They take twenty-five dollars out of your pay every month and send it home to the family." He looked at his mother. "It will help a lot, Mama. You won't have to work so hard. And imagine twenty-five dollars a month! What a difference it will make."

Augusta stood and walked to her son. She laid her hand on his arm. "I don't mind working. And even with the extra money, my income will still be needed. I just can't imagine you living so far away. Please reconsider. We can make it without this job."

"No, Mama. It's the right thing for me to do. I'm a man, and I need to work." He looked directly into her eyes. "I am going."

Tears brimmed in Augusta's eyes. Abruptly she turned and walked into the kitchen. "I'll make some tea."

Pavel looked serious, his face creased into a frown. "I understand, Son. It's something you must do." He shook his head. "We'll miss you."

"You're going away?" Samuel asked, only now seeming to understand what was happening.

"I have to, but I'll be back."

"When do you have to go?" Tatyana asked, her voice trembling.

"I catch the bus day after tomorrow."

"So soon?"

Dimitri shrugged. "That's when all the workers have to leave. But that means I'll be able to send money home sooner."

Nine-year-old Ella let the corn drop to the floor. She looked at it, then at Dimitri. "I don't want you to go."

Dimitri stooped and picked up the vegetables. "I wish I didn't have to."

He looked at Tatyana. She gazed at the floor and wouldn't meet his eyes. He wondered if his leaving would make any difference in how she felt about him.

As Augusta served the soup, the Broido family was quiet. With no more than a "thank you," they dipped their spoons into the hot broth. The sound of silverware clinking against the glass bowls sounded loud.

Pavel took a sip. "This is good, Flora. Thank you."

The old woman nodded and smiled.

"I've heard Nebraska is very different from here," Pavel continued. "They say it is flat, and there aren't many people."

Augusta hadn't touched her soup. "You make sure to wear your long underwear and . . . oh, I wish I had time to knit you a new hat. I heard Nebraska has very cold winters." She stirred her broth. "Maybe the church has some warm coats. I'll make a trip there tomorrow."

"Thanks, Mama," Dimitri said, hating how this was hurting her and wishing there were another way.

When they had finished, Augusta began to clear away the dishes.

Tatyana hadn't said anything during dinner, and she'd barely eaten. She stood and picked up her bowl.

"Tatyana, I was wondering if we could take a walk," Dimitri said.

Augusta took the bowl from Tatyana. "Please go. I will finish."

The evening air felt cool, and the city had quieted. Dimitri and Tatyana strolled down the nearly empty sidewalk. Dimitri longed to take her hand but refrained.

Tatyana took a slow, deep breath. "Fall is coming. I can feel it."

"They say we're going to have a hard winter this year." Dimitri's mind frantically searched for a way to say what he truly wanted to say.

"When I walk at night, sometimes I think I can smell the farm." She sighed. "I do not think I will ever stop missing it."

"The place you grow up always stays with you, I think. When I'm in Nebraska, I know I'll miss my home here. I don't remember much about Russia, except skating with friends and helping Papa cut wood. Most of the rest I know only because Mama and Papa told me."

As they approached the soda shop, Dimitri asked, "Would you like to go in and get something?"

"It is too much money."

"I have a little left, and now that I'll be making a good salary, I think splurging this once is all right."

Tatyana nodded. "All right."

Dimitri ushered her inside.

"We can sit at the counter?" she asked.

"Sure."

Facing the bar, they each sat on a stool, a strained silence separating them.

Dimitri was grateful when Bruce, the soda jerk, approached.

Wiping down the counter, then flipping the towel over his shoulder, he asked, "What will you have?"

"I would like a Coca-Cola," Tatyana said.

"Me, too." Dimitri looked at Tatyana. "I remember when you hated Coca-Cola."

"At first it tasted awful, but I like it now."

They watched while Bruce filled their glasses. He set the soft drinks on the counter, poked a straw into each, and slid them across the bar. "That'll be ten cents."

Dimitri dug into his pocket and plunked down a dime. "Soon I'll be able to buy you a pop any time."

Tatyana sipped her drink but didn't reply.

Leaning on the counter, Dimitri looked at her. "Day after tomorrow, I'll be leaving."

"I'll miss you," she said quietly. "I . . . I wish you were not going away."

"Yeah, me too. But, I'd be foolish to turn down such a good job."

Bent over the sink, Bruce looked over his shoulder at Dimitri. "So, you got a job, huh?"

"Yeah."

"Congratulations." He straightened and dried his hands on a towel. "Who you working for?"

"The CCC. I'll be going to Nebraska. They're building bridges and new roads. The pay is good—thirty dollars a month."

"Not bad. I know about a better job, though. My brother-in-law just sent me a wire, asking if I knew of any men who'd like to go to work for his lumber company in Washington State. It pays real good. He says a man can make $2.50 a day and some weeks they work seven days. That figures out to about $75.00 a month."

Dimitri stood. "No kidding? Seventy-five a month? A man could do a lot with that kind of money." He looked at Tatyana,

"Even take care of a family." He turned back to the young man. "How can I find out more about this?"

"Well, hang on a minute. I've still got the wire. I'll get it for you." He slipped through a door at the end of the counter and disappeared into a back room. When he returned, he unfolded a piece of paper. "I've been meaning to do something with this, but you know how it is."

Fearful the jobs were already gone, Dimitri asked, "How long ago did you get it?"

"A few days." He smoothed out the wrinkles and handed the paper to Dimitri. "I'd go myself, but I'm kind of attached to New York. I don't think I'd do well up in the woods."

Dimitri studied the wire. "Says here, they need several men, and they need them right away." He slapped the message down on the counter. "I'll take it!"

"Dimitri, what about the other job? Didn't you promise to work for the CCC?" Tatyana asked.

"Well, yeah, but this is a lot better." He drained his glass. "I can't believe I went so long without anything and now I have my choice of two jobs!" He looked at Bruce. "How am I supposed to get out to Washington?"

"That's easy. I owe my brother a telephone call. I'll talk to him tonight and make sure the job is still open. He said the company would pay the bus fare for new employees. I'm sure he'll be interested in you. You're a big fella. I bet you can fell a lot of trees in a day."

Dimitri grinned. "I like the sound of working in the woods, and I've heard Washington is a beautiful place." He took a deep breath. "Fresh air, tall trees, and open country! Sounds good!" He set his glass on the counter. "Tell your brother-in-law that if he's still looking, I'm available."

"I'll see if I can get through tonight and let you know tomorrow."

Dimitri stood up and shook the man's hand. "Thanks, Bruce. I'll be back first thing."

✳ ✳ ✳ ✳ ✳

Dimitri could barely contain himself as he walked toward the soda shop. He'd slept little through the night. All he could think about was the seventy-five dollar job offer. With that much money, he could save and still send money back to his family— perhaps even make enough to buy a real home so Tatyana would reconsider and marry him.

He pushed open the door and stepped into the shop. No one was behind the counter. "Bruce, you here?" There was no reply, so he paced the floor and waited.

A few minutes later Bruce came from the back room. "Morning. Good to see you." He reached out and shook the big Russian's hand. "Congratulations! You've got a job. My brother-in-law said he'd wire you the money and asked if you'd come out right away."

Dimitri couldn't believe his luck. He pumped Bruce's hand up and down. "Thank you! Thank you! Anything I can do for you, just let me know. I owe you."

"Nah, you don't owe me anything." He wiped down the counter. "I'm happy for you. My brother said he'll send all the information you'll need when he wires you the money."

Dimitri nearly ran home. It was all he could do to contain his excitement. When he reached the tenement, he took the steps three at a time and burst through the apartment door. "You won't believe it!" He grabbed his mother and spun her around.

Her spatula still in hand, she squealed. "Dimitri! Stop!"

He ignored her. "I got it, Mama. I got it!"

"I said stop!" Her voice sounded sharp, and this time Dimitri obeyed.

"I got a job working for a timber company in Washington State! It pays seventy-five dollars a month!"

"I thought you were working for the CCC in Nebraska."

"I was, but I heard about this job last night. I didn't want to say anything until I was sure. This morning I found out I got it, Mama. The company is sending bus fare, and then I'll be on my way."

"Washington? That's further away than Nebraska. It's almost on the other side of the world."

"It's a long way, I know, but I'll be making enough money that you can come and visit."

Tatyana walked into the kitchen, still half asleep. "You got the job?"

"Yes! And I leave as soon as the bus fare arrives!" He looked at Tatyana and remembered how many miles would separate them, unless he could convince her to go with him. "I'd like to talk. Could we?"

"Right now? I am not dressed."

"Yes, right now. Please."

Tatyana studied Dimitri. "All right. I will comb my hair and put on some clothes. I will meet you on the roof."

"Okay. I'll wait for you there."

"We meet in ten minutes?" she asked.

Dimitri nodded, and she left the room.

He met his mother's eyes, and the pain he saw there grieved him. He gave her a fleeting smile, then as casually as he could he stepped out into the hall, closed the door, and walked up the stairs to the roof.

CHAPTER 24

Tatyana took a deep breath and pushed open the door. She knew what Dimitri wanted. What would she do? Not until he told the family about his job and that he'd be moving did she understand how much he meant to her. As she considered the days and weeks without him, life looked bleak. *I love him,* she realized. *Dear Lord, I love him.*

For so long her heart had yearned for home. She'd longed to return but never considered what her separation from Dimitri would mean. Even now she couldn't bring herself to abandon her dream of returning to Russia. She would have to accept this new sorrow.

When she stepped onto the roof, Dimitri stood on the opposite wall. His arms folded over his chest, he stared down at the street. She closed the door quietly, still uncertain what she would do. She took another deep breath and prayed, *Father, help me to know what is right.*

A gust of wind lifted the scent of roses, and Tatyana looked at the small rose garden Dimitri had carefully tended all summer. The flowers were beautiful, their blossoms full and bright. She bent and picked a yellow one. Holding it to her nose, she smelled deeply of its fragrance.

"They're beginning to fade."

Startled, Tatyana looked up to find Dimitri standing close and looking at her. "They are still beautiful."

He glanced at the dark clouds that had settled over the city. "Soon winter will be here. They will die." Plucking a white blossom tinged with golden brown edges, he said, "They like sunshine and warmth." He held the rose out for her.

Tatyana took it and added it to the yellow one. "They are very pretty to look at, but it is their smell that is most wonderful."

Dimitri's expression turned tender. "Like you—beautiful on the outside, but your spirit is even more exquisite." He took Tatyana's hand and gently caressed it. "I still have little to offer you, but I'll give you all I have. My new job will make it possible for me to . . . "

"Please, Dimitri, I—"

"Why do you try to keep me from telling you how I feel? You know I love you. I cannot change that. You are forever part of me. I am leaving and may never return. We do not know what our future holds. I don't want to face mine without you. Please, let me say what I must."

Tatyana longed to comfort him, to tell him what he wanted to hear, but she was too afraid. It would mean giving up too much.

"Will you listen?"

Nodding and blinking back tears, she said, "Yes."

Dimitri allowed his eyes to wander over the garden. The leaves of the bean plants had yellowed and wilted. Many of the carrot tops drooped and lay in the soil. There was bare dirt where plants had once bloomed. "I always feel sad at the harvest. The plants have given all they can and then they die, and it is over."

Tatyana plucked a carrot whose top had gone to seed. "But these, if put in the ground will grow a new garden. They never really die."

Dimitri gripped Tatyana's arms. "When I think about leaving you here while I go across the country, I feel I will never produce anything good again. There will be no gardens in my life. Without you my future is empty."

Unable to meet his eyes, Tatyana looked at the roses in her hand. Her voice quiet, she said, "Our lives do not always turn out the way we plan."

"Don't you think we should do the best we can to make them good?"

"Yes, of course, but what is good? Is it what makes us happy? Or what is best?"

"Is there a difference?"

Tatyana was confused. Her heart longed to love Dimitri, but she knew it could only be at the expense of a reunion with Yuri. How could she know the right answer?

"Please, marry me and come to Washington. We'll make a home there. After we're settled the rest of the family can join us. It will be a new beginning for all of us!"

Tatyana's confusion only grew as she looked into Dimitri's pain-filled eyes. A strand of blonde hair had fallen onto his forehead. She wanted to reach up and brush it aside. Instead, she took a deep breath, looked away, and stepped back a pace. Without looking at him, she said, "I have moved too many times. The only place I want to go now is home to Russia."

Running his hand through his hair, Dimitri swiveled on one foot and looked at the brick building across the alley. "Russia, Russia, Russia! Why would you want to go back to that awful place? Stalin has destroyed thousands, maybe millions of his own people! I don't understand."

Feeling protective of her home, Tatyana could feel her frustration rise. Her voice tight, she said, "That is the problem. You cannot understand. What I feel does not make sense, but it *is* here," she said as she pressed her hand on her chest, "like a wound. It is a pain that does not go away." A petal fell into her hand, and she caressed its velvety surface. "I am longing for home, and I do not understand why." Blinking back tears she continued, "My family is there." She wiped her wet cheek. "When I came to America, I hoped Yuri and the others would also come one day, but no one answers my letters. I write and write—no answers." Fresh tears spilled onto her cheeks. "I do not know what is happening to them. I must go back."

Dimitri stepped closer. His voice gentle, he said, "It may be something you will never know." He took her hands, pressing the roses between their hands. The prick of the thorns almost went unnoticed.

"If you return, you're risking your life. Do you think the Russian government is going to let you walk back into the country without consequences? You left it. That makes you disloyal. I've heard some of the things that happen to people they believe are traitors. You can't go."

"When things change I will return to my family."

"That may never happen."

She caught her breath. Dimitri was too close. She couldn't think. She pushed against his hands. "The thorns are hurting."

Dimitri immediately released her. "I'm sorry."

Tatyana set the flowers aside and studied her palm. A small drop of blood stained it. She looked at Dimitri. "If things get better in Russia and I want to return, would you go?"

Dimitri didn't answer right away. "I . . . I don't know what I would do. I haven't thought about it. This is my home."

"This is *your* home," she repeated softly. "I know you would never leave. And I do not think I can bear never returning to mine."

His eyes gentle, Dimitri said softly, "This won't be your home until you allow it to be. There is so much for you here. Don't you see you already have roots in this land? You have family here. What will you feel when you are in Russia and your family is here?"

Tatyana had been so set on returning that she hadn't thought about what she would lose by leaving. She swallowed hard and tried to comprehend it all.

"There is no perfect answer," Dimitri said as he picked up one of the roses. "Just as there is no perfect flower. Even this beautiful rose with its extraordinary scent is imperfect." He turned her hand over, exposing her cut. "It has thorns." He closed her palm. "And eventually it loses its fragrance, wilts, and dies. Don't you see, you will not find happiness by substituting one home for another. You must find a way to be content where you are. No matter how much you want it to be so, you will never have everything. You must choose what is best."

Tatyana knew he was right. *Oh, God, what am I to do?* Burying her face in her hands, she wept. "I . . . I can't do it. I can't turn my back on Yuri and Russia forever."

"And what do you lose when I leave for Washington? What happens to us?"

"There is no us!" Peering through her tears, Tatyana could see the pain she inflicted on Dimitri. "I have tried hard to make sure there is no us. Why is it you do not understand?"

Dimitri flung the rose to the ground. "Why? Are you saying you don't love me? If you are, I don't believe you. I have seen it in your eyes. Even when you've tried to hide your love, it is there."

Tormented, Tatyana looked into his eyes. For so long she'd denied her heart. How could she continue the lie? Nothing good could come from it. "All right. All right. It is true. I do love you. I tried not to, but I do." She stepped into his arms and softly repeated, "I love you, Dimitri. I love you."

He cradled Tatyana and gently stroked her hair.

"What will become of me here?"

"You will be my wife." Gently Dimitri held her away from him. "I'll take good care of you. We can face the battles together. It is always better to have a partner to share joys and sorrows."

She wiped at her eyes and sniffled. "How do I forget my family, my country?"

"You don't forget, you remember. Didn't Yuri send you here because he loved you?"

She nodded.

Then honor him by doing what he asked. He loved you enough to let you go. Now, love him enough to stay."

"When I think of never seeing him again, it hurts too much."

"You have to let go."

"I do not know if I can."

"I'll help you. Please let me." Gently he wiped away the dampness from her cheeks. "We can build a new family."

"But that cannot replace the one I already have."

"No, but love eases pain."

Tatyana looked at Dimitri and, for the first time, believed she could know happiness with him. Her love surged in a rush of emotion. "I will marry you."

Dimitri smiled. "I will be good to you," he said as he folded her in his arms.

For a very long time they held each other, their burdens lighter, now that they were shared. Tatyana understood better that sorrow didn't have to be her plight and that joy emanating from within was attainable. She had Dimitri and a family who loved her. Could she ask for more? She stepped away and smiled at him. "Your . . . our family will want to know."

※ ※ ※ ※ ※

Dimitri's bus fare arrived the next day with instructions to report to a logging camp outside of Seattle in one week. There was little time to plan a wedding, but the entire family worked together, and in two days they were ready.

Tatyana's demons returned the morning of the wedding. Her mind whirled with questions. Was she doing the right thing? What if she realized she couldn't remain in America and be happy? Would she be allowed to return to Russia? Would Dimitri join her? If not, could she live with that decision? Their declaration of love was still so fresh, and she felt uncertain of its substance. Was it something that would last? She'd had so little time to consider the ramifications of her decision.

She stood in front of the mirror and looked at herself. Flora's pearl white wedding gown made her look like someone else. She smiled as she remembered the older woman coming into the front room with the dress draped over her arms. She held it out to Tatyana. "I have kept this packed away for many years. It would be better if it were worn again."

Tatyana's eyes brimmed with tears at the memory. Flora had been her first friend in America. She had stood beside her as they traveled across the sea. Once they arrived in New York, Flora stayed with her and helped her find a home and friends.

Tatyana looked at her reflection. The dress looked as if it had been made for her. A tiny satin bow decorated the high neckline, and delicate lace covered the fitted bodice and waist, accentuating Tatyana's tiny waist. Two tiers of skirt hung loosely from her hips, flowing freely to the floor. Flora had been taller than Tatyana, but all it took was a little hem for the dress to fit her perfectly, brushing the toes of her shoes.

Tatyana lifted the skirt. *I'll have to be careful so it doesn't drag on the floor.*

A knock came at the door. Before Tatyana could answer, Augusta peeked inside. "May I come in?"

"Yes. Please." Tatyana smiled. Fearful Augusta would see her uncertainty, she quickly returned to studying her image.

"Turn around and let me get a good look at you."

Tatyana held out her arms and carefully turned and faced Augusta. She was careful to keep her eyes on the floor.

"You look lovely."

Studying the skirt, she said, "It is kind of Flora to let me wear her beautiful dress."

"She is happy you can. She never thought it would be used again." Carefully she unfolded a lace handkerchief and held it up. "This was my mother's. I wore it on my wedding day. I thought you might want to use it." She tucked it into the wrist of Tatyana's sleeve. "It will bring good luck."

"Thank you." Tatyana chewed on her lip as her emotions overwhelmed her. "I wish my mother were here."

"She would be very proud of you."

"She will never know my husband."

"Oh, but she will. Our life here is not forever. One day she will meet him." Augusta looked more closely at Tatyana. "There is something else troubling you? You look worried."

Tatyana glanced at the mirror. "You know me too well." The veil had been laid over a chair, and she picked it up. "Can you help me?"

"Of course." Augusta took the veil. "You will have to sit. I am not tall enough."

Tatyana sat, careful to keep the dress from wrinkling.

Gently placing the veil's comb in Tatyana's hair, she said, "You look so pretty with your hair down. You should wear it like this more often." She pinned the comb and stood back to examine her work. "Take a look."

Tatyana stared in the mirror. Her eyes met Augusta's.

"Now, do you want to tell me what is bothering you?" the older woman asked.

Tatyana didn't know what to say. How could she tell her future mother-in-law she wasn't sure she should marry her son? But as she looked at the kind woman, she knew there was nothing she couldn't share with her. "I do not know if this is the right thing to do."

"You mean marrying Dimitri?"

Tatyana tugged at the handkerchief in her sleeve and twisted it. "I love him. He is a special man, kind and gentle." She pulled the handkerchief completely free and studied its delicate design. "I could find no better man."

"Then, what is it?"

"I am still uncertain because I am Russian and, although he once was, he is no longer. I am haunted by my family and my homeland. I feel I am leaving them behind forever. What can I do? I fear one day I will hate Dimitri if I am forced to forsake them."

Augusta met Tatyana's eyes. She took the young woman's hands in hers. "Is it your family and homeland you love most or Dimitri? Think carefully, because you will have to live without one of them."

Tatyana's eyes brimmed with tears. "Why must life be so hard?"

Augusta patted her hand. "Would you like to know what I think? You and Dimitri love each other. I have known it for a long time. And if two people love, I believe it is God's will for them to marry. He is the one who brings couples together. The love between a man and woman is a special gift and very powerful." She gently tucked a strand of hair into Tatyana's veil. "God will watch over you and help you work through the difficulties. But, you must trust him if it is to be so." She smiled and stepped back.

"And what of Yuri? I am afraid for him. I do not even know if he lives."

"Sometimes there are mysteries in our lives—mysteries that will never be answered." She took Tatyana's hands. "I believe God is with Yuri. I have an assurance here," she said as she placed her hand on her heart, "that he is living. I think he is in difficult times, but God has not forgotten him. And I believe that one day you will meet again." She kissed Tatyana's cheek. "God loves your brother the same way he loves us all."

Tears welled up in Tatyana's eyes, and she hugged her dear friend. "Thank you, Augusta. You are wise." She dabbed at her eyes, then straightened and looked at herself in the mirror. "Do I look ready to be married?"

"Yes. You are a beautiful bride. And I know where to find a young man waiting for you." She smiled, kissed Tatyana on each cheek, and left.

A moment later a knock came at the door. Pavel peeked in. His mustache had been trimmed and his graying hair slicked back. He stepped in and straightened the jacket of his suit. "How do I look?"

"You are very handsome."

Grinning, he asked, "Are you ready?"

"Yes. I think so." Tatyana smoothed her skirt.

Standing very tall, he held out his arm. "I'm proud to be the one to walk you down the aisle. We are happy to have you as a permanent part of our family. Dimitri is very lucky."

With a renewed sense of well-being, Tatyana took his arm. As they made their way to the sanctuary, butterflies danced in her stomach. She took a deep breath to calm herself.

They entered the foyer of the church.

Allison had been waiting for them. Her layered silk georgette dress swished away from her as she hurried toward Tatyana. A large rhinestone cinched the waist of the gown.

Although it hung loosely on Allison's tiny frame, the pale green emphasized her hazel eyes, and she looked stunning.

She gripped her bouquet of carnations so hard they shook. "Tis a grand day for a wedding. I've never been a bridesmaid before. I hope I do everything right." She gave Tatyana a quick hug. "Thank ye' for asking me."

A prim-looking woman whom Tatyana knew as Mary sat at the organ. She looked at the pastor and the guests, then turned and placed her hands on the keys. Deep, rich tones filled the room. Allison quickly turned and faced the front of the church, taking one step inside. Tatyana tightened her grip on Pavel's arm. She thought of her family so far away and wished they could share this day. Tears burned her eyes, and she blinked hard to hold them back.

Allison stepped into the sanctuary, doing her best to keep pace with the music. She held her spine straight and her shoulders back.

Tatyana stopped just inside the sanctum doors. She could see Dimitri standing at the front. He gazed at her, and she felt herself blush. He looked very handsome in his borrowed suit, so tall and robust. As always, a lock of blonde rested on his forehead.

When Allison arrived at the altar, Pavel grasped Tatyana's arm a little tighter and took a step forward. Tatyana's legs felt stiff, and she was afraid she might stumble.

Pavel patted her hand and smiled reassuringly. "You are beautiful," he whispered. "Everything will be fine."

Tatyana squeezed his hand and walked with a little more confidence.

Dimitri gazed at her, his eyes glowing with admiration. Tatyana trembled inside as she studied the tall blonde man who was about to become her husband. The first time she'd met him she believed him to be rude and inconsiderate. How could she have been so wrong?

Pavel stopped a few feet before reaching the altar. The music ended, and Tatyana stood between the two men. Trembling inside, she took a slow deep breath, closed her eyes a moment, then looked into Dimitri's eyes. Her knees shook.

"Who gives this woman to be wed?" the minister asked.

"I do," Pavel said, as he placed Tatyana's hand in Dimitri's and took his place beside Augusta.

Dimitri's hand was large and warm, his grip strong. Tatyana felt secure. She smiled at him.

The couple faced the minister and repeated their vows, promising themselves to each other for life. As prayers were said and vows exchanged, the words settled over Tatyana like a warm blanket. She and Dimitri belonged to each other. It felt good, like being anchored in a stormy sea—something she hadn't known for a very long time. Although she didn't know what the future held, peace settled over her. She was assured of God's guardianship, and she knew he had chosen this man for her. He would sustain them.

A final blessing was said, and the pastor looked tenderly upon Dimitri and Tatyana. He smiled. "You are now husband and wife." He nodded at Dimitri. "You may kiss the bride."

As Tatyana faced her husband, she felt unexpected panic. She'd never kissed a man before, and she didn't know how. As Dimitri placed his hands on her shoulders, she swallowed hard and forced a smile. He bent and gently pressed his lips to hers. Immediately her fears were swept away by the powerful love they shared.

They parted, smiled at each other, then turned and faced the guests. As organ music filled the room, the couple linked arms and walked down the aisle. Tatyana felt a joy she could not contain. She couldn't remember knowing such happiness.

Had it been only a few days since she'd been bereft at the thought of losing Dimitri? How could things have changed so quickly? *It is God,* she thought. *He has done this.*

Even when she caught sight of Reynold Meyers standing among the guests, her joy didn't falter. She tipped her head slightly as she passed him.

After that they were steered into a reception room where guests lined up to greet them. Tatyana saw Reynold Meyers waiting in the line and wondered why he'd come to the wedding. As he approached she could feel her stomach knot. What did he want now?

Dimitri protectively circled his arm around Tatyana's waist and pulled her close.

Mr. Meyers looked at him. "Congratulations to you. You're a very lucky man."

"I am that," Dimitri said, locking eyes with his former employer.

He took Tatyana's hand. Gently pressing it to his lips, he said, "You are beautiful. Congratulations." His voice sounded gentle. "I can see your joy, and I am truly happy for you."

Shocked at his demeanor, Tatyana could think of nothing to say.

Mr. Meyers reached into his front pocket and removed a white envelope. "I have something for both of you. I behaved badly and would like to make amends. You lost wages because of me." He handed the envelope to Dimitri. "I hope this will help you get a start on your new lives."

He looked at Tatyana. "I am sorry."

Tatyana thought he looked genuinely remorseful.

"We can't accept this," Dimitri said, holding out the gift.

"Please, keep it."

"No. It wouldn't be right."

Reynold looked hard at Dimitri. "Don't be stupid. These are difficult times."

Keeping his voice quiet, Dimitri pressed, "And why do you care?"

Reynold Meyers looked at the ground, then at Tatyana, and back at Dimitri. In a voice barely above a whisper, he said, "You are a stubborn fool if you let your pride keep you from taking care of Tatyana. She deserves better than what she has. I want her to have a few comforts. Please, keep the gift."

Never taking his eyes off his former employer, Dimitri pressed the envelope into his palm. His hand closed into a fist. Gripping the rejected gift, Reynold Meyers turned and walked away.

Tatyana's heart constricted as she watched him. His stride was no longer arrogant, but wounded. What had happened?

Allison touched Tatyana's arm. "He's seemed very changed since the box social. No one is sayin' what happened t' him, but something has."

"I hope he is all right."

The afternoon passed in a blur of well-wishes, music, and dancing. It was the celebration of two lives fused into one.

When the festivities came to an end, Tatyana and Dimitri left the church beneath a shower of rice. Tatyana tossed her bouquet of roses, and a surprised Allison caught it. Farewells were said, and the couple hurried into a waiting taxi.

Still laughing, Tatyana leaned against Dimitri and waved at the onlookers. He held her close as the car merged into traffic. Resting against the crook of his arm, she sighed. "It was a wonderful day!"

"It was that, Mrs. Broido."

The name sounded strange. "It will take me a while to get used to being called Mrs. Broido."

"You have a long while to get used to it," Dimitri said and kissed her soundly. "I plan to be married to you the rest of my life, and that will be a good long time."

"Oh, yes." She gently stroked his cheek. "Thank you for waiting for me, for believing in me, for loving me."

Dimitri tightened his hold. "How could I help myself? You are extraordinary. I could do nothing less than wait for you."

Tatyana snuggled against him, feeling content. "I love you," she whispered.

As they passed through the city, her mind wandered home, and a shadow pressed down on the young bride. Tatyana's heart ached as thoughts of Yuri swept over her. *May only good things come to you, Yuri. I pray we will be reunited one day. Please, Father, watch over my brother. We are like seeds scattered in the wind. May we not be lost from each other forever.*